WHEN
there are
NO MORE
STARS *left*
to COUNT

María Martínez

sourcebooks
casablanca

Published by Sourcebooks Casablanca, an imprint of Sourcebooks
1935 Brookdale RD, Naperville, IL 60563-2773
(630) 961-3900
sourcebooks.com

Originally published as *Cuando no queden más estrellas que contar* in 2022 in Spain by
Crossbooks, an imprint of Grupo Planeta. This edition issued based on the paperback
edition published in 2022 in Spain by Crossbooks, an imprint of Grupo Planeta.

Cataloging-in-Publication Data is on file with the Library of Congress.

Printed and bound in the United States of America.
LB 10 9 8 7 6 5 4 3 2 1

To those who wish upon a falling star

We need a farewell before we can see each other again.

Fighting yourself is exhausting.

Fighting against the undeniable fact that nothing will ever be the way it was before. Against the fact that the things that have happened can't be changed, however much you dream of returning to the moment when they could. The exact second when everything fell apart.

And yet you try. You return to that fateful instant. It doesn't matter if you're asleep or awake, because for some time now your longing and your impatience have made it impossible to distinguish between nightmares and memories. You stand before your destiny, and instead of taking a step forward, you take two steps back. Just two, enough to avoid disaster. You recreate the scene nonstop in your mind. You sink into an infinite loop of watching your feet step back and carry you away from the pain. From the suffering. From that cracking sound when a dream shatters into pieces so small, you know you'll never be able to put it together again.

Two steps. Just two. Enough to keep you from the siren song of tragedy. To bring you back to applause and admiration.

To that world where you matter, where you aren't invisible, where you flourish every time you step on the stage.

The world where you exist. Where you are in control.

That's why you keep trying. You close your eyes, go back to that decisive second, and as you hold your breath, you take two steps back. Your heart's tense like a fist and you're praying in silence: *Please, please, please….!* As if that word you repeat like a mantra were a spell and you had the heart and mind of a witch.

And yet, what's happened can't be undone. There's no spell that can unmake the past. I took a step forward, and that car couldn't dodge me.

Maybe it was written.

Maybe it was chance.

I couldn't predict it.

I stopped being a princess and became a swan forever.

The end.

And the beginning…

1

Maybe Antoine was right and it was my fault. It had been weeks since things had started going badly for us. Too many arguments, and always about the same thing: my attitude. I wasn't the same person I used to be. I was cold and uninterested. Absent.

And it was true, in a way. The past six months had been torture for me. The operation, recovery in the hospital. Returning home and the weeks of rehab. My grandmother's constant reproaches, how easily she made me feel bad for everything that's wrong with the world. Probably the polar ice caps are melting because just once, I did something without her permission.

Just because I wanted to.

Once, and the punishment was brutal.

Deep down, I think she was happy about the accident. The satisfaction on her face every time she said *I told you so* or *If only you'd listened to me* was a cruel pleasure she liked to wallow in. Her eyes shouted *You deserve it* every time they caught me in their stare, and then, with a condescending smile, she would forgive me under the sole condition that I sacrifice every second of my existence to her.

No one should be responsible for making another person's dreams come true. It's impossible to live up to the expectations of a person who has failed to achieve her own dreams and desires.

But the hardest thing for me to bear was the uncertainty.

The wait was consuming me inside and I was incapable of thinking of anything else.

Maybe Antoine was right and I was pushing him away just as I was everyone else. Still, I would have appreciated a little empathy from him. A little more patience and compassion. I had known Antoine since I was fifteen, when his family moved from Paris to Madrid for work, and he began to take classes at the Mariemma Royal Conservatory of Dance, where I was studying, and I knew he was emotionally stunted. Not just that: he didn't even know how inept he was at trying to put himself in someone else's shoes.

Despite that, I'd learned to love him along with his defects. As a friend at first, and something more a few years later, when we both entered the National Dance Company as soloists. At twenty-two years old, the strongest relationship I'd had, apart from with ballet, was with Antoine. That was the only unconditional love I'd allowed myself.

For that reason, I was scared of losing him. I needed his affection. And I was scared, closing my eyes and holding my breath when he curled up tight to me beneath the sheets and, still sleepy, slid his hand between my legs. He pressed his hips into my buttocks, and I could feel he was aroused. I took a breath and let it out slowly, concentrating on his fingers, how they caressed me, the warmth of his chest against my back. The way he pulled me tight.

I opened my eyes and looked at the hands of the clock.

His finger tried to work its way inside of me. I flinched and grimaced. I tried to relax, but I couldn't. I couldn't feel anything at all.

"I've got to go," I whispered.

Face beside my neck, Antoine grunted, nibbled my shoulder.

"Come on. Look what you're doing to me."

He pushed into me again. I was starting to get agitated.

"I'll be late."

"Just a quickie," he said, using his French accent like an aphrodisiac. But it got on my nerves.

I jerked away and got up, glancing at the clock again and feeling anxiety in my stomach. I grabbed my dress off the chair. Still in bed, Antoine huffed and lay on his back, staring at me.

"Are you for real? Dammit, Maya. We never do it anymore, and I–I have my needs."

I pulled my dress over my head and glared back at him. "Never? What was yesterday, then?"

"Getting it on in a bathroom with our clothes on doesn't count."

I rolled my eyes and sat down to tie my shoes, looking for a moment at the scars on my leg. Their color was lightening, and the swelling was starting to go down. Or at least that's what I thought. I didn't dare to actually touch them. I stood and grabbed my cell phone off the table.

"Are you seriously leaving?" he asked, as if it weren't obvious from the fact that I was heading for the door.

"I can't stay any longer, OK? I've got a doctor's appointment in less than an hour."

He jumped up, looking surprised, and I couldn't help but eye up his nude body. A whole life devoted to ballet had transformed him into a perfectly proportioned, walking sculpture. And yet, I felt nothing.

"It's today?" he asked, and I nodded, feeling a hint of panic at what I knew he'd say next. "Shit, I'm sorry! I completely forgot."

"It's fine."

"You want me to come along?"

"No need," I told him. "I'd almost…rather go by myself."

He looked relieved, and that made me feel bitter as he came over, wrapped his arms around me, and kissed me on the forehead.

"Everything will be fine, you'll see. You'll dance again, you'll go back to being principal, we both will, and we'll travel the world together. They'll talk about us the way they did about Fonteyn and Nureyev. You and me onstage, Maya… We're something else."

He grabbed my chin and forced me to look him in the eyes—those eyes so green it was hard to believe they were real. I smiled softly. It was true, onstage we were so in synch we moved as one body, one mind, and we trusted each other completely. Never once had I feared that he'd drop me.

If only the same was true in our personal relationship.

"I'll let you know," I said.

"Sure, just text me. I've got class and then rehearsal today, so I'll be back late."

"OK."

I gave him a quick kiss on the lips and hurried into the bathroom, washing up a little and taking a look at myself in the mirror. My eyes were so dark I could hardly see my pupils. My brown eyebrows framed them, just as my brown hair framed my face, still with a few tangles in it I hadn't managed to brush out.

I leaned in close and thought about how different I looked from the rest of my family. My grandmother, my aunts and uncles and cousins, my mother…all of them were blond with light-colored eyes, their features a reflection of the Ukrainian blood in my grandmother's side of the family. Even on my grandfather's side, the Spanish side, most people had pale skin and straw-colored hair.

I was the exception. And whenever I noticed those differences, I couldn't stop thinking about how somewhere, there were similarities. Traits that resembled another person. Him. Wherever he was.

I walked off down the hall and heard voices in the living room: Matías and Rodrigo, whom I found at the breakfast table. They formed part of the corps de ballet and shared the apartment with

Antoine. It's funny how small the ballet world is, like a little army you serve in and give your all to. You work sixteen hours a day, six days a week. You eat, sleep, and breathe ballet.

Maybe that's why we dancers rarely associate with people outside the world of leotards and pointe shoes. You have to be in it to understand it. We spend almost all our time together, training together, rehearsing together, touring together.

"Good morning!" I said.

"Good morning," Matías replied.

Rodrigo stood and pulled a chair close to the table. "Want a coffee?"

"No thanks. Caffeine's the last thing I need today."

I looked around for my bag and found it on the sofa. Then I grabbed an apple Matías handed to me. He was always so attentive. I thanked him with a peck on the cheek.

"Today's the big day," he said.

"Or the worst day," I responded.

Matías was my best friend, the only one I could tell everything to without any worry of being judged. I could share my worries with him, the loneliness that comes with that disciplined, competitive lifestyle. I could cry in front of him. I could show him all my shortcomings, even the ones I buried deep.

"It's all I know how to do," I told him. "I can't lose this."

"You won't. Worst-case scenario, Natalia will put you with the corps de ballet until you get your rhythm and confidence back. Then you'll be principal again."

"You really think that?"

"Of course I do. Ever since she came on as director of the company, she's done everything in her power to keep you in the ensemble. She's been following you since the conservatory days."

I nodded, wishing with all my might that he wasn't wrong.

I started dancing when I was four, and I hadn't done anything since. I'd given up all other studies to focus on ballet. Climbing slowly to a summit everyone thought I was predestined to reach. I had what I needed to achieve it. And even if the fear of injury is something that stalks every one of us, I never thought it would happen to me, and not in such a ridiculous way.

2

I said goodbye to Matías and Rodrigo and left.

My stomach was growling, and I forced myself to eat my apple as I took the three flights of stairs to the street. Outside, the sun was shining bright. It was nine in the morning, but it was already warm out. Summer was hitting Madrid with full force, and this June was hotter than usual.

I put on my headphones and chose a random playlist on my phone as I walked to Lavapiés and raced downstairs to catch the train to the hospital. Thirty minutes later, I was walking through the door of the outpatient clinic and toward the D wing with a knot in my stomach.

I signed in and sat in the waiting room.

I stopped cold when I saw her there with her back to me. So straight. So haughty. Her blond hair was pulled back perfectly, neither too tight nor too loose, and not a single hair had fallen out of place. She had on big sunglasses that covered much of her face, and I knew behind those dark lenses were those cold green eyes surrounded in eyeliner as meticulously applied as her red lipstick.

Olga Yarovenka, my grandmother. The woman who had raised me after my mother abandoned me at four years old, because taking care of her own daughter was just too much for her.

She stood when she saw me.

"You should have been here already," she said.

"What are you doing here?"

"You didn't come home last night."

"I went out with Antoine. It got late, so I stayed at his place."

"I see you're not too worried about this appointment. Your life's hanging by a thread and you're busy going out with this would-be player who thinks he's the next Sergei Polunin."

The contempt in her tone struck me like a whip.

"How can you say I'm not worried? There's nothing I want more than to keep dancing," I said.

"If you'd listened to me, you'd never have had to stop. But you think you know everything, and look where that's gotten you."

"It was an accident. I had nothing to do with it."

She was about to reply, but a nurse's voice interrupted her.

"Maya Rivet Yarovenka?"

"That's us," my grandmother responded.

"Your number's been up on the screen for some time."

"Sorry," I told her. "We got distracted."

The nurse showed us which office to go to, and my grandmother entered first.

I almost told her to go outside and wait. I was an adult, after all; I could ask for privacy if I wanted it. But I got scared, and the words died on my lips. My grandmother wasn't a woman to be contradicted, and if you tried to confront her, she could make you shudder with one cruel look. I knew from experience. I had lived my entire life under her iron fist.

"Doctor Sanz, nice to see you again," my grandmother said.

"The same, Mrs. Yarovenka," my doctor replied, sitting at his desk.

"Call me Olga, please. I'm not that old."

The doctor nodded and grinned, then told us to sit before typing something into his computer with a concentrated expression. His eyes scanned the screen and his forehead furrowed. Then he looked over at me kindly.

"Well, Maya. How are you?"

"Good?"

"Still doing your physical therapy?"

"She goes religiously to every session," my grandmother responded.

Doctor Sanz nodded, but didn't take his eyes off me. "Pains, cramps, inflammation…"

"No, none of that. Everything's perfect," my grandmother responded again. I agreed, though it wasn't true. My knee and ankle ached when I overdid it, but I wasn't going to tell him that. Pain is a part of ballet: You don't need an injury for that to be true. You get used to it, and it's just another part of your day-to-day routine. Besides, I wanted to get back on the boards, and I wasn't going to risk that for the sake of something that could be controlled with anti-inflammatories and painkillers.

"Very good," he said.

He looked back at the screen and clicked around with his mouse. I could see X-rays, test results, other data from a few days before. I was getting nervous, and I started scratching at a flake of skin on my finger.

"Will she be able to dance again?" my grandmother asked, sounding almost wrathful.

The doctor's eyebrows rose, and he said, "Of course she will…"

"Thank God!" my grandmother exclaimed.

As I expelled a breath, he continued. "But not professionally, the way she did before. I'm sorry about that." His tone was compassionate, but I felt the ground open at my feet as tears welled in my eyes. He didn't take his eyes off me as my grandmother peppered him with questions, barely stopping to take a breath.

"Maya, your CK enzymes are very high still, and that leads me to think the damage to the muscle is permanent. And the other tests back that up. Your leg can't take another year of professional ballet. Maybe not even six months. Even before the accident, you had bursitis, tendinitis, reduced bone mass..." He leaned forward, making sure he had my complete attention. "You're just twenty-two years old. You have your whole life ahead of you. Do you want to live it with a cane or, more likely, in a wheelchair?"

I shook my head. Obviously no one just decides to spend their life in a wheelchair. And yet...

"There's nothing I can do?" I asked in a thin thread of voice.

Doctor Sanz leaned back in his chair and joined his hands on his desk.

"Maya, you're not the first ballerina I've worked with, and I've seen firsthand what it does to a body. When your leg is in the condition that it's in, there *will* be further injuries. It *will* get worse. If you go back to dancing professionally, you'll lose a lot more than just your career."

3

My grandmother kept cursing as we got in the car to leave. For forty minutes, I had to hear how disappointed and hurt she felt, and how I could never make it up to her, and how she'd sacrificed so many years to get me to where I was and I'd spoiled it.

All she'd cared about was my future, she told me for the ump-teenth time, from when she first started giving me classes and I was just a little girl. She'd devoted her time to molding me at her dance school, and years later, when I moved on to the conservatory, she continued guiding me from the shadows. She managed my time, dictated my studies, told me when to sleep, what to eat, how to dress, and who to hang out with.

I grew up under her wing, eyes fixed on the goal she had chosen for me: becoming nothing more and nothing less than the primary in the National Dance Company. Only that would do, and she never changed her mind, not even when other companies tried to woo me.

I eventually realized there was a personal motive hidden behind her obsession. I discovered this by chance, when Fyodora, one of my teachers at the conservatory and later a répétiteuse in the company, let slip that for years, Olga had gotten rejected at every audition she showed up for. She had never even been part of a corps de ballet.

She wound up opening her own school in Delicias in Madrid, where she went to live with my grandfather after they married. There, they trained dozens of boys and girls, preparing them for various conservatories and dance schools. *My little angels*, she liked to call her students.

Even once she'd parked in the garage and we were in the elevator, she didn't let up with her reproaches. Only once we were inside and I saw my grandfather sitting on the balcony did I stop listening. Carmen, the woman who helped take care of him, was sitting next to him and reading him the paper. When she saw us, she stopped.

My grandfather's head lolled aside and he scanned the living room when he heard our voices. His diabetes made his vision worse every year, and he'd gotten to where he could distinguish little more than light and shadow.

"What's going on?" he asked.

"What's going on? It's over, that's what's going on. Her entire career down the toilet. Years of effort, dedication, and money invested in her education. All of it in the trash can!" my grandmother shouted.

I couldn't believe what she was saying. Money? I had worked myself to the bone to get one scholarship after another since I was sixteen. It had been six years since I'd needed help from her. In fact, I passed her money from my skimpy salary whenever I could. And now that skimpy salary was gone. Which made the house of cards that much closer to collapsing.

"Maya?" my grandfather called. He reached up and I took his hand, kneeling next to him and letting him stroke my cheek with the other hand. "Are you all right, honey?"

"Don't treat her like a victim. Don't you see it's all her fault? If she'd listened to me the way she should have... For God's sake, she was this close! A few more months, and she'd have made it," my grandmother grumbled.

I clenched my fists and fired back, "Are you talking about me or you? Which one of us would have made it?"

Standing still and glaring, she said, "How dare you insinuate such a thing? With everything I've done for you. I sacrificed my life for you, to give you the opportunity to be someone, and we were almost there, right up until you…"

"I didn't do anything," I exploded, standing again. Grandpa squeezed my hand and whispered my name, trying to calm me down. "A car ran a light and hit me. Stop blaming me for it."

"We both know how that ended up happening. You had an option: You could have listened to my advice and done the right thing, but no, the life you have here wasn't enough for you. You wanted to go off to the middle of nowhere and be just one more mediocrity instead of becoming the prima ballerina assoluta. Well, this is your prize. You're a failure, just like your mother!"

Tears streamed down my cheeks. It wasn't fair for her to treat me this way. But then, why was I surprised? She had been cruel and pitiless with me for a long time, pushing me past my limits in a way even my harshest professors couldn't compete with. And still I wasn't enough.

I had never felt love from her, or security, or protection. It didn't matter what goal I achieved, she never congratulated me or encouraged me, because being the best and climbing to the top were things she simply expected. But if I made a mistake, she wouldn't hesitate to show her contempt. She was implacable.

I had never been her granddaughter; I'd always been her project. I knew that more than ever just then. She had transformed me into a skittish marionette: obedient, head always lowered, staying in my place. Though every fiber in my body rebelled against the thought, I could understand why my mother had run away. Even if running away meant she had abandoned me, too.

I realized I was about to break down. But I wouldn't give my grandmother the satisfaction, and I sure as hell wouldn't ask her to forgive me. So I walked out without a word and shut the door of my bedroom, opening the window to get some fresh air and sitting down on the bed.

I looked at the poster of Maya Plisetskaya on the wall. They named me after her. They had my whole life planned for me the day I was born. If only I'd inherited her free, wild spirit. Her will to defend herself and be exactly what she was.

Despite my best efforts, the pain, sorrow, and bitterness were too much for me. What was I going to do? I took out my phone and called Antoine. It rang a few times and went to voicemail. I hung up and texted him: Not good. Call me when you can, please.

Then I wrote Matías: You there?

He asked me how it had gone. I wiped my tears away and blew my nose and responded, Bad. He wrote that he'd pick me up in thirty minutes, and when I asked, What about your classes? he responded, You're more important.

I smiled. I adored Matías.

I looked out the window and waited to see him come up the sidewalk. When he did, I waved to him and told him to wait for me downstairs. My grandfather was alone in the living room. In the kitchen, I could hear Carmen and my grandmother putting together the shopping list. I rested a hand on Grandpa's shoulder and whispered, "I'm sorry."

He grinned. "You didn't do anything wrong. Don't worry about her. She'll get over it. She's hard on you because that's how she was raised. If you'd met her mother, you'd understand."

I bit my lip and nodded, even if I didn't agree. My grandfather adored his wife and had always forgiven her, and he tried to clean up her messes as best he could. But not everything was fixable. Especially not people. You can't just glue the pieces of a broken spirit back together again. It's like the water that runs through your fingers and soaks into the dry ground. Like the ash left after a fire that a brief gust of wind blows away. An ice cube in the sun. It vanishes and you can never get it back.

"Sure…" I told him.

"I know it feels like the end of the world, Maya, but it isn't, I promise. Don't forget, when one door closes, another one always opens."

"Yeah, but what if that one shuts, too?"

"Then beat on the damn wall till you knock a hole in it."

I smiled even though I knew he couldn't see me, then kissed him on the cheek.

"I'm going to take a walk," I told him.

"Be careful," he responded.

I scurried softly down the stairs, and Matías received me with open arms, squeezing me against his chest as if we hadn't seen each other in months. Noticing my eyes were red and swollen, he clicked his tongue.

"We need a beer and a bite."

"It's eleven in the morning. Besides, what about your diet?"

"Screw my diet. I won't eat dinner tonight and I'll be fine."

"Matías…" I groaned.

I worried about his health, because he would do anything to keep his weight down, and there was a thin line between sacrifice and an eating disorder that wasn't hard to cross. I'd seen it many times through the years, and not everyone managed to crawl out of the hole.

I had known Matías since I was eight, and we had auditioned for a place at the conservatory. We were in the same group, and we were both terribly nervous. Weeks later, we were back there, but as classmates. And we grew inseparable.

I weaved my arm through his and we headed downtown.

"What did the doctor tell you?" he asked.

"That I can't go on dancing professionally. My leg's a disaster, and if I keep it up, I'll need a cane to even walk. Or worse."

He froze. He clearly hadn't expected that. "You'll get a second opinion, though, right?"

"What for? Eloy Sanz is the best trauma specialist in the country. If he can't fix me, no one can. It's over, Matías, I'll never dance on the stage again."

He expelled a breath of air, exasperated. Then he hugged me again, tight, but differently from before, with an emotion that stirred me in my deepest depths.

"Shit, Maya, I'm so sorry. I don't know what the hell to say."

My face still buried between his neck and shoulder, I asked, "So now what? I don't know what the hell to do."

Matías began walking again with his arm over my shoulder.

"You could teach. You're still in time to apply at María de Ávila. I don't think you'd have a hard time getting in."

"That's a four-year degree! Anyway, I don't know if I'm built for teaching."

"You could study choreography. You're creative, and you've always had an incredibly artistic sense."

I thought it over. I didn't know a world apart from ballet shoes, the barre, steps. Becoming a teacher would keep me close to what I'd always considered my home, but I wasn't sure if I had what it took. Choreography, though… That had always fascinated me. Making a story arise out of nothing, transforming it into movements, gestures, expressions…emotions that people can feel.

"I'll think about it, but I need to look for a job first. Whatever I end up doing, I need money. I couldn't even pay my registration fees as is."

"There you go—focusing on the future. I like that. No regrets."

"Matías, I'm a wreck," I confessed. "I feel like I'm in a nightmare and can't wake up."

Matías shook his head and bent over and kissed me on the temple.

"I know. How'd your grandmother take it?"

"What do you think?" I asked, my bugging my eyes out and sticking out my tongue. "It was like it was her life falling apart and not mine. She says I'm a failure, just like my mother."

"She's a heartless bitch," he replied.

"Don't say that."

"It's true, though."

"She's still my grandmother, and at least she never abandoned me. Maybe she loves me, in her own way."

"Well, her own way is pretty damn weird," he responded.

We walked off into the multitude whose lives were so different from ours. Dozens and dozens of stories. Little worlds, each with its own problems and joys, hopes and deceptions.

"You're not a failure," he continued, "so don't you dare think she might be right. You're amazing, Maya. You always have been." He gave me a smile full of tenderness.

I smiled back, thinking of my mother, a woman I might have seen ten times in my whole life. My grandmother rarely mentioned her, but when she did, her voice was full of pain and bitterness. She resented her, the same way she had resented me that morning.

I closed my eyes and tried to remember if I'd ever truly seen my grandmother happy. I didn't think so. Maybe when I passed my audition and became a soloist. At that moment, her eyes shone bright for just a moment. Then she told me, gritting her teeth, that I'd better not disappoint her.

4

At twelve years old

"Again."

Her voice was like shattered glass.

I took a deep breath and walked to the center of the room. It was Saturday, and I had spent the entire week taking classes at the conservatory, apart from school and rehearsal for our end-of-the-year performance, and all I wanted was to lie down in front of the TV and do nothing.

I was panting and my feet hurt. My grandmother put on music again and stood in front of me with a frown on her face, scrutinizing me as she said, "One, and two, plié, passé…" Again, she went through the steps and I followed her directions, "Demi, demi, full, port de bras and up. Second port de bras, back. Four… Steady on your feet, Maya."

I did as she said and kept moving, feeling my toes scrunched inside my shoes and my fingers tingling. I ignored the pain. I ignored my spine, overstretched, twisting until I thought it would crack.

"Plié tendu, three and four. Développé croisé, plié en arabesque… Maya, use the music, use the tempo! Shoulders down."

I pursed my lips. I hated her shouting at me… It didn't matter if I did a good or bad job, her voice rose until it bounced off the walls and struck me like a bolt of lightning.

"Come on, Maya, up, up… Extend your leg and jeté." When I put my foot down, I twisted my ankle, and she cursed in Ukrainian. That meant she was starting to get pissed off. "Maya!"

My muscles were so tense, they burned. But I took my position again and repeated the steps. I watched her nodding almost imperceptibly as she walked around me, analyzing my movements.

"Don't look at the floor, dear. Back, back, arabesque… Pas de bourrée, five and up until the passé…"

I continued struggling for another half hour, concentrating on dancing with my head because whenever I let go, my heart took over. And then I made mistakes, and she always noticed. I hated dancing and thinking about it: It just wasn't fun.

When I first started ballet, what I liked about it was that it was a game, one I was very good at. I learned the steps and the choreography quickly and then all I had to do was dance and feel the music. Jump, turn, fly. Flap my wings like a butterfly without a thought in my head.

As I progressed, my grandmother turned my favorite pastime into a competition, and I ceased to enjoy it. Or I didn't enjoy it in the same way. I stopped being motivated by what I felt when I danced and became addicted to the slight shows of approval she gave me every time I bested other girls and myself. The need for approval kept me always tense, always on the verge of cracking.

"Good… arabesque, pirouette, and finish in the fourth position."

I stopped, chin raised, chest rising and falling quickly in search of air. I looked her in the eyes, expecting a reaction. I had done well, better than well, and I was sure of it. I was just twelve years old, but I was head and shoulders above most.

My stomach growled, my cheeks burned. I could control many things, but not my stomach, and I was hungry. I hadn't eaten anything since my breakfast of an apple and yogurt. My grandmother's eyelids sank a moment, slowly, showing no emotion but indifference. Or perhaps disgust.

"Repeat it from the beginning, and this time, try to move with elegance," she said softly.

5

Matías and I wound up spending the day together. We ate in a bar close to El Retiro Park, had a shaved ice near a pond, and slept in the garden under the shadows of the trees. It was almost eight when I got a message from Antoine apologizing for not responding earlier. He was sorry about the bad news and asked me to wait for him at his place.

I put my phone in my pocket and tried to ignore the unease that was roiling in my stomach. No more rehearsals for me. I needed to talk with Natalia, the company's director, and tell her what had happened. It wouldn't be pleasant. She had trusted in me from the beginning and had done everything possible after the accident to keep my place open in case I got better.

"Are you all right?" Matías asked. I shrugged. "Was it Antoine?"

I nodded and forced a smile.

"He says he's still got a few more hours of rehearsal."

Matías looked away with a slight scowl. It only lasted a second, but I could see the tension in his spine, the way his head turned upward. I knew him too well not to read his mood.

"What?" I asked.

"Nothing," he responded, grabbing my arm at the crosswalk. "I'll call Rodrigo to see if he's home and can open up for you. I left my backpack and keys in the changing room."

"Don't worry," I said. "I'll go with you."

"Are you sure you want to come?"

"Yeah, don't worry, I can handle it. Plus it'll give me the chance to talk to Natalia. The sooner the better, right?"

"Maya, it's just so fucking unfair!" Matías said, looking upset.

I tried to smile. It was nice knowing someone cared about me.

Eventually, we got tired of walking and caught the bus. Fifteen minutes later, we were walking along Paseo de la Chopera toward the company's building. When we entered, the lights were off in all the rehearsal rooms and nobody was there but the doorman. Strange, I thought: Antoine had only written me fifteen minutes before.

"They all finished early and left," he said.

"I forgot my backpack. Do you mind if we go get it?" Matías asked the doorman.

Squeezing Matías's hand, which I'd been holding since we were outside, I told him I needed to go to the bathroom.

"Again?"

"You know I've got a small bladder. I'll see you inside in a minute."

Matías went for his things and I ran to the bathroom, almost jumping up and down as I lifted the lid and pulled up my dress. I jerked down my panties and sighed with relief as that feeling of urgency faded away.

I was washing my hands when I heard water pouring down in the showers and a laugh I knew all too well. My heart skipped a beat. I listened closer and heard a groan and another laugh, higher pitched. It can't be, I thought. I walked to the changing room, barely able to take a breath.

The steam was already filling the air and condensing on the tiles.

I peeked into the showers. I could see a body, a back under the falling water, the silhouette of arms, hands on buttocks.

I froze, shuddered.

It was Antoine. But he wasn't alone. Just past him was a smaller, thinner woman's body. He was hooking up with someone else! He lifted her up in the air and she wrapped her legs around his back. Then I saw who it was. Sofía, my substitute. The same one who texted me every day telling me to get well soon. The hypocrite!

I felt myself dying inside.

I wanted to turn around and run out, but I couldn't stop staring. The way his hips moved between hers, as if their bodies already knew each other well and he was searching for the angle that gave her the most pleasure. The sound of their bodies rubbing together. Grunts, groans. Panting echoing off the walls.

On the verge of vomiting, I stepped back.

Pain. Disappointment.

Just then, she opened her eyes and stared straight at me. For a moment, she couldn't react. Then she shouted, "Maya!"

Antoine turned his head, and he looked like a deer in headlights. I ran off, prey to an agony that was eating into my entrails. I was trembling, I was furious, I could barely even see. Behind me, I could hear Antoine shouting at me.

Matías was waiting for me at the end of the hall. I ran toward him. The tears burned my eyes. With a startled expression, he looked at me and then past me, trying to figure out what was going on and why my boyfriend was chasing me and shouting my name.

"Maya, wait!" Antoine begged. "Let me explain. It's not what it seems!"

I turned and scowled at him. "It *seems* like you were banging Sofía."

"I don't even know how it happened. We were just rehearsing, and… My God, I'm sorry!"

He was disgusting, standing there completely naked, his member still defiantly erect.

"You're a pig," I hissed, turning toward the exit.

"Maya, please, wait. I'm sorry. I didn't plan it, I swear."

"I don't give a shit how it happened. I never want to see you again."

"It was the choreography that did it, you know how the pas de deux from *Carmen* is. All those hours rehearsing together... I think the character took me over."

I stopped, my hand on the doorframe, and looked back over my shoulder. Did he honestly think that excuse was going to cut it?

My face was hot from rage and shame.

"Fuck you, Antoine. Thanks for making this shitty day even worse."

I walked outside and covered my ears to stop hearing him shout my name.

At every step, the pain was more intense, and I didn't know what to do with it. It was burning me, stabbing me inside.

I wouldn't look back, I told myself, and I didn't. I didn't want to ever see that bastard again.

Matías ran up and stopped me, grabbing my shoulders and looking at me with his dark eyes. He didn't need to say anything. I could read his face like a book.

"You knew."

"I suspected."

"Why did you never tell me anything?" I asked furiously.

"Because I wasn't sure, Maya. I couldn't risk screwing up what you guys have when I wasn't certain. I'm sorry."

"How long have you suspected?"

"A few months, give or take."

"A few months, seriously?"

"He started acting weird after Natalia asked Sofía to step in for you. She praised him to high heaven and he obviously didn't mind, but still, it never occurred to me that Antoine would do anything. I mean, he fucking adores you! But I did start seeing things, and…"

"Just let it go. I don't even want to know…"

I leaned into him and cried, my tears soaking his T-shirt. I could feel his hand on the nape of my neck and the other hand stroking my back as he kissed me on top of my head.

"He's a dickhead," Matías said. "He doesn't deserve you… What will you do now?"

"We're close to the train station. When the high-speed line comes through, I could throw myself in front of it. If I jump right in front of the engine car, I don't think I'll survive."

I could feel him shaking as he laughed in silence. "That's not funny," I whispered.

"It is, though."

"I want to go home."

"Let's go home, then," he said.

We didn't say anything more as we walked. He held me up as he always did, and I let his affection warm me inside. I loved him like crazy, and just having him there made me calmer than I would have been.

My phone wouldn't quit ringing, and the sound was driving me crazy. I knew who it was. I stopped a moment to block his number. Then I erased it.

"Are you sure that's a good idea?" Matías asked me cautiously.

"He cheated on me. Who knows since when, and with how many girls. There's no way I'm going to talk to him again."

We reached the doorway to my building, and I pulled away from him reluctantly.

"Are you going to be OK?" he asked.

"Yeah, don't worry."

"I can stay if you like."

"You know how my grandmother is."

"I love ignoring her, and I'm good at it," he joked.

"Yeah, that's why she can't stand you."

"Good thing I don't care."

I looked down at my feet. I didn't really want to say goodbye, because I knew once he left, my life preserver would be gone and I'd be unable to remain afloat in the sea of self-pity.

"You know you and I would make the perfect couple," I murmured.

"We already are the perfect couple, dummy."

"We should make one of those promises to each other like they do in the movies: that if in ten years, you haven't met the man of your dreams and I'm still going out with the same dickheads, we can get married and grow old together."

"Sounds good. What about sex, though?" he asked.

"Sex is overrated."

"Only a person who's never been laid properly would say that."

I narrowed my brows and smacked him on the chest, and he broke out laughing and pulled me in close. I loved his laughter, I loved his arms around me. He was my little boy, my refuge.

People walked past us.

The world kept turning.

Time advanced inexorably.

The immensity of the universe enveloped us, and in that infinite space, my problems and I were nothing more than an invisible dot.

It was terrifying, feeling so insignificant.

6

The next day, my grandmother changed her torture strategy and decided to ignore me, pretending I didn't exist and taking it so far that at midday, she didn't even set a place for me at lunch.

I'd be lying if I said it didn't hurt.

Matías had told me before that what Olga did with me could be considered abuse. But I never wanted to listen. That sounded repulsive to me. Sure, my grandmother had been harsh, but she did it to motivate me. She pushed me to work hard because the world was competitive and if you wanted to make a name for yourself, you couldn't settle for being just good.

The problems arose when I started to have dreams of my own. Wishes that were different from hers and that I ended up sacrificing for her sake. She always ended up getting what she wanted, and I just went along with her to avoid arguments.

Maybe from inertia.

Maybe from force of habit.

Maybe because Matías was right and I had always been afraid of her.

My grandparents were the only family I was close to, the people I had grown up with. When I was born, my two uncles, my mother's older brothers, had already moved out of Madrid and only visited for the holidays. I was never close to them or their families.

All I had was my grandparents, and the possibility of losing them had terrified me since I was little. If it had been so easy for my mother to leave me, wasn't it possible they could do the same? But now that fear was lessening, and my dignity, my pride was taking over. I knew I didn't deserve to be humiliated. I hadn't done anything wrong, and for six months now, my grandmother had made my life a hell of reproaches and nasty comments.

From the dining room table, Carmen watched me with pity in her eyes as I helped my grandfather eat. I smiled at her: I didn't want her to worry about me. I went to my room, feeling an immense emptiness creeping in through all my pores. I turned on my phone and the notifications rolled in.

I was surprised to find a few messages from Sofía, which I erased without reading. It was too late for her to try to act like we were sisters.

An unknown number had written me dozens of times. I opened my messages and immediately got a bitter taste in my mouth. Antoine. I erased all of them and blocked that number, too.

I saw several missed calls from Natalia that made my heart race, and I sent her a message asking if we could meet that afternoon. She said yes, and we agreed to see each other at six at the company building. I needed to talk with her as soon as possible and let her know that, despite what we'd both hoped, I wasn't going to get better. No more projects. No more plans. Or not with me, anyway.

I lay in bed, put on my headphones, and turned on Spotify, closing my eyes. A song played, then another, and I let the music fill me, losing myself in the notes, in the melody, and standing and moving to the rhythm without even realizing it.

Without being self-conscious.

Without worrying.

I let myself go, and I flew. I rose higher and higher and my arms shook and my body twisted. My heart quaked and my lungs contracted.

And I tasted the saltiness of tears.

I turned on my tiptoes.

Once.

Twice.

Maybe, if I wished harder, they'd appear.

I closed my eyes tight and my movements became a furious dance.

And for a second, I could almost feel them under my skin, bursting through my back.

Almost.

My invisible wings.

The wings that would take me out of there and make me free.

As they did for my mother.

I wanted freedom so badly.

7

At four years old

I walked into the academy with my grandfather, who had picked me up from day care. He kissed me on the head and left to run some errands. I followed the music to the hall and entered without making noise. My grandmother hated it when I interrupted her classes.

I sat on the floor, back close to the mirror, and watched my mother, smiling.

"Again, Daria," my grandmother said while my mother moved around her. "Pirouette en dedans, attitude derrière… Pirouette into attitude and arabesque. Don't bend your knee! Good, développé to écarté devant, attitude derrière… Grand allegro…jeté, jeté and grand jeté."

When she touched the floor, my mother stumbled forward.

"Sorry," she quickly excused herself.

"My God, you look like a novice. Concentrate!"

"I've been here for hours. I'm tired."

"Your auditions are around the corner. You can't let up now," my grandmother replied severely.

I watched my mother close her eyes and take a sudden, deep breath. I don't know why, but I wanted to cry. She always seemed so sad, so forlorn, surrounded by a halo of desolation.

My grandmother's voice echoed off the mirrors, frightening me. She said something in Ukrainian, turned off the music, and hurried out. I didn't move. I just stared at my mother as she walked over to the window and rested her hands against the glass, staying there a long while, trembling, then rocking back and forth as the thin rays of sun made strange reflections on the floor and lit up her feet.

She stood on her tiptoes. An inaudible beat guided her hands, her arms, and her legs. She turned, jumped in the air, descended with the elegance of a feather. The music was playing inside her, and I couldn't stop watching her.

My mother was gorgeous. Her hair was blond, her eyes gray, and they always filled with tears when she looked at me. Maybe that was why she didn't do it that often, preferring to stare at the ground.

I felt a heaviness in my chest. Her emotions reached me, but I didn't understand them. I did feel them, though. I had never seen her dance that way, and it was beautiful and terrifying.

"Why are you dancing like that, Mom?"

"I'm not dancing, Maya."

"What are you doing?"

"I'm flying. Can't you tell?"

She jumped again and flapped her arms with a swanlike delicacy.

"But Mom, you don't have wings."

"I do, though, they're just invisible, that's why you can't see them."

I grinned and imitated her, hopping and moving my arms as my grandmother had taught me.

"I want to do it, too, Mom. Can I have invisible wings like yours?"

"Sure, Maya. You'll realize one day you already do, and you'll fly very, very far."

"To where?"

"Wherever you want, because the place doesn't even matter. What's important is you'll be free."

She grabbed my hands and turned me, and I saw tears in her eyes and a big, bright smile on her face. She threw me into the air, and I laughed.

"Freeeee!" I shouted.

"Free," she repeated. She hugged me and spun with me in her arms. "I'm sorry, Maya. I'm so, so sorry."

"For what, Mom?"

"Not being stronger."

I didn't understand what she meant. I thought she was the strongest person in the world. She was making me fly and I didn't even have wings. She looked me in the eye in a way she'd never done for a long time. Then she kissed me and put me down.

That same night, she left without saying goodbye.

Without telling me where.

She just left.

8

Happiness doesn't depend on what happens to us, but on how we perceive what happens to us. I still hadn't learned that, though, when I met with Natalia and her team. So I walked out feeling as if I'd been fired, thinking about the facts and their meaning and not how I felt about them.

And the facts were simple. I'd hurt myself. My professional ballet career was over. I was twenty-two years old and I had devoted eighteen of those years to ballet. My only goal had ever been to become principal in a major company. I had dreamed of joining the Ballet de la Opéra in Paris, or the Mariinsky, or the Bolshoi. And because of that, I had lived in my own world where nothing except dancing mattered. A world that demanded a great deal of sacrifice. A world that could be painful if you didn't stand out. A world I had given myself to body and soul, and that now no longer had a place for me.

The door had closed in my face.

All I could think about was what a failure I was. How disappointed my grandmother would be. How all the work I'd done was lost and how I'd suffered to scale every step and had defended my position tooth and nail.

But I didn't stop to think about how I actually *felt*. About that chain that had been so tight around my chest and was starting to fall away. That breath of fresh air sinking in among all that accumulated unhappiness. Layers and layers of unhappiness that had clung so tightly to my skin, it seemed I was born with them.

I walked briskly to the exit. I didn't want anyone to see me crying.

The music of the second act of *Giselle* emerged from the rehearsal studio, and I could hear my friend Mar's voice repeating the steps for the ballerinas. My skin was standing up on end and I wanted to peek in. I didn't, though. My heart wouldn't let me.

I was nearly outside when I felt a hand on my shoulder.

"Maya."

That voice.

I pushed the door and walked out without looking back.

"Maya, please," Antoine insisted.

I stopped and turned around, looking him in the eyes with a blend of contempt and repulsion. He had deep bags under his eyes, and the green of his irises didn't shine as it had before. He was shirtless, in cotton pants and leg warmers, his torso gleaming beneath a layer of sweat.

"What?" I shouted.

"I'm sorry."

"And what, exactly, are you sorry for? Hooking up with her for more than a month straight, or me catching you?" His eyes opened wide in surprise, and that was enough for me to confirm I was right. "Do you think I'm an idiot?" I went on. "I know yesterday wasn't the first time."

He looked down, embarrassed, and murmured, "I love you."

"Well, you sure know how to show it."

"I'm sorry I hurt you. Sofía means nothing to me. At first, it was all just a game. We seduced each other as we danced, trying to find a little chemistry because, at first, we were like two robots. It was nothing like when you and I dance." He ran his hands through his hair, frustrated, and looked straight at me. "It got out of hand. And I regret it. I was an idiot, Maya."

"So what? You want me to feel better now? Because I don't."

"Forgive me, please. Let me fix it, let me make it up to you. I won't see Sofía anymore. I'll ask Natalia to change my partner, I'll do whatever you want, just…forgive me!"

"I'm sorry, but I can't. I don't trust you anymore."

"Maya, please."

"No. It's over. And I hope for your sake you didn't give me anything. Because from what I saw yesterday, you didn't even have the decency to use protection…"

"I did, always. I would never risk giving you something. It's just that yesterday…"

"Yesterday you were horny like a dog and couldn't help it?!" I sighed. "I don't care, I'm going."

"Maya, don't leave! Talk to me. We can work this out."

"No! There is no working this out, and you know what? It's actually better. This is the best thing that could have happened to me. A clean break with all this shit. That'll make it easier to get over. Sorry, Antoine, but you and I are done."

"I made a mistake! It won't happen again! I can't lose you, though."

"You should have thought of that before," I told him, turning around and walking off.

"Maya…Maya, please."

I ignored the pleading in his voice and the fact that he was following me out.

A bus passed and stopped about fifteen feet ahead, and I ran up to it and edged through the doors just as they were closing. With a knot in my throat, I walked down the aisle and held onto one of the bars. I looked through the glass and saw Antoine on the sidewalk, immobile, shrinking as we pulled away.

I forced myself to breathe, but the air refused to enter my lungs. It was all I could do not to break down then and there right in the middle of those strangers surrounding me, who knew nothing about me and the drama I was going through.

I went straight home, though it was the last place I wanted to be. The tension between my grandmother and me could have been cut with a knife. It was stifling in there, heavy, and she didn't even need to speak to me to make me feel bad.

I was still thinking of Antoine as I opened the door. I didn't really know how I felt about him. He had cheated on me, and we had broken up after a whole year together.

I should have been angry, sad, broken…

But what I felt was…

Nothing. I actually felt nothing. And that concerned me.

I heard voices in the living room. They were talking softly, but I could tell they were arguing. I peeked in and saw my grandparents sitting on the sofa. I was surprised: They never disagreed, at least not openly. They adored each other and got along perfectly. They were very different, but they complemented each other and always had.

She was the wave that swept everything away, and he was the foam it left behind.

She was the shout, he was the echo.

She would say jump, and he would always ask how high.

Olga looked up, saw me, and stood, putting an end to their conversation.

"Hey," I greeted them.

"Hello, darling. Is everything good?" my grandfather asked.

"Yeah, I'm going to my room."

He nodded and smiled. But he didn't look especially happy. I started away, but turned back when I heard her clear her throat to get my attention.

"Have you thought about what you're going to do?" she asked.

"About what?"

"About your life from now on, obviously."

Once again, I felt like I could barely breathe, like I was still flailing with my head just above the surface of the water. No: I still hadn't thought about what to do with my life. I shrugged and remembered what Matías had said.

"I might go back to school. Go to María de Ávila, become a teacher."

She sighed, and I prepared myself for some nasty response.

"You need to get a job. As quickly as possible."

I nodded and left, and once in my room, I made an appointment with my doctor. Then I lay back on my bed and remained there for hours, sometimes sleeping, other times awake, until my sense of time vanished.

My mind was empty.

I was thinking of nothing.

And of everything.

Waiting for an explosion that wouldn't come.

For a crack.

For a collapse.

For the rubble to fall at my feet.

The rubble of myself.

But there was none of that. Just tears. Bitter, salty tears. Hot, painful. Leaving me empty and numb.

Tears that had no real reason to be, because when I thought of Antoine, all I could hear was a little voice telling me this was how things went: Relationships start and end, and that's it. I looked around in myself for rage, wounded pride, pain, the sense of betrayal and rupture. But I didn't find those feelings anywhere.

And that terrified me, because what did it say about me? About him? About us? Was there an *us*?

Those tears didn't have a clear motive, but when I thought of my now-vanished career, all I could feel was anxiety, fear of my grandmother. Her rejecting me. Her indifference. Losing her, too. She had only ever loved me in exact proportion to the perfection of my pirouettes and sautés. Would she still love me now that I was just me?

I was scared because if the answer was no, what was left?

Just me.

And who was I?

9

Several days passed between my most recent medical tests and the phone call from my doctor giving me the results. I breathed easily once I learned I had nothing to worry about. No STDs. Everything was in order.

I thanked him, hung up, and felt relaxation flow through my body.

I looked up at Matías. We were having a coffee outside at the Starbucks on the Plaza del Callao. "Good news?" he asked.

"Yes. My vagina is still a perfect little garden. No crabs, no syphilis, no nothing."

Matías burst out laughing, his cup to his lips, and splattered coffee all over the table. I looked down with horror. I had a pile of résumés sitting there. It had taken me forever to get them right, the printer wasn't what you'd call cheap, and now he'd spit all over them!

"Shit, Matías! You ruined them." I sorted through them, pulling out the decent ones as he kept chuckling. "Is me saying 'vagina' really that funny?"

"It's the ugliest word ever."

"Sure, and I guess 'penis' is music to your ears."

"Now that you mention it, yes it is," he said.

I narrowed my eyes maliciously and started repeating, "Vagina, vagina, vagina, vaginaaaaa…"

A woman frowned at me from the next table over, but the man with her, who I assumed was her husband, grinned, looking past his newspaper.

With an innocent look on my face, I told the woman, "He's my gynecologist."

Matías was cackling now, bent forward with tears in his eyes, resting his head on the table. He glanced up and said, "You're crazy."

"And you're a child. Apart from paying for the coffee, you owe me five euros for the résumés."

"It wasn't my fault!" He kicked me under the table. "But whatever. What do you want to do now?"

"I don't know. Some window shopping, maybe? You can hand out a couple of those CVs."

Matías offered me his hand, and as we stood, I gave him a hug, feeling like a baby koala as he kissed me on top of the head. What would I do without him? He was my one constant in the midst of so much uncertainty.

We spent the rest of the morning stopping at shops, restaurants, and cafes, and at lunchtime, my feet hurt and my cheeks were aching from smiling at all the people I hoped might hire me.

"Do you think anyone will call?" I asked him as he left me at my place.

"You'll see. Something will come up."

"I hope so. I'll need to start squirreling away now if I'm going to make it through the winter."

Brushing a hair out of my face, he said, "Talk to an adviser or something. Maybe you can collect unemployment or disability or something."

"Sure, I will."

"I've got to go," he said. "I promised Rodrigo we could have lunch together."

"You and Rodrigo sure have been spending a lot of time together."

"Of course we do, we live together, Maya."

"And you don't seem to mind."

Looking a little embarrassed, he told me, "He's not interested."

"His loss."

We hugged each other for a long goodbye, and for that brief moment, I managed to tell myself everything would be all right. Calm, at ease, I climbed the stairs. When I reached my floor, I found Carmen walking out of the apartment, eyes red, expression distressed.

Worried, I asked, "Carmen, what is it? Is my grandfather OK?"

"He's fine, Maya," she replied, trying to pretend everything was all right.

"What is it then?"

"I'm going. Your grandmother doesn't need my services anymore."

"She fired you? Why?"

"Just go in." She took a deep breath. "And good luck. If you need me, you know where to find me. You can call me anytime, OK?"

"Sure."

"Bye. Take care, now."

I watched the door to the elevator open. She stepped inside, looking back at me with a maudlin expression before she disappeared.

At home, I could hear voices. I entered softly and shuddered when I saw one of them belonged to my uncle Andrey. What was he doing there? He lived in Alicante, and he didn't usually come around much.

"I don't agree with any of this. This isn't right," my grandfather said.

"We've talked about it already, Dad. You need help with everything, even eating, and Mom can't take care of it all anymore. Besides, you're both all alone here. It only makes sense for you to come with

Yoan and me. You can be closer to us, to your grandkids," my uncle said.

Wait—were they talking about leaving Madrid? And just like that, from one day to the next?

"This isn't the right way to do things. We both know perfectly well the real reason you want to leave Madrid," my grandfather replied.

"We're getting old, and we're far away from our children. There's nothing for us here anymore, Luis," my grandmother replied.

"You're punishing her."

"Don't be ridiculous. I don't want to argue about this anymore!" My grandmother's voice was straining. "The movers will come the day after tomorrow, and the Realtors have already found a couple interested in renting the apartment. We're going."

"Yeah, Dad. Mom's right," Andrey said.

I walked, trembling, into the living room, where they were sitting. "You're renting out our home?" I asked.

All three of them turned. Even my grandfather, who couldn't see, squinted in my direction.

"Yes," my grandmother said.

"Maya, dear…" my grandfather began, but my uncle cut him off, "Dad!" Nervously, Andrey continued, "I'm taking them with me. They need a change of scene, and the sun and sea will be good for them. Uncle Yoan, Aunt Ana, your cousins…all of us want them down there."

"But what about me? Why didn't anybody ask me anything? I live here, too. This is my home," I objected.

"No, it's my home," my grandmother countered.

I was confused. My heart was pounding. Unease overtook me. Where did I fit into this plan? I didn't know, but it couldn't be anywhere good. The idea of dropping everything and moving to Alicante with them was out of the question. But how the hell could I stay in

Madrid with nowhere to live? I needed to find a place, and I barely had a cent to my name.

"What will I do?" I asked.

My uncle didn't beat around the bush. He was like my grandmother in that way. "Sorry, Maya. I've only got one room free. And…"

"And…" my grandmother said, "you're an adult, you're twenty-two years old. At your age I was already making a living and no one helped me. It's about time you looked for a job and went out on your own. Live your own life. Isn't that what you wanted anyway? To move away to New York?"

She was being sarcastic, reproachful, and I could tell. She thought I was a total failure, and she wasn't even trying to hide it. Wickedness impregnated her words. She knew perfectly well that my ship had sailed and wouldn't come back. And she knew how much missing that opportunity had hurt.

"Olga!" my grandfather said.

"Am I wrong? She was ready to leave us here after all I've sacrificed for her. All the time I spent trying to make her into something."

I opened my mouth to defend myself, but I couldn't. I didn't have the strength to say a word. I was beaten, defenseless, frozen. I felt a part of me had died inside, and she hadn't even budged as she'd spoken those words.

"How much time do I have?"

"The apartment needs to be empty in three days."

I nodded and walked automatically to my room. Once inside, I shut the door and leaned against it, feeling suffocated. They'd kicked me out with no warning, without offering me a shoulder to cry on. I was alone, the way I'd always felt with my family.

There had been a division there since forever: them on one side, me on the other, divided by a thick line, like rivals on opposite sides of the field. I never knew why, though. If it was because I looked different, or because my mother left me. My mother—the black sheep of the family. Or maybe it was because my father was some stranger who didn't even know I was alive.

I had been a mistake, and nobody had wanted me. I invaded their lives. I shattered a dream, and now they wanted me to make that better. But I couldn't. I couldn't fix things.

I walked to the window and lowered the blinds. It was hot in there. Someone knocked on the door. I saw the knob turn, saw my grandfather's face peeking in.

"Maya?"

I walked over and took his hand. "Do you need something, Grandpa?"

He squeezed my hand and shook his head. I guided him over to my bed and helped him sit down.

"I can't make her be reasonable. When she gets something in her head, she just can't see any further. She won't listen." I could tell he was upset as he told me this.

"Don't worry about it. I don't want you to have to argue with her because of me."

"How can I not worry, honey? Leaving you here, all on your own."

I settled down next to him, feeling resigned.

"I'll make it. I'm not a little girl anymore."

"You've never been a little girl," he mused. "I wish there was something I could do, but since I went blind, they've treated me like a damn fool. A zero, someone whose opinion doesn't even count. I'm blind, not stupid! My brain works just fine."

"Of course it does. But you know… Maybe it's not such a bad idea, you two moving down there. Andrey's got a great house, with a huge yard. You can sunbathe and take walks on the beach."

He clicked his tongue in displeasure. "I hate the beach."

I giggled and rested my head on his shoulder. I loved him so much.

I can't say he was like a father to me—he never tried to be—but he did give me the best upbringing he could, and he was always there for me with open arms.

"Everything will be OK," I whispered.

"That's for me to say." He waited a moment before continuing. "Maybe I shouldn't have loved her so much. If it had been different, maybe I'd have had the strength to face her. To tell her she should think twice before raising our granddaughter the way she did. But I didn't do it."

Neither did I, I thought.

In the background, I could hear the traffic and the washing machine rumbling down the hall.

"What are you thinking about?" he asked me after a couple of minutes had passed.

"How I don't know where to put my things," I said, looking around.

The pain in my chest wouldn't go away. In fact, it got worse as I realized that a day would come when other pictures would decorate my walls, other clothing would hang in my closet, another person would live in my bed.

"You can take it down to the storage room in the basement. We won't rent it out."

"OK."

"Everything will be fine," he said softly, feeling around for my hand.

"I know," I told him.

And in silence, I prayed that I really did.

10

"And here's the bathroom. It's a little small and doesn't have a window, but for a shower and a dump, you don't really need much else, right?"

I looked at the guy and blinked in a state of utter shock. He was wearing a pair of tighty-whities and a sleeveless shirt that clearly hadn't seen the inside of a washing machine in ages. A joint was hanging from his lips, and the scent of it was making me sick to my stomach. He smiled and scratched his temple. I glanced around again at the mildew on the walls and in the gaps between the weird, yellowish tiles. It looked like no one had cleaned in months. And the stench...

I wanted to puke.

And yet, it was the nicest apartment I'd looked at so far, and more importantly, I could afford it. As long as I could learn to hold my breath the entire time I was there, it would be all right.

Behind me, Matías must have sensed that I was getting close to saying yes, because he grabbed me by the arm and pulled me back, saying, "Thanks for showing us around, pal. We're going to think it over and we'll let you know." His tone was chipper as he dragged me toward the door.

"Let us know soon, dude," the guy said. "There's a lot of people interested."

"Right, no problem," Matías said.

We made it to the landing and Matías tried closing the door three times before managing to get it all the way shut. He walked me quickly down the four floors, and once we were outside, he gave me a serious look.

"Have you lost your mind? Are you actually thinking of living in this place? It's a trash heap, and that guy…"

He shivered with disgust.

"Matías, we've been looking at apartments for two days and this is the only thing I've found that I can afford. I hardly have any savings, I don't have a job, and tomorrow I have to leave my home forever. I can't afford to be picky."

"You can stay with me until you find something."

"Your bed's too small."

"Take the couch. No, I'll take the couch." It was funny how quickly he changed his mind.

"And see Antoine every day? I don't think so." I leaned against the wall of the building and rubbed my face. "I don't know what I'm going to do."

Matías grabbed my hand and pulled me toward him, walking off.

"For now, we're going to eat something. Then we'll cross our fingers and look at the other three apartments on the list."

When I got back home in the early evening, I could feel my heart cracking inside. The living room and hallway were full of boxes. Andrey had tape and a marker and was sealing and labeling all our possessions. For the first time, I truly knew the nightmare was real. That the only family I had was abandoning me when I needed them most.

I ran to my room and shut the door. On top of the bed were a bunch of empty boxes. Very subtle.

I threw my purse on top of the dresser and took off my shoes. There was no point in drawing this out, so I gathered my things, starting with the books that filled my shelves, then the clothing, then the shoes. With every drawer I opened and shut, a deeper anxiety overtook me. I still didn't have a place to live, and time was getting away from me, and I didn't know what to do.

I hadn't gotten lucky with any of the apartments I looked at. One of the rooms was already rented; the second one wasn't even a real room, just a bed out on a glassed-in balcony someone was trying to charge three hundred euros a month for; and the third I rejected outright when I saw a falling objects warning in the doorway.

One of the women who lived there told me, "It's termites. But I've been here for ten years, and nothing's ever happened. It is noisy, though…"

I sat on the bed after taping the last box shut. My knee hurt, so I grabbed a painkiller from the box on the nightstand, chewing it up and trying to keep a clear head.

My phone screen lit up with an Instagram notification. The company had tagged me in one of its posts. I opened it, feeling anxious, and saw a photo of one of my rehearsals taken just a few days before last Christmas. A few days before everything fell apart.

Goodbye, Maya. You'll always be dancing in our hearts, the message read.

"I'm not fucking dead," I murmured.

I mean, I guess it was nice, but it was depressing as hell, too, like this was the end of me as a person.

I looked at the rest of my notifications and messages, but there was nothing there that mattered. I expected that since I hardly ever posted. On an impulse, I unblocked my mother's account and found myself reading her posts. The last one was from December 31, just before midnight struck. She was with Alexis, the guy she'd been with for the past ten years, on a beach with a bag of grapes in her hand. Guille, my little brother, was between them.

My brother.

That word still got stuck in my throat. He was five now, and I'd only ever seen him once. I took a deep breath and slid my finger over the screen, looking at photo after photo. Faces, gestures, laughter, hugs. Special moments. They looked so happy.

Even though I didn't want to, a part of me envied that boy for having with him the mother I never did. She had never looked at me with that light in her eyes, with that genuine smile. She had never hugged me so tight I struggled to get away, or kissed me until my cheek ached.

I stopped on one picture of my mother's face and peered in close. We basically had no relationship apart from the birthday present she usually sent me and a couple of phone calls every few months that lasted just long enough to ask how we each were amid awkward silences and pointless phrases that left a bitter taste in my mouth.

She didn't come see me when I had the accident, and in a way, I was even grateful.

They say time heals all, and I wondered all the time how much time I would need to get over her abandoning me. Leaving me there like a hostage so she could be free.

For a moment, I wanted to call her.

For a moment, I wished I was brave enough to go look for her.

But I didn't. I just stood and carried out the first box.

I grabbed the key to the storage room, which was hanging on the door of a cabinet near the apartment door. I walked out, got into the elevator, and went down to the garage. The door to our storage closet was a little tough to open—the lock clearly hadn't been used for years. The air inside smelled dry and dusty. The light blinked, and I looked around. It was a little bigger than I'd expected. If I moved the bike and piled up the plastic crates on the floor, I could make a place for my things on the shelves.

A half hour later, my entire bedroom's contents were piled up there in that unventilated concrete room. I set down the last box and rubbed my chest. My pride felt wounded, and I was angry and heartbroken.

When I turned around to go, my pants pocket caught on something. I jumped back just before a wooden box fell and landed on my foot. It struck the floor and cracked open, the lid tearing free from the hinges. And from inside, I heard a series of harmonious notes, as from a barrel organ.

It was a music box.

I crouched down and picked it up, regretting my clumsiness.

It was precious, painted blue and gold. I looked closer at it. It must have been very old. Inside it held a porcelain ballerina. I touched it and sighed with relief. Miraculously, it hadn't broken. I turned it over and over in my hand to see if I'd damaged it and saw the bottom part pulling slightly away. A piece of paper peeked out.

I pulled it open and found several photos inside. In them were my mother and a brown-haired guy. I stood and looked closely at them under the bare bulb hanging above. I was stunned.

The guy…

The guy in the photos looked exactly like me.

I've always struggled to see it when someone says so-and-so is the spitting image of their dad or their uncle, but in this case, it was so clear… As if someone had taken my face and plugged it into one of those apps that show you what you'd look like if you were the opposite sex. He even had the same mole over his eyebrow that I did.

I picked up the pieces of the music box and put them back on the shelf. Then I stuffed the photos in my pocket and walked out, confused. My hands were shaking as I entered the elevator, and my body was in a cold sweat.

My mother had always told me she had no idea who my father was, that she got too drunk one night and had sex with a guy she didn't know from Adam. She didn't know his name, his age, or where he was from. He was a ghost.

No one ever questioned that.

It never occurred to anyone that what she said might not be true.

But the photos told a very different story.

I grabbed my purse and went out impulsively. I knew Matías would still be up, and I needed someone to tell me if I was going crazy, seeing things. I caught a cab, and five minutes later it stopped in front of his building. I sent a message asking him to come down, and soon he was there.

"What's up? Are you OK?" he asked, worried. I reached out and handed him the pictures. Confused, he said, "What are these?"

"Just look at them and tell me what you see."

Matías blinked a few times and looked attentively at the photo. Even in the shadows beneath the streetlights, the resemblance was evident. "That's your mom, right?"

"Yeah, but what else do you see?"

"That's the vestibule at the Royal Conservatory, and she looks young, so I guess she was still studying there."

Impatiently, I took the photo from him and held it next to my cheek. "Look closely at the guy next to her." Then I pulled back my hair and pointed at my face. "Notice anything?"

Matías brought his face close to the photo and shook his head.

"No way!"

Nervously, I asked, "I'm not making it up, right? There's a major resemblance there."

"You're like the same person."

I felt weak in the knees and had to lean against the wall. "She always told me I was a slipup, that she'd hooked up with a stranger, that she knew nothing about him and he was impossible to get in touch with. But that's not what the pictures say. Plus they were hidden. If that box hadn't broken…"

Matías shook his head and leaned next to me. "What are you going to do?"

"I don't know. Not having a dad never really mattered to me that much, especially one who didn't know I existed. But now… I don't know. What if he's out there? What if he does know about me? Where is he?"

"You need to confront your mother and make her tell you the truth."

"It's been twenty-two years. Don't you think she would have told me if she'd wanted to? And why should I trust her, right? If the man in the pictures is who I think he is, then she's gone out of her way to make sure I don't know about him."

"So?"

"I don't know, Matías. I'm freaking out right now. I don't know what I feel—if I even want to know who he is, if I want to meet him… Maybe it's just a coincidence that we look alike and I'm overthinking it." I shook my head, unable to clear my thoughts, feeling lost in all that uncertainty.

"Listen, if I had a daughter wandering the world, I'd want to know," Matías said.

"What if he does know?"

"Even if he does, the question is what *you* need. You don't have to respect his decisions when they affect you like this."

I closed my eyes and thought about what he said, trying to silence the voices in my head that came from the more rational part of myself. The part that was debating between what was the right thing to do and what was the easy thing to do. The part that was scared to suffer and that preferred to ignore the truth. The part that thought of others before myself.

Matías was right. I wasn't just born from nothing. I had a father and a mother and no relationship with either of them. They had made that choice for me. But what about what I wanted? Why should I just accept things as they were when they affected my life?

The words emerged on their own, pushed by anxieties I didn't know I had before then. "I need to know who my father is. I need to meet him. I need to know his name, his age, where he lives, what he does for a living. If he has a family. What his voice sounds like, what he smells like. I need to know if he ever thinks of me."

"Then do it, Maya. Go look for him."

I nodded, more and more convinced that this was something I had to do.

"I will."

11

There's always a first step. One that puts us on a certain path and shapes everything that will happen afterward. It's like a compass pointing us in a certain direction. Finding those photos was the first step on a journey whose destination I still don't know today. That's what life is like: random, unpredictable, impossible to plan. And you just have to keep living it until the day you die. The end—that's the only real destination.

When that moment comes, the moment when everything changes and your path turns in a different direction, you know it. You feel it. Maybe you just feel a slight tickle. The air grows thinner. You can't concentrate, you get a feeling in your chest, you keep needing to look over your shoulder.

Still—you know it.

And I knew it that next morning, after a sleepless night.

I got up early and went to the Royal Dance Conservatory. I was absolutely certain that my mother wouldn't give me any answers if I had nothing to base my questions on. And that meant I needed a lot more than a photo of someone who looked like me.

I knew Fyodora was still giving classes on Tuesdays and Thursdays from nine to eleven, and that she liked to arrive early. I waited for her at the door. I felt like a bundle of nerves. When she arrived, I ran over to meet her.

"Maya, what are you doing here?" she asked, glad to see me. "You look wonderful."

"I'm here to see you."

She must have known something was up, because her smile vanished and she put a hand on my back and guided me off to a corner. I had known Fyodora since I started ballet at the conservatory at eight years old, and she had always been kind to me. A mentor.

"Did you see my message? I'm so sorry you had to quit the company."

"I did see it. Thank you. But that's not why I came," I said.

"Is everything OK?"

I took the photos out of my purse and showed them to her. "Do you know this guy who's with my mother?"

"Honestly, no."

"He looks like a student. See, in this picture he's wearing tights." I pointed to a stairway in the vestibule. "Those are the same steps, right?"

"They are."

"And you were already teaching here when my mother was a student. Is it possible you taught this guy? Does he really not ring a bell?"

"I'm sorry, Maya," she responded. "I have no idea who he is. Maybe he wasn't a regular student. Maybe he was just here for a summer class. Why are you so interested, though?"

"I think he's my father." Fyodora was astonished. I continued. "I need you to help me figure out who he is. If he was here, maybe there's a file, a name, an address…something that can help me find him."

"That's against the rules, Maya. You know I can't give out personal information."

"It's been decades," I argued. "Please. That could be the only clue as to who he is and his whereabouts."

"What even makes you think he's your father?" she asked.

"Take a look and tell me he's not."

She looked at the photos and licked her lips with their pretty pink lipstick. Then she sighed.

"You do look a lot alike," she mused.

I begged her, "Fyodora, I realize maybe this is a dead end, but what if he's my father? I have a right to know."

She hesitated, and in her eyes I could see a flood of contradictory emotions: anxiety, loyalty toward me, the need to do the right thing, uncertainty as to what the right thing was.

"Fine, I'll try. I'll call you if I find anything."

"No. I'm going to wait here," I insisted. "My grandmother wants to leave Madrid, and they've already rented out the apartment. I'm basically on the street. I have no idea where I'll be tomorrow."

"Olga's leaving Madrid?"

"She made the decision as soon as she found out I couldn't do ballet anymore."

I couldn't quite gauge her reaction. She looked alarmed but unsurprised, as if she couldn't have expected anything different from my grandmother. One thing was clear, though: learning that had tipped the scale in my favor.

"Wait for me at the café in Puerta Bonita, I'll do what I can do find out who the guy in the photos is. You deserve it, even if I'm not sure it will get you far."

"Thank you."

I walked to the café, ordered a tea, and sat outside. I don't know how long I sat there, almost twitching from anxiousness, but it felt like an eternity. I asked myself questions: What if I got a name? An address? Would I just show up there out of the blue and tell him, *Hi, my name's Maya and I think I'm your daughter?*

It wasn't perfect.

But did I have another option?

I toyed fretfully with my hair, waiting for Fyodora to appear, and when she did, I shot to my feet.

"Did you find something?"

"Barely," she responded.

Barely. That wasn't the same as nothing. It meant there was a possibility, small though it may be. I felt the world revolving around me.

Fyodora sat down and handed the photos back to me.

"There wasn't anything in our files from the years when your mother was here, but on a hunch, I decided to look at the group photos we used to take of the students at the end of each semester, summer included."

I dug my nails so deeply in my thighs that it hurt.

"And?"

Fyodora set before me a xeroxed copy of a photo: black and white, a little dark. But I could still see the guy I was looking for in the group. He was fourth from the bottom. Under the photo was a caption with a list of names.

"Going from left to right, one, two, three… Giulio Dassori."

Holding my breath, I repeated that name to myself: *Giulio Dassori, Teatro di San Carlo Ballet School, Naples.* Fyodora and I looked at each other, and she rested her hand on mine. I gripped her fingers, feeling comforted, and told her thanks, even though I could barely speak.

"My father used to say if you see a sign, you have to follow it. Because once you leave it behind, it might never come back," she told me.

"What do you mean?"

"I think this is your sign, Maya. And you need to follow it. My father also said there was no such thing as coincidence, that everything happens for a reason. Fate is pulling the strings, guiding us—not like marionettes, though. It's asking us to be the heroes of our own stories, not bit actors in the stories of others."

"You say that like I was an actor in a play and Fate was the director."

"Sure, why not? I mean, life is made up of interlocking stories, and the world's the stage. It's that simple and that complicated."

I looked down at our hands, which were still joined. Complicated—sure. Simple—I didn't know about that.

"Do you really think this is a sign?" I asked.

"It would be worth it to find out. What do you have to lose?"

Looking at Fyodora, I felt a security that was unusual for me. Excitement, almost. A yearning I had stifled as long as I could remember to finally know my father.

"I don't want to get too emotional. It might not even be him."

"It might not. But what if it is?"

What if it is? I thought. Would I ignore the signs? Would I grab the line Fate was throwing me? Would I become the hero of my story or would I go on letting others' decisions guide me?

An invisible hand seemed to be crushing me. There were so many opportunities that it was frightening.

I kissed Fyodora twice on the cheek to say goodbye, and full of gratitude, I walked to the bus stop, unable to stop thinking about the man in the photos with my mother. They were clearly close. So comfortable together, holding each other… When two people care about each other, there's something in their eyes you can't deny.

I wondered what could have happened between them that would make her never even mention him.

Maybe he had gotten scared and left her hanging when he learned she was pregnant.

Maybe he was one of those guys who was incapable of taking

responsibility or thinking of anyone but himself. The world *was* full of men like that. Cruel, stupid, egotistical men.

But I forced myself to put an end to those negative thoughts. Maybe he wasn't anybody like that and here I was accusing him of terrible things for no reason.

I grabbed my phone and googled his name. There were several links. I clicked through them as I waited for the bus to arrive, but didn't find anything that helped. So I went to Instagram, hoping I would find his account.

I looked through dozens of photos before finding one with a profile photo that caught my eye. It was him. He was older, more mature looking, with a stubbly beard that hardened his features. But the eyes were the same: alive, awake, childlike. So similar to mine that I couldn't help but tell myself: *This is him.*

I grunted when I saw the account was private. But there was still some information there under his name:

Giulio Dassori
Scuola di Balletto Giselle
Sorrento

I got on the bus. It was packed with passengers, and I had to tuck my phone away to squeeze in. All I could think about the whole time was Giulio. I wondered if that school was his. If he worked there. If he had a family. A wife. Kids. My mind was like a pressure cooker about to explode. I wasn't used to feeling this way. Uncertain. Scared. Free. Because I was now: free, completely free, and I didn't know to do with that freedom when my entire life I'd been ordered around and obedient to routines and schedules and someone telling me what to do and when, where, and how to do it.

I got home a little past eleven.

My grandparents and my uncle were arguing in the living room. That's all they had done for the past three days, and it always had something to do with me.

I scurried down the hall and locked myself in my room. Leaning against the door, I looked at the bare walls and empty shelves and drawers. There was nothing left of me in there, just a sad suitcase, a handbag, and a pile of clothes. It was the most depressing thing I'd ever seen. Almost as depressing as the idea that in a matter of hours, I'd have to leave my home, and I still had no idea where to go.

I sat on the bed and took out my phone. Looking for Giulio's school, I found a public account with a bunch of photos. He wasn't in any of them. There was an address, though, and I memorized it.

I thought of my mother. She had always been hard to talk to. But I needed to do it now. I dialed her number, and it rang several times before going to voicemail. I fretted a few seconds then sent her a message. If you knew who my father was, you'd tell me, right?

A few seconds later, I saw she'd gone online and the message was marked as read. I could feel myself shaking as she started to write back. For a moment, there was nothing, then she resumed. I waited and waited, then finally gave up: She wasn't going to respond.

There had been a time, long ago, when I'd told myself nothing she could do or not do would ever hurt me ever again. That was a promise I made to myself, but I never managed to keep it. At best, I half succeeded at putting her out of my mind.

But now, looking at the screen, I hated her more than ever.

In the living room, they were still arguing, and I was starting to feel trapped. My chest hurt, just under my sternum. I was struggling to breathe, and my whole body was shivering as if I'd been locked in a refrigerator. But I wasn't cold; I was hot all over. I felt something like an electric shock.

I stood, grabbed all the clothes I'd left on the chair, and stuffed them into my suitcase. The door opened, and my uncle walked in. He looked irritated. His chin raised, he tossed something at me, an envelope that landed on top of my open suitcase. Why did everybody treat me that way, like even talking to me was some kind of burden?

"Just so you know, I'm not on board with this," he said bitterly. "When I was your age, I made my own living and nobody did a thing for me. I don't know why he's so soft on you. If it was me…"

His voice trailed off. Unsure what he was talking about, I grabbed the envelope and felt the blood draining from my face when I saw there was money inside.

"This is for me? Why?"

"Ask your granddad. But if I was you, I wouldn't take it."

He walked out furiously, and the shouting in the living room resumed. It was just my grandmother and uncle at first, repeating over and over that Grandpa was a fool for what he'd done.

He replied, "It's my money, and I'll do as I want with it. I'm not going to leave Maya high and dry."

"You do know you have other grandchildren who deserve to be treated equally?" my uncle asked him.

"I do. Or do you think I don't know that your mother paid for your two children's driving lessons? Or the down payment for that new car you didn't need?"

"Since when do I have to ask you for permission to help out our children?" my grandmother interrupted him.

"Then why should I ask you for permission to help out my granddaughter?"

"Are you serious? After all she's done!" his wife said.

"What has she done, Olga? When are you going to realize you can't live through other people, expecting them to make your dreams come true and destroying them in the process? First it was Daria, then it was Maya… Who's next?"

"Dad!" My uncle cried out.

"How dare you talk to me that way," my grandmother said.

"I'm starting to realize I should have done it a long time ago," he responded, and she shouted his name, "Luis!"

I covered my ears to keep from hearing any more.

Everyone has a limit, and I had been pushed past mine a long time ago. I'd been limping along, stumbling, trying to keep my balance… and I couldn't anymore. I couldn't bear the reproaches, the silences that hurt more than words, the glances that made me recoil from guilt. Just because I existed and wanted to be the person I was.

I jumped on the bed and went back to packing my clothes in a rush, sitting on the suitcase to get it shut and throwing whatever was left in my purse. I threw it over my shoulder and stomped off toward the door. I needed out. I needed away. I needed distance between them and me, even if that meant I had to fight through my own resistance, that fear that always held me back.

As I gripped the doorknob, I realized I didn't have anywhere to go.

That realization struck me like lightning, and it seemed to fry my brain as it did so, but I clenched my teeth and walked outside without saying goodbye.

The same way my mother had many years before.

Like a thief in the night.

Like a convict breaking out of jail.

Relieved. Enraged.

Guilt flapping inside me like a butterfly in a jar.

For a second, I was in my mother's shoes.

For a second, I understood her.

Not enough to redeem her.

Not enough to forgive myself.

Maybe it ran in the family. A hatred of that word or what it implied… I wasn't sure, but I could never say goodbye. I didn't like to say it, I didn't like to wave, I didn't even like to look back. There was a feeling there I couldn't allow myself and that I crushed beneath layers of pretended indifference.

I've always thought the word *goodbye* was synonymous with hopelessness.

And when the hope is gone, there's nothing left at all.

Everything vanishes.

But in that moment, without knowing it, I was betting on a hope: one thin as a breath, the only one I had left, banking it all on a desperate impulse.

12

When I realized how crazy what I'd done was, I was already flying over the Mediterranean on a plane headed to Rome. It was the cheapest flight I'd found that would get me to the Italian capital as quickly as possible.

I panicked and almost stood up and screamed that I wanted out. I nearly did, but the way the woman next to me glanced over made me sit back down. She had a mixture of fear and distrust in her eyes, as if she thought I was a hijacker ready to bring the plane down.

So instead, I waited a moment, then walked to the bathroom, apologizing every time I bumped someone with my bag. When I was in the tiny stall, I closed my eyes and tried to relax. I started the faucet and wet my face and neck, then rested a hand on each side of the mirror and concentrated on my own eyes.

Inhale. One, two, three…

Soon, I'd managed to lower my heartbeat and the anguish had gone away. When I returned to my seat, the woman who was sitting next to me leaned over.

"Better?" she asked with a friendly smile.

"I am, thanks," I said.

"I've had panic attacks for years. I can recognize them from a mile away. Thank God they're temporary. You feel like you're going to die, but you never do, right? That's what I always try to tell myself, that it'll pass."

I nodded, unsure what to say. She took a handful of candies out of her purse and offered me one. I accepted, just to be polite. I wondered where she was from. She spoke perfect Spanish, but not from Spain, and I struggled to identify her accent.

"Thanks," I said.

"Are you vacationing in Rome?" she asked.

"No, I'm headed to Sorrento, but the ticket to Rome was way cheaper."

"I know Sorrento! Is it your first time there?" I nodded. She went on, "Don't miss the cathedral. It's amazing. And if you have time, visit the ruins of Pompeii. They're not far. My daughter's been living in Rome for years and I go visit her every summer. I usually stay for a month and do some sightseeing. My Lorenzo, though, he doesn't like planes. He prefers to stay in Toledo. He's so hardheaded and so dull! You know, I still don't know how I wound up marrying him and getting stuck in Spain!"

She stuck out her tongue with disgust, which I found funny.

"Where are you from?" I asked.

"Chile. I was just eighteen when I came to Spain with my parents for a family wedding. You know what they say, one wedding always leads to another. My Lorenzo happened to me there, and he always has had the most beautiful eyes you can imagine. Even if he just uses them to look around his hometown." She laughed, and I laughed with her, and she told me her name was Chabela.

"I'm Maya."

"What a pretty name."

Chabela went on talking without taking a breath. She told me about her husband, her children, and her grandchildren, whom she adored, especially the little one, who was more sensitive than the others. She recommended some self-help books to keep my anxiety under control and even gave me a recipe for a yogurt cake. No oil— butter only. She was a charming, caring woman, and her constant laughter was infectious.

I couldn't stop looking at her. She must have been my grandmother's age, but she was so different… If only I'd had a Chabela in my life instead of an Olga.

We got out of the plane together and walked arm in arm to get our luggage. I stayed with her until she found her family, and we hugged each other goodbye.

"Just follow the signs, it's impossible to miss the station," she said. "Buy a ticket for Naples, and once you're there, look for the Circumvesuviana train, it leaves every half hour and it's five euros max. But look out for pickpockets and don't leave your luggage anywhere. It's not the most amazing trip, but it's worth it once you get there."

"Thanks for everything, Chabela."

"Don't mention it, Gorgeous, and take care. Single women on their own need to be careful."

"I will."

She said goodbye, and I watched her walk off without responding. A blast of hot air hit me when I walked out of Fiumicino Airport.

I stood there on the sidewalk, more aware than ever of where I was. I thought of turning around and catching a flight back to Spain. Now that I was myself again and not just some woman in a blind panic, my mind was functioning lucidly. My grandfather had given me three thousand euros. It was a lot of cash, enough to rent a room somewhere and eat in Madrid until I could find a job.

Going back would be the sensible thing.

The prudent thing, given my situation.

And yet, I didn't. My feet were anchored to the ground. People kept walking by me while I stood there like a statue. Thinking. Hesitating. What did I really have waiting for me back in Spain? Nothing, just Matías. And he had a life of his own. Plus, he was about to go on vacation with his family in Gijón.

Oh, Matías!

I regretted leaving without telling him anything. I took out my phone and turned it on. A long thread of messages appeared, all from him, asking where I was, how I was doing, if I felt like going out. In the last one, he seemed angry and threatened to call the cops and report me missing. I wrote him back, telling him I was fine and I'd let him know what was up soon.

As I put my phone away, I remembered Fyodora's words: *I think this is your sign, Maya. And you need to follow it.*

I was starting to think that, too. And I needed it to be true. But I had no idea what I was looking for or what I hoped to find. I didn't even know what was behind this urge. I just knew I needed to go to that town and see Giulio.

I bought my ticket and walked to the platform. The next train to Naples was leaving in five minutes. I got in, put my suitcase on the luggage rack, and chose my seat. A feeling of vertigo made me grab hold of the armrests. I closed my eyes.

And they remained that way until I felt someone patting me on the arm.

"Mi scusi, signorina. Siamo arrivati a Napoli." I opened my eyes and found the ticket collector standing above me and smiling. I must have fallen asleep. He pointed out the window. "Siamo alla stazione di Napoli. Capisce?"

I shook my head, not understanding what he was saying; then I nodded: He was telling me we'd arrived in Naples. I didn't catch everything, but I'd been lucky enough to have a professor at the conservatory who was from Genova and spoke to us all the time in his native language.

"Grazie," I replied.

I stood and retrieved my luggage and stepped out into Napoli Centrale. It was a huge station, and I needed a moment to find directions to the Circumvesuviana platform. I bought a ticket and walked downstairs. There was a giant crowd waiting: backpackers, tourists, families, workers on their way back home. I was surprised it was so packed on a weekday.

I found a small empty spot near the doors of the train and sat down on top of my suitcase. I put on my headphones and picked a random playlist. All the other sounds vanished as I heard Kodaline's "Everyone Changes." All of a sudden, there were no more voices, there was no more laughter, no more screeching of rails. The world fell silent and the music played on; the landscape shot past and my heart beat rhythmically.

I started singing to myself. On the other side of the glass, the countryside started to change. Chabela was right; it was beautiful. Big cities, little villages, earth tones, deep greens. Once in a while, the sea would peek over shyly behind some hill, its blue ranging from indigo to turquoise.

When we stopped at the Sorrento station, it was almost nine in the evening. The sun was dying over the rooftops, and the streetlamps had begun to illuminate the streets.

I walked from the station into the heart of the city. It seemed impossible that I'd woken up in Madrid that morning. I had the feeling it had been years since I'd spoken with Fyodora, since I'd run away from what had once been my home and climbed into an airplane without even stopping to ask myself what I was doing.

I took a deep breath, and the scent of food filled my nostrils. My stomach grumbled and I realized I hadn't eaten or drunk all day except for a tea and the piece of candy I'd been given on the plane. I was starving, but before I could deal with my hunger, I'd have to find a place to sleep. That was something else I hadn't thought of before then.

Looking around, I saw a park at the end of the street. I walked there and sat on a bench, turning on my phone to look for hotels and hostels. There were lots of them, but the response I got from the first one I walked to was just a taste of what was to come.

"I'm sorry, but all our rooms are booked up. Tomorrow is the Festival of Sant'Andrea in Amalfi and people come from all over to go there."

"Do you know where I could maybe find a room?" I asked.

The receptionist smiled at me with sympathy.

"I don't, sorry. I doubt there's anything open. People make these reservations weeks or even months in advance. Sant'Andrea is one of the most important holidays here. We get tourists from all over. Amalfi's not big, and since Sorrento is close, people often stay here."

"Thanks anyway," I said.

"Maybe try Airbnb or Booking.com. Lots of people rent rooms out in the summer months."

"Thanks, I'll try."

I left the place despondent, and everywhere else I tried, the response was always the same: *No vacancy.*

I didn't know what to do. I was hungry and tired and needed a shower.

Up in the sky, the first stars had just started to shine.

Unsure where I was going, I wandered down streets packed with people, past crowded bars and patios. When I turned a corner, I saw a sign that caught my eye. Now I no longer felt hunger in my stomach. Something else had replaced it. My pulse raced as I walked to that place with the yellow walls and the wooden door.

Scuola di Balletto Giselle, the sign read.

"Ciao, Adriana."

"A presto, Giulio."

The woman who had uttered those words, dressed in an apron, was waving from a liquor store a few yards away. A man waved back at her. I recognized him, and it was like standing on the edge of a volcano.

It was him. I was sure of it.

He passed by me without noticing, and I pretended I was looking at my phone. Only when he was walking away did I look up. I followed him without thinking twice. What were the chances I would run into him as soon as I'd arrived in a city of 16,000 people with another 16,000 tourists there ready to celebrate the start of summer? It was virtually impossible, and yet there he was.

Was this a sign, too? I needed to know.

Keeping a prudent distance, I did all I could not to lose him in the crowd. Sorrento is a labyrinth of tiny streets, squares, and colorful buildings, though, and it's easy to get lost.

All at once, the city ended abruptly at a cliff with a lookout giving a view of the horizon. The sea shone under a starry sky and I could see ships bobbing near the coast. In the port, there was a narrow beach with docks. Bars and terraces seemed to emerge from the sheer stone of the mountain; tables crowded the edges of the shore, and people were gathered, dining and drinking, on the boats in the wharf.

I looked back and saw Giulio hurrying away, and I lost him as we stepped into a park. My suitcase made a racket as I dragged it behind me. I could hear myself wheezing. When I got to the other side of the park, he was gone.

I looked all around, disappointed.

Close by was a restaurant with outside seating. I weaved my way between the packed tables, looking down at the pizzas and pastas, the fish, the toasted bread that smelled of oregano and olive oil. My mouth was watering, and I was exhausted.

A couple got up, leaving one of the tables free, and I sat down there in a hurry, body buckling in the chair. For a long time, I just stared at the sea. My legs were like lead, and my throat was parched.

I tried to comb my hair with my fingers, thinking how horrible I must look.

"Buonasera."

I looked over at a young man with a tray and a cloth in his hand, and reciprocated his cheerful smile. He quickly cleared away the dirty plates, wiped off the table, and offered me a menu.

"Grazie," I said, and he vanished no sooner than he'd appeared. I looked through the dishes, which all sounded delicious, but all that fat, all those carbs, all those calories would do me in, and I...

I remembered something. I didn't have to watch my weight. I didn't have to make sacrifices to stay thin or control my hunger. A silly chuckle escaped me at the mere thought of hot, oily, melted cheese, and bread and more bread.

Just then, a man's hand swooped down before my eyes, setting down a clean plate and silverware.

"Buonasera, chè cosa ordina la signorina?"

13

I looked up and saw a pair of grayish-blue eyes staring at me with curiosity. I opened my mouth to answer, but I wasn't sure what he'd asked. He had a soft, welcoming face and a rebellious strand of hair that fell over his brow until he blew a brusque breath of air and it settled back into place.

In a moment like that, you don't know. You never do. No one recognizes the moment that changes their life forever. It's just minutes that come, that pass, that leave things as they were before. And yet, it's happened. There's been a change, and there is no turning back.

The same way no one recognizes the person who's fated to change them forever. It's just a person, after all. They show up one day without you expecting it, and they look at you. You don't know it, but something's happened. Your pupils dilate, you feel their breath on you, and your hair stands on end. You hold each other's stare for too long. These are nearly imperceptible details, you chalk them up to something else, but in fact, they're the beginning of something important. Something that may drown you or save you. Because some waves carry you back to the shore, and others drag you down to the seafloor.

"Ha bisogno di pensarlo ancora un po'…?" the guy said, pointing at the menu.

I was pretty sure he was asking if I needed more time to think it over. Which meant he was in a rush for me to order. I looked back at the menu.

"Voglio mangiare una pizza ai quattro…" I tried to say it in Italian and shook my head, cursing to myself, "Dammit, I don't even know if that's how you say it!"

He giggled and asked, "Española?" Relieved, I nodded. "From what city?" he continued.

"Madrid."

I asked where he was from, too, but I was already beaming because his accent left no room for doubt. He nodded, looked at my bag, and uttered the words I was waiting to hear. "I'm from Madrid, too."

"What a coincidence!"

"You'd think that, but you wouldn't believe the number of Spanish people living around here. Anyway, what would you like?"

I looked up and down the plastic surface of the menu until I found what I wanted. "This: a four-cheese pizza, a Coke, and some of that toasted bread they have on the other tables."

"Sure. So for bread, we've got oregano, onion, capers, black olive…"

"I don't know, which one do you recommend?"

"Black olive. It comes with a spicy oil, you'll love it."

"That works, then."

He wrote everything down on a little pad and told me it would be up in around fifteen minutes.

I watched him turn and disappear into the restaurant, then drew a long breath of air. It tasted of salt. I didn't bother trying to conceal my curiosity about the other tables. I wondered whether I'd really seen Giulio or had just wanted to. I wasn't sure.

My phone dinged and I took it out of my bag. It was a text message from Matías:

Can I call you? I'm worried.

I barely had any battery left and I didn't know when I could charge up again. I couldn't waste it.

It's a bad time. But I'm fine. I promise.

Then tell me what's happening. At least tell me you've got somewhere to stay.

I felt bad not telling him the truth, but if he knew where I was and why, he'd worry. Then again, he was already worried, so what's the difference.

His name's Giulio and he's Italian. He lives in a town close to Naples.

Are you talking about the guy in the photos?

Yeah. I need to meet him. You're the one who told me to look for him.

You're in fucking Italy? You just left without saying anything?

I did, and I promise I'm fine.

You've lost it, just running away like that. And so far.

Like you've never done anything crazier.

So you do admit it's crazy.

I rolled my eyes. When his protective side came out, it got on my nerves. And yet, it made me love him even more.

> You trust me, right?

Like I have a choice.

> I promise I'll write you every day and keep you informed.

K.

> I love you.

I love you too, but I still think you're a crazy bitch.

I turned off my phone and put it away as the waiter returned with his tray. He laid a basket of bread on the table and an olive oil dispenser with herbs and peppers floating inside it, setting down beside them a glass of Coke.

"The pizza will be up in five," he said.

"Thanks."

I brought the drink to my lips and moaned as its sugary flavor touched my tongue and the bubbles exploded just under my nose, tickling me. I tore the bread into little strips and bathed it in oil until it was almost swimming. I closed my eyes as I took the first bite and felt myself rising into heaven. It was incredible. I ate two slices before I'd even stopped to think, and was about to wolf down a third when my mouth started burning.

Shit! It was spicy!

I drank, fanned myself, took a drink again. I stuck out my tongue and felt my eyes tearing up.

"How much oil did you use?" the waiter asked as he dropped off the pizza. I wanted to respond, but couldn't. It was horrible. "OK," he said, "don't worry, and don't eat anything else. I'll be right back."

A few seconds later, he returned with two glasses, one of milk and one of water. As he handed them to me, he sat down across from me. Grateful, I began to drink the milk. Slowly, the burning started to fade.

"Better?" he asked. I nodded. "Did you not notice the peppers in the oil?"

"Yeah, but I didn't think they'd burn like that. Where did they come from, hell?"

He laughed and rested his forearms on the table. He seemed to find my difficulties amusing. Without asking, he pulled off a slice of pizza and offered it to me.

"Here. Eat. It will make it go away faster. The fat in the cheese helps."

"Thanks."

I bit into the slice and began to chew, closing my eyes and hearing the sounds of my swallowing.

"It's incredible," I said, mouth full.

When I opened my eyes, I saw him leaning forward and staring at me shamelessly. His hair was brown, unkempt, wavy, covering the tops of his ears and his neck. His eyes, hidden behind long, thick lashes, were intense, like a sea in winter, the kind of eyes that drill through your skin and see everything inside you.

But what really caught my eye was the freckles all over his face: that map of brownish stars radiating out from his nose. I'd never thought freckles were sexy before, but now I did. They made him look like a mischievous little boy, and that was awakening feelings in me I hadn't imagined would come to me this early in the trip.

"My name's Lucas," he said.

"Mine's Maya."

We leaned clumsily across the table to exchange two kisses on the cheek. His skin was soft, and it smelled good, woody and slightly citrus, an aroma I could almost taste.

"It's nice to meet you, Maya. Now, if you don't need me to put out any more fires, I actually need to get back to the bar."

He winked seductively and stood. I bit my lips.

"The bar?"

"I don't usually wait tables, I'm really the bartender. Speaking of, the milk's on the house."

I felt stupid for gawking at him, but I couldn't help it, and I think he felt the same. But then he ran his hand over the back of his neck and turned away. He was tall, taller than he'd seemed at first, with long legs and a firm step. Handsome, but not in a conventional way, not a knockout, but pure, simple. He didn't look fake, and he didn't look like he was trying. Everything about him was at ease, and that caught my attention, along with his relaxed good humor.

I blushed. What was I thinking? I never looked at guys like that, just because they were attractive and had said a few friendly words to me. It was my circumstances, I guessed: I felt lost, vulnerable.

I'd only broken up with Antoine a few days before.

Antoine...

I hadn't thought of him since, and doing so made me feel strange. Cold.

We'd been together for a year, and he'd cheated on me with another girl. I should have felt something, right? Something. But inside, I was totally empty.

I tried to forget all of that and enjoy my meal.

I ate the entire pizza and got an ice cream for dessert. There wasn't really room for it, but I had to keep eating if I wanted to keep sitting there, stretching out the hours on a night when I had nowhere to go.

Little by little, the clientele departed and the servers began cleaning and packing up the tables. I paid, grabbed my bag, and started off. The lights on the terrace had been turned off, and only the streetlamps brightened the darkness.

I looked back into the restaurant and saw Lucas behind the bar, drying glasses in a rush. I don't know why, but I wished he would look up and our eyes would meet.

Because that's nice when you see it in a movie, right? That connection that's like fate and that hits you with the force of a tsunami. You dream of it, but at the same time, you run from it, because love at first sight is impossible.

It's just a dream.

And everyone should know that by now.

That love that explodes like a supernova from out of nowhere doesn't exist. It's an idealization, something we confuse with attraction, which is just a chemical reaction. It makes you look at a stranger's lips and yours open like a simple reflex. Your hair stands on end whenever that other person looks at you. You quiver inside, and your muscles contract and your breathing turns shallow. It makes you feel good things. Sweet things. Unknown things. It's that unique, personal aroma that unleashes your endorphins, and they invade your blood like a drug and turn you into an addict.

And soon you need another dose.

A smile.

A stare.

A scent that clings to your tongue and that you savor for hours afterward.

And that attraction transforms into desire.

The kind that hurts rather than calms you.

But Lucas didn't look up, and I started to walk away.

And that could have been the end.

But no—it wasn't destined to be that.

It was just a chance to ignore the signs. To run.

And I didn't do it. I stayed.

Because sometimes, a train comes only once.

And never passes that station again.

And you get on, even though you know it's going to crash.

Because it's easier to live with the certainty of what wasn't than with the uncertainty of what could have been.

It just is.

14

I walked aimlessly, my suitcase wheels echoing on the sidewalk, thinking how strange, how pathetic that night had been. The more steps I took, the more certain I was that I'd lost my mind. Going over a thousand miles away, with nothing more than what could fit in a travel bag and a maybe on my mind. Without thinking. Without examining the consequences. I'd never done anything like that. I'd barely ever done anything on my own, and the few times I had, I'd thought it over for hours, days, weeks.

And yet, there I was. I'd jumped without a parachute.

Someone whistled behind me, and I jerked, my entire body tense. I heard steps and didn't dare to turn, instead speeding up. I was alone, and the street was empty. When I reached a crossroads, I turned left. There were stairs there. I picked up my suitcase and started walking downward.

Soon I regretted it. The steps seemed never to end. They were narrow and steep, and it was hard to see where I was putting my feet. From what little I could see, the stairway seemed to lead to the beach. I finally reached bottom, and nearby there were still a few bars open. In the light they gave off, I saw lines of umbrellas and beach chairs on the thin stretch of sand along the shore.

I walked toward the one farthest away, near a few stranded boats, and lay in it after stowing my suitcase underneath it. The sky was full of stars that shimmered up high, the breeze was cool, the air smelled strongly of salt. I was so tired I could barely keep my eyes open.

My eyelids fell closed and sleep carried me away.

And then I shuddered awake, my heart racing, with no sense of time. I'd heard a noise. I was sure of it.

I looked around, but I didn't see anything.

Then I noticed the smell of tobacco.

I heard a breath and saw a coppery glow before a cloud of smoke emerged.

Squinting, I managed to make out the shadow of a man leaning against one of the boats. I remained still, thinking he hadn't noticed me and hoping he'd finish his cigarette and leave as soon as possible.

Then something warm and damp touched my arm. I jerked and shouted. Was that a dog? Where the hell had it come from? I scowled at it and begged it to go. Dogs have always given me the creeps.

As I shook my hand at it, it grunted and ran off.

"Tutto bene?" a gravelly voice asked. It was the guy from the boat hurrying over.

"Sì, sì, grazie," I said.

I crouched down and pulled on my suitcase, which had gotten stuck in the sand, so hard that I fell on my ass. I heard a click: the striking of a lighter. Someone standing over me. I blinked several times and stared.

"Maya?"

"Lucas?"

"What are you doing here?" he asked. I tried to answer, but everything that occurred to me was embarrassing, and before I could open my mouth, he continued. "Were you honestly thinking of spending the night here?" He shook his hand and the flame went out. "Goddammit, I burned myself."

"Are you OK?"

"I'm fine, what about you, though? You know it's not safe to stay here by yourself."

"I do know, but I don't have any other options," I replied.

"Why not?"

"I didn't make a reservation," I said. "I thought I could just get a room somewhere, but tomorrow there's this important festival of some saint or other, and there's not a single bed free in all of Sorrento."

"Sant'Andrea in Amalfi," he said, and I was sure he was grinning at me in the dark.

"Yeah, that one."

"Thousands of people come every year."

"I'm sure it's just amazing," I responded sarcastically.

He rubbed his face, and the silence stretched on long enough that I started to get uncomfortable. I didn't like not seeing him clearly. At last, he said, "There's one bed free in Sorrento."

"Where?" I asked, full of hope.

"At my place. You can crash there if you like."

I couldn't believe it. I had a place to sleep, to change clothes, to wash. It was incredible. But then, I didn't know him at all, and that scared me.

"Don't get offended, but…" I paused, unsure how to continue. "I don't know you, and going home with you is, uh…"

"You don't trust me?" His voice was serious.

"It's not that I have a reason not to, but then, I don't have a reason *to* trust you either." I hugged myself, tired and cold from the damp air condensing around us. "I'm sorry, I just don't know…"

"I get it. It's normal." I felt terrified when I thought he was going to turn and walk away, but he added, "Wait a sec," and now that I was used to the darkness, I could see him taking something from his pocket. He turned on the flashlight on his phone.

"Here." He reached out and handed me his ID. "Take a picture of it and send it to one of your friends, or your mom, or your boyfriend. You can tell them where I work, too. Does that make you feel more comfortable?"

I only needed a few seconds to respond. Lucas seemed like a good guy, and he was opening his home to me. He was trying to make me feel safe, and now he'd done it. It was a kind gesture, and it had worked.

"I don't have a boyfriend," I replied. Why was that the first thing I'd said? "I mean, I used to, but we broke up. He cheated on me with another girl, and that was that. So yeah, I could definitely use that spare bed if you really don't mind."

He smiled, making me nervous, and said, "Sure, no problem,"lifting up my suitcase as I grabbed my handbag. He told me to follow him and we walked in silence. He took a few coins from his pocket, walked past the stairs I'd taken before, and arrived at what looked like a tunnel carved into the stone with a sign next to it that read: LIFT-ASCENSORE.

"Are you serious?" I grunted. "There's an elevator! I almost killed myself going down those damn steps!"

He laughed and shook his head. I followed him toward a ticket window where a woman was watching a tiny TV. He bought two tickets, passed them under a scanner, and guided me in. The elevator doors opened and we entered, and soon we were stepping out into a park overlooking the bay.

"This way, my car isn't far."

"What were you doing on the beach?" I asked.

"When I'm working the night shift, I always take a walk here and smoke a cigarette and listen to the sea before going home."

"What is that, like your ritual?"

"It's just something I like to do. So what are you doing here? Does it have to do with your boyfriend? Some kind of spiritual journey to mend your broken heart?"

I looked away. His gaze was too penetrating.

"Ex-boyfriend," I corrected him. "No, he doesn't have anything to do with it. We broke up, so now it's done. No drama. I mean, what's the point of feeling bad or of doing something stupid over a person who hurt you on purpose?"

"There's no point, but it's also normal to suffer when someone hurts you. Maybe even inevitable. And that is a thing people do, even if you call it stupid: running away somewhere, getting as far away as possible, with no plans, without reservations."

I had the feeling he wasn't just talking about me. I looked down the street and thought about Antoine in the shower with Sofía. It had hurt me bad. I'd felt abused and betrayed, even if it had just lasted a moment. Then that pain became muffled, like an echo, losing intensity over the following days.

Something suddenly made me uncomfortable. Did this mean I'd never really loved Antoine? No, that couldn't be. You can't be with a person a whole year, sharing as many things as we'd shared, and not love them. Or can you?

I realized I was holding my breath and let it out.

"How did you end up here?" I asked him.

Turning his head, he began, "I helped out someone who was in a bind. She invited me to have an ice cream and then...she made me an offer I couldn't refuse. That was two years ago, and here I am."

To judge from his smile and the gleam in his eyes, this *she* had to be someone very special.

"Someone in a bind the way I am?" I asked. And I immediately regretted doing so. I didn't even know where that question had come from, or why I'd asked it. I felt something strange: goose bumps, butterflies in my stomach, racing heart. We stared at each other a moment in the eyes.

"No, not like you," he replied, which made me blush.

Then the meaning of his words hit me: There was someone in Lucas's life. "Hey," I told him, "now that I think about it, maybe it's best if I don't stay at your place."

"Did I say something wrong?"

"No, but since you mentioned a woman… I guess it must be your girlfriend, right? Or wife, or friend with benefits, I don't know… Maybe she won't like you showing up with a stranger in the middle of the night."

He grimaced.

"The *woman* you're talking about is my landlord, and I'd marry her in a heartbeat, but she refuses. I haven't given up, though. She told me that at seventy years old, with two husbands in the grave, she's not interested in burying a third. It stung, but I understood."

For a minute, we seemed to be staring each other down, and he was especially serious. Then we both burst out laughing until we could hardly breathe, and when we were done, all the tension was gone.

A few streets further on, Lucas stopped in front of an old red car. He took out his keys, opened the trunk, and stashed my suitcase inside. Then he opened the door for me.

He needed to crank the motor three times, and the way it shook and rattled, I worried the entire vehicle would fall apart. The vibrations worked their way down into my bones, almost like in one of those massage chairs.

"Where'd you get this piece of junk?" I asked.

"Hey! Don't be nasty. This is a 1975 Fiat 128 Coupe. I traded a watch for it. A rather expensive watch, if you're wondering."

"For real?"

"Why would I lie to you?"

"I don't know," I responded, "but you must have your reasons."

For a few seconds, he struggled with the gearshift before finally getting it into first and starting to pull out. It was stuffy inside. I tried to roll down the window, but the lever wouldn't budge.

"Wait, there's a trick to it," he said, leaning across me, and I tried to lean back to give him space and to ignore how close he was to me—close enough that I could smell the scent of coconut in his shampoo. "There you go. That's as far as it will go down."

"Then I guess that will have to work," I said.

"Cool. Off we go."

Lucas stepped on the gas and the car lurched away. Instinctively, I grabbed the seat and only let go when the car stopped bucking and rattling. We left the center of town behind us and headed south. The tiny streets of Sorrento seemed to hug the cliffside, and once we were on the highway, the views of the Gulf of Naples were astonishing. The starry sky melted into the sea at the horizon like a black blanket enveloping the coast, and far off, I could see the unmistakable outline of Vesuvius crowned by a tiny crescent moon.

"My God, it's beautiful," I whispered.

"Wait till you see it during the day."

The mere thought of it made me tingle with anticipation. Lucas slowed down and put on his turn signal, veering left and parking next to a wall behind a white van with the logo of a florist painted on the side.

"Here we are."

He got out and grabbed my suitcase, and I followed him, awed by the silence. There was nothing visible except that wall that seemed to extend off into infinity. Around the corner, we saw two lights hanging over an archway and double doors of wood beneath it.

I wasn't ready for what I saw when I walked through them: an immense garden, with trees, bushes, and stone flowerpots full of flowers. Climbing roses, jasmines winding around an iron trellis forming a natural canopy of leaves. In the middle of that oasis was a three-story building with earth-tone walls and wooden shutters. It was huge, and there were lights hanging from the facade illuminating the doorway.

"There's no way you actually live here," I said. "This place is amazing!"

"Welcome to Villa Vicenza!" Lucas said proudly.

"I feel like I'm in a movie. I can't imagine what it feels like to wake up to this every day."

"I got lucky," he responded. "Finding my apartment here is probably what got me to stay."

"Are there other people here?"

"Yeah, it's six apartments in total, two on each floor. The first floor is the owner and her family. On the second, there's a Galician couple, retired: Iria and Blas. They're nice. Roy is there, too, he's a painter from Mallorca. Weird, but cool. On the third floor is Julia and me. Julia's Spanish, too, but she's been in Sorrento almost fifteen years. She has a hair salon downtown. Her nephews are here right now, but not for much longer if I have anything to say about it. They spend all night making noise on their stupid video-game console. Oh, there's also a couple of cats around. You're not allergic, are you? I should have asked earlier."

He actually seemed nervous, timid even, which I found charming. "I don't know why I'm telling you all this," he concluded.

"I asked," I said. "Anyway, I'm not allergic to cats. Not that I know of. I don't usually get too close to animals. I don't think they like me."

"I can't imagine why."

Those words in that deep voice of his made me blush. He opened the door, and I suddenly felt apprehensive, as if all this was just too much.

"So everyone here's Spanish?" I asked.

"Almost."

"That's a coincidence!"

"The owner's Spanish, and she's turned this place into a commune, or a shelter, or whatever you want to call it. I love it here. Hold on, though. I don't want you to trip over anything."

I stood still as he turned on a light that flickered a few times. I looked up and saw a bronze lamp with chandelier bulbs. The vestibule was large, with whitewashed walls and blue hand-painted borders. It was crumbling in places, but rather than making it look run-down, that just added to the naturalness and authenticity of it. On either side of us was a door with a straw mat in front of it. A stone staircase with an iron handrail led to the upper floors, and further back, I could see another large set of wooden doors like the ones we'd just walked through.

I followed Lucas up the stairs to the top floor, where the ceiling was a little lower. He slid the key into the lock of the door on the left, turned on the lights, and invited me in, apologizing for the disorder. I took a quick look around. It was a roomy apartment with the two bedrooms, the kitchen, and the bathroom extending off the living room. I couldn't imagine a person needing anything more. The walls were bare, and there was no more furniture than necessary: just a sofa, a table with four chairs, a sideboard, and a couple of shelves. Aside from that, there were an end table and a TV hanging on the wall. I liked it; it was very cozy.

"You can sleep here," Lucas said, turning on the light in one of the bedrooms and rolling my suitcase in. There was a bed without sheets there, a closet, a dresser, and a desk with a chair. It was a nice size, with two windows that must have let in lots of light during the day.

"Thanks so much for letting me stay the night," I said. "I'll be gone in the morning. I don't want to bother you any more than necessary."

"There's no rush. My old roommate moved out last week and I still haven't gotten any calls from anyone interested. So for now, it's free."

"You're renting it?" I asked.

He nodded. "Believe it or not, I'm not getting rich at the restaurant. Renting the room out helps me make it to the end of the month, and thankfully, my landlord doesn't mind."

"I could pay you."

"Come on, now, I don't charge by the hour. I'm doing this because I want to, OK?"

"OK." My nerves were making me need to pee, and squeezing my thighs together, I asked, "Can I use the bathroom?"

"Sure. There are towels in the closet in there, too, if you want to take a shower. Make yourself at home."

"Thanks."

I tossed my purse on the bed, took out my shower kit and a T-shirt and underwear, and went inside. I don't know how long I sat there on the toilet, pants and panties around my knees, face buried in my hands. I was exhausted, and that was the first time all day that I had finally felt comfortable and relaxed. In the bathroom of a stranger, of all places—a man I was staying with because he'd taken pity on me.

I looked in the mirror. I needed that shower, all right. My hair was knotty and frayed. I stripped, pulled back the shower curtain, got inside and let the water run till it was hot, then stayed there for a good long while. I don't know why, but I decided to use Lucas's coconut shampoo, and the smell of it made my pulse race. I could have asked myself why—why it aroused such feelings in me—but I decided not to.

When I came out, all the lights were off except for a small lamp on the sideboard. I could hear Lucas breathing deeply and evenly in his bedroom. When I walked into my room, I found he'd made the bed and left a quilt doubled over the chair. The sweetheart.

I plugged my phone charger in, turned off the light, and got in bed. The scent of lemons and jasmine came in through the window. It was silent except for the murmur of the wind shaking the trees and water in what must have been a fountain. It was so relaxing, and I balled up and closed my eyes.

I felt weariness overtake my body.

I felt sleep gathering around me.

I felt tears stinging my eyes.

A knot in my throat.

And like that, I fell asleep.

15

When I woke, the sun was pouring through the windows. I opened my eyes and looked up at the ceiling fan. White. Everything in that room was: the ceiling, the walls, the windows, the curtains…

I liked that.

I sat up and rested my feet on the floor, wiggling my toes and staring down at them, surprised not to see broken nails or bloody blisters. And they didn't hurt the way they had when I practiced every day, even if they were still ugly. Deformed.

I found some socks in my suitcase, slipped them on, and opened my messages on my phone. Matías had written me early that morning, and another text from an unknown number had insisted on talking to me and had begged for another chance. I erased that one. I saw the little photo of my mother in the list of chats, and touched it, though I knew the harsh reality that awaited me.

A question without an answer.

An eloquent silence.

Once again, the confirmation of a certainty.

I erased the message I'd written her. Then I erased her number, too. Fuck her. I was over it. Over her. Over a family that had never been a true family to me. Over everything and everyone.

I threw open the window. The sun shone bright and there wasn't a cloud in the sky. The sight was so perfect, it was like a picture post-card. Looking out, I witnessed an explosion—there's no other word for it—of shapes, colors, and scents, so varied my senses couldn't keep track of them.

There was so much to look at that my eyes didn't know where to pause: on the flowers in their assorted pots, on the stone fountain shaped like a woman's body, on the cypresses bordering the wall with their strong smell of resin, on the grapevines with their clusters of green grapes on the trellises, or on the chirping birds hopping from place to place.

That garden was a fantasia.

A scene from a fairy tale.

I leaned out a little further, and my hand slid on the windowsill, my phone slipping through my fingers.

"No!" It fell into a bush, bounced, and disappeared. "No, no, no, no, no!"

Half my life was on that phone. Instinctively, I hurried out, down the stairs, and into the vestibule, jerking the door open and dashing out. I reached the bush, which was gigantic and covered in tiny blue flowers, and pulled apart the branches, sinking half my torso inside as I searched.

With a sigh of relief, I found my phone intact.

"Va tutto bene?" a man's voice asked behind me.

I twitched, remembering that all I had on were a T-shirt and a pair of panties with the image of a doughnut on the back and the words *I'm so sweet*, which anyone behind me would have had a panoramic view of. I turned, grabbed the hem of my shirt, and tugged it down, preparing myself to answer. But when I saw the face in front of me, I lost my voice.

OMG, it was him. Him! Giulio!

What were the chances of something like this? One in a hundred thousand? One in a million? I had no idea. But there he was.

"Stai bene?" he asked, looking disconcerted.

I bumbled something that didn't make any sense as I examined every inch of him. He must have been around forty, like my mother, but he looked much younger. He was incredibly handsome, with dark, curly hair and eyes so dark I could hardly see the pupils. His skin was toasted by the sun and his enchanting smile showed off his bright teeth. And there it was, over his right eyebrow—a mole exactly like the one I had.

Trying to concentrate, I managed to get out the words, "What did you say?"

"Oh, you're Spanish?" he said with a heavy accent and, when I nodded, continued. "I was asking if you were all right. Because you were about to disappear into that jasmine…"

I laughed as I felt the blood rush into my cheeks. I lifted up my phone, felt my T-shirt rise with it, then hurriedly jerked it back down. "I dropped this."

"Sure… We haven't met before, have we?"

"No, I just got here last night."

"You're not Iria and Blas's granddaughter, are you? I thought you weren't coming for a few more weeks."

"No! I'm staying with Lucas."

His expression turned knowing, as if we'd been up to something naughty, and he said, "Ah, with Lucas! Va bene."

A woman inside the house called his name, and he shouted back, "Sto arrivando, Mamma," without looking away from me. "My mom. She has to have her coffee in the morning. You coming in?"

"Yeah. I should probably get dressed."

"I doubt you'll bother anyone here," he said with a chuckle.

I tried not to stare at him as we went inside, telling myself to relax and not succeeding in the least. I was a ball of tension and anticipation.

"Your Spanish is really good," I told him.

"In this place, you need to speak it. I get… How do you say it? I can get on?"

"I think you mean you can get by."

"Exactly," he said. "I can get by. My mom's Spanish, anyway. She came to Italy with her family when she was a kid."

In the vestibule, a woman opened the door on the left and said, "Giulio, the coffee maker's not working." Then, examining me with curiosity, she added, "Who's she?"

"Mamma, this is…"

I introduced myself. "My name's Maya."

"She's staying with Lucas," he explained.

She smiled and responded, "Hello, Maya, I'm Catalina. You're renting the room from Lucas?"

"No, I, uh, I just…"

She grinned and said to Giulio, "L'estate è per i giovani amanti," in a near whisper.

He laughed, and when I inquired what she'd said, he responded, "The summer is for young lovers."

"Lovers!" I almost shouted. "No! We're… That's not what we are. We're…" I couldn't get the words out. This woman was old enough to be my grandmother—maybe she *was* my grandmother—and there I was, half-naked in her vestibule.

"It's a joke," she said.

I tried to laugh along with it, but I was dying from embarrassment, and I thought I'd faint if I stayed there any longer. My legs felt like rubber, and I wasn't sure how much longer they'd hold me up.

"I should get back upstairs, speaking of," I said. "I accidentally dropped my phone out the window and I came down to find it. It was nice to meet you, though. It was nice to meet both of you."

Pulling my T-shirt down until I could hear threads popping, I climbed the stairs with all the dignity I could muster, knowing that both of them were looking at me. I could hear voices from one of the apartments: children and a woman chewing them out. Overwhelmed, I reached the third floor and found the door locked.

Brilliant, I thought to myself.

I rang the bell, and soon the door opened and Lucas appeared with a towel wrapped around his waist and water dripping from his hair. I wondered which of us looked more ridiculous. I guessed it was me. He stepped aside, not bothering to conceal his amusement.

"I dropped my phone out the window," I said, trying to pretend that was something normal, and walked toward my room.

"It happens to me all the time," he replied blithely. "You in the mood for breakfast? I don't have any doughnuts, but I do have some crumb cake. Maybe if you stick your fork in it hard enough, it'll say 'I'm so sweet,' too."

"Just a second," I said.

I blushed like a teenager and let go of the hem of my T-shirt, which jumped back up above my waist. Whatever. He'd already seen everything anyway.

This whole thing was crazy, and I had no idea what I should do. Not even two days had passed since I'd seen those photos, and here I was in a building shared by a man who might be my father, and the first thing he'd ever seen of me was my ass.

My father…

Just thinking those words filled me with fear, because I'd never considered the possibility that I might meet him. I felt the need for him, of course, but I'd always stuffed that longing away. I had grown up surrounded by people who looked different from me, I'd known I was different, I'd even asked questions.

Questions that were never answered.

And I just accepted that.

And I forgot him.

And I grew up without even missing him.

Or maybe I did miss him, and that's why I was there, obsessed with the fact that he had a mole over his eyebrow, or had made a similar gesture, or seemed to have some trait I'd inherited.

And the most ridiculous thing of all was, scared and uncertain as I was, I wanted to stay there. I wanted to be brave, to find the moment when I could show Giulio those photos and learn the truth hidden behind them. If there was any truth.

To learn if he was that part of myself my mother had stolen away from me.

16

At seven years old

"Promise me you won't tell Grandma."

I wondered why my grandfather was saying that, and I asked.

"Why?"

"Because what we're going to do today is a secret."

"But Grandma says secrets are bad."

"Not all of them. This is a good one. I promise."

I agreed, not entirely convinced, and looked at the people rowing in the pond at El Retiro Park. But then I got impatient and asked, "How good?"

Squeezing my hand, he replied, "Very good, Maya. And if you like it and you want to ever do it again, then Grandma can't know. She'll get mad and she won't let us come back."

I didn't want her to get mad. I hated when she shouted and broke things. It scared me, and I'd run off and hide, even though that only made her angrier.

"OK, I promise I'll keep it secret."

Grandpa looked slightly tense as he looked around at the crowd. Then he smirked and got emotional, eyes filling with tears. He let go of my hand and walked off a few steps, stopping in front of a person I couldn't see well and throwing his arms open.

"Daria!"

"Hey, Dad."

"It's been so long, honey. And I missed you so much."

"I did, too," the woman said. "Thanks for doing this for me."

"She's your daughter. How could I not?"

Grandpa stepped aside and let me see who he was talking with: a tall, blond woman with gray eyes and thin lips. She walked over and crouched down in front of me, taking one of my hands in hers. She was trembling, I noticed. Then she looked up and my heart started racing, though I didn't know why.

"Hello, Maya," she said.

"Hi," I whispered.

"Do you know who I am?"

I shook my head, even though a part of me suspected, as if my body recognized hers and she awakened some buried memory within me. My mouth was almost too dry to talk.

"No," I said.

"You don't remember me? Maya, it's me. I'm your mother."

We spent the day together. We ate ice cream, rode around in a boat, and talked about all kinds of things. It was an amazing Saturday. I didn't have to be a dancer. I was just a girl talking about girls' stuff with her mother.

Grandpa stayed with us the whole time, looking overjoyed. I think it was the happiest I ever saw him.

Later that afternoon, we were sitting on the patio of a bar. Grandpa had gone to order lemon ices, and she and I were alone. I had my coloring book and markers she had bought me on the table and was flipping through the pages. Nearby there was another girl eating with her parents.

I couldn't stop looking at them, even though it made me sad.

"Why don't you live with us?" I asked my mother.

She forced a smile, though I could tell she was sad. "Because Grandma and I don't get along very well," I said.

"How come I don't live with you, then? I want to live with you."

"Because you're much better off with them, I promise."

"But kids usually live with their parents, I know because all the kids in my class live with their parents."

She sighed. "Not all of them do, Maya. Sometimes it's impossible and the kids have to go live with other people who love them as much as their parents do."

"I don't know if Grandma does love me, though," I told her.

"Why do you say that?"

I shrugged. I didn't know how to answer the question; it was just something I felt. My mother's expression turned sad, and I went on, "Like sometimes I don't even feel like dancing. I like it, but I also want to go to basketball with my friend Estrella, or to the park, or to birthday parties...and Grandma won't let me."

"I understand," she said.

I looked back at the little girl, whose father had sat her in his lap and was giving her a bunch of kisses on the cheek. They laughed and laughed, and even I couldn't help smiling when I saw them. A thought came into my head unexpectedly.

"Can I live with my father?" I asked.

I was seven years old, and I knew by then that all mammals had a mother and a father. My teacher had told us that at school. That meant I must have a father somewhere. Maybe he didn't get along with my grandmother, either, and that's why he didn't come to see me.

My mother grabbed my hand and squeezed it.

"You don't have a father, Maya."

"But all mammals..."

"I don't know who your father is. I don't know his name, I don't know where he lives. Nothing. So forget about him, because you'll never meet him. All right?"

I was surprised by her severity, but I nodded. "OK."

"There is no dad somewhere thinking of you, all right? He doesn't know you exist."

"OK," I repeated.

"This is how life is sometimes. You'll understand one day when you're older."

"OK."

"So promise me you won't think about it again."

"I promise," I said.

And so that longing remained buried deep down inside me, and I forced myself to forget it was there.

"And promise me you'll be a good little girl so I can keep coming to see you."

"I promise," I told her.

And I did. I was a good little girl. I always did everything right. And a year later, she came back and spent a day with me. And the same thing happened a year after that. But at some point, I guess I stopped being good, even if I didn't realize it, because she quit coming to see me.

17

I looked through my suitcase and nearly freaked out. Where were my clothes? I was sure I had kept more than those few dresses, those three pairs of shorts, that half-dozen T-shirts, some of which were so old I couldn't even wear them outside.

I dug through it all again, as if the garments might multiply just because I was moaning like a baby. Then I sat on the floor, resigned and embittered, and tried to see the bright side of it: I wouldn't have to fret over what to wear.

I chose the least wrinkly of my dresses, put on a shorter pair of socks, and slipped on my sneakers. I was nervous as I walked out of the bedroom, still thinking about my encounter with Giulio. Was it a coincidence, or something more? Or did I just want to think it was something more?

They say your decisions mark out your destiny, but what if my destiny had chosen me? What if all this was part of its plans for me? Was it sending me more signs?

The scent of fresh coffee distracted me from these ridiculous ideas, and I followed that aroma into the kitchen, where I found Lucas with his back to the door, leaning over the counter, busy with something or other. He was dressed in beige linen pants and a white shirt with the sleeves rolled up.

"Good morning," I said as if we hadn't seen each other half-naked a moment before.

He turned and smiled. "Good morning. You hungry?"

"Very," I confessed.

He motioned for me to sit down. His shirt front was open, and I tried to look no longer than necessary as he took the Moka pot off the stove and set it on a cloth in the center of the table before retrieving cups from the cabinet and two spoons from a drawer. He set out a few slices of cake as well, then sat across from me, poured two cups of coffee, and offered me one.

"Thanks," I murmured. The coffee was thick and strong. I took a sip and grabbed a piece of the cake, which I started nibbling. "This is amazing," I said.

"And sweet," Lucas replied while chewing.

Idiot! I wanted to say, realizing he was making a joke about my underwear. "Don't tell me you've never seen a girl in a pair of dumb panties before..."

"They weren't dumb," he responded. "Actually, I thought it was a pretty sexy ensemble."

I shook my head. Everything about him, every least movement, was so calm, so casual, so confident. And it was contagious. And I guess that was why, before I even knew what I was doing, those words emerged from my mouth. "Lucas, will you rent me that room?"

He glanced at me skeptically over his cup. I'd clearly caught him off guard.

"You want to rent the room? Why?"

"Have you looked around here?" I asked. "It's amazing, I love it."

"Maya, I rent it out by the month, not the day. I'm not allowed to do vacation rentals."

"I was thinking about sticking around for a while," I said like it was the most normal thing in the world. When I saw he was suspicious, I added, "I've got money."

He looked curious as he observed me, and I could see he wasn't the type to rush things, even if you would have thought a guy so calm, so easygoing, just took things as they came. Finally, he took a long breath and said, "It's three hundred a month, utilities included, plus one-seventy-five for a deposit."

"Sounds good," I responded. Between my paltry savings and what Grandpa had given me, it was doable. Plus, I wanted to be close to Giulio, and what better way was there?

"We split the chores, and you can have half the space in the closets, the fridge, and the bathroom. Having friends over is fine with advance notice, but no parties. The same goes for me. Your room is your castle: Whatever happens in there is your business."

"Sounds good. Let me go grab the cash."

I started to stand, but he stopped me, resting a hand on top of mine that seemed to give me an electric shock.

"If you're going to live here, I need to know some things about you. Those are Catalina's rules, but they're mine, too."

I felt immediately defensive, and asked, "Like what?"

"Nothing weird, I hope." He leaned back and I checked out his bare chest before glancing quickly away at the little scratches on the surface of the table. "Look," he continued, "the people who live in this villa are like a big family. When they say hi because they run into you on the landing, it's not just good manners. We truly live together here, and we share our days with each other. I'm the person who's been here the least amount of time, and I've been here two years. What we have here means a lot to me, and I can't let just anyone in… It's nothing personal, Maya."

I nodded, I got what he wanted to say, and I understood why he was worried, even if I couldn't help but feel judged.

"Fine," I said. "What do you want to know?"

"Let's start with the basics: age, and are you working or studying. Why you're in Sorrento and how long you're thinking of staying. Criminal record. Anything that will help me get to know you."

"Are you serious? Do I look like a criminal? Do I need to take a medical or psychological test, too?"

"Listen, it is what it is," he said.

He was calm and I was tense, and I didn't understand why this was getting to me so much. I didn't have anything to hide, except for things he hadn't asked me to share. Things that were for me and no one else to know.

"OK," I said, "my name's Maya Rivet, I'm from Madrid, and I'm twenty-two years old. Until a few days ago, I was employed by the National Dance Company, but they had to let me go because of an accident I was in a few months back. I live... Excuse me, I *lived* with my grandparents, but they decided to rent our place out and move to the coast."

I took a sip of coffee. My mouth was getting dry. Lucas remained attentive.

"I caught my boyfriend, who was also my dance partner, banging one of our soloists, and I broke up with him. My plan had been to shut myself up in my best friend's apartment and cry my eyes out in his arms all week, but he happens to share his place with my ex. Under the circumstances, I decided the best thing I could do was catch the first flight out of Madrid and get a change of scene. Distance, you know, so I could try to forget it all... I landed in Rome, I heard a group of tourists talking about Sorrento, and here I am." This last part was a lie, but I didn't even blink. There was no need for him to know everything about what had brought me there. "I've never committed a crime, and I don't know how long I'm going to stay, honestly. But you can trust me. I won't screw you over."

He downed the rest of his coffee, his expression still strangely intense. I tried to ignore the way those blue eyes made me feel: how they looked dreamy in some moments and stormy in others.

He smiled. "Honestly, you had me in the bag as soon as you didn't ask for milk for your coffee. For me, that's a deal-breaker."

I giggled. In part because I was so anxious, and in part because I was elated that I could stay. "Is that a yes, then?"

"You bet it is."

"Thank you, Lucas!" He tried to shrug off the significance of it as I stood and told him, "If I'm going to stay, I need to buy some stuff. Is there a mall or something around here?"

He shook his head and stood as well. "Sorry, the closest thing would be in Pompeii, and that's thirty minutes away by car. But there are some nice little shops around here." He started clearing off the table.

I wondered what to do. I realized maybe the villa was a little out of the way. "Can I walk, or take a bus maybe?"

"I'm not sure about the bus, but if I were you, I wouldn't walk. It's a couple of miles probably."

"Sure," I said, downcast.

"But I'm off today, and I've got some shopping to do, too, so I can take you."

"Amazing."

"Just give me a minute to get changed," he said, "and we'll go."

I nodded, unable to suppress a smile. And yet I was agitated inside, feeling as though I were crossing a threshold and there was no turning back. On his way out of the kitchen, Lucas stopped and told me, "By the way, I'm respectful of other people's freedom and their quirks. So, uh…if you want to walk around the house in your underwear, that's fine by me, no problem. Just pretend I'm not here. You can wear your doughnut panties, or cookie ones if you have them, or whatever. I've got a sweet tooth."

Without thinking, I grabbed a lemon out of the fruit bowl and threw it at him. He caught it, just barely, and ran into his room. I wanted to tell him off, but as I leaned my hands on the table, I felt something. Something different. An inner warmth. As though something inside me was thawing out. I felt silly, but I felt happy, too. I grabbed my bag and waited by the door. A few second later, Lucas appeared in jeans and a black T-shirt, sunglasses propped high on his head and a cigarette behind his ear. He tucked his wallet in his back pocket and grabbed some keys from a bowl on the sideboard, tossing them to me. I had to juggle them in the air before I finally caught them.

"Here, these are yours. Shall we?"

I agreed and we walked downstairs. Outside, I felt the magic the place emanated once more. The scent of citrus fruit was intense, and the damp from the sprinklers hung in the air around us, making tiny rainbows in the sunlight.

Under the arbor, I saw Catalina pruning rose stems.

"Good morning," Lucas said.

She turned and flattened her hand over her eyes.

"Good morning," she responded, examining me briefly. "Headed out?"

"Gotta fill up the fridge. By the way, *Nonna*, this is Maya. She's going to rent the room, as long as you don't mind."

"Of course," Catalina said. "If she's good enough for you, she's good enough for me." She laid down her clippers and walked over to give me a brief kiss on each cheek. "Hello again, Maya. Is your phone working?"

I could feel myself blushing as I told her, "Yeah, I think the bush broke the fall."

Surprised, Lucas asked, "You two know each other?"

"We met this morning in the vestibule," I told him, "when I had to come downstairs and rescue my phone."

The way they looked back and forth at each other, they seemed to be communicating something, and finally Catalina raised her arms and said, "A new renter! You know what that means?"

"Barbecue?" Lucas ventured.

"A barbecue!" Catalina said. "We've got to welcome our new guest. And how long has it been since the last one? I can no longer remember."

"It was when Paulo came here about a year ago, I think," Lucas answered.

"Tell me about this barbecue?" I asked.

Catalina explained, "We always have a little welcome dinner when someone new moves into the villa. It's a way to get to know them. And now it's your turn!"

Get to know me? I wasn't sure if I liked the sound of that.

"There's no need for all that," I told her. But they both told me there was. And when I asked them not to go to so much trouble over me, I started stumbling over my words, and they said, almost in unison, "It's a tradition," with Lucas telling me it would be a nice way to meet the neighbors and Catalina adding, "And a nice way for them to meet you."

I think Lucas knew I was scowling at him, but he didn't let it bother him. He just flashed that same innocent smile at me.

"Great, I'll tell everyone," Catalina said, heading inside. "I'll ask Giulio to buy what we need, and Blas will take care of the firewood."

"We'll get drinks," Lucas said.

"Good, va bene."

Catalina disappeared inside. I was torn between anxious and angry, and Lucas was clearly amused to see me in such a state.

"Are you seriously going to get all these people together to meet me?"

"I told you, we're like a big family."

"I didn't think you meant that literally."

"That's how it goes here," he said.

"And you like that?" I asked as we walked toward the car.

I don't know why, but the idea of meeting all those people weirded me out. I'd always thought of myself as sociable, friendly. But now I felt deeply insecure. Maybe it was the circumstances, or maybe it was a little voice in my head making me feel like a delinquent getting ready for her next caper.

Lucas lowered his sunglasses and put his hands on my shoulders.

"Maya… Look around you. Do you see how pretty all this is? Can you feel the sun and breeze on your skin? Can you taste the salt from the sea on your tongue? All that is telling you something: you're here. And from what you've told me, I think this is the best place you could be. A place to get away from everything and forget. So pay attention to someone who came here for similar reasons: Don't think, just let things happen."

He was leaning in close as he said this, and his aroma encircled me. I nodded over and over, and his voice drowned out the rest of the world. As we looked at each other in the ensuing silence, a moment passed, a moment that didn't need to be anything else.

And yet it was.

It had turned us, without our knowing it, into something like two drops of water on a pane of glass playing hide-and-seek. Pretending to be two things when already we were mixing and melting into one. We didn't know because there are some things you can only see when you close your eyes, and we couldn't stop looking at each other.

18

Getting to know the town with Lucas made it so much lovelier than I could have imagined at first. He told me there were two ways you could live in Sorrento. One was as a tourist. The other was the way the locals did it. And that was how he liked it. So he showed me the stores where the locals shopped, which were cheaper and cozier, and the restaurants and bars where the locals ate and drank, and the feeling was almost intimate. Away from the tourists, you could breathe freely, getting lost for hours in little corners of the city where the multitudes never bothered you.

As we did that, we talked about everything and nothing, sharing ice creams, laughter, and jokes. Filling in at random the blank sheet of paper that was our lives. Writing a next chapter that neither of us imagined.

"Land of mermaids... Are you serious?"

"Yeah," Lucas said, "there are many legends about them from around here. This is where Homer had the meeting between Odysseus and the sirens take place when he was returning to Ithaca. I love places like this, places you can breathe art, culture, and history. Lord Byron, Dickens, Goethe, Nietzsche, all of them were here. Is it not just fucking incredible to know you're walking the same streets they walked down so long ago?"

I didn't know much about those poets and writers apart from their names, but seeing him so inspired brought a smile to my lips.

"I've never read any of them," I said, shrugging when he seemed surprised. "Honestly, I haven't read anything in forever."

"Don't you like reading?"

"I used to love it, but for so many years, ballet just sucked up every free moment. I barely even had time to sleep. Now that all I have is time, though, maybe I should pick it up again."

I looked at the ground as we walked down a narrow alley with shops and homes with colorful awnings. I had seen understanding in Lucas's eyes a moment ago, but now I saw something else: curiosity, the same curiosity I felt for him. I wondered what had brought him here and why he'd decided to stay. How he could go from a place as different as Madrid to Sorrento.

"Lucas," I asked, "what did you do before?"

He turned around and started walking backward in front of me.

"Want to guess?" he asked.

"I don't know. I could imagine all sorts of things, but it sort of depends on how old you are."

"I'm twenty-seven."

I'd been wondering that all day. "All right, then. I think you used to be a high school teacher. You taught history, or maybe philosophy. You used to ride a bike to school and you had black-framed glasses and wore V-neck sweaters and carried a shoulder bag full of books. Like Robin Williams in *Dead Poets Society*. The cool teacher, you know."

"Cool?" he repeated timidly.

"Yeah, like a little bit of a dick, but also cool."

He laughed and turned back around, walking so close beside me that our arms, which were wrapped around shopping bags, started to graze each other.

"You struck out," he responded. "I studied law and business administration with a certificate in enology. And after that, I started working in the family business."

"What's the family business?"

"Wine. My family has a winery in La Rioja. They also export fancy olive oil, and I think they just opened a hotel in the countryside in Huelva. One of those high-end getaways."

That *I think* struck me as odd, and I could tell there was more to the story. It was hard to imagine him sniffing a wineglass or sitting in an office keeping the books, calculating revenue vs. profit, and that kind of thing. It just wasn't him.

"What did you really want to do, though?"

That question made the air seem to thicken around us, and he turned tense, as if I'd overstepped a line.

"Why did you ask me that?"

"Sorry, I didn't mean to…"

"No," he interrupted me. "I'm serious, why?"

"Nothing," I said. "Maybe I just liked the version of you I made up more than the real one. Wine snob… I don't know, it just doesn't suit you."

I saw a mix of emotions on his face as he looked away and kept walking. Something had happened, but I didn't understand what, and I wasn't sure whether things were OK with us or whether he was mad at me. We crossed the square and made our way to another street full of shops with their wares on display outside, stepping into a doorway to let a man with a baby carriage pass.

"Same," Lucas finally said in a soft tone.

"Same what?"

He grinned, and that allowed me to recover a bit of my

self-confidence as he continued, "I prefer your version, too. I don't even like the taste of wine. I mean, I hate it, actually. I don't know what I would have done if I'd had other options. I didn't, so I never thought about it."

His vulnerability just then made me curious. His story and mine had a lot in common, and I wanted to know more.

"So what now?" I asked him.

"I don't know. I haven't found what I'm looking for. So I'm just living for today until I do."

"You really don't know what you want?"

"Is there something wrong with that?" he responded.

"I don't know. You *are* twenty-seven."

He laughed, and that gave me a jolt of adrenaline.

"Sorry, is there a maximum age on that? If I reach thirty without knowing, will someone force me to go live on a desert island with the other failures?"

"Of course not," I responded, blushing and feeling a little stupid. I was judging him, and of all people in the world, I was the person who had the least right to.

We walked back to the main road, and after seeming to meditate, Lucas said, "The thing is this, Maya: I don't know what I want to do with my life, but I'm also not worried about it because right now, this is perfect. Plus, I do know what I don't want to do."

"And that is…?"

"I don't want to be the person I was before I ended up here. And if I can stick to that, I'll be satisfied."

I remembered what he'd told me that morning: *Pay attention to someone who came here for similar reasons.* He thought I'd come to Sorrento fleeing the disaster in my life, looking for space, looking to forget. What was he running from, then? And what was he looking for? And had someone told him to just let things be, too?

"What would you have done if you weren't a ballerina?" he asked me.

"I don't know. I didn't really have options, either. There was never any notion of things going a different way until they did. Everything fell apart, and now I don't know what to do or what I want to be. My life is like a boat adrift." I didn't bother to conceal the fear and frustration I felt about my situation as I told him this.

"Yeah, but what's the rush?" he asked.

That threw me off, and I struggled to find the words to describe how uneasy I felt without my stability and my routine. I felt secure knowing when I got up in the morning I had a purpose, a plan, an agenda. It had been that way all my life, and now I felt I was nothing without it.

"I'm not in a rush," I replied. "I just… I don't know."

Lucas walked around in front of me, stopping me, and I felt pierced by his eyes, as if they were looking for something and failing to understand it.

"Have you ever let yourself be guided by what you want and not what's expected of you?"

"What do you mean?"

"I mean living according to your instincts, according to what your body wants from you."

The answer was yes, I had. Once. I'd bet everything on a hunch. A dream that never was anything more than a dream. And because of that dream, I lost other things that would matter much more later.

"What if my instincts suck?" I asked.

"They don't."

"How do you know?"

"Because instincts come from inside you. That means they *are* you. And if you're truly in touch with yourself, you can't be wrong about what you want." He looked over my shoulder and pointed to something with his chin. I turned around and saw we were in front of a pastry shop. He continued, "See that chocolate cake?"

On a platter with a glass top was a dark chocolate cake with rasp-berries. It looked delicious.

"Yes."

Leaning close and whispering in my ear, he said, "As soon as I saw it, I felt it: instinct, impulse, desire. I could feel that cake in my stomach, in my mouth. I want a piece. It's tempting me, and I know beyond a shadow of a doubt that I'll enjoy it."

"I don't know what you're getting at."

But I felt his breath on me, hot, and smelled his hair, and every-thing about him was so close... I could have pulled away, but I didn't. It wasn't uncomfortable, but it was strange...tempting.

He lowered his voice, "I could pay attention to that impulse, go inside, and buy a piece, eat it and lick my lips and gobble up every last crumb. Or I could convince myself that I don't actually need it. I could tell myself it will spoil my supper and an apple is way healthier. Fewer calories, no saturated fats. I mean, I *am* getting older and those *are* the things people worry about. Maybe I should turn around and walk away, even though I want that piece of cake more than anything in the world."

Looking at his profile, the outline of his jaw, I could feel my heart racing. This guy I barely knew had reduced my entire life to the image of an apple, and worst of all...he was right! I wanted that cake! I always had! And I'd always refused it to myself!

"I want the cake," I said with a sigh.

"Are you sure?"

"Yes. I don't care if everyone wants me to eat the apple, I want the cake, and that's all that matters."

"Give it a shot, then, Maya. Try it, let go. You might be surprised by all you find out about yourself if you do. Who knows? You may even learn who you want to be."

For the first time I could remember, I felt a weight being lifted off my chest. I turned to the shop window, then to Lucas, whose handsome lips were tugging upward, and in his eyes, there was something impossible to resist.

"Fine, I'll try it."

He looked over a moment and said, "Cool, I'll be right back."

He walked into the pastry shop while I stood there, thinking about the conversation we'd just had. I'd known him for less than twenty-four hours, and I'd already shared thoughts with him I'd never shared with anyone before. Never had anyone made me feel so safe that I could just open up like that. And I couldn't find an explanation for why. Two strangers just shouldn't trust each other that way. But there I was, feeling closer to him than I did to people I'd known my entire life.

19

Night was falling when Lucas knocked at my door.

"Be right out," I told him.

I buttoned my pants and slipped on my slippers. There in my room, my clothes were now in the closet. The bed looked different with the new sheets and cushions I'd purchased, and the wall was less cold with the printed kerchief I had hung over it like a flag. It felt like my space now, and that comforted me.

When I opened the door, I found Lucas there waiting for me, carrying all the drinks we had bought for that evening.

"Let me help you with that," I said.

"No, you carry the cake."

The box from the pastry shop was sitting on the sideboard. I felt my stomach growl. I realized I would never look at a chocolate cake the same way again, without thinking of the time Lucas had whispered in my ear how badly he wanted to taste it.

We walked down the stairs together, and when we reached the vestibule, we found the door that led to the backyard wide open. I could hear voices, music, and the crackling of a bonfire.

"I'm nervous," I told him.

"You shouldn't be."

"I only know a couple of phrases in Italian. How will I talk with anyone?"

"Everyone here speaks Spanish. Don't sweat it."

I was speechless when we reached the garden. Beneath my feet was pea gravel that stretched out toward the huge stone flowerpots of stone and terra-cotta at the other end of the patio. Wreaths with tiny light bulbs hung from the trees, shining brighter as the sun went down. In the center of it all was a huge table with seating for twenty covered in plates, glasses, and silverware.

It was homey, welcoming, with white wicker chairs and orange and blue cushions all around.

To my left, by the wall that enclosed the property, a grill was giving off smoke as the flames burned into the firewood. Giulio was there tending it. I could feel my throat closing up.

"You're here."

I turned and saw the origin of that voice, Catalina, standing up from her chair and coming toward us. Her hair was pulled back in a ponytail and she was wearing a pink caftan so long that all I could see was her bare feet. She looked wonderful.

"Lucas, there's a tub with ice over there on that chair. Put the drinks inside." As he obeyed, she looked at the box in my hands and asked, "Did you bring dessert?"

"Chocolate cake," I responded.

"Oh, the children will lose their minds!" she exclaimed.

"They're not what you'd really call children, though," said a man I hadn't met before, who introduced himself with the words, "Ciao, I'm Marco, Angela's husband."

"Hi, I'm Maya," I said, and we exchanged kisses on the cheek as well as we could with the pastry box between us. "You speak Spanish!" I added.

"With this family, you have to!"

"Who's Angela?" I asked him.

"Angela's my daughter," Catalina interrupted us. "Come on, set that down on the table and I'll introduce you to everyone."

Trying to remain calm, I followed her to the edge of the patio. Like a person about to give a speech, she shouted, "All right, everybody pay attention. I want to introduce you to Maya." I felt my cheeks flush as she took me by the arm and introduced me to a brown-eyed woman who was cutting bread into slices. "This is Angela," she said.

"Pleasure to meet you," she said, but soon her smile turned to panic as she shouted, "Gianni, get those scissors away from your sister's hair right now!"

I turned to see a boy of around eleven chasing a little girl with a pair of blunt-tipped scissors.

"Mamma, he says I'm a plant and it's time to trim me. I don't want to be trimmed," the girl shouted in Italian, trying to protect her curly hair with her hands.

"Chiara, your brother's just playing. He's not going to cut anything."

"Will, too. That way she'll grow better."

I tried not to laugh, but the whole scene was too ridiculous.

Now, Angela turned to Marco and called out, "Marco, can you stop eating cheese and take care of your children, please?" Marco jumped and gulped down one last bite before telling his son, "Gianni, if you try to cut your sister's hair, I'll cut off something of yours."

Chiara egged him on to do it, giggling maliciously. We all wanted to act like adults, but it was impossible not to crack up with her.

"They're little demons," Angela told me, "and they can't keep still. If they ever bother you, though, just tell me."

"No, don't worry, I'm sure we'll get along wonderfully."

Catalina took my hand and said, "Come on, I want you to meet the others." She walked me over to a group of people standing at a round table of wrought iron and ceramic, drinking wine and chatting. Pointing to an older woman with short white hair and huge eyes, Catalina told me, "That's Iria, and next to her is her husband, Blas. They came here on vacation five years ago and never left. The guy smoking the pipe is Roy, he's our local celebrity, he's a writer who's published a bunch of travel books and articles." Finally, Catalina rested her hand on a pregnant blond woman's shoulder and informed me, "And this adorable couple is my niece Monica and her husband, Tiziano. They live in the house across the street."

I waved and said hi, and they all answered back: "Hola," "Ciao," "Bienvenida," "Benvenuta."

A woman then walked over pulling two teenagers with her, almost as though she were hauling them around against their will. The boys' heads were hanging down and she was talking so fast she was almost impossible to understand.

"You two are going to stay here and have dinner with everyone else and socialize. No grunts and murmurs. I want words, complete sentences. Words with more than one syllable, if you think you can manage that. Understood? What did I just say?"

The boys tried to mumble their way out of it, but when the woman kept insisting, they finally said, "Yes, Aunt Julia."

She rolled her eyes and walked toward us energetically, smoothing down her hair, which was dyed strawberry red.

"Those two bums, I swear they never move," she blurted out when she reached us. "All day playing video games and grunting and groaning. I go to the salon in the morning, and when I come back at midday, they're in the same position. There's a permanent outline of their butts on my sofa."

"Teenagers today are just like that," Iria said as she chuckled.

"They're seventeen years old. Wouldn't it be more normal for them to be out there trying to buy alcohol and lose their virginity? That's what I was doing when I was their age."

Roy interrupted her. "You make it sound like virginity was a bad thing."

"Not all of us held onto it like an heirloom," Julia replied. Roy laughed in response. The way they looked at each other, with sympathy and understanding, made me think there was a story there. But before I could speculate any further, she said, "Hey! You must be Maya."

"That's me!" I said.

"Welcome to the madhouse! I love your hair, by the way. It's so pretty. But if you ever decide you want a makeover or just a trim, stop by my salon. I'll give you a discount. Now where's the wine?"

Someone turned up the volume on the music and I found myself with a glass of red in my hand. Once Catalina had introduced me, I ceased being the center of attention and became just one of the crowd. They tried to include me in the conversation and make me feel at home, but nobody pried. People just seemed to accept that I was there, and any apprehensions I'd had just melted away.

More of Catalina's friends and neighbors showed, and there ended up being around twenty of us in the garden. Iria told me they did this often, that the house was generally full of life. All over, people were talking in small groups or helping with dinner. Gianni and Chiara were now playing and laughing with two other kids who had shown up.

It felt almost surreal as my eyes settled on Giulio, who was still working on the fire. After a few seconds' hesitation, I walked over to him and said hi. He turned, looking content, and said, "Hi. Having fun?"

"Yeah, everyone here is just great."

He set aside his poker and grabbed his glass of wine off of the sill of the woodshed.

"Yeah, they're all good people," he affirmed.

I had to stop looking at him, even as I was entranced by his face, his eyes, the tone of his skin. His fingers were long, his nails oval, his ears big, his eyebrows arched. He looked different from in the photos in my suitcase, older, more masculine, but the resemblance between us was still unmistakable.

He was right there. All I had to do was open my mouth and say it. Utter my mother's name, tell him I knew that they had known each other, admit that I thought he might be my father. Terrified, feeling the cold sweat gather on the nape of my neck, I told myself, *Just do it*. But then I found Catalina looking at me, and I heard Angela scream and run after her husband, trying to whip him with a kitchen rag. Giulio laughed, and I asked myself: What if this is my new home? The people were so kind and caring; they clearly adored each other and everyone else, too. It was as if they lived to open their arms up to you and make you feel you were part of their universe.

And I had always dreamed of that: a family that was truly a family. A family that could be mine.

Say it.

The children ran past, and we had to jump back to keep from getting our toes trampled.

"Bambini, per favore!" Giulio exclaimed. "They're little monsters."

Squeezing my glass tight, I asked him, "Do you have any children?"

"Me? No!" He responded as if the mere idea were insane. "I'm not made to be a father."

"How do you know?"

"You just do, don't you agree?"

I asked if he didn't like children.

"I love children, I adore my nephews. But I don't have any need to be a father. It's an impulse I've just never felt. The idea of being responsible for another person, someone needing me for the rest of their life, and especially the idea that I might not be up to it... All that scares me. It's too big a commitment for me. Why, do you have kids?"

"No."

"Of course not. You're too young." He took another sip of wine and licked his lips. "Do you want them, though?"

I thought about it. I tried to imagine myself with a big belly like Monica's. Holding a baby, taking care of it... It was terrifying. Not because I didn't want to be a mother. I just thought of that baby growing up and being someone like me. I didn't want to make another person unhappy the way others had with me. Bring someone into the world only to hurt them.

"I don't know," I replied.

Looking down into the purple liquid in my glass, I felt the pain of the knowledge that Giulio didn't want to be a father, had never wanted it. I knew it shouldn't hurt, but it did.

And there I was, without certainty.

Without the truth.

Without proof.

Giulio raised his hand and looked off in the direction of a man in his mid-thirties who walked over to us. He was tall and thin, with long, curly hair somewhere between light brown and red, pulled up in a man bun with a few stray hairs hanging down from it. Giulio embraced him. Then the other man cupped Giulio's face in his and kissed him on the lips. Deeply. Both men closed their eyes. They giggled, whispered, gave each other a few more pecks, then held hands as they walked over to me.

"Vieni, voglio presentarti la nuova vicina," Giulio said. Still in shock, I stood up straight and forced myself to smile. "Dante, this is Maya," he continued.

"Ciao, Maya, piacere di conoscerti."

"Grazie. I don't speak much Italian."

"I'm still learning Spanish, but we'll understand each other," Dante said. "Giulio told me how you met."

OK, now I was embarrassed. The idea that my panties were a topic of discussion around here made me want to hide my head in the sand like an ostrich.

Giulio elbowed him in the ribs and shook his head, and Dante smirked apologetically.

"Dante's my husband," Giulio said.

Husband?

I managed to tell them what a precious couple they made, and to ask how long they'd been together, despite my astonishment.

Dante looked pensively at Giulio and said, "Twelve years, I think…"

"Thirteen," Giulio corrected him.

"Right. Thirteen. But we've only been married for four."

"Wow, that's like forever," I said.

"It's symbolic; gay marriage isn't allowed in Italy," Giulio informed me. "We don't care, though. We don't need anybody's permission."

I could see in their eyes how much they adored each other, and their bodies showed it, too: the way they were always trying to touch each other, whether it was holding hands or just brushing shoulders lightly. They were in love. It was beautiful to see two people so close. At the same time, it made me bitter.

Marco walked over with a dish of grilled vegetables and meat, and I used this as an excuse to walk away, wondering if I was wrong. Giulio was gay, in a long-term relationship. Maybe I'd only seen my father in those photos of him because I'd wanted to, needed to.

Maybe—but that wasn't everything. He had known my mother. They might have been together. People changed, their needs changed. And I still needed to know. Now more than ever.

20

"Don't make me feel even stupider," I groaned.

On the other line, Matías was trying to stop himself from laughing.

"I'm sorry, Maya, but it's a stupid question. Of course you can be gay and be a father. You know my first time was almost with a girl?"

Excuse me? I sat up in bed, holding the phone tight to my ear. "You never told me that," I said.

"I was sixteen. I was spending the summer with my grandmother in Gijón. One day I sort of suggested to her I might like guys, and she did *not* take it well. She's very religious, and she started talking to me about how God had created men and women to be together, and anything else was a perversion, and lust was a mortal sin and so on. And that made me question myself and the whole thing drove me crazy. I had to go out with a girl, I thought, like that was going to be the solution. And it was then that Paula showed up. She liked me, and she wasn't shy about letting me know. So we hooked up."

"Are you for real?" I asked, not because I doubted it, but because Matías had always been so sure of himself and his sexuality that it was impossible to imagine him questioning himself. And one thing I had never seen was him taking interest in a girl.

"Yes, for real, we hooked up, and one night we almost went all the way. At the last minute, I got cold feet, but we were almost there."

"Wow…"

I went to the kitchen and poured myself a glass of water. I took little sips of it and looked at the sky through the open window. Matías went on talking.

"There are people who need time to figure out what they want, and others who know from the beginning but cover it up by engaging in hetero relationships. Maybe Giulio slept with your mother, freaked out when she got pregnant, and that's what made him realize what he really wanted, and now he's married to a guy. The real question is, what are you going to do now?"

"I guess I'll stay here until I find a good opportunity to talk to him."

"So you're not in a rush…"

I walked to the living room and lay down on the sofa. Lucas had left before I got up, and I was able to relish the silence. It was so nice, having all that space to myself.

"I like this place, Matías. It's like another world. Time passes differently here, slower. It's so calm. And the people… Everyone I've met is just amazing, and Giulio's family… You can't imagine what they're like, but they don't resemble mine at all, and that's a huge relief. What if Catalina was my grandmother? I barely know her and I like her so much already. There's nothing wrong with me just embracing that and riding it out for a little while, is there?"

"Of course not," Matías said. "But be careful. Maybe Giulio is your dad, but maybe he isn't, and I don't want you to get too wrapped up in that idea. Just in case, you know."

"Don't worry, I know what I'm doing."

"OK, then talk to me about the important stuff. This Lucas, is he hot?"

I covered my eyes with my arm and sighed. "I'm not going to answer that question."

"OK, so he is. That's what I wanted to hear. You're a grown woman now, and I know you don't need me telling you what to do, but use a condom and don't put anything in your mouth that I wouldn't."

"Matías!"

"What?" he replied innocently. "You've repeated his name thirty times in the last five minutes, so it's obvious you like him. And I know how much you need to have fun, experiment, maybe try a regular old fling for once. So promise me you will, and promise me you'll tell me all the dirty details."

"I'm not promising that."

"Fine, I'll take a video instead."

Matías always cracked me up with those remarks. He never hesitated to step over the line, and I loved him for it.

We said our goodbyes and I took a shower. After getting dressed and eating breakfast, I walked around the apartment, turned on the TV, and wasted half an hour watching a talent show. Then I grabbed the keys, walked out the front door, and took a stroll around back to the garden. The sun was shining in the cloudless sky, and I could already tell it would be a hot day. A grating sound was coming from the trees, constant and monotonous, and I looked up into them trying to find the source of it.

"It's locusts," Roy announced from his wicker chair in the shade. He was wearing a white suit and a beige shirt with a Panama hat and a pair of printed cloth slip-on shoes.

"Oh, I didn't see you there. How are you?" I said.

He adjusted his hat to cover his eyes a little more. "Good, how are you?"

"Fine, just looking around a little bit." I pointed to the open book lying on his stomach. "What are you reading?"

He lifted it up to give me a better view of the cover. It looked like a romance novel. "Julia lent it to me. She said it's incredible."

"And you…?" I asked.

"The history part could be done better. It jumps back and forth so much it should have a time machine in it, and the love story's rushed. And yet, I can't put it down." As he said this, his eyes looked awake and bright with intelligence even with his forced cynicism.

"I should let you keep reading, then. I'm going to walk around a bit."

I left him sitting there and walked along the wall until I reached an iron gate. Behind it was a field of lemon trees, green leaves and yellow fruits gleaming in the sun. As I plunged into the grove, I tore off a few of the leaves and rubbed them on my palms, savoring their scent.

I left the grove behind me and caught sight of the coast. I sat down there on the ground, knees pulled to my chest, and enjoyed the view. The sea was a symphony of turquoise tones and my mind was a concert of contradictory emotions.

I was happy to be there, but I was sad because I was far away from my family, and the physical distance was the least of it. They didn't care about me, and even the ballet company, where I'd spent every second of every day, hadn't left me with any real bonds, any true friends. Maybe it was me. Maybe I hadn't known how to open up enough. But still, it hurt. It made me feel alone.

"The views are incredible, right?"

I recoiled and looked over. Catalina was behind me with a basket of lemons hanging from her arm.

"Hey." I stood and shook the dust off my pants. "Those look great. Do you want a hand with them?"

Grimacing, she replied, "Now that you mention it…" She handed me the basket, which was so heavy I had to hold it with both hands. "I come here almost every morning. My grandchildren like homemade lemonade." She passed her hand across her forehead. "It's hot. Do you mind if we go back?"

"Of course not," I told her, and we walked back through the lemon grove. I added that my grandfather used to love making lemonade at home.

"Used to? Did he pass?" Catalina asked with worry.

"No, he's OK! But he went blind because of his diabetes a few years ago and there are a lot of things he stopped doing."

"Aw, that's so sad."

"Yeah," I said, "it was a tough blow for him, but he's better now. He's not the type to give up."

I looked at her and noticed she was smiling, and that her smile was exactly like Giulio's, tugging a little bit higher on the right.

"You must really love him," she said. "I can tell from your voice."

"Yeah. I grew up with him and I love him more than you can imagine. He's like a father to me. He and my grandmother are the ones who took care of me from the time I was born."

Hands on her waist, she asked, "What happened to your parents? If you don't mind telling me…"

"My parents?" It felt strange to just be telling Catalina everything, almost like it was all slipping out of me. "Nothing. I don't know, sort of." I couldn't find the words. Catalina reached up and tucked a stray hair behind my ear, and I looked away, as if I were trying to hide some secret from her.

"You don't have to tell me anything if you don't want to," she said. "I'm just a nosy old woman who asks too many questions."

"No, it's not that," I responded, still feeling stifled. "It's just… I don't know who my father is. My mother doesn't know either. She left me with my grandparents when I was four, and I've barely seen her since. That's all."

Is it possible to tell the truth and a lie at the same time? Of course it is, I was doing it, and I felt deeply ashamed.

"I'm sorry," Catalina said, "but you know something? What's important is that *somebody* loves us when we're growing up, that we feel cuddled, protected, loved. That's what everybody needs. And as a grandmother myself, I can say growing up with one is nice. They spoil you more. Just ask my grandkids!"

I shuddered as she wrapped an arm around my shoulder and I told her, "Your grandkids are lucky. You're a good person."

She studied my face, and she must have seen something in it, because she inquired cautiously, "So what's your grandmother like?"

Uncomfortable, I replied, "Olga is… I don't know, she's…" I didn't want to say anything, because I couldn't find anything nice to say. "Olga's just Olga."

Giving me a squeeze, she said, "Don't worry, when people ask about my late husbands, may they rest in peace, the best thing I can find to say is that they were very clean. Clean! Can you imagine? And they were wonderful men, I could fill a book with all the reasons why."

"You lost two husbands? I'm so sorry."

"Yep, I'm a widow twice over. Now no man in the village will go out with me." She chuckled.

Walking among the lemon trees with the sounds of cicadas in the background, Catalina told me about the two men. Vicenzo was her first true love, a man bursting with character, impulsive, impassioned. Their life together was intense, but a heart attack brought it to a quick end. All she had left of him were her memories and her wonderful son, Giulio.

Years later, she met Alonzo, and again she felt things she thought were impossible. For thirty years, they lived a life of sweet and serene love, and with him, she had her daughter, Angela. She told me that she still kept his clothes in the closet even though he'd died three years ago. And every night, she opened the doors and smelled his shirts before going to bed.

Little by little, I got a feeling for what her life had been like, and as I learned who she was, I wanted her story to be a part of mine, too. To feel that I was the fruit of something special, no matter how idealistic or stupid that sounds.

21

It took me an hour to overcome my nerves and leave the house, and I had spent that hour at the window, listening to the voices rising up from the garden. I had now been in Sorrento for four days. Four days, and I'd never stopped feeling like a stranger, never stopped hearing those hundreds of voices telling me to run away and forget all that had happened.

It wasn't just about me anymore. It wasn't just about finding answers. Any step I took would affect other people, changing their lives with no turning back, and why? Because of some photographs that might mean nothing?

I felt on edge as I walked down the stairs. I toyed with my ponytail. This had turned into a tic, and I was doing it constantly, the same way I used to always press my hair down when I had it pulled into a bun. I'd had these habits for years, but I was only now becoming aware of them.

The back door was open, and from the vestibule I could see the wreaths of lights hanging in the trees and illuminating the space warmly. Outside, I found everyone around the table except for Marco, Lucas, and Julia's nephews.

A waitress at Lucas's work was sick and he was taking over her shifts, so I'd hardly seen him since the barbecue. He only came home long enough to sleep and shower.

As soon as everyone saw me, they made a space for me at the table. Giulio cheerfully served me a glass of some liqueur, and his good mood instantly made me feel better. I took a sip and shivered. It was strong, but it tasted good. "Thanks. What is it?" I asked.

"Limoncello," he replied, sitting back down next to Dante.

"So, Maya, how do you like it here?" Iria asked.

"It's great," I said. "Everything is so calm and so pretty."

"Where have you been, then?" Julia inquired. "We've barely seen you."

"At home. But I've gone out to take a few walks."

Julia continued, "You never told us about your life in Madrid, what you do for work, if there's a boyfriend in the picture…"

As Roy rolled his eyes, Catalina chastised her. "That's because it's none of our business. We're here to listen, not to ask questions. If Maya wants to tell us something, she knows where we are."

We exchanged a trusting glance, and I was grateful she had done that for me. She must have been able to tell I struggled to talk about my past. Was I that easy to see through? It was just that anything I said could lead Giulio to think something. Especially anything about ballet, the conservatory, or my mother.

"Hello, everyone."

I heard Lucas behind me. "Did you start the party without me?" he went on.

Catalina threw her arms around him and he gave her a kiss on the cheek. She told him he looked tired, and he replied that he was exhausted. Then Dante announced, "Daniella's better. She'll be back tomorrow. You can take the day off."

Collapsing into the chair next to me and yawning into his hand, Lucas asked, "For real? That would be amazing." He bent over, grabbed a glass, and added ice and a little limoncello before leaning back and patting me on the knee, saying hello. The warmth of his hand was comforting, even magnetic. But Roy interrupted the moment by asking him how to connect some cable or other to the TV, and Lucas promised he'd help him with it the next day. Blas told us he was watching a German series about time travelers, and Iria butted in to say she'd seen four episodes and still didn't really know what it was about.

"You'd understand better if you didn't always fall asleep five minutes in," he said, to everyone's amusement.

The conversation flowed on easily, with discussion of travel, TV series, gossip, politics, and anything else that popped into people's heads. I listened along and tried to participate, but I could hardly get a word in edgewise. I didn't know anything about anything, and I was starting to feel bad about it, as though they came from one planet and I came from another.

Saying I needed to stretch my legs, I stood and walked off. My head was hurting. I let down my hair and combed my fingers through it. Feeling relieved, I asked myself why I didn't just leave it down all the time. Why I kept walking the way I did, bending the arches of my feet or resting them on my toes to keep the swelling down with my own warmth. There was no need for any of that now.

I heard steps behind me. It was Lucas coming close.

"You all right?" he asked.

"Yeah, I just needed to get the blood flowing a little bit."

"Good excuse. Now tell me the truth."

"Excuse me?" I asked, surprised.

"Maya, you've got a very expressive face. You're not good at hiding things."

"Maybe you're just watching me too close."

"That, too," he said, and I blushed. The bastard. He went on. "I'm serious, tell me why you ran away."

"I didn't run away."

"You did, though."

"I just…" I needed a second to gather my thoughts. "I don't know how to get along with normal people. I try, but I just don't."

"Are you saying you're not normal?"

"No! But I've started to realize I was living in a bubble, and now that I'm outside of it, I feel like an alien that landed on the wrong planet."

"On your planet, is everyone like you?" That question irritated me for some reason, and I turned around to walk off. He grabbed my wrist and said, "Wait, sorry! I was just joking to try and stop you from being so serious all the time. I'm listening!"

"You can listen all you want, but you won't understand."

"Try me."

"Look," I told him, "every single person I've been around since I was four was part of the ballet world. I'm talking family, classmates, teachers, boyfriends… Even my best friend is a dancer. So you can imagine I have basically one thing I know how to talk about."

"Let me guess…ballet?" he said jokingly.

"Even in the little free time I had, I basically watched YouTube videos of performances and documentaries about the lives of dancers."

"Well, I won't deny that's a little obsessive, but it was your job, your career. It makes sense. I've got a friend who's a high-level athlete, and trust me, he's even worse."

His hand slipped from my wrist to my fingers, which he interlaced with his.

"I don't know how to have a conversation with anyone," I said, "because I don't know what to say. I haven't seen all the big TV shows, I've barely read any books, I definitely don't read the newspaper, and I have no idea what's going on in the world." I frowned. "I don't have any opinions about anything, and I don't even have a good sense of humor."

"Are you saying that because you didn't laugh at one of Dante's jokes? Because if so, trust me, you're not alone. He's not funny."

"No, that's not it. I'm just boring."

I looked down at his hands. He hadn't let mine go, and I hadn't tried to get him to.

"That's not true. And you're a good talker. You're talking to me right now."

"You make it so easy though," I whispered.

I glanced over and got lost in his eyes. That was easy, too. I didn't know why I opened up that way with him. Maybe it had something to do with that glass of milk he offered me on the first night. Or the fact that he didn't leave me hanging out on the beach. He didn't know me at all, but he'd worried about me, and I needed that from someone desperately.

Did that mean I needed him?

I felt his thumb tracing circles on my skin as he listened to me. Then he started pulling me back home.

"You know what you need?" he said. "You need to go out. And I'm going to make sure that happens."

"What? Where?"

"Who cares? Just let it happen."

Let what happen? I wanted to ask.

He looked over his shoulder with mischievous excitement and expectation. As if he didn't know what the hell we'd be doing either. He was improvising by the minute. Letting life happen to him. That attitude was different from anything I'd ever known, and it was pushing me to see the world in a freer, less rigid way.

Maybe that was one of the reasons why I found him so special. So different. He was the opposite of everything I was. Everything I knew. And I wanted to try to be a little more like that.

So I squeezed his hand and let him drag me along and share his spontaneity with me. I decided I would let things happen, even if I didn't know what the hell that meant.

I felt alive.

For the first time in my life, I felt connected to something.

To someone.

22

Broken. I don't like that word when it's applied to a person. It's so cutting, because not everything broken can be repaired. I prefer incomplete, I prefer to say something's missing. And if whatever that is can't be found, maybe you can replace it with something else that's even better.

I like thinking we're like a puzzle in a box, a bunch of pieces waiting for someone to help fit everything together. That person can move us, try us out in one place, turn us upside down, until they help us connect with the other pieces and create a new, complete image. And some people are even capable of making new pieces to replace the ones that are missing.

Before I met Lucas, all I could see were the scattered parts of myself, as if I were being reflected in a cracked mirror. With him I learned that words may say one thing, our mind may say another, but it's what our body feels that really matters. The body can't lie. It reflects what we desire. Impulses shake it. Sensations make it move.

I learned with him that you have to let your emotions take hold of you. Feel them. Even if they hurt, even if they scare us. Because when all of them come together, that's what we are. They give us shape, draw us with our lights and shadows, show us from different angles in all our dimensions.

He taught me that there are journeys without a destination.

That the destination is itself a journey.

With no map, no compass, no stars to guide us.

Because the route doesn't matter.

It doesn't matter whether you're going nowhere.

In the end, where you end up is always where you belong.

Your destiny. Your destination.

23

Lucas took me to a pub on Corso Italia, the main street in Sorrento. It was a small, picturesque place called Banana Split. We took a table outside.

"What do you feel like having?" he asked.

"What are my options?" I replied.

Lucas pointed to the wall where there was a huge board with the drink menu. I couldn't believe how many they offered. I read attentively until I reached the section called SEXY DRINKS. I felt as shy as a little girl as I read: Golden Dream, Sex on the Beach, Against the Wall with a Kiss, Orgasm, White Lady, Sixty-Nine. I burst out laughing and couldn't stop. I'd been nervous for days and I was finally exploding. And it was liberating, letting all that tension go.

When I regained my composure, more or less, because I was still giggling—a little like the aftershocks of an earthquake—I said I was sorry.

"Don't apologize for my sake," Lucas responded. "I think it's great."

"What, seeing me acting hysterical?"

"Oh, whatever. You've got to loosen up. I'm serious."

A waitress came over and said, "Hello, Lucas."

"Hey, Stella, what's up?"

"Just the usual. I'm good. I haven't seen you around in a while."

She looked like she was hanging on his every word as he responded, "I've been busy. The restaurant is insane right now."

"That's summer for you," she told him. "Do you know what you two want?"

Lucas looked over at me, but I shook my head and told him to pick.

"Yeah, we'll take two Big, Big Tits, but easy on the tequila."

Of course, I cracked up again, and Lucas did, too—I'm pretty sure he ordered those drinks with the express intent of making me feel ridiculous—and when we calmed down, we found ourselves looking at each other, and I felt almost weak in the knees. I started fiddling with my hair to distract myself, but his eyes wouldn't leave me in peace. "What?" I asked.

"Nothing," he replied, but I couldn't help noticing how he glanced down at my lips just then. His pupils were like two black holes in a very blue ocean. Something clicked in that moment, and we saw each other as the people we truly were.

Attraction—it's a mystery, right? Every day you pass people by, and people pass you by in turn. You meet eyes for just a second, you talk, and none of it matters. You don't feel anything.

But then there's a change. Unpredictable. Instinctive. Something makes you shiver. A look that's different from the others, and your pupils dilate. You get a tickle in your stomach. The air thins. Your mouth dries out. Your stomach contracts until it hurts. And that's attraction. It's not the same as love. Love germinates and grows. Attraction explodes.

It was like feeling the ground shift beneath you. I'd never felt anything that intense before.

The waitress brought our drinks. I sipped mine through a straw and started coughing. My throat burned. I wasn't used to drinking at all, and certainly not anything that strong.

"Are you all right?" he asked.

I nodded and winked. He looked over at the cocktail menu again and made fun of me for when I said the list of drink names was a bit much. "It sounds like a porno-movie catalog," I told him. He accused me of thinking about sex, and I protested that I wasn't.

He whispered back to me, "I am. I think about it all the time."

Taking another drink through my straw, I tried to pretend he wasn't staring at me. But it went on for what felt like an eternity. I was feeling uncomfortable. I needed to think of something else. Right then. So I remarked, "You didn't tell anyone anything about me. Not even Catalina. Why not?"

He shrugged. "You could have lied to me just to make a good impression and get the apartment... But instead, you were sincere in a way I absolutely did not see coming. The stuff you told me was personal. And I respect that." He ran his finger meditatively around the rim of his glass as I thanked him. Then he confessed bashfully, "I looked you up on the internet. There wasn't much there, but enough to give me some ideas about you."

"Like what?"

"Well, I know you're good. At what you do, I mean. Why am I saying good? You're amazing! And I'd guess if you can dance like that, you're probably good at everything else, too. You seem methodical."

"If by methodical you mean an unbearable perfectionist, then yeah, that's me. That's one of the other things I think I'd like to get away from."

"I find you pretty bearable," he said.

I flicked a bit of my drink at him with my fingers, making him smirk. "Anyway, I'm not that good anymore," I replied.

"Don't be stupid. Talent is something you're born with, not

something you pick up and then lose. Maybe you can't show it the same way you could before, but it's still there."

"You can say that again," I told him. "Still, though, it's hard to accept."

"Did you really like it that much? It's just a job, right?"

"It's not, though, Lucas. It's a way of life. I was going to dance at the American Ballet Theatre! I was going to go live in New York! Forty dancers from all over the world came to my audition and they picked me for the one open spot. Me!"

He grinned as he edged closer to me. "That sounds incredible."

"I'd devoted every minute of my existence to achieving it. You can't imagine the sacrifice and effort something like that takes."

"I'm sorry it didn't work out," he told me.

"Yeah, me too."

He reached out and touched my knee, and his fingertip brushed the scar that I still hadn't managed to bring myself to touch. He did it slowly, softly, following its entire outline. Then he grabbed my calf and held it.

"What happened?" he asked.

It was hard to respond with his touch there, feeling like a hot iron brand, but I began. "A car blew a red light and destroyed my leg. They had to operate on me a bunch of times. The doctors did what they could, but it's still screwed up. You know, I got my admissions letter from the ABT the same day it happened."

"Man, that sucks."

"It does," I agreed, looking down and toying with the ice in my glass and feeling his fingertips sinking into me. Despite the burn of the tequila, I swallowed down everything that was left.

"You in the mood for another?" he asked. I nodded, even though I wasn't usually much of a drinker and could already feel my head getting cloudy. "The same, or something different?"

I looked up at the menu, biting my lip, and responded as I read the ingredients, "I'd like to try another one. I'm between the Orgasm and the Sex on the Beach. Which do you recommend?"

"I mean, there's a natural order there." I could tell he'd thought that was funny. He tried not to laugh as I stared over at him and he raised his eyebrows. With a snicker, he ordered another round from the waitress, and bent over to see if he could ask me a question.

"Of course," I replied

"The guys...the male ballerinas... I saw those tights they wear and, like, they're very snug! What do they do so you don't see their, uh...their junk?"

Oh my God. Was he actually asking me that?

"They wear a special kind of belt," I murmured, "that gathers everything up into a little package."

"Got it. That makes sense."

"Why were you thinking about that?"

"No reason."

"Come on, Lucas, spit it out!"

"You know what tucking is? The thing drag queens do to hide their stuff..."

I nodded, deeply entertained at the thought of Matías trying to do that. "You mean like with tape and all? No, of course that's not what they do!"

He clicked his tongue. "How am I supposed to know? Anyway, my mind always tends to go in a kind of perverted direction."

I saw a little sparkle in his eyes with their crow's-feet next to them, and the dimples that bordered his lips when he grinned.

And I stopped resisting.

I let myself go.

I let things happen.

Because deep down, I wasn't strong.

I wasn't firm.

I was an exhausted girl who wouldn't allow herself to feel what she wanted.

Tired of pretending to be in control when inside me, everything was chaos.

Hounded by the wish that something would change, but unable to let that wish sprout wings.

24

We left the bar and walked to Piazza Tasso. A girl walked up to us and gave us two coupons for discount drinks in a nearby club. They'd have live music that night.

"You in the mood?" Lucas asked.

"Yeah!" I responded enthusiastically.

I couldn't remember the last time I'd had that much fun, and I didn't want the night to end. Not yet. The club was called Fauno Notte. It was in the basement of a building on the corner of the park. We walked down the stairs and through a long hallway until we reached a huge room packed with people. Strobe lights gleamed in all corners, and colored beams and neon flashes spun round and round like a kaleidoscope.

Lucas grabbed my hand and walked me to the bar, cutting a path through the dancers jumping up and down to the music of a DJ. He ordered drinks and we settled down in one corner. It was hot, and the lights were making me a little dizzy, but just being there was exciting.

Lucas said something and I shook my head. The music was two loud for me to hear. Only when he spoke slowly did I manage to read his lips:

"Let's dance."

"No!"

No way I was going to go hop around to some horrible techno garbage in the middle of that huge crowd.

"Yes!" he said.

"No."

Lucas took my empty drink out of my hand, set it down on the bar, and grabbed my wrist. "Come on," he insisted.

I tried not to. It was embarrassing. That's how seriously I took myself. And my resistance lasted until he got behind me and lifted me by the waist. He actually carried me out onto the dance floor. When he set me down, I turned to face him. A spotlight was shining on our faces. Good God, he was handsome. I could feel myself melting for him.

One song ended, and the next one began. It was a slower song, a little more normal, but the rhythm sped up faster and faster as the volume rose and my eardrums were bursting and I could feel the floor shake.

And I danced. I danced!

I let the music and the torridness carry me away. Sweat dripped down our bodies as we got closer and closer, moving back and forth, brushing each other accidentally.

Or maybe not so accidentally.

His hand looked for my waist. My hand touched his stomach.

His hips rubbed my hips. My back leaned against his chest.

The lights flashed. Damp curls of hair jostled across his forehead and neck. I could see his eyes were focused on my lips. I could see he was hesitating, tense, lost. I wanted him. And the feeling of wanting him scared me. And I took a step back.

"It's too hot in here!" I shouted. He bent over to listen better, and my mouth touched his ear. It wasn't premeditated, but it might as well have been, the way the scent of his hair and the taste of his sweat turned me on. "I'm hot. Should we go out?"

He nodded and grabbed my hand. We went back outside and I caught my breath, thankful for the fresh air. My hair was so wet, it was glued to my head and neck. I pulled it up in a bun and knotted it.

"What do you want to do?" he asked.

"I don't know, you?"

"I've had too much to drink to get in the car. Should we take a walk?"

"Sure."

The evening was cool and pleasant. We were very close together, drunk, unsure where we were headed. We talked about everything and nothing: stories, memories. We laughed. We walked on. The minutes slid past without us having any idea where they had gone.

"Wait, what?" I said suddenly, interrupting him—he'd been telling a story, but my mind had wandered, and now I wasn't sure if I'd heard him right.

"I'm serious," he responded. "I got hammered. It was the summer before I entered the enology program. My dad was dead set on me taking this private class with this super-famous French sommelier. There were just four students, and none of us had the least idea what was going on. For two hours, the guy droned on about the mysteries of wine tasting, aromas, subtleties, and we tried to detect all this stuff with all these different wines. He thought we all knew what we were doing, so he didn't say anything, and every time we tried a glass, we swallowed."

"So?"

"We were supposed to spit!"

"Gross!" I shouted.

"At any given class, we might try up to twenty different wines, so even if it is gross, it's what you have to do. So an hour passed and I could barely stand. I was sick as a dog, and the next day I had the worst hangover in history. I've hated wine ever since."

I shook my head. "And yet you still did the degree program."

"I didn't really have any other options," he said, staring off into the horizon.

We were looking out onto the Gulf of Naples. All over Sorrento, there were places to catch sight of it. On the horizon, there was the thinnest gleam of sunlight.

"Are you hungry?" he asked. "I'm starving to death."

"Me too," I said. "But everything's got to be closed, right?"

Instead of answering, he just winked, grabbed my hand, and pulled me away.

"Where are you taking me?" I asked.

"You'll see. For now, just try to figure out how you're going to thank me."

I gave him a friendly slap. Soon afterward, I saw a familiar restaurant with a terrace. Lucas took the keys out of his pocket and opened the door, then turned off the alarm.

"Won't you get in trouble for this?"

"No! Dante's a good guy. He knows me and trusts me. Come on, let's go to the kitchen."

Lucas turned on the lights, and I stood in the doorway, apprehensive, not really sure what to do. The walls were immaculate white, the tables and cabinets and appliances were all stainless steel. It smelled like air freshener and disinfectant.

Lucas took bread out of a cabinet and put it on the table, then opened the two huge double doors of a refrigerator.

"What are you in the mood for?" he asked.

"What is there?"

"Come take a look."

I peeked over his shoulder and saw what resembled a smorgasbord. And everything looked delicious.

"Tomato and cheese," I said.

Lucas grabbed the ingredients and took them to the table. I got comfortable on a barstool and watched him cutting the cheese and tomato into slices. His hands moved quickly and skillfully. He had a knack. Then he broke open a long loaf of bread and filled it with these ingredients, adding oregano, pepper, and oil. He cut it in half and stuffed it into a paper bag.

On our way out, he walked behind the bar and grabbed two sodas. When he'd locked the restaurant, he took me to a nearby park. There wasn't a soul on the streets. It was deserted.

We sat on the lawn and ate in silence.

It's incredible how quickly a person can get used to happiness.

To feeling good.

To living as though life had always been beautiful.

25

When we finished, Lucas took off his shoes and laid his feet in the grass, and I did the same. My bare skin shivered as my legs stretched out and the humid ground touched them. My head was still spinning from the alcohol, and my limbs felt like they were made of rubber.

"Do you care if I smoke?"

I shook my head and Lucas removed a pack of cigarettes from his back pocket, pulling one out and lighting it. He took a long drag and breathed it out before looking at my feet.

"You should take your socks off."

"Nah, I'm good."

"I mean, you should take your socks off sometime. You never do."

I blushed and pulled my knees into my chest. "I like wearing socks," I said.

Grimacing, he said, "Come on, now, tell the truth."

"Why should I?"

He took another drag off his cigarette and narrowed his eyes when the smoke got into them. "Lying's bad for you," he said.

"Have you ever seen a ballerina's feet? The feet of a person who's done nothing but dance for fifteen years straight?" As he shook his head, I informed him, "Well, they're ugly."

"Let me get this straight: You won't take your socks off because your feet are ugly?"

"Exactly."

"They can't be that ugly. Let me see them."

"No!"

"Please?"

"No!"

He took a last drag from his cigarette and dropped the butt in his can of cola. He looked sly, like he was planning something, and before I could react, he leapt at me and I shouted. I wrestled against him and he pinned me to the ground, and at one point I kicked him in the stomach by accident, and he pretended to bite my leg in response. Soon he was raising his arms, victorious. My socks were in his hand, and I was trying to hide my feet, but he grabbed my ankle in both hands and pulled me toward him.

"Oh, come on!" he shouted. "They're fine."

"They're hideous."

"What about mine? You can't exactly call them appetizing. They're hairy all over. They look like they belong to a hobbit."

Even once he'd gotten what he wanted, he didn't let me go, and the slight, warm pressure of his hands felt like a caress. Then he lay on his back and looked up into the sky, my foot resting on his chest. I tried to retract it, but he wouldn't let it go, and I just had to settle for the fact that a guy I barely knew was there stroking a part of my body that I hated.

Still, I enjoyed the intimacy of that moment. The kindness of that gesture, the strength of his hands, and their delicacy.

"Did you know, if you could travel at the speed of light, supposedly it would take you forty-six billion years to cross the universe? It's full of galaxies and solar systems, planets and satellites, asteroids and comets, and stars," he said.

"I had no idea."

"It's so immense, and you and I are just two microscopic points inside it. It's a little frightening," he responded meditatively.

I looked up, too. "It scares you?"

"No, it just makes me ask myself if there's some other planet millions of light years away where there are two other little points that are drunk and talking bullshit."

I giggled. "Maybe it's us, but in an alternative reality."

"I like that idea."

"I read somewhere that a star shines brightest just before it's about to die."

Lucas grunted. "Remind me not to ask you to cheer me up if I'm ever feeling down."

"Dumbass," I replied, rolling my eyes. "It's because they explode, and that explosion is so powerful that it leads to the formation of nebulae, and inside them, new stars can be born. I'm not sure, because I'm improvising here, but I like to think that the end of something always brings about new life, that it doesn't go away, that there's an infinite cycle there."

"When I was little, I used to look at the stars with my granddad. We could spend hours lying on the ground and looking up at the sky. My grandmother thought we were out of our minds and used to ask us, *When the hell are you two going to come inside?* Granddad would tell her: *When there are no more stars left to count.*" He paused and took a deep breath. "I'd crack up then, you know, because there are millions and millions of them. That was his way of telling her to leave us in peace."

In the ensuing silence, as the stars faded into the lighter blue of morning, I glanced over at him, saw his mind was elsewhere, preoccupied, maybe, and I said, "Lucas, can I ask you a question."

He turned his head and said, "Shoot."

"How long has it been since you last saw your family?"

His expression changed. "What makes you think I don't see them?"

"Something you said the other day, and then... I don't know. Look at this place. I wouldn't blame you for not wanting to leave here."

He sat up and rested his elbows on his knees. He was tense. I could tell by the way he was clenching his jaw and opening and closing his fists.

"Two years. I haven't talked to any of them for two years except my sister, and her just barely. We wish each other a happy birthday, we chat on the holidays, that's about it."

"I'm sorry."

"Don't worry about me. I'm better than ever."

"What happened?"

He shrugged and chuckled humorlessly. "What didn't happen? My family's very conventional, very religious, one of those where the patriarch sets the rules and everyone else has to obey. And my father has always been a tyrant, and incredibly demanding. So that should give you a bit of a picture of how things were."

I thought of my grandmother, of her domineering, severe character, and that helped me imagine what it must have been like for Lucas, living in that family. Lucas kept talking as he slipped on his shoes, "I think Dad already had my future planned for me long before I was born, and from my very first day on earth, he started training me to fulfill his expectations. It didn't matter so much when I was little, because I wasn't so aware of what was going on, right? But when I turned twelve, I made different friends and I turned sort of rebellious. I wanted to go out and play and sign up for the soccer team instead of going to tutors in the afternoon."

"And your dad wouldn't let you."

"No. According to him, those things would distract me from what was really important, and the Velascos only cared about what was important." He sounded hurt and scornful as he uttered those words. Picking up our trash, he stood. "Anyhow, even my tutors couldn't keep me from failing math. I remember when my report card came, he lost it. He started shouting at me like a crazy person and he kept getting more and more pissed off, and then all of a sudden, he clutched his chest and fell to the ground."

"He had a heart attack?" I asked.

I hurried to put on my socks and shoes as Lucas stretched a hand out to help me up.

"Yeah. He almost died." He pulled me to my feet. "We were alone at home when it happened and I could hardly even call for the ambulance. And I felt like it was my fault, and so after that, I tried as hard as I could to do whatever he wanted."

"Lucas," I told him, "how could something like that be your fault?"

He squeezed my hand, looked away in anger, and tossed our bag into a trash can. "I don't know, but they think it is, and maybe I do, too. And another thing is, after his heart attack, he had complications, his heart was weak, and his doctors told him he had to remain relaxed at all costs. And Mom used to remind me of that all the time."

My heart broke as I thought of twelve-year-old Lucas feeling guilty for his father's illness. It just wasn't fair. "So you decided to become the perfect son," I said.

"I did. I went to the schools he told me to go to. I chose the major he wanted, I spent the summers in La Rioja learning how the winery worked. When I got my degree, I worked for the company, and I went on doing everything he told me. Then a moment came when I just couldn't anymore."

"What happened?"

He shook his head and I didn't press him. He barely knew me. A week before, he'd had no idea I existed, and I was sure that without the alcohol, he wouldn't have revealed anything so private, so personal to me. And yet, when I'd assumed he would let the matter go, he started speaking again, "They lied to me about something really important, and that opened my eyes. I realized I didn't mean shit to them; all they cared about was the stupid fantasy world they were living in. So I left one day without saying anything."

His words were bitter, and all I could do was squeeze his hand and try to comfort him.

"Are you never going to go back?"

"No way," he said cuttingly. "My family thinks I'm their puppet, and I refuse to be manipulated. They made me feel like I was nothing. I still don't get it. I need to be far away from them if I'm going to have my own life, OK? I can't fall back into the trap. Anyway, I like it here. I love it, actually. I can do what I want."

He seemed better after his confession. He smiled as he swung our hands and I tried not to think about how wonderful it felt, being with him.

"And you can be yourself," I added.

He rolled his eyes at me as the breeze shook his hair. "Why does everyone always say that? Be yourself. What if I don't want to? Like, there are some times when I'd prefer to be anyone but me. And what does it even mean to be yourself? I think a lot of people hide behind those words to justify being selfish and not worrying about the effects of their actions on others."

There was something sweet in his indignation. I asked him, "Who would you like to be then, if you don't want to be yourself?"

"I don't know. Depends on the moment. A famous actor. A porn star. A cat?"

"Really? A cat?"

"Cats are the best animals in the world," he said. "What about you? Who would you like to be?"

"How can you ask me that? You're the one person right now who knows the crisis I'm going through."

"The only one?" he asked, clearly pleased. I nodded. "So that makes me your confidant. Does that mean you're going to tell me all your dirtiest private fantasies?"

I flipped him the bird and he grabbed me around the waist and picked me up, eliciting a shout. A wave of emotion ran through me. I didn't fight back, though. I let him wrap his arms around me. The murmur of the sea, the scent of summer, made it impossible to put up resistance.

And for the first time in ages, I felt like me.

Just me.

And I didn't want to be anyone else.

26

The morning sun crept through the wooden slats of the blinds in thin golden rays that divided the room in a pattern of light and shadows. I opened my eyes, blinked, and tried to focus. I felt as if I'd slept a whole day straight. And I had, in a way.

The day before, Lucas and I had returned home after dawn. We were exhausted, and we shut the doors to our rooms and slept until late in the afternoon. Then we made dinner and got comfy on the sofa, dozing off at times and at times watching TV.

We barely talked. We just sat there. The silence was comfortable. There was no need to fill it with words.

I did catch him watching me, though. And he caught me watching him, too. Then we'd freeze. But we didn't take it any further. We wanted to. And we were scared that we would.

Restrained.

But the question wasn't if; it was when…

I got out of bed and dragged myself to the shower. With the hot water streaming down my face, I swore to myself I'd never drink again. My stomach was still killing me.

I dried my hair with the towel, leaving it down, and looking at myself in the mirror. It was the same reflection I'd seen a million times looking back at me, but there was something new there: a glimmer in my eyes, color in my cheeks. Something throbbing, something light, something alert, something living.

A few minutes later, someone knocked at the front door. I opened up and found Giulio standing there.

"Hey," he said, and I struggled to come up with a reply. Even the simplest words were hard to get out with him there. Maybe because I was too busy staring. It was almost as if I thought the answers to all my questions lay in his face. Only after I'd blinked a couple of times did I notice the cruising bike behind him, leaned against the wall, cream-colored, with a little basket and a pink helmet inside it.

He looked over at it and said, "It used to belong to my sister, and I thought maybe you could use it while you're here."

"For real?"

"She never touches it."

"That's amazing. Thank you."

"It's no car," he added with a shrug, "but you can get around on it, go to town or whatever you feel like."

A strange feeling overcame me. Every kid dreams of getting a bike from their dad. It was happening to me more than a decade late, but who cared? A world of possibilities opened before me. "It's amazing," I said. "Seriously, thank you."

"No worries. Be careful, though, all right?"

"I will. I promise."

I couldn't help but glance up quickly at that mole on his brow. I wondered if he'd noticed mine, too. Maybe. Maybe not. Maybe he thought it was just a feature of my face, while I thought it was the key to half of who I was.

Giulio grinned, waved, and took off downstairs, and I felt myself start to tremble as I shut the door and leaned against it. I'd been in Sorrento a week, and every day I kept coming up with different scenarios in which I'd confess to Giulio that I'd come there looking for him. These dialogues would come to life in my mind, but in the real world, I couldn't do it. I fell silent whenever I saw him. The fear—the possibilities—paralyzed me.

I opened the door back up and looked at the bike again. It was cute, even if the pink helmet was awful. Who cared, though? I sure as hell didn't.

I felt so free, pedaling around and soaking in the landscape. I still couldn't get over the views. Sheer cliffs dropped straight into the clear blue waters of the Mediterranean, a sea I had seen but felt as though I'd never really known. From up high, I could look down on the tiny idyllic beaches bordered by rocks, the houses on the hillsides, the orange and lemon trees in terraced fields like balconies overlooking the bay. All of it bathed in a blinding light that made the colors almost burn my eyes.

I turned off the main road and took a small street into town.

July had brought mobs of tourists in, and it was hardly possible to walk in some places. The parks and squares were full of people waiting to pounce on a patio table or step into the shadows to get a break from the heat.

I walked my bike through there and looked at the stalls selling clothing and shoes on a street parallel to Via San Cesareo, which, with Corso Italia, formed the backbone of Sorrento and housed many of its stores.

I found a small shoe shop that sold gorgeous sandals. I saw a red pair, flat, with little crystals on the straps. I felt something strange as I looked at them and then down at my own ugly feet in their socks and sneakers. I'd had a complex about them for as long as I could remember.

But I told myself to stop letting it get to me, and I bought them and a pair of flip-flops, too. At another stand, I got some bikinis and other stuff to wear to the beach. Finally, I stopped in at a funky shop to buy a couple of dresses marked down from the season before and a flouncy lace skirt and matching top.

I hung my bags on the handlebars and checked the time. I was thinking of grabbing a bite to eat, but then I heard someone shouting my name and found Monica waving at me. I waved back and said, "Hey!"

As she reached me, she responded, "I wasn't sure that it was you."

She stopped and rested her hands on her hips, and I noticed her belly was popping out. I hadn't realized during the barbecue that she was so far along. She was huffing and puffing and evidently fatigued, and I felt a little worried for her.

"Are you all right?" I asked.

"Yeah, it's just the heat and all the extra pounds."

"How far along are you?"

"Six months, if you believe it, but I'm going to have twins. That's why I look like a balloon."

I chuckled, then covered my mouth and said, "Sorry, I don't mean to laugh."

"Relax, I would too if I it didn't make me piss myself. What are you doing around here?"

"A little shopping. What about you?"

"My flower shop is down that way," she said. "I just closed for midday. Have you eaten?"

"No. I was just about to look for someplace."

"Forget that," she replied. "You're coming to my in-laws' with me. When Tiziano has to go to work in Naples, I always eat lunch with them."

"I don't want to be a bother, though."

She took my arm. "They'll be overjoyed to have you. You'll see."

Monica's in-laws instantly made me feel like part of the family. They were kind, gentle, a little saucy. I was stuffed to the gills, but I didn't complain. Everything was delicious. For the first time, I had a pasta frittata and a gateau di pattate. For dessert, we had sfogliatella, a dessert of layered puff pastry filled with cream.

They had just poured the coffee when Monica got a call from a deliveryman waiting in front of her shop. After saying goodbye to her in-laws and promising to visit again soon, I accompanied her back to work.

"I told them last week over the phone that I was only opening in the morning and that the deliveryman had to come early," she told me, getting angry.

When we arrived, the deliveryman looked irritable from waiting. But Monica didn't bend. They argued briefly—I could hardly understand a word of what they were saying—and he opened his van and took out several plastic buckets full of flowers, carrying them inside and apologizing.

"Don't leave your bike outside," Monica told me once they were done.

"Are you sure?"

"Yeah. Stand it up by the counter."

She was going to move the buckets herself, but I stopped her, warning her she could hurt herself and telling her I would take care of them if she'd just tell me what to do. After double-checking that I was serious, she thanked me. "Honestly, every single thing I do lately takes twice the effort, and I'm so fat I can barely see my feet." She rubbed her belly. "You can start by taking those flowers to the back. We'll cut the stems, put them in water, and stick them into the refrigerator."

"Sounds good."

I followed each and every instruction to the letter, cutting the stems at an angle, being careful not to crush them, and putting them in a special blend of preservatives she taught me to mix up that would keep them from wilting. Finally, we placed a few orchids in cardboard boxes, and she explained that they lasted longer if stored in that way.

"Flowers need special care. But you're a natural," she told me, closing the door to the refrigerator.

"Really?"

"I wouldn't tell you that just to flatter you."

I thanked her and told her I'd happily come another day. "Just call me."

"Seriously? Because I know you're on vacation and I don't want you doing me any favors, but if you don't mind coming in a few hours in the morning and helping me spruce up... I mean, I'd pay you, obviously."

Perplexed, I asked, "Are you offering me a job?"

"Something like that."

I wasn't sure what to say. The last thing I'd expected was someone offering me a job there. I thought it over. I could use the money, even if it wasn't much. And it would give me something to do with my time. Without any distractions, the days were starting to get long.

"Thanks, Monica. I'd love to."

"Perfect, Maya!" She hugged me as best she could in her state. "Does tomorrow at ten sound good?"

"I'll be here."

I said goodbye to her and pedaled to Villa Vicenza. As I did, with the sun at my back and the sea breeze striking my face, I was happy, excited, and I felt secure in a way that was almost unknown to me. I dropped my bike in the vestibule and ran upstairs with my bags.

I opened the door just as Lucas was coming out, and we ran into each other before each jumping back to let the other through. We hesitated, then moved, then ran into each other again. Finally he stood aside. "You first."

"Thanks," I said.

"Where have you been?"

"I was in town," I said.

"How'd you get there?"

"Bike. Giulio brought one up for me and said I could use it as long as I was staying here. I went shopping. I got a ton of stuff: clothes, some sandals, bikinis. I hope it all fits. I didn't try any of it on."

"I'm sure you'll look great. But if you need an objective outsider's opinion, I'm here for you."

I blushed. I hated how I always blushed when he was around!

"Are you leaving?" I asked.

"Yeah. Night shift tonight. I won't be back till late, I'll try not to wake you."

"Sure, no worries."

After a stare that lasted a little too long, he said, "Goodbye." I couldn't make myself respond. I shut the door and listened to his footsteps as he left.

My mind was shouting for him.

My heart was shouting for him.

My body was shouting for him, too.

I liked Lucas. In every sense of the word. And with each day that passed, I liked him more. Not just because he was handsome; he was also nice, funny, and a little naughty.

And he'd made me think about something besides me and my problems.

My world had started to revolve around him since the first time I laid eyes on him. If that wasn't a sign, I didn't know what was.

27

"Matías…"

"I'm just telling you: Be careful, and think clearly about what you're doing."

"I am!" I replied like an angry little girl.

I got up, feeling smothered, and walked over to the cracked window.

"Let me remind you," he said, "you went there for a reason. And now you've rented an apartment…"

"A room…"

"Whatever. You've moved into this place, you've gotten a job, you've got the hots for the guy you're living with, and the way you talk about him, I think you're actually falling in love. You're bonding with these people, and…"

"And what, Matías?"

"You still don't know if that guy's your dad, and that's the whole reason you went there."

"I know," I said, "but I need to choose the right moment."

"Well, choose fast before this all blows up in your face."

"Fine," I hissed, leaning my head against the windowpane and closing my eyes. He was right: Being silent, drawing things out, could only create problems. "I've got to go. I need to leave for work in a few minutes."

"Sure. We'll talk soon."

"Hey, Matías? I love you, OK?"

His tone eased. "Love you, too."

I hung up. Lucas had been awake for a while, and I wondered what he was doing. I walked out in my pajamas and found him standing there with his back turned in a pair of baggy drawstring pants, drying plates and putting them away in the cabinet.

"Good morning," I said.

He turned and smiled. "Good morning! There's still coffee left, and Catalina just brought up a fresh-baked cake."

"Thank God. I'm dying of hunger."

He took the Moka pot off the stove and poured me a cup. "What about that cake?" I asked.

"It's on the table under that cloth."

I lifted a tea towel, and the rich scent of sweet dough struck my nostrils. I cut a slice and sat down, eating while he put away the silverware in the drawer and wiped off the counter. His bare back tensed as he moved, his pants hung low on his hips, and that spectacle, all that bare skin, made something stir inside me. I was so entranced that I didn't notice he was staring at me, too. Then our eyes met. It was almost like a duel: He was direct, transparent, seductive; I was insecure, but no less intense. I tried to take a breath. I didn't want to think about what all this meant just now.

Then I saw the clock and leapt up in my seat.

"I'm late!"

"Late?"

"I've got a job! I'm helping Monica out at the florist. Incredible, right?"

Entertained, Lucas asked if I needed a ride.

"No, I can handle it on the bike. But I appreciate the offer."

I ran to my room, put on a strap dress with a loose skirt, and dug around in my drawers for a pair of socks. I sat back on the bed to slip them on, then noticed the box for the sandals, which was sitting in the same place I'd left it the day before. I decided to open it, and I felt strange when I put them on, but a glance at the mirror showed how well they went with the dress.

I rushed into the bathroom, brushed my teeth and hair, and washed my face. When I came out, Lucas was lying on the sofa. He eyed me up and down, lingering a little too long on my feet.

"Very nice," he said.

"Thanks. You don't look so bad yourself," I fired back, feeling incredibly nervous as I did so.

I ran out and down stairs, dying from embarrassment.

You don't look so bad yourself? How corny. "Idiot," I said to myself.

"Idiot?" someone else said, and I looked up and found Dante entering the vestibule with bags from a home decor shop. Behind him was Giulio. As always, I was happy to see him.

"Don't worry about it," I said. "I was just talking to myself. You guys were shopping, huh?"

"Yeah, getting decorations for the living room. We just rehabbed it," Giulio replied. "Are you leaving?"

"Yeah," I said, "I'm heading into town."

"Be careful."

"I will."

His being so kind with me made me feel bad, and that feeling grew with each day that passed without my saying anything to him. But I couldn't find the time or the place—or the way—to admit to him why I'd come there.

I pushed the bike past them and rode away. At the flower shop, I saw how overwhelmed Monica was between the phone, taking down orders, and handing off orders that had already been prepared. There was a line of customers at the counter, and they were starting to get impatient as I pushed past them to greet her. She looked relieved when she saw me.

"Thank God you're here! Put on that apron so you won't get messy and give me a hand with these roses."

"These white ones?"

"Yeah, they're for a wedding. We need to separate them into bundles of twelve."

"All right."

We were busy all morning, and I had to learn to do everything on the fly. I cut thorns, made bouquets, tied bows, filled out cards. I also ran all over town making deliveries. When I arrived back home, my body was aching as if I'd gotten a beating. But when I went upstairs, I smelled something delicious that made my stomach groan so loudly that you could probably hear it all through the building.

Lucas peeked out of the kitchen and asked, "Hey, do you like fish?"

I loved it, as it happened, and I told him so as I dropped my bag on the couch and walked over to him. I found the table set with cloth napkins and wineglasses. In the middle was a vase with sweet-smelling flowers from the garden.

"Is all this for me?"

He nodded as he brought a casserole dish of fish and potatoes out of the oven, setting it down on the counter. "Since you got a job, I thought we should celebrate. Take a seat."

I did so, deeply moved. No one had ever done anything like this for me before, not even Antoine in all the time we were together. Little gestures, moments of togetherness… We'd never had any of that. Nor seduction or intimacy, just the sexual act itself. Feeling emotions of the kind that were now running through me like electricity was something completely new.

Lucas opened a bottle of wine for me, and I remarked, "I thought you hated wine."

"This is for you," he said. "It goes great with the fish. I'll have a beer myself."

Sitting across from me, he looked in my eyes and I thought I saw a special gleam in his stare. The roasted fish was so good, I had a second helping. He knew what he was doing in the kitchen. Certainly better than me: The most elaborate dish I'd ever made was an omelet with cheese. He asked me about the flower shop, and I told him in detail everything I could about the business. What had really interested me there was the relationship between flowers and different feelings, colors and their meanings.

"Like pink symbolizes love," I said. "Yellow is friendship. White orchids express purity, red is for desire. Gardenias are for secret love. And sunflowers are a symbol of happiness."

"You learned all that in one morning?"

"Monica's quite the talker, and I realized I've got a knack for memorizing these things. I guess having to remember all those choreography routines was good for something."

Lucas stood and started gathering the dishes. "I'm not surprised," he said.

"I am. It's a miracle I got my high school equivalency."

"So what, Maya. You did other things. Much more important things."

I nearly sighed. Why did my name sound so wonderful on his lips?

We cleaned the kitchen, then sat together on the couch. I kicked off my sandals and pulled my feet up under me. Lucas had closed the blinds and turned on the ceiling fan to relieve the heat a bit. At that hour, the sun shone directly on the roof. Leaning back and relaxing, Lucas turned on the TV and started flipping channels. Then he stopped.

"Shit! I love this movie!" he said.

"Doesn't ring a bell for me."

"You can't be serious!"

On the screen I saw strange images, wacky, old-fashioned. I was sure I'd remember if I'd seen it before.

"It's hilarious," he said. "It's about this doctor and his helper who go to Transylvania to confirm their theory that vampires actually exist. The plot gets super complicated from then on. There are some slapstick scenes that are just brilliant."

I grabbed a cushion and tucked it under my head. "Have we missed a lot?"

"No, they're just reaching the inn now. I think it's just been a few minutes. Why? You don't want to watch it, do you?"

"Maybe I'll like it."

"You'll love it," he said, settling down and edging even closer to me. His leg now grazed mine, and his arm was resting against my side. My head was close to his shoulder, and whenever he spoke, I could sense his breath on my temple. No matter how much I tried to focus on the film, I couldn't ignore him, I kept thinking how I could just reach out my pinkie finger and touch his hand.

But then I fell asleep. And when I woke, my mouth was dry and my hair matted and covering my face. At first, I didn't even know where I was. Then I noticed Lucas was gone. I stood and stretched out my arms. The TV was still on, but the volume was turned down. I shut it off and went to the kitchen for a glass of water.

The clock on the microwave told me it was six thirty.

I put on my sandals and looked at the books on his shelf, finally taking down one he seemed to have read many times. I leafed through it as I walked downstairs to the back garden.

Roy was out there, sitting in a hammock under his favorite tree, typing on a laptop that was in his lap. I waved at him and he tipped his hat courteously. He was quite a character.

I walked on toward the lemon fields and found a comfy spot under the leafy branches where I could sit and lean my back against one of the trunks. As I read, the hours passed without my realizing it, and I followed the lives of the characters, who kept drawing me deeper and deeper in.

I closed the book when it had gotten too dark for me to make out the words. Then I held it to my chest and stood. I wasn't in a hurry to get back: My head was still too full of stories, too full of the feelings those stories had aroused.

"'Melancholy' is such a dramatic-sounding word, but sometimes it's the right one. When you're feeling both a little happy and a little sad," the story had said.

Melancholy—that was how I felt most of the time.

Happy sometimes, because I was learning that life was full of new beginnings. That you can lose things and the void they leave behind can be immense, but that you can treat this as a new place for new things that may fulfill you better than whatever was there before.

Sad sometimes, because I was more aware than ever of how alone I'd been as long as I could remember, and that loneliness had led me to confuse my urges with my longings, my deficiencies with desires. To convince myself that I deserved anything bad that happened to me because I wasn't enough. Because I had always been lacking.

I put those thoughts aside as I passed through the gate into the garden.

The light bulbs were shaking in the breeze, and music was coming from a window on the ground floor. The kids were running around and shouting, chased by Marco, who was pretending to be a monster. Angela was pacing and talking on the phone, and she waved as soon as she saw me. Roy had emerged from his hiding place and was listening to Julia tell him in a torrent of words about a new technique for shaping hair that was apparently *the bomb*. Sitting at the table, Catalina, Iria, and Blas were playing cards and waved me over.

I felt light in the chest just then, because I could sense them there. My wings.

The wings that had carried me there.

28

My routine didn't change much over the coming days. In the mornings, I'd help Monica out at the florist, then go home and eat with Lucas. We'd watch TV for a while and drowse on the sofa, knocked out by the heat of a July that was almost over.

In the afternoon, Lucas would go to the restaurant and wouldn't be home until late. I would take a new book out to the lemon fields with me, then come back and share what remained of the day with all those people there who were starting to become a part of me.

One day I opened my eyes, dying from the heat and looking up at the ceiling fan that was spinning round and round with a slight hum. I heard something, then turned and found Lucas next to me, his head leaning back, his mouth open.

I was surprised at first, but then I remembered he didn't have to work that day. I looked at his square jaw, his straight nose, his thick eyebrows. His five-o'clock shadow made his features look a little harder and framed his luscious lips. I loved his freckles, abundant but so small and light you could hardly see them. On his left cheek were some that I'd swear formed an M if you looked at them right.

M. Like Maya.

Could I be any more ridiculous? That was the kind of thing a teenage girl would scrawl in her notebook.

His voice surprised me, and I brought my hand to my chest, startled. "If you keep looking at me like that, I'm going to start thinking you like me."

"I wasn't looking at you."

With a lazy grin, his eyes just slits, he said, "Hey, I don't mind. I look at you, too."

"I wasn't looking at you! But wait… What do you mean, you look at me?"

He held up his index and pinkie fingers and pointed at his eyes and then at me. "Don't think I don't notice. There's nothing wrong with it."

"Speak for yourself."

"You speak for yourself. You were watching me sleep. I know you were. But…I like it."

His voice was soft, suggestive. I got up, my heart pounding, feeling the blood rush to the surface of my skin. I remembered what Matías had said about me falling in love, and I felt almost dizzy. I tried to get up, but Lucas took my hand.

"Sorry, I'm a disaster when I try to be seductive," he said.

"And lots of other times. But who's keeping track?"

He laughed and pulled me down next to him, bending over me, and said, "Tell me more." I tried to think of something funny to say, but couldn't. Of course, he was anything but a disaster: He could captivate me effortlessly. He had a gift for it, and everything he did or said I found fascinating. I looked down at his lips, burning with desire. I hadn't sensed it coming, and it had taken hold of me intensely. Like a storm, a whirlwind, taking over my body.

"What would you say to a trip to the beach?" he asked.

"In this heat… Yeah, let's do it."

He stood, and I gathered my composure, and a few minutes later we were getting into his car with a backpack with bottles of water, some munchies, and a towel. Lucas drove toward Amalfi. It was five thirty in the afternoon and the sun was blazing. With the air streaming in through the windows, I couldn't hear the music from the radio or Lucas's voice, so I distracted myself by looking at the landscape.

Thirty minutes later, Lucas parked on the side of the road and we walked a half mile on a dirt path toward a steep hill. It was a gorgeous place, full of vegetation, and the views of the sea were incredible. Soon we reached a stone staircase carved into the hillside, and he told me, "Be careful. They're wet and it's easy to slip and fall."

I told him, "OK," but that didn't keep me from stumbling a few times, maybe because I couldn't stop looking up at the cove ahead of us, small, hidden between cliffs and the ruins of an old Roman villa. We set down our towels on the tiny pebble beach. There wasn't much room for us, but who would want to lie down when we could sink into that crystalline water shimmering with reflections of sunlight as if it were made of diamonds.

I left my clothes by the backpack and adjusted my bikini. Lucas was pretending not to watch, but I knew otherwise. I felt a little nervous, exposing myself to him. And that's exactly how I felt: exposed.

"Will it be cold?" I asked.

"Just a little bit. Come on."

I followed him to the water's edge, and when a wave lapped my feet, I jumped back. It was freezing.

Lucas jumped right in and started floating on his back, looking over and asking, "Do you want me to come get you?"

"Just give me a minute to get used to it," I said.

"Don't think about it. It doesn't make it any easier."

I took a deep breath and jumped in, and the salty water covered me up to my scalp. I came up for a breath and laughed reflexively. Then

I looked around for Lucas, but I couldn't see him anywhere until he popped up just ten inches away and splashed me.

"Hey!"

I splashed him back and we took turns dunking each other, just like two little kids. But we were adults, and this was just an excuse for us to touch each other. He put his hands on my waist; I rested mine on his chest. At another point, he grabbed me from behind, and I felt his stomach on my back as our legs intertwined.

We swayed back and forth with each other, and I wasn't sure whether we were still trying to pretend something wasn't happening or not. With the passing of minutes, we finally dared to look at each other. It felt like the first time. His eyes looked gray under the light, and I noticed the tiny droplets clinging to his eyelids and the reflections of the sun on his brown hair. When a wave came through, the water would wash over his lips.

More people showed up, and we decided to get out of the water. I lay on my towel and closed my eyes, feeling the heat of the sun. Lucas sat down beside me. I heard him digging around in his backpack, and then I heard the sound of the lighter. The crackle of burning tobacco. Inhale, exhale.

"When did you start smoking?"

"In college. Then I quit for a few years, then I got hooked again."

"You should quit. It's bad for you, and it stinks."

"Yes, Mom."

"No one likes to kiss an ashtray," I said.

His stare seemed to weigh down on me as he asked, "Oh…were you thinking of kissing me?"

"What would make you think that?"

"Well, you implied it."

"I didn't though," I told him.

"Well, if you change your mind…"

"What?" I asked. "You'll stop smoking?"

"It might motivate me."

"Where's my motivation?"

"I'm one hell of a kisser," he affirmed.

He lay down beside me and I soaked in the sun, listening to the murmur of the sea and smelling the salt breeze and Lucas's masculine scent.

"How long are you going to stay?" he blurted out.

I opened my eyes and looked over, seeing him there in profile, and asked if he was planning on kicking me out.

"Nah," he replied. "Just curious."

"I don't know. I hope that's not a problem."

"Not in the least. Stay as long as you like. I mean that."

Was he asking me or just letting me know that I could? Because there was something slightly urgent in that word *stay*. He closed his eyes and I turned up to the sky, and for a long time, we said nothing as our arms lay at our sides and our hands so nearly touched.

And our breathing rose and fell like the waves.

29

"Are you sure you don't mind?" Catalina asked again.

"Yes, I don't mind," I replied patiently.

"I wouldn't have asked you if there was anyone else, but Angela and Marco are spending the day in Positano with the kids, Roy still isn't back yet, and Blas is a terror behind the wheel."

Rubbing her arm, I reassured her, "Don't worry, just tell me where I need to go."

"It's Piazza Sant'Antonino. On the corner, there's a street with an arch over it and you'll see a little boutique. My friend Donata runs it. Just give her this and tell her it's from me."

"Sure," I said, looking at the bag with curiosity.

"And be careful, it took me a month to sew it and I won't have time to do it again."

"I'll be careful, I promise. But what is it?"

"A bridal veil. Donata's daughter is getting married next week and she asked me to make one."

"I didn't know you sewed," I said.

"Well, professionally I don't. I don't do anything anymore, but I worked for a haute couture house for years. I did this as a personal favor. Donata and I have been friends forever and I couldn't say no."

"Well, I'll make sure she gets it intact," I told her.

"Thank you, Maya, you're a dream come true."

I closed my eyes as I let her hug me. She smelled of jasmine and pie crust—a scent that I loved. Her kindness moved me so deeply in my soul that it was hard not to ask myself what my life would have been like if I'd grown up with her and not with Olga.

I placed the bag in the basket of my bicycle and pedaled downtown.

The boutique wasn't easy to find. When I finally located it and entered, I heard a bell chiming over my head. A little woman in a tight cherry-red dress hurried out to greet me. She looked like Sophia Loren, but blond: She had the same big eyes and oval face. Her breasts were bursting from her push-up bra, and she had a wasp waist and hips to die for.

After handing over the veil and conversing a moment in my newly acquired Italian, I said goodbye to her, and we kissed each other on the cheek.

On my way out, I wondered whether to pass by the restaurant and visit Lucas. He normally worked the day shift, and I often only saw him at lunchtime. And every day, our time together felt shorter and shorter, when all I wanted was for it never to end.

How can a person you've only known for a few weeks come to feel so essential? I don't know the answer, but Lucas had done it. He was a part of my days now, and I couldn't imagine them without him.

Traffic was crazy that day—it always was at that hour—and I decided to get off my bike and walk it on the sidewalk before someone ran me over. I reached an intersection, and that's where I saw it: the ballet school.

I couldn't resist the urge to go there. The sign was lit up, and the lights were on inside, too. I tried to just peek in, but the glass was too dark and I couldn't make out anything.

"Hey," I heard a deep voice say right beside my ear.

I flinched and found Giulio smiling a few inches away from my face. In one hand, he was carrying a case of water.

"Hey! What are you, um… What are you doing here?" I asked.

I don't know why my first impulse was to play dumb. Maybe because no one had mentioned the school yet, not even Giulio. Everything I knew, I'd found out on my own, and I wasn't sure I wanted to come across like a stalker.

"It's my school. Didn't I tell you?"

"No. You've barely told me anything about yourself."

"Well, then, my name's Giulio Dassori. I'm a dance instructor, and this is my school. Pleased to meet you," he joked. He placed his arm in the fifth position and with a humorous expression on his face asked, "Would you like to come in?"

"I don't want to be a bother," I said, almost terrified.

"You won't be. Come on, you first," he insisted.

I gave up, or gave in, to his eyes, his sincere smile, the little wrinkles in his forehead, and that mole on his brow I was now obsessed with as a mark that proved our kinship.

"Fine."

The door led to a small sitting area with a glass counter and chairs around a small table. On the walls were photos of girls performing and posters of some of the most important ballets, like *The Nutcracker*, *Romeo and Juliet*, *Sleeping Beauty*, and *Le Corsaire*. A shelf held trophies and decorative plants.

"You can leave the bike here," he said, pointing to a spot next to the counter.

Looking around, I told him, "This place is amazing."

"You like?" I nodded. "There's a class going on right now if you'd like to take a look. Just come with me."

He guided me down a hallway and paused at a pair of doors. On one was a drawing of a tutu, on the other, a pair of pointe shoes. From the second came the sound of piano playing.

"The kids love to have an audience," Giulio whispered.

He pushed the door open and my stomach fluttered as he invited me in and we stood against the wall to avoid interrupting the class. A dozen students were doing their exercises with the barre. None was older than seven, but they were disciplined and attentive as their teacher showed them the moves and a woman marked rhythm with the piano. It was enchanting, but the slight echo of a ringing phone interrupted it.

"I'll be right back," Giulio whispered.

I murmured an *OK* and remained there, observing, until the teacher paused to let the students go to the bathroom and get a drink of water. She nodded to me as she passed by and walked out into the hall. The children all broke up into their little cliques except for one girl who remained at the barre, very concentrated, trying to execute a pirouette.

She tried and tried, and each time she stumbled.

I noticed her posture wasn't right—her back was too arched, and she was putting her weight on the wrong foot. She groaned. Her frustration was moving to me. I had been just as hard on myself when I was her age.

I came close to her, smiling to make her feel more comfortable, and gestured for her to observe me. I got into position, and she did the same. With a hand on her back, I showed her the correct posture, and with the other hand, I tugged at her chin to get her to lift her head and look up. She did and managed a perfect turn. She radiated happiness as we both clapped our hands.

From behind me, I heard Giulio say, "The Balanchine method?"

"No, Vaganova," I replied without thinking. Then I stiffened as I noticed the curiosity in his eyes.

"I knew it the first time I saw you," he said. "The way you walk, your posture... Where did you study?"

As the blood drained from my face, I told him, "The Mariemma Royal Conservatory of Dance."

Hie eyes opened wide. "I took two summer classes there! When I was eighteen. I had a scholarship, and I was auditioning at the Ballet of the Opéra de Paris, and I spent several weeks in Madrid."

The world seemed to be spinning around me and I felt pressure in my chest. That was the moment I'd been waiting for. All I had to do was tell him what I knew. This was why I'd come there, to get to know him. I could mention my mother, tell him she'd gotten pregnant that same summer and I'd seen the photos of the two of them together... Tell him he might be my father...

I opened my mouth over and over.

But I couldn't.

Panic seized me, and the words got caught in my throat, and I told myself over and over this just didn't make sense. "What a coincidence!" was all I managed to say, my tone forced.

"It is!" He was looking at me as if he'd seen me for the first time. "So you dance professionally?"

"I did. I was a part of the Royal Ballet company, and then I joined the Spanish National Company as a soloist. I was prima ballerina."

"Wow, and so young. That's impressive."

"It's not such a big deal," I told him timidly.

"What's your favorite thing to perform?"

"Oh, there are so many pieces... The third act of *Swan Lake*, the second act of *Giselle*, the 'Dance of the Sugar Plum Fairy'..."

"Those are all pas de deux."

"Yep."

"What about *Romeo and Juliet*," he asked. I nodded, and he replied jovially, "It's the absolute best! Dance it with me."

He offered me his hand and brought the other to his heart, pleading. I took a step back.

"No!"

"Come on," he urged me. "The kids will love it, and it's not every day an opportunity like this comes along."

He said something to the students I didn't catch, and they all started shouting and jumping up and down. The pianist played the first few chords of Act III, Scene I: *Juliet's Room.*

"I don't have shoes," I said by way of excuse.

"I do. What size do you wear?" He wouldn't give up, and as soon as the teacher came in, he said, "I'd guess you two wear the same size. Marina, le tue scarpe da punta?"

"Sì," she replied.

It pained me to see his expression, and at the same time, I was about to do something I'd always dreamt of: dancing in my father's arms. I used to think of it before I even knew he existed. What little girl doesn't want to dance with her father? I nodded, and Marina handed me her pointe shoes. They made room for us and I tied the ribbons and stretched out a few seconds. Barefoot, Giulio approached with his arms extended.

"Ready?" he asked.

"I guess so."

The piano started again, and I took my position. Giulio walked to the opposite side of the room. He drew a breath, grinned, and then his face transformed into the lover forced to leave his beloved. And the story came to life.

It was magical. I still remember it as though it had just happened. Innocent Romeo in jeans and a white shirt, Juliet in her blue dress, tormented by a secret. Two souls condemned to disaster.

We danced, each in our roles.

Juliet's hands reached out, trying to keep Romeo from leaving, but pulling back from his hands in tragic despair.

Romeo finding Juliet with every leap, pirouetting and calming his somber disappointment.

A wordless goodbye.

Anticipation filled with suffering.

The music turns furious as the leave-taking approaches.

Juliet covers Romeo's face with hysterical kisses.

Promises of love. Of seeing each other again.

Romeo departs and Juliet remains, shattered, agonizing.

End of the act.

The room filled with applause and Giulio ran over to me, hugging me and lifting me off the floor. I held him with closed eyes, tight. I could feel myself wanting to cry, struggling to breathe through so much emotion. It was almost impossible to let him go. I wanted to stay there forever, his heart beating against mine.

"My dear," Giulio said, setting me down. I was confused, but then he went on. "Did you see how magnificent she was? I was right about her."

I turned to see Dante standing in the doorway watching us with his arms crossed. He nodded, content, and said, "Bellissimo, amore."

"Are you done at work?"

"Sì, Andiamo a casa," he said, and made a walking motion with his fingers to show he was suggesting we go home.

"Good," Giulio responded. "I'm tired. Maya, you'll come with us, no? That way we can keep talking."

Nervously, I told him no. I didn't want to bother, and I felt as if I'd done something wrong. That feeling had been hounding me for days now. But then Dante caught my eye and waved me toward him, "Andiamo, come with us."

"What about my bike?"

"We'll put it in the trunk."

"OK," I said, seeing that arguing would get me nowhere.

30

When we got home, Giulio said we should spend some time out in the garden. He was clearly excited to know someone he could share his passion for ballet with. And I was still on a cloud. I would have done anything he'd said.

We sat on the patio as the sun was about to vanish over the orange-tinted horizon. The breeze shook the tree branches and the crickets began singing in the grass.

Dante brought us something to drink and snack on, then went inside to make dinner. Giulio kept peppering me with questions about my career and where I had studied, and I told him everything: my years at the conservatory, the scholarship I got when I was fourteen to take a summer course at the Ballet de la Opéra in Paris, the one I got to continue my studies in London when I was seventeen. How I became an apprentice at the Royal Ballet and graduated from the English National Ballet School when I was twenty with certificates in classical and contemporary dance. My return to Spain, my rise in the company. How much it had meant when the American Ballet Theatre called me, how I'd never been able to accept that post. Finally, I talked to him about the accident and its far-reaching consequences.

"It's sad for your career to be cut short like that, but you can still dance," he remarked, turning his beer bottle around in his hands. "You didn't lose that freedom."

"I put dance before everything else, and without it, I'm no one. I'm nothing."

I'd promised myself I would stop thinking about that, stop letting it obsess me. What's the point of worrying over things that simply can't be? But the words had just come out of me. Was it consolation I wanted? Pity? Or did I just need to share every piece of myself with him?

"First of all, Maya, you still have dance. All you left behind was an elite culture that has as many bad things as it does good. Now you're just you. And that's all you need. To be yourself."

"But, like… I don't even know how to do anything else."

Giulio pushed my hair aside and lifted my chin to look at me. "Why are you so obsessed with that?"

I shrugged, almost ashamed. "When I danced, I stopped being invisible, you know. People loved me." My eyes filled with tears.

"Maya, if they loved you for how good you were on the stage, then they never really loved you at all. And you're not invisible. I can see you. You're a beautiful girl with tons of talent and your whole life ahead of you. You lost your dream. I get it—it's horrible. But dreaming is free, and you'll find another one. More modest, maybe, but it could well make you even happier."

"What if I don't, though?"

"You will, but first you need to learn that you can't keep looking for acceptance from others, especially not people who measure how much you matter according to how perfect your grand jeté is or how many doubles you can do in a row. Love yourself for who you are, and when you wake up tomorrow, do the same again. That's how you keep going. OK?"

"OK."

"You'll meet lots of people who will love you unconditionally. We already do," he said. He bent over to dry my tears with his thumbs and I found myself holding on to his shirt. When I finally managed to pull away, I grabbed his beer and took a sip to see if it would relieve the knot in my throat.

The sun had nearly set, and the scent of fresh food was wafting from the apartment house. The two cats that were always roaming around walked over the garden wall and jumped to the ground. I was calmer now, calm enough to say to Giulio, "Tell me something about you. When did you open the school?"

There were so many things I wanted to know about him. He replied, "The school belonged to a woman who helped me to realize I had a bit of talent as a dancer."

"I think you've got more than a bit."

I wasn't saying it to kiss up. For the minutes I had danced with him, he'd shone like a star. He had innate talent, and the mere idea that I might have inherited some of it made me feel a special connection.

"Thank you, Maya. My sister was the one who started teaching classes there, two days a week after school. I would go there and pick her up. I would always wait outside, but then one day I went in, and…everything had changed! Nicoletta—that's the owner's name—saw something in me. She taught me all she knew and helped me get into the ballet school of the Teatro di San Carlo in Naples, one of the most prestigious ones there is. I graduated, then I went to Spain for a summer, and that same year I got into the ballet at the Paris Opéra."

"Are you serious?"

"Oui, mademoiselle. I worked there until I was twenty-six and had become the danseur étoile. Then the Bolshoi made me an offer and I was with them for three years. After that, I gave it up."

"Why?" I asked, astonished. I couldn't understand. Those were among the top five companies in the world. You couldn't get much higher. He had been a star.

"Do you want the honest answer or the one I give people when they look at me the way you're looking at me now?"

"The honest one," I said, feeling slightly embarrassed.

"I know it sounds crazy, but I couldn't deal with the stress. It was too much: too much pressure, too much work, no life outside of class, rehearsal, and touring, and I just wasn't made for it. And believe it or not, being gay in that world isn't so easy, especially not in Moscow. Let alone for a foreigner like me. And by then, I'd met Dante. I was in love with him, he was the world to me. He still is," he said, looking serious and shaking his head.

"So you left it all for love."

"That was a big part of it, yeah. He was here, I was there. We barely ever saw each other, and the job didn't make up for it. Besides, I was tired. Very tired."

"And you came back," I said.

"I came back and I helped Dante set up the restaurant. And he helped me with my diving company…"

"Your diving company?" I asked, surprised.

"Yeah, you didn't know about it? It's small, just a couple of boats and four instructors, but we're growing. The undersea world has always enchanted me."

"What about the school?"

"When I came back, Nicoletta was already sick. That school was her life, and losing it would have killed her. I helped her keep it afloat—I owed that to her. When she died, she willed it to me. I haven't been able to let it go. I doubt I ever will. I still love ballet. That's the truth."

"It was nice dancing with you," I told him.

"Likewise." He smiled. "Speaking of, how long are you going to stay here?"

That question put me on edge. "I'm not sure. Why do you ask?"

"Well…I don't like to close the school in the summer, because it's almost like a day care. Since this town survives off of tourism, many of the parents are working in hospitality and can't get time off, and they don't know what to do with their kids. I don't mind, but staffing's always an issue, and…I wonder if you'd like to give classes there. I've got some kids who are really talented and have lots of potential, and I think it would help them, learning from you."

"I've already got a job at the florist," I reminded him.

"Yeah, in the morning," he said. "I'd only need you at the school for a few hours, three afternoons a week. And I'd pay you, obviously."

"I've never taught. I studied dance, not dance education."

"You've got experience, and you know what it is to learn. That's more than enough."

"I don't know what to say," I admitted.

"Then say yes," he told me.

We both laughed, and I agreed we could try.

"Good, let's try then. This is incredible, isn't it?"

"What?" I asked.

"This! You and me! How similar we are, and how we just happened to meet each other. And now we're here sharing things most people could never understand. It's one hell of a coincidence."

I smiled and nodded, but now I was starting to feel bad. It wasn't a coincidence, and not telling him was making me miserable. My silence, at this point, was no better than a lie.

"Giulio…"

"Yes?"

I had the words, but once again, fear turned them into empty air. Weeks before, when I arrived there, I'd had nothing to lose. Now I felt I could lose everything, even if none of it really belonged to me.

"Nothing," I told him, and we looked up as the sun vanished over the horizon.

"They say the past is made of memories and the future is born of dreams," he whispered. "What's happened can't be changed, and regretting it is a waste of time. Who knows what's to come. No one, I can promise you that."

I turned my head aside and looked at him in profile, asking, "What about the present?"

Grinning, he said, "Maya, the present is made of moments." He took my hand. "Focus on those moments, on the little things every day, and live them in your heart. Dream of tomorrow and don't hide from the past. We're made of memories, my dear. That's everything we are."

I nodded and looked down at my legs, resting a hand on my thigh, tentatively bringing it closer and closer to my scar until I touched it with the tip of my finger. The skin was soft there. I hadn't thought it would feel like that. I pressed it harder, and memories flooded me like a river inside my head.

And I did it. I faced the past with open eyes. Without guilt, without remorse. Because I didn't have time for them anymore.

31

At twenty years old

June.

I squeezed the phone tight.

"You know perfectly well I just took a post at the Royal Ballet," I said with a trembling voice.

"So what?" my grandmother responded scornfully on the other line.

"Are you not listening? They gave me a full scholarship for two years. They paid for my studies, my lodging, they helped me graduate, and now they've offered me a job. A good one! It's one of the best ballet companies in the world! I'm lucky."

"Lucky? You'll be lost in the crowd up there. Here you can triumph, be somebody in your own country. Prima ballerina, probably. Do you not understand how much that means? You can't just let all the work we've done go to waste."

She always spoke as if she was the one who had accomplished everything and I was just a nobody, when I was the one who had done it all, with my hard work and dedication.

I had sacrificed so much…

And it had been so hard to escape…

I let myself slide down the wall and ended up sitting on the floor of my dorm room. I liked living in London. I'd been there for two years, and it was the happiest I'd ever been. I didn't want to go back to Madrid.

I couldn't live with her again.

"Please, Grandma, I want this," I begged.

"Stop with the nonsense, Maya. I want you here this Sunday at the latest. Monday we'll start getting ready for the audition. We've got less than a month."

"But…"

"Don't make me come look for you."

I covered my mouth with my hand to hold back a sob. I wanted to scream. To howl: *No, no, no, no, no.* But I didn't. I gave in the way I always had. I shrank till I nearly disappeared. I folded. Because I was scared. Because it was what I'd always done. I swallowed my rage, suppressed my wishes, and said what she wanted me to say:

"Fine."

A month later.

They were supposed to call on Monday, and it was already Wednesday, and the tension was killing me. The unpleasantness in the air was weighing down on me like a tombstone.

"You should have tried harder," my grandmother said from the sofa.

At the table, I stared at my untouched salad. "I did a good job," I murmured.

"Not good enough, clearly."

"There were lots of talented people there."

"And you allowed them to outperform you," she replied contemptuously. "You failed."

I pursed my lips, not wanting to let her see me trembling, and tried not to draw a breath. My hands were under the table, my nails were digging into the flesh of my thighs. The pain extended through my body, but I couldn't hold back the tear that streamed down my cheek.

My phone rang. I looked at the screen and saw that it was the National Dance Company. My grandmother stood, but I answered before she could snatch it away from me.

"Yes?"

"Good afternoon, I'd like to speak to Maya Rivet, please."

"Speaking."

"Hello, Maya, this is Natalia Durán, I'm the director of the National Dance Company."

"Oh, it's a pleasure to hear from you."

"Likewise." She paused. "So, the team and I were very impressed with your audition and we'd like you to join our family. As a soloist."

"Seriously?"

"Seriously. So if it sounds good to you, maybe you can come by tomorrow and we can have a chat and I'll give you all the details in person."

"Yeah, of course," I responded.

"Will nine in the morning work for you?"

"Sure, perfect."

"Excellent. Then I'll see you tomorrow, Maya. And congratulations."

"Thank you!"

I hung up and rested my elbows on the table. The adrenaline was coursing furiously through my veins. I could feel the throbbing in my jugular and pinpricks all over my body. I had done it. I had. For the first time in days, I looked my grandmother in the eye.

"They gave me the position," I told her.

Her only movement was to exhale a breath through her nose. Her expression, her posture didn't change. After a moment, she nodded slightly.

"Now don't screw it up. Prima ballerina, that's your next goal."

I had achieved something important. A dream thousands of dancers work tirelessly for and never achieve. And yet, I wasn't happy. I felt like I was drowning. Like a weight was bearing down on me.

There I was again, back at the beginning. With her. Without an escape hatch. Or maybe I just wasn't brave enough to run away. I had so much to say to her, years' worth of resentment to unload. But I couldn't. I had never been able to.

And of course, I owed it all to her—that was what she'd told me till she was blue in the face: *You owe it to me, you owe it to me,* as if that were a tattoo on my skin.

I owed her, and she made me pay.

A year later. Early November.

"What's up?" I asked.

"Nothing bad. The opposite, actually."

Fyodora took my hands and made me sit next to her on a park bench where we'd agreed to meet.

"You seemed like you were freaking out on the phone," I said.

"I am!" she almost shouted, then patted me on the knee to calm me down. "I've got something to tell you, OK? I have a friend at the American Ballet school and a few weeks ago she told me they were looking for a new dancer. It was invitation only, they weren't holding open auditions, but I applied for you, and I sent a video in, too."

"You did what?"

She took an envelope from her purse and handed it to me. "They picked you! You've got an audition in three weeks in New York!"

I shivered, and it had nothing to do with the temperatures dropping that fall. I had always dreamed of working for Alexei Ratmansky, and he had been the choreographer for the ABT for years now. "You *are* kidding, right?" I asked.

"No, Maya. They chose you. This is an amazing opportunity."

I opened the envelope and read the letter, then held it to my chest. It was true. I thought of my own company in Madrid. I was about to become prima ballerina there. I had worked hard to achieve it. And then there was Antoine. A relationship like ours had almost no chance of surviving that much distance. And then there was my grandmother...

She'd say no. She'd never let me leave.

"Fyodora, I can't."

"Maya, you can and you should. Go to New York and knock their socks off. Fly, babe."

"How will I pay for it?"

"Don't worry about that," she said.

Just thinking about it was painful, and I was incapable of concealing the desperation that was running through me. Wanting to, being unable to. Being able to and not knowing if I wanted to. I was walking on a thread, and it was terrifying. I would have to change my life. Was I ready? Was I ready to change my future, everything I had known?

"But..." I began.

"No buts. We're doing this. Is your passport up to date?" she asked.

"Yes."

"Then all we have to do is pick your routine."

Three weeks later.

"You're ruining everything," Olga shouted.

"It's just an audition, and there's a zero percent chance they'll take me."

"Then why waste your time? You could still go with the company to Seville. It would be your first performance as prima ballerina. For God's sake, Maya, get ahold of yourself."

I shook my head, praying she would understand me. That for once in my life, she'd take my side.

"Natalia agrees," I said. "She's fine with it, she supports me, she's happy I got this chance."

"Of course she is. What does she care? If she doesn't have you, she'll just find someone else."

"If I don't make it, they're not going to fire me."

Drilling into me with her cold eyes, she asked, "And what if it goes well?"

I didn't dare respond. I couldn't tell her that if the ABT accepted me, I'd run away from Madrid without looking back, leaving her behind and finally having a life of my own. One she couldn't control for me anymore.

I grabbed my suitcase and headed for the door.

"Maya, I forbid you to leave this house."

I didn't turn around.

"Don't you dare leave," she continued. "You're squandering everything."

I turned the knob and opened.

"Maya, you can't do this to me. Not now. You owe me."

I closed the door behind me and didn't stop.

This time, I was going to be brave.

A month later, three days before Christmas Eve.

"The postman just brought it," Matías said over the phone. Pulse racing, I adjusted my earbud. The traffic was roaring past and I could hardly hear.

"You mean the…?"

"Yep, the response from the ABT."

"Did you open it?" I asked.

"Of course not. You should."

"Why can't they just send an email like everyone else in the world?" I whined.

"I don't know, I like all that ceremony: official letterhead, fancy signatures. It makes the whole thing look cooler."

"Dickhead!" I flipped the bird at a bicyclist zooming down the sidewalk.

"Excuse me," Matías said. "Did you just insult me?"

"No, it was this jerk that almost ran me over." I turned the corner and went on zigzagging through the crowd. "I'm just so nervous, Matías."

"What about me? I can't stop thinking about it, so move your ass and get home so we can open that damned bottle of champagne I've been saving since the dinosaurs roamed the earth."

"Your Moët? You'd really open it for me?"

"Only for you, Maya. You're my best friend."

I stopped in front of a crosswalk and stared at the little red man in the light telling me to wait.

"I'm almost at the bus stop."

"Well, hurry! I'm jumping out of my skin," he shouted.

"New York! Can you imagine?"

His excitement was adding to mine, and when the light changed, I hurried into the street.

I saw him coming, but I thought he'd stop.
And he didn't.
I heard shouts. The squealing of brakes. Felt the blow.
My body flew through the air.
After that, nothing.

32

I got up early on Saturday. I'd been thinking of taking the bus to Naples and looking for a specialty shop where I could get the shoes and clothing I'd need to start giving classes the following Monday. That would also give me an excuse to get to know a new place.

I showered, put on a long white skirt and matching top, pulled my hair back in a ponytail and put on some makeup. Nothing fancy, just eyeliner, foundation, and a strawberry-flavored lip gloss.

Walking out, I ran into Lucas.

His eyes were two slits just barely showing his blue irises, and his hair was sticking out in all directions. I tried not to notice that he was naked except for his underwear. He blinked as he saw me, still half-asleep.

"You work on Saturdays?" he asked me hoarsely.

"No."

"Then why are you up?"

"I'm going to Naples."

"To Naples? How?"

"On my bike."

That shook him out of his stupor. "Maya! You can't ride your bike to Naples!"

I burst out laughing: I don't know if it was his expression of surprise or my anxiousness at seeing him undressed. "I'm taking a bus, Lucas! Did you honestly think I was just going to pedal there?"

"With you, I never know what to expect, honestly."

I pushed him to make my way out of the doorframe and into the kitchen.

"I'll take you," he called from behind me.

Looking over my shoulder, I asked, "Don't you have to work?"

"Not till Monday. Let me take you."

"You wouldn't rather go back to bed and rest?"

"Nah. Just let me shower quickly."

He seemed out of it as he ran his hand through his hair, and I reminded him, "Listen, you don't have to do this for me, OK? It's your time. You don't have to feel obliged to help me. I don't need a babysitter. If you're feeling sluggish, trust me, I can go and come back on my own…"

"Maya…" He cut me off. "I want to go with you."

As I saw that smile of his reappear—so sly, so manly—I wondered if he knew he'd caused my heart to stop. Just for a second. Before it started galloping again.

"All right," I said.

If someone asked me to describe Naples in one word, I'd have to say: color. The streets, the buildings, the shops…everything was color, so immense, so varied, that it seemed to knock you over. And yet, Naples was much more than that. It was Vesuvius in the distance, the blue sea, music in the streets, cheerful people, terrible traffic. A chaos of squealing tires, yelling people, honking horns.

"Careful!" Lucas shouted, pushing me against a wall as a motor scooter with two people on it passed a few inches from us on the sidewalk.

Scared to death, I brought a hand to my chest and muttered, "Fuck!"

"Are you all right? You're trembling."

I nodded. I didn't tell him that every time a car passed or I heard brakes, my entire body tensed, waiting for the impact. That the memory of the accident came back to me clear as day, with phantom pains for the few seconds until my rational mind reminded me that all of that was behind me, and I was all right now.

"They drive crazy here," I said.

Lucas looked back and forth and tucked a lock of hair behind my ear. He pulled close to me, protecting me as people roved all around us and he pushed his way through them.

"'Vedi Napoli e muori,' they say."

"What's that mean?"

"See Naples and die. The idea is supposed to be that it's so beautiful, you can die after, but I'm starting to think it's really because you're lucky to get out of here alive."

I relaxed, leaning back on his chest and taking a moment to gather myself. I could feel his breath on my temple and his hand on my back, soft at first, then firmer as we walked on. Protective. Possessive, maybe. And it calmed me. So much so that when he asked if I was ready to keep walking, I was tempted to tell him, *No, I want to stay like this forever*.

But instead, I whispered, "Yes," and we walked on. I didn't need to ask him to keep holding me: he threw his arm over my shoulder and I moved close to his side. We fit together perfectly, like two parts yearning to be one.

I looked at the map on my phone. "I think it's the next right."

"I think I know where it is," Lucas said.

And when we turned the corner, I saw it: a tiny shop with a little window decorated with paper garlands and tulle clouds.

I bought leotards, tights, tutus, demi-pointes and flats, with ribbons and with elastic straps. The shopkeeper was nice and patient, and she even gave me a sewing kit on the house, which I thanked her for profusely.

"Do you have everything you need?" Lucas asked once we were outside.

"Yeah. We can head back to Sorrento whenever you want."

"Or we could spend the day here…"

"Do you really want to?"

"I do," he said. "Do you?"

I shrugged, trying to feign indifference, until I couldn't contain myself and started hopping up and down.

"Yes I do!"

I discovered that day it was impossible to get bored with Lucas. Before we'd finished doing one thing, he was already proposing the next and planning whatever we'd do afterward. All you had to do with him was let yourself go and enjoy the conversation, the laughter, and the crazy thoughts that passed through his head.

I loved hanging out with him. He was so charming. His cheekiness, his *whatever* attitude, the way he looked at me. One minute I felt he was stripping me bare, and the next it was as if he were wrapping me in a big, warm blanket. Beside him, I stopped thinking and focused on the moment. On the now.

We bought ice cream and headed to the Piazza del Plebiscito. Once there, Lucas was set on making me cross the square blindfolded, from the gate of the Royal Palace to the entry of the Basilica of San Francesco di Paola. It was a tradition, and the idea was to go in a straight line and pass between two equestrian statues. I managed it on the third try and took a bow before a group of tourists that applauded me.

We ate at a place called Sorbillo. Lucas told me they made the best pizza in the world, and he was right. Then we went to a nearby pastry shop for sfogliatella, a kind of puff pastry filled with ricotta. I'd never had anything so rich in my life.

We spent the afternoon in Spaccanapoli, an area dividing the old city into north and south, running from the Spanish neighborhoods to Forcella, the soul of Naples, a labyrinth of tiny streets full of artists and artisans, scents and little portraits of the city's daily life.

We were stopped at a stand selling trinkets and jewelry when all at once, the sun vanished. I looked up and saw black clouds covering the sky. Thunder roared overhead, and a current of air whirled around our feet. A drop of water struck my cheek.

"We need to get to the car," Lucas said.

He took my hand—he was doing that more and more lately—and we walked away, hugging the buildings as the rain started to come down. There was a crack of thunder, and a bolt of lightning lit up the sky.

No sooner than we'd jumped into the car than a storm overtook the city. Rain struck the glass with a deafening sound and it was impossible to see outside.

"Let's wait for it to die down a bit. I don't think it will last too long," Lucas said, wiping off his face with his T-shirt's tail. He turned in his seat, eyed me over, laughed, and said, "You're soaked."

I looked down and saw my skirt, almost transparent, sticking to my legs. My T-shirt was clinging to me, too. I've never been one for wearing a bra if I didn't need to, and most of the time, I don't. But the realization that I didn't have one on then, and that thanks to the rain, I wasn't leaving much to the imagination, made me feel timid. I crossed my arms and rubbed them, pretending to be cold.

We sat there watching the rain. I could hear Lucas breathing audibly, and his left leg was bouncing up and down. He seemed tense, and he wasn't the only one. I didn't know what to do around him anymore.

I was a bundle of feelings and sensations, and I couldn't stop asking myself if he felt the same way. If attraction flowed both ways between us as friendship clearly did. If the intensity was the same. If he was holding back as much as I was.

"Lucas," I asked him, "the other day on the beach… How come you asked me to stay?"

He grabbed the wheel and slid his fingers down one side of it, tensing his jaw.

"I don't get the sense that anything important is waiting for you back in Madrid, and it seems like you like it here."

That wasn't the answer I'd expected, and it was a little bit disappointing. But then, what had I wanted? A declaration? An admission that he liked me? Yes, of course that was exactly what I was dreaming of.

"Am I wrong?" he added.

I shook my head. "I mean, I don't even have a home to go back to. My grandmother tossed me out on the street without blinking."

"Are you serious? Why the hell would she do something like that?"

I shrugged as if it didn't concern me, but tried to answer, "Because I never mattered to her. Not as a granddaughter, anyway. She tried to live her own dreams through me and controlled my every step. She took advantage of my need to be loved to manipulate me, and I allowed it. But then the accident came and everything kind of crumbled. When they confirmed that I wouldn't be able to dance professionally anymore, she cast me aside with no concern whatsoever and went off to live with my uncles. She took my grandfather with her. He was the only one who ever cared about me."

"What about your parents?"

"I don't know my father, I don't even know who he is," I lied—or half lied, because I still wasn't sure about Giulio. "And my mother couldn't stand living with my grandmother, so she left when I was four. Unfortunately, she forgot to take me with her."

"She abandoned you?"

"Without thinking twice about it," I murmured with contempt. "So yeah, to answer your question, there's nothing waiting for me in Madrid or anywhere else."

"That must hurt, huh."

"It's my family!"

Lucas bent so close I could count each of his eyelashes. He seemed to be trying to memorize the details of my face as he looked me in the eye.

"Don't waste another second thinking about those people. Fuck them. They don't deserve you. If they weren't there for you, why should you be there for them? You don't need them."

"I wish it was that easy."

Lucas looked out through the windshield and exhaled.

"It would be if we didn't grow up with this idea that family's forever, that we have to love them no matter how horrible they make our lives. Honor thy father and mother—sure, but what if your father's an asshole? What if all your mother did was bring you into the world and after that she only ever thought of herself? We can't just let that hold us back, Maya. Blood is just blood. It's not a justification for another person to fuck up your life."

His words moved me, above all the resentment and rage in them, the sorrow that impregnated them. He added, "If I ever have children, I can promise I won't treat them like my property or like a means to achieve some goal. Bringing a life into this world is selfish enough. The least you can do is let that person take their own decisions and live the way they want. And I sure as hell wouldn't abandon them and leave them in the care of someone who wouldn't care for them."

The power of words is inestimably strong. It can lift you up to the sky or make you sink down into the void. At that moment, I didn't know where I was. But I could see Lucas. And all around us were stars.

33

The next morning, the scent of coffee woke me. I kicked the sheet down to my feet, still a welter of sensations as I remembered the day before. My dream had left me feeling warm in my chest and between my legs.

I pressed my thighs together and rolled up into a ball. I'd never felt that kind of frustration—probably because no one had ever turned me on in that way. I'd never wanted anybody the way I wanted Lucas. I hid my face in my pillow and slid a hand down my stomach and into my underwear.

Panted.

Felt a tickling.

Yes...

In the living room, the vacuum cleaner turned on.

I bit the pillow to muffle a shout and got out of bed. Lucas was shirtless and shoeless, vacuuming the rug. The windows were open and the curtains were shaking in the breeze. Music was coming from the speakers, and he was bobbing his head and shaking his shoulders as I leaned into the doorframe to watch him.

I thought to myself that I could easily get used to spending every morning of my life that way, watching him clean up half-dressed, with the smell of lemons, coffee, and the sea. The smell of home.

"Good morning, sleepyhead," he said, pulling me out of my daydreams.

"Good morning."

"Are you going to stay there devouring me with your eyes, or are you going to get to it?"

He gestured toward a pail on the table with rags and cleaning products inside. With all the endorphins, pheromones, hormones, and whatever pumping through my body, I'd hoped he meant something else by *get to it*.

"I need a coffee first," I told him.

I had almost made it to the kitchen before I realized I was naked except for a T-shirt. I hurried back to my room and heard him giggling behind me.

Lucas and I spent the morning cleaning up. Around one, Catalina showed up with a lasagna that smelled amazing. As she helped us cut and plate it, she told us how Iria and Blas's granddaughter had shown up the afternoon before and there would be a barbecue that evening.

"What's her name?" I asked.

"Judith," Catalina said. "She's a lovely little girl."

"Little girl? How old is she?" Lucas inquired.

"Eighteen."

Lucas grabbed forks from the drawer and glasses from a cabinet, handing them to me to set out on the table. As he passed me on his way to the fridge, he bumped me intentionally with his hips. He loved trying to get on my nerves, and I always played along.

Catalina was watching us. Then she looked around as though seeing the place for the first time. I caught her looking at me with a special kind of tenderness. I barely knew her, but I adored her in a way I struggled to understand.

I walked her to the door while Lucas finished setting the table. She looked back at me before stepping out and reached up to stroke my hair.

"Giulio told me about the classes and about what happened to you. I'm so sorry," she said softly.

"It's fine."

"I hope so. Anyway, you seem to be fitting in well here. I'm glad."

"Me too."

I had the sense she was looking deep into my heart as she told me, "You know, everybody's got to find a place where they fit in. People they can trust, people they can tell their hopes and fears to. We all deserve for someone to look in our eyes and tell us we're good. That we matter."

I nodded and looked down, not wanting her to notice how her words were affecting me. I didn't know if I really deserved what she was saying, but it was something I'd always wanted. I wasn't used to having anyone there to pick me up when I fell. I wasn't used to the warmth of someone holding me up so I wouldn't drown. I felt myself clinging to her tight as she told me, "I'll see you at dinner," and I replied, "You sure will."

I looked at myself one last time in the bathroom mirror. I barely recognized myself. The bags under my eyes were gone, my cheeks were pink, I'd put on a little weight, and my tan made the white of my dress stand out. It was a little skimpy, with a square neckline and lace straps.

I was nervous as I walked out, and Lucas looked up at me from the travel magazine he'd been reading. He took his time examining me before telling me, "You look incredible."

Shyly, I asked if I hadn't overdone it.

"I wouldn't change a thing." He rubbed his hands on his jeans as he stood and said, "I'll take the drinks if you'll carry down the appetizers."

We were the last people down there. Iria and her granddaughter came over as soon as they saw us. Judith was petite, her face round, her hair short and dyed blue. She was wearing a shirt with a band logo I didn't recognize and platform boots with laces. She was a nice girl, and smiled easily, and I liked her right away.

"You're into them?" Lucas asked, pointing at her T-shirt.

"Yeah. What about you?"

"They're not really my thing. But some of that British alternative metal I'm into."

"Yeah," Judith said. "That stuff is too soft for me."

"You young people don't have an ear for music," Iria said. "Carlos Gardel, Rodolfo Biagi, Nat King Cole…now that was music."

"Nat what?" Judith asked.

Iria rolled her eyes and hugged her, dragging her off to see Julia's nephews.

"Grandma, I don't want to," Judith protested.

"They're sweet, and they're your age," Iria responded.

Marco announced dinner was ready, and we sat around the table, which was overloaded with food. Everyone talked and joked, the silverware clanged, glasses clinked, platters moved from hand to hand. Angela was next to me and wouldn't stop refilling my glass. When the cork came out of the second bottle, my only choice was to get away from her.

Amid the chitchat and stories of people whose names didn't even ring a bell, I felt good—good and full. I was a part of them. It was as if this had always been my home, my people, my family.

Lucas and I locked eyes over dessert, and I got lost in the contours of his eyes and the curve of his lips. Julia was saying something—I tried to listen—about a new technique she'd learned for hair cutting that she wanted to try out on me. I found the idea horrifying.

When we were done, Dante brought out a few bottles of liquor and Roy turned on his old radio. I sat down on the wicker sofa between Julia and her nephews. Catalina and Dante danced, and Giulio walked over with outstretched arms, wanting me to join him as well. I tried to resist, but it was impossible, and in a matter of seconds, he had dragged me out there, resting his hand on my waist and weaving the fingers of his other hand into mine. We swayed to the rhythm and when the chorus came, he spun me around several times. I laughed, clutching his shoulders so I wouldn't slip on the grass.

The song ended, and during the pause, I went to pour myself a drink. It was hot, and the damp air felt thick around me. I struggled with the soda bottle, and finally Dante appeared beside me and opened it.

When I thanked him, he said, "Prego," and asked me in Italian if I was having fun.

"It's impossible not to," I told him.

He studied me with his penetrating stare and said, "So, you're going to work in the scuola di danza. Bene, Giulio will have more free time. He needs it."

"Why?" I asked after taking a sip of my drink. "Does he work a lot?"

"Yes, especially in summer." Giulio, just then, was jumping around with Chiara on his back. "We promised each other we would spend less time at work and more time together. Il tempo è importante, especially if you want to start a family."

"Family?" I asked, gripped by a kind of horror.

"I want to adopt a child, or due, or tre... I've always dreamed of being surrounded by a bunch of kids."

I was happy he was at least telling me most of this in Spanish. I didn't want to miss a detail. Still, he talked so fast, and his accent was a little strange.

"What about Giulio?" I asked, trying to look less interested than I was.

"He says he doesn't have, eh…l'istinto paternale?"

"Paternal instincts, right."

"But I think he's starting to change his mind."

I felt so uncomfortable—and guilty because I still couldn't bring myself to ask Giulio that burning question I needed the answer to. I knew he must have noticed the changed expression on my face. The idea of Giulio having children was so strange to me. It made me almost jealous. And I hated myself for that.

"I'm sure you'll be wonderful parents."

"Grazie."

I took another sip of my drink and watched how everyone there was enjoying themselves. Some were dancing, some laughing, and I was trying not to burst into tears. I had the sense that someone was watching me and turned around to find Lucas on the other end of the yard. We were trapped briefly in that moment, not even pretending not to look at each other.

Another song began. I recognized the melody. Lucas smirked, left his drink on the windowsill, and walked over. *No*, I thought. He wouldn't. He couldn't. Did he have no sense of shame?

I started shaking my head, and he nodded. I tried to run off, but I didn't make it far. He grabbed me around the waist and turned me around. "Please, no," I said as our bodies met.

"Come on, it's summer, you're in Italy, and Eros Ramazzotti is playing. One day you'll look back and remember this as one of the best moments of your life."

"I doubt that."

"You'll remember me!" he said.

"Oh, and that's supposed to be a good thing," I replied, and he pretended to be offended, calling me wicked. He wrapped my arms around his neck and pressed my lower back to bring me closer to him. With his other hand on my waist, we started swaying. I felt his hot breath on my neck as he sang. I couldn't understand the words so well, but I could tell it was a love song. A man said he didn't remember how it started, but he sang to a woman one time, and words of love weren't enough to tell her how beautiful she was. How unique…

We were squeezing together tight, and we fit together perfectly. I was hot, tense, my eyes pinned to his lips. It was ridiculous, special… perfect. I had never danced with anyone that way. So intimately. Our bodies saying all we couldn't say with words. I longed for him, and I knew that moment would remain burned into my memory. Burned by the fire of happiness.

The singer wondered how the years pass but his love never changes…now: *How is it years pass, and my love for you never does, infinite…*

I was trembling as I drew in a deep breath.

We weren't alone, but I no longer cared.

Let yourself go.

Let it happen.

My hand stroked his neck…

34

A bolt of lightning crossed the sky, and the garden lit up as though the sun had just risen. Thunder rumbled far off, and again lightning seemed to tear through the clouds like a crack across a mirror.

Amid a gust of wind, Lucas and I pulled away from each other. The desire was still there, though. The hesitation as well.

Someone said we should walk to the cliffside to watch the storm over the sea, and soon we were all marching toward the lemon grove using our cell phones as flashlights. Roy tripped and cursed, and Chiara repeated what he'd said like a parrot, provoking merriment.

"Really, you all," Angela chided them.

What I saw on the cliff left me speechless. On the horizon, the clouds were glowing, the sea was choppy, and lightning came down from the sky like fire. The roar of the waves and the howl of the wind drowned out everything else. It was terrifying, but also fascinating. Beautiful, but also savage.

The electricity in the air made my hair stand on end. I walked forward, and the wind caught me like a sail, and the breakers striking the rocks far below reminded me of how high I was. How close I was to the void.

I walked forward a little more, and my toes hung over the edge. Adrenaline shot through me.

A drop of water fell on my cheek. Another on my forehead. It was starting to rain.

Everyone rushed off to the lemon grove. I heard their shouts and laughter as they vanished. I didn't move, though. The storm had hypnotized me.

I closed my eyes and leaned my head back, stuck out my tongue and licked the rain that hammered my lips, soaking my hair and clothes. I'd always wondered why there were so many scenes with rain in movies. What was supposed to be so pleasant about letting water soak into your bones and plaster your hair to your head and cover your feet in mud?

Now I knew. I felt Lucas's body behind me, and my heart started to beat faster. He touched my stomach, pulled me back from the edge, and stayed there, holding me. My nerve endings were raw. It was exhilarating.

I felt something soft. Lips brushing me.

I couldn't breathe.

I turned, trembling, and the sky glowed above us like a sparkling ball of fire. I looked up at Lucas, and he looked down at me, pressing his forehead into mine. He had pulled me back from the edge of the cliff, but I was at the edge of something else now—a different abyss, one I couldn't escape, one I was ready to hurl myself into.

I understood those scenes set in the rain, the magic that surrounded them. The pleasure of cold rain on hot skin burning with desire. Begging to be touched, begging to come close.

Even the air between us felt like an insult—something keeping us apart.

This was no dream.

This was no fantasy, recreated in my mind a thousand times.

This was happening.

I felt his hand on my cheek. His lips just inches from mine.

One second. Two. Three…

It was agony! Torture! But a part of me didn't want it to end. The anticipation was driving me mad. That moment, while he hesitated between kissing and not kissing me, was the most intense I had ever experienced. The most erotic. Erotic: That was a word I'd heard before, but I'd never known what it meant.

Four. Five. Six…

I decided for both of us and sought out his lips. I kissed him because the desire was causing me to ache. It was clawing to get out of me. Lucas pulled back to stare at me.

One second. Two. Three…

And his lips struck mine again, hungry and firm. I moaned as my tongue felt his tongue, as I tasted his flavor. As I kissed him as though the world were on the verge of ending and nothing could save me but that kiss.

Lucas was breathing hard as his hands clutched my face with desperation, pulling me close so he could feel me. Feel it. Feel what we were together. Two bodies quivering with desire under wet clothes.

The lightning ripped once more through the sky overhead. I could see it even through my closed eyes. We looked up, it struck again, and the rain turned to a downpour, thick drops coming down in a fury.

Lucas took my hand and we ran off through the orchard, reached the garden, hurried into the house. The lights in the vestibule and the stairway were off. The power had gone out. We walked upstairs carefully and reached our door.

The living room was pitch-black and silent apart from the sound of our breath and the storm beating the roof and shaking the shutters. I couldn't move… I didn't know what to do. I was scared. Timid. As if my determination had stayed behind on the edge of the cliff. But I still wanted him, more and more as my eyes adjusted to the darkness and I saw his outline standing still before me.

We were in our element. We, too, were two raindrops on a window, coming together, one now, blind, in need of each other. Unable to see that they were on opposite sides of that window, that something invisible separated them…

Lucas leaned in, pushed my hair out of my face, and grabbed me by the nape of the neck. I opened my mouth again. One second. Two. Three…

I leaned back, and his lips found mine. Our tongues weaved together and our longing grew, as if each caress were kindling, the beginnings of a bonfire. We were hungry, we were wild, we were tender, we were soft. I tugged at his T-shirt, and he stepped back and pulled it over his head.

He turned me around and pushed me against the wall, unzipping my dress and pressing his chest into my back, warm and firm. His hands gripped my stomach as I felt his teeth on my shoulders, my neck, my jawline. He kissed me and spun me back around. My dress fell to the floor and I shook off my sandals. All too anxious. All too alive.

Unable to stop touching each other, we made it to his bedroom. I ran my fingers through his hair. I had wanted to do it for so long… to see what it would feel like.

"I need to ask you," he said breathlessly. "How far do you want to take this?"

I smiled. Licked his lips. I thought it was obvious. I unbuttoned his pants and pulled them down.

"As far as you're willing to take me."

He bit my lip, making me hotter.

"Then get ready for a long trip."

We fell into bed, I pulled him close, and I arched my hips, ready for him. I felt his hands all over me, his lips, his teeth, impatient, groaning, thirsty.

I could hardly stand it when he paused to open the nightstand. Every few seconds, lightning exploded across the sky. Then I could see him, his shimmering skin, his tense muscles, his firm stomach, those eyes I loved so much fiery with desire.

Lucas pressed one hand into the mattress and had the other around my neck, and was tracing the outline of my lips with his thumb. I shook, tried not to show how badly I needed him, kept my eyes open because I didn't want to miss a single detail.

His hips pressed into me, his rhythm was soft, and I let myself be dragged away as if by the tide. I pushed into him… I wanted to feel him deeper. We were two waves dancing. Breaking on the same shore. Turning into foam.

"You know why I asked you to say here?" he whispered. I nodded, incapable of words. "Because I want you, Maya. I need you. Bad. You're the most gorgeous woman I've ever seen."

I closed my eyes, hyperventilating.

"Because you drive me crazy, the way you look at me," he went on, "and I can't take my eyes off you."

"Lucas…"

I felt so full of him as he told me how he'd spent days and days trying to imagine holding me like this. And he went faster. Harder. Deeper. "This is incredible," he said.

Our lips joined, I felt myself rising.

I let myself go.

We let ourselves go.

Together, trembling.

Then we lay in silence, listening to the rain.

And eventually, we fell asleep, legs weaved together, weariness overtaking us.

Late at night we felt each other again, like a calm sea.
And the next morning, I was on top of him, looking down.
Taking possession of him, or starting to.
Making him fly high with the sunlight toasting our skin.
And in that moment, in his arms, I found my wings.

35

Lucas fell asleep with his head on my chest and I ran my hands through his hair. In the window, motes of dust floated in the air. The room was silent apart from his deep respiration.

I bent down and looked at him: his face, the constellations of freckles. They were adorable, as were his nose, the arches of his eyebrows, the shadows his eyelashes cast over his cheeks, the little wrinkles on each side of his lips from smiling.

I pushed aside my thoughts and let myself feel. I refused to analyze what was happening, what consequences that might have. I didn't want to understand it; I just wanted to enjoy it, to be carried along, guided by instinct. I wanted to get to know the person I was becoming. The person I had always been, but hadn't allowed myself to be.

Lucas cleared his throat, yawned, stretched like a cat—a huge cat that covered my body and buried its muzzle in my neck as it purred. "Hey," he whispered next to my ear. Then he left a trail of kisses that led to my breast.

The clock on his nightstand read nine o'clock.

I wanted him, I wanted to melt into him again, but I didn't want to be late to the florist's. And I was sore in places I hadn't known could be sore. It was a sweet aching, but an aching nonetheless.

"Lucas," I murmured, resigned.

I could feel him tense up as he responded, "Don't. Don't say it."

"What?"

"That what happened was a mistake. That we're roommates. That this makes things too complicated. I don't know! Just don't say it, OK!"

"I wasn't going to say anything like that."

"No?" He raised his head.

"No, I was just going to ask if you'd take me to work. I'm not sure I'll make it on the bike."

With an almost exasperated look, he said, "Obviously I'll take you to work. Don't freak me out like that. What's wrong with your bike, though?" That was a dumb thing to ask, it should have been obvious that it was me, not the bike. When he realized that a second later, he nodded. "Ahh, sorry. I understand. Sorry."

I slapped him softly and told him not to laugh at me, and he swore he wasn't. But his weak attempts at suppressing a grin told me otherwise. "Idiot," I said, trying to push him off of me.

He stood and grabbed a pair of pants off the chair. "You shower first," he said. "I'll make breakfast."

I went to my room for some clean clothes and saw everything I'd bought next to the bed. I took my pointe shoes out of the bag and looked at them, whispering to myself, "What the hell are you doing?"

I looked around and saw that my room there was mine in a way nothing in Madrid ever had been. I had two jobs, so I had some stability. I'd found a place for myself in that big family of people in the villa, and I'd hooked up with a guy I liked a lot. And he liked me too, and he'd asked me to stay.

I was building a life for myself!

And now I was getting scared of losing it.

36

"Maya, dammit, I don't know what to tell you. You went to that town to talk to him and find out the truth," Matías reminded me on the other end of the line.

"But what if I open my mouth and I ruin everything?"

"Why would you ruin everything?"

"I don't know. There's all kinds of reasons, and I'm scared."

I finished putting the roses in a vase and leaned on the counter, grunting, because he was supposed to be encouraging me. At least about this one thing.

"Maya, you're talking about moving to another country. That's not a small decision. I feel like you've gone on one of those radical makeover programs, but instead of changing your appearance, they've changed your brain."

"Don't joke around."

"I'm being serious."

"I love it here, though," I told him. "I feel as if I could stay here forever and be happy. I don't need anything else."

"Yeah, you don't need anything else except for Lucas and his big old…"

"Hey!" I cut him off. "Don't go there. I shouldn't have even told you."

I could hear his chuckle as he said, "Admit it, Maya, you're falling for him. At least tell me he's treating you right. Because otherwise, I'll fly there right now and kick his ass."

"I love you, Matías," I replied. "You know how much I miss you, don't you?"

"I miss you, too. But you didn't answer my question."

I found myself nodding, even though I knew Matías couldn't see me, as I rested a hand on my hip. "Lucas is a good guy. Seriously. He's trustworthy, nice, attentive, giving…"

"I don't doubt that. It sounds like he's been *giving* it to you for two days straight."

"Matías!" I shrieked. But I couldn't help but laugh along with him.

He complained that I'd gone a week without telling him what was happening between Lucas and me, and I reminded him that he'd been too busy to call. I could feel him fiddling around in the kitchen, pouring himself a glass of water, as he explained how Natalia had decided to do a new version of *Don Quixote* next season. "It's madness," he went on, "but Maya, I've always got time to talk about sex. And I want details. Lots of details."

"Perv."

"Honey, I haven't gotten any in ages. So I'm going to need to live through you."

"I didn't think straight sex turned you on."

"Listen, Maya, I'll just omit you from any scenario you tell me about and focus on the part about your naked boyfriend."

I never liked to share the dirty details, but I was about to give it my best shot when I saw Lucas on the other side of the window, approaching quickly. I hadn't been expecting him.

"Hey, Matías, sorry," I said. "I've got to go. I'll call you back soon."

"Are you all right?"

"Sure."

The bell rang over Lucas's head as he opened the door and he greeted me with a *Hi* muttered in that gravelly, seductive voice that turned me on so much. I waved at him as Matías made a terrible joke about Lucas being like Harry Potter and coming to show me his magic wand, and then he begged me to put the call on speaker so he could hear Lucas's voice or, better still, FaceTime.

"That's not going to happen," I responded.

"Don't be greedy. I want to see!"

"I'm hanging up now."

"Maya…"

I put my phone down on the counter, and Lucas asked if he was interrupting something.

"No," I said, "it was just my friend Matías. I've told you about him."

"Aren't you supposed to be closed by now?" Lucas wrapped his hands around my waist and looked me in the eye.

"Yeah, why?"

"Well, it is Friday, and if you and I are both off, I was thinking maybe you'd like me to take you out to eat. Or…?"

"I'd love it," I said as he toyed with the bottom of my skirt.

"After that," he went on, "maybe we could go home and…"

Now his hands were under my skirt, and I was holding my breath. "And…?"

He leaned his head to the side, his mouth just a few inches from mine. "I don't know. But I'll bet we can come up with something."

One second. Two. Three…

How I loved it: that brief, eternal moment before our lips met.

37

Until then, I hadn't known you could be addicted to someone.

I'd never felt the need to have a person as close as I wanted Lucas. At every hour of the day.

No one had ever made me feel that longing that burned me up inside, made me tremble, filled me with life.

I hadn't known until then that I could provoke those same emotions in another person. That someone could look at me the way he looked at me. That anyone could touch me the way he touched me.

And I couldn't imagine doing all that with anyone else.

I couldn't see myself elsewhere, with a different life.

I felt certain, and I made a decision. I would put those photos away forever, and I'd say nothing to Giulio. It was enough just to see him every day and to know he was there, that he cared about me. That he was close.

38

The days passed calmly, with my routine of the mornings at the florist that glided into the afternoons at school. I barely even noticed time was passing.

I felt freer than ever, lighter, happier. Leaving behind my life in Madrid, the life I'd fallen into and had never wanted, was like being reborn. Opening my eyes for the first time to a world that allowed me to feel like a part of it.

But the best of all was the time Lucas and I shared.

Those moments when we stripped off each other's clothes with our eyes and opened ourselves up to get to know each other better. The hours between the sheets. The sex. The pleasure. The sleepless nights holding each other. Sharing caresses with our hands and our lips. Gazing. Or now, nearly falling asleep in a bathtub full of cool water to stave off the heat, my back against his chest, my legs over his legs.

"What time are you done tonight?" I asked.

We were holding hands, and they emerged from the water covered in suds and wrinkly from being in there so long. He kissed my fingertips and told me, "Elevenish. I'll come get you and we can watch the fireworks."

It was the end of July, and Sorrento was celebrating the Feast of Sant'Anna, one of the most important holidays. It would end at midnight with a spectacular display of fireworks over the sea.

"Sounds good," I said.

My phone dinged. It was the sound it made when I got some notification on social media. I leaned over the pile of clothes where I'd left the phone to see what the message was and managed to read the first few words. Then I groaned.

"What is it?" Lucas asked.

"Nothing. Antoine. He's got terrible timing, and he doesn't know when to quit."

"Your ex? He's still writing you after all these weeks?"

"He wants another chance, and he won't shut up about it."

"Are you going to give him one?"

What was that question about? I tried to turn away, but he squeezed me in his arms so I couldn't move.

"No way," I responded. "Never. What would give you that idea?"

"I don't know. You just never talk about him, so I wasn't sure."

"Do you want me to?"

He slid his fingers up and down my arm, kissed my neck, tickled me with his breath. "Not especially. How many boyfriends have you had?"

I looked back at him. "Why do you care?"

He bit his lower lip, and for the first time, I saw him as vulnerable. "Because I'm insecure and gossipy and I get nervous when you duck my questions."

That was strange. We'd been sleeping together for two weeks, and it was evident we liked each other, that we were both very attracted to each other. Day or night, it didn't matter, we were always struggling to keep our hands off each other. That was it. And I knew I was starting to have even stronger feelings for him, emotions that had taken root without me realizing it and were starting to grow.

But as for Lucas… I wasn't sure until just then.

"I've gone out with three guys," I told him. "The first one was just a summer hookup. His name was Daniel, and he was a stuck-up jerk. We were both seventeen and he broke up with me when he found another chick who would let him touch her boobs."

"Yeah, he sounds like an idiot," Lucas said.

"When I moved to London, I met Eddie. We were together for seven months, then I found out on Instagram that we were apparently in an open relationship."

"Oh no!"

"It wasn't as bad as it sounds. I mean, I liked him, but whatever. Then it was Antoine's turn. We knew each other, we had studied together at the dance conservatory. We met up again when I came back from London and I joined the company. I guess all those hours together added up and we found ourselves going out."

"You fell in love with him," Lucas said, and I wasn't sure whether it was a question or a statement.

"I thought so, but now I'm not so sure."

"Why?"

"I mean, I didn't have anyone to compare him with in that sense."

"And now…?" Lucas asked.

I didn't have the courage to tell him yes. That I'd never felt emotions as intense as the ones he provoked in me, and that now I was questioning every choice I'd ever made. That I wondered whether I was falling love with him or if the whole situation in Sorrento, the intensity of everything there, was making me lose my bearings.

"You're nosy today," I said, turning and splashing a little water over the tub's lip. "Why don't you tell me about you? Have you had a bunch of girlfriends?"

He stroked his jaw and leaned back. "Since I got here, I've only had hookups. Nothing serious."

"What about before?"

"I was with the same girl for ten years."

"Ten years? That's like a lifetime."

"You're telling me," he said.

He stared off into the distance as I sat there dying of curiosity. I wrapped my legs around him and sat in his lap.

"What happened?" I asked.

He told me he'd never talked to anyone about this before.

"I'm not just anyone," I replied.

Pulling me in tight, he drew a deep breath and began. "Her name's Claudia. Our fathers knew each other from their school days and had been friends ever since. They went to college together, they were godparents to each other's kids, they went into business together... You get the idea. So Claudia and I grew up together. I barely have any memories without her in them. Since we were little, our families joked about how one day we'd get married, and either we really did fall in love or just hearing that all our lives sank in, and so we started going out at fifteen..."

He seemed for a moment to try to be ordering his thoughts, then he went on. "We never had what you'd call a great relationship. It was never healthy. Claudia's impulsive, she's flighty, and she always needs to get people's attention. When she was with me, she wanted more, and when we broke up, all she wanted was to have me back. She tried a million times. First it was, *I need to meet other people, I feel stifled, I don't know what I feel*, then she fell on her knees and begged for me to forgive her. And I never knew how to say no to her, no matter how much she hurt me."

"They say love's blind."

"That wasn't love, Maya. That was pain. And the older we got, the less things changed. It's not just that she was constantly leaving me hanging and only tried to fix things when she thought I was slipping away from her, it's that she was actually cheating on me, and then she had the nerve to tell me it was my fault because I was always working or studying, and she didn't feel that I *valued* her. And I actually bought it, and I tried even harder, and I fucking forgave her."

"Lucas, there's a name for that: codependence and emotional abuse."

"Yeah," he admitted. "It was hard for me to see it that way, but I know that now. Finally."

"Your family didn't say anything?"

"My family was no help whatsoever. Anytime I'd gather the courage to break up with Claudia, they'd intervene and I'd end up folding. My parents organized our engagement, bought the ring, set us up in an apartment. Claudia's family handled the wedding and the honeymoon and paid all the expenses."

"How...traditional."

"It sucked." He pinched the bridge of his nose. "Then Claudia got pregnant and our families wanted to push the wedding forward. But no one asked me what I thought. Whether I was in agreement, whether I even had an opinion. They just decided without giving me a chance to reply."

I froze. Pregnant? Did Lucas have a child? I didn't dare ask. But I could feel my throat swelling as he spoke on, "Claudia had a near-miscarriage a few weeks later, and the doctors told her she'd need to rest for her entire pregnancy. The wedding got put off. It was a horrible time. They gave her a C-section as soon as they could, and right away, we noticed something was wrong with the baby."

"I'm sorry," I whispered, fearing the worst. They must have lost the child, I thought. Lucas looked up at me with his blue eyes, deep, wounded, defeated. And for a moment, I saw all that they were hiding.

"The doctors said they thought he might have Marfan syndrome. It's a genetic disorder. Claudia and I ended up taking a test for some study or other."

"And…?"

"The baby wasn't mine."

I brought my hand to my chest. "Whose was it?"

"I don't know and I don't care," he replied, now furious. "It was a nasty blow. You can't imagine. And worst of all, no one seemed to care. I'd been naive, I'd been cheated on, and they still thought I was such a dumbass that I would go on with the wedding, raise some other asshole's kid, and keep my head down all for the sake of appearances."

"But you didn't."

"No. I gathered what little pride I had left and I took off that same day. I've never talked to any of them again, and I don't plan to."

"I'm so sorry you had to go through all that, Lucas."

He tried to smile, tried to let me know he was OK, but I knew he couldn't be. I had picked the scab and dug my finger into the wound. A wound that was deep, that was probably still infected.

He kissed me quickly and stood, getting out of the bath.

"I'll pick you up later, OK?" he said, wrapping a towel around his waist.

I stayed there for a while after Lucas left, thinking about all he had told me. It was hard for me to understand how someone could be so sure of himself, so strong, so composed, and then could allow people to abuse him like that. And it was abuse. There was no other way to describe it. They had manipulated him, lied to him, threatened him, and he had just put up with all of it. He hadn't reacted until he had to. And if he hadn't, he'd have disappeared completely.

But why should that surprise me? I had been just as blind with my own family. With my grandmother. Matías always told me she mistreated me. That it wasn't just that she was standoffish, or bossy, or severe. Matías, too, had used that word *abuse*, had tried to tell me she had no right to run me down the way she did and make me feel insignificant for no reason.

No one deserves to be treated that way. No one.

I realized then that Lucas and I were like two mirrors, and I had needed to see my reflection in him to understand that a love that hurts, that wounds, isn't really love.

39

It was a little after nine when a knock came at the door. I put aside my popcorn and lowered the volume on the TV.

"Hey!" I shouted at Giulio when I opened the door.

"Hey, sorry to bother, but…"

"Don't apologize. Do you need something?"

"I was in the garden, about to leave, when I noticed the light was on." He stuffed his hands into his pockets. "You know, everyone's gone into town to see the fireworks. You don't want to come along?"

"Yeah, Lucas is going to come pick me up when his shift ends."

"That'll take hours! Why don't you come with me? We'll go to the restaurant, see everyone else there, and have a drink."

"Sure," I agreed, beaming, and told him, "I j-just need a moment."

I hurried off to the bathroom to brush my teeth and comb my hair. I sprayed on a little perfume and tried to find my sandals in the bedroom. I looked all over for them before remembering I'd taken them off in Lucas's room. When I crossed the living room on my way there, I found Giulio looking around curiously.

"Sorry," I told him, "just a sec."

"No rush."

I stepped into my sandals, which were lined up by Lucas's bed, and stumbled out to find Giulio standing there grinning.

"What?"

"Nothing!" He shrugged.

When I saw the mischief in his eyes, I chuckled and said, "Yeah, it's exactly what it looks like."

"I know. I've known for a while now."

"How?"

"I pay attention to details," he said.

"What do you think, then?" I don't know why I asked him that. It wasn't anybody's business, and I didn't know why he should care.

"You and Lucas being together? Why would I get in the middle of it?"

"Sure." I grabbed my purse and dropped the keys inside. "Ready," I told him.

The restaurant patio was so packed that it took us several minutes to get inside. Giulio went looking for Dante and I stayed by the door. I noticed Lucas long before he noticed me. He was walking back and forth behind the bar, pouring drinks, opening bottles, clearing glasses. He had the same smile as ever on his face. I wanted to rush over and kiss it.

A girl walked up to ask him for something, he bent down to hear her better, and in that instant, our eyes met. Seeing him smile at me, I thought I would explode inside.

Lucas got his coworker to assist the girl, walked out from behind the bar, and approached me.

"Hey, sorry," I said. "Giulio stopped by and convinced me to…"

I couldn't say more, because his lips pressed into mine, silencing me. I felt our tongues touch, and the entire world vanished. My feelings for him crested like a high wave on the sea, trapping me, swallowing me, dragging me off in their current. As I caught my breath, he took my hand and muttered into my ear, "Come on, I'll take you to where everyone is."

I followed him onto a porch where a table had been placed. Everyone from the building, even Julia's nephews, was there. Catalina waved at me and motioned for me to sit beside her.

"Are you hungry?" Lucas asked. I nodded. My stomach growled at the smell of food in the air. He told me he'd bring me something. As we talked and joked, time flew by. Giulio soon joined us with a tray of pastries in his hand, and Lucas came and sat next to me, draping his arm around me and pulling me in for a kiss on the lips. That was the first time we'd done anything like that in front of everyone else. Revealing that we were more than roommates, more than friends. I could feel everyone looking at us and hear their giggling, and I noticed Roy nudging Julia in the ribs.

"I told you," he said proudly.

I understood better than ever then what Lucas had said to me that first day: *The people who live in this villa are like a big family. When they say hi because they run into you on the landing, it's not just good manners. We truly live together here, and we share our days with each other.*

I felt so thankful to have them in my life.

Not long before midnight, Dante walked out and sat next to Giulio, and I observed them: the way they looked at each other, the way they smiled, the way they seemed to become one person when they touched. It was nice to see them together, to see what real, lasting love was like.

I looked up at the moon, which was shining over the warm waters of the calming sea. Dante said something and Giulio's expression changed. As they exchanged a few words, I could see they were tense. Giulio shook his head and pulled his hand away from Dante, who looked up and saw that I was watching them. He stiffened, and there was something cold in his eyes. It sank into my skin, below it, making me uncomfortable.

Instinctually, I sought refuge in Lucas, who squeezed me tight and kissed the crown of my head. As I breathed out, a sharp hissing pierced the night, and a bright trail rose and ended in an explosion over our heads. As the fireworks began, I silenced the anxiety that was growing in me.

I let myself be embraced by my favorite scent.

By the perfect hug.

By the man who was making everything I'd thought impossible come true.

40

The next few weeks were a blur.

Just as in Spain, August 15 is a national holiday in Italy. There, they call it Ferragosto, and it coincides with the Assumption of Mary, which is a huge deal for the Italians. There are processions, parades, concerts...

Lucas wasn't working that day, and he said we should go to Positano, which was only about twenty minutes by car from Sorrento. They call Positano *the city of staircases*, and my knees soon discovered it wasn't just some random nickname. Still, it was precious, wedged between sky and sea, vertical, with houses clinging to the mountain over the Gulf of Salerno, looking stacked one atop the other.

The view was incredible. It was like a dreamland.

We ate a curry risotto in a restaurant on the terrace of a hotel with incredible views of the coast. Then we spent the afternoon wandering the maze of streets and squares, walking through archways, looking in the stores of craftsmen and soap and limoncello makers that stretched through all the different neighborhoods.

As night fell and the lights turned on, I had the feeling I'd been transported elsewhere. A film set. We found hidden squares, shadowy balconies with fig trees, secret stairways. And wherever we turned, we were watched by dozens of cats strolling along the tops of the walls.

We decided to have dinner in a place called Franco's Bar. We sat on the patio, waiting for the fireworks to start. On Lucas's lap, with his arm around my waist, I saw the sky light up and felt the solitude I'd always known my whole life vanish. It was that simple, that easy.

We went home not long after the show ended. We were tired, but we were also happy.

When we pushed open the front door, we could hear music playing out back. We found everyone sitting around the table on the patio except for the kids, who were sleeping on the wicker sofa, covered by a blanket. The adults were arguing about something and seemed to have split into two sides.

"What's going on?" Lucas asked.

"We're having a debate about first love," responded Angela, who was wrapped in her husband's arms. "Julia says your first love is always the most important, the most intense, the most special."

"Because it's new, and you're discovering things, and you never forget it," Julia butted in.

"Whereas I think 'first love' is just a fancy name we give to our first sexual impulses. You're young, you're innocent, and you confuse love with arousal, you feel that urge for sex like butterflies in your stomach," Roy said.

Julia chided him. "Easy with the scientific words: 'impulse,' 'arousal.' You sound like a dictionary. I swear I could choke you sometimes."

Instead of responding, Roy simply raised an eyebrow and grinned.

"I think your first love is the most important, too," Iria said. "It depends on your experience of it, of course, but still, it marks you forever, and it has an effect on every relationship that you have afterward.

If that person hurt you, you'll be more cautious about opening your heart next time. But if it was happy, then you haven't built up any defenses. You know what I mean?"

"Not really," Blas said. "Because unless I'm mistaken, I'm your first and only love, and yet you sound like somebody who knows all about the subject."

"There's no way you actually believe that," Iria said mirthfully. Blas looked shocked, and she laughed and kissed him on the cheek. "You really are an idiot," she added.

"I think first love is overrated," Lucas said.

I looked at him out of the corner of my eye and he fingered the ice cube in his drink.

"Do you now?" Catalina asked.

He nodded. "The last love is the one that counts. The person you choose to stay with."

He glanced over at me and grinned enigmatically, and I shivered, hugging my arms to my chest.

"Are you cold?" he asked.

"Yeah," I said. "I think I'm going to go grab a sweater."

"I'll bring you one back," he replied. "I need to go up and pee."

"Just look in the first drawer in my closet," I told him, and he replied that he'd be back in no time, hurrying off.

Now Dante took the floor. "I think what marks you isn't your first love, but the first time a person breaks up with you. The first time your heart's broken."

Angela agreed. "A breakup always stings, especially if you're the one who gets left. I still haven't gotten over Francesco dumping me in grade school."

"The kid with the glasses and the lisp?" Catalina asked, giggling.

Our conversation turned toward innocence, first times, memories, confessions, and in the midst of it, Giulio announced, "There's a famous phrase: 'Your first love is the one you love the most, but the other ones you love better.'"

"I like that," Catalina said.

I was struggling to listen along, and as everyone drank more, their words were becoming less coherent. Lucas was taking forever, too, and that was worrying me. I excused myself and went to look for him, climbing the stairs to the third floor. The light was on in my room. I peeked in and found Lucas sitting on my bed, elbows resting on his knees, my photos in his hands. The dresser drawer was still open.

My heart started pounding and I felt an abyss open at my feet. He looked up at me with an expression so frightening I took a step back.

"I told you to look in the drawer in the *closet*," I said defensively.

Lucas's eyes were shimmering with anger. He stood and walked over to me, shaking the photos in my face, along with the documents Fyodora had found for me. "What is this?" he asked. "Why does the girl in the photos have your last name?"

"Give them back!" I reached for them, and he pulled his hand away.

"Why the fuck is Giulio with her?"

"It's not your business."

"It's not my business? Bullshit, Maya. It sure as hell is my business. It means you've been lying to me since the moment you showed up here."

"I never lied to you."

He walked past me in fury, dropping the photos on the living room table and grabbing his pack of cigarettes. He lit one. I could feel the rage coming off of him in waves.

"I didn't lie," I repeated. "I just left some things out."

"Same thing," he said.

"No, it isn't. I told you what you needed to know to rent me the room."

He kept sucking in more and more drags as though his life depended on it.

"Maya, I can't deal with lies, and even less with liars. Lies hurt people. They make people suffer. They ruin people's lives. A lie can destroy you!" he shouted.

I felt myself shrinking. Did he hate me now? Was that it? He was comparing me with Claudia. I could see it in his eyes, and it hurt me that the thought came to him so easily.

"Why should I have told you?" I asked, confronting him. "I didn't know anything about you, and I'm supposed to tell you something so personal? This is my issue. It belongs to me. No one else, OK?"

"Well, what about now?" he growled. "You know everything about me now. You don't think after fucking me for all these weeks you could have found the time to be honest with me about these fucking photos?"

"Who are you to be placing demands on me?"

"You used me."

"No!" I shouted, on the verge of tears. "How can you even say that?"

I saw the anger in his eyes, but behind it was desperation and fear.

"What do you want me to think?" he asked, picking up the photos again. "Because I see clues here, and they don't look good. You showed up here with these. Looking for Giulio. Why?"

I couldn't answer, couldn't get out the words, and he went on, "You know what? I don't care. It doesn't matter. I don't even want to know. Just go."

He slumped down, defeated. That smile I had always found on his face was gone, and in its place was a cold mask I couldn't recognize.

"What are you saying?"

"Get your things and go. I don't want you here."

I felt myself falling apart. Everything had changed in an instant, and now I had to face the reality, a bitter reality I could have avoided if it had been just a little warmer out, or if he hadn't opened the wrong drawer.

"Lucas, you don't understand. You're right that I came to Sorrento for Giulio. What you don't know is that I think he could be my father."

"What?" His expression changed. His eyes wide, his mouth gaping, he looked almost funny, and I might have laughed if the situation had been different. But I was shaking as he went on. "You told me you didn't know your father."

"I was telling the truth. All I have is these photos, some dates, and a likeness." I blinked, wiped the tears out of my eyes, and pointed to my face. "Tell me you don't see it."

I slumped down on the sofa, trying to find the strength to fight off despair, as Lucas looked at the photos for what felt like an eternity. Finally, he murmured, "I don't understand."

"My mother told me over and over that she didn't know who my father was. Just a stranger, she said. Then I found those photos in her things and I tried to ask her again, but she wouldn't even answer. Giulio spent a summer in Madrid. He knew my mom. I was born nine months after that. Look at me and tell me it's not possible."

Lucas slowly approached the sofa, his stare shocked and confused, and sat on the opposite end. Was he still angry with me? I didn't think so, but I couldn't tell. I continued, trying to order my thoughts, "I didn't even think about what I was doing when I got on the plane and came here. It was an impulse. But once I did it, there was no turning back. And then, as soon as I reached town, I ran into Giulio, almost like it was fate. I followed him through the streets to a scenic lookout, where I thought I lost him, and I even asked myself if I hadn't just imagined it. Then I saw the restaurant, the packed patio tables, and that free table that seemed to be waiting there just for me. And then you appeared."

Lucas glanced up at me and looked away, leaning back and pinching the bridge of his nose. I hoped he would say something, but when he didn't, I forced myself to keep talking. I told him everything. About my family, about how my life had been in Madrid. About my relationship with my mother. I stripped myself down to the bone, confessing every fear, every yearning, every thought that had brought me to where I was then. Everything that had brought me to that couch where we were sitting next to each other, with an abyss now between us.

"Since I got here, every night when I've gone to bed, I've promised myself I'd say something to him the next day, but then I wake up and I'm scared and time keeps passing…" I looked down. "Lucas, I never wanted to hurt you. I never wanted to hurt anyone. That's why I decided not to say anything and just leave things as they are. I was looking for a family, and I've found so much more than that, and I was scared of risking that and losing everything. It was my secret, just mine, and I wasn't hurting anyone by keeping it to myself."

"You were hurting you," he whispered.

"Yeah, but everything else made up for it. And anyway, what if it wasn't true? What if all this was just a bunch of coincidences and not a sign? Maybe my mother was telling the truth and my father was just some stranger who'll never know he has a daughter."

"Or maybe Giulio is your father and he'll never know."

What was he saying? That I should tell Giulio? Or that he was willing to keep my secret?

"What he doesn't know can't hurt him," I said. "And it's got nothing to do with you. It's my thing."

"Yeah, but now I know."

"And you also know what it feels like when other people make decisions for you. When they take the freedom to do so away from you."

Our eyes met, without filters, without masks, without deceptions. So close...and at the same time, so far away.

And then he stood and walked out without a word.

41

That conversation with Lucas left me exhausted and empty. It was the calm before the storm, and I knew that fragile, crumbling dam that protected me would soon fall to pieces. It was just a matter of time. And then reality would strike me mercilessly, and I didn't know if I could take it.

I put the photos back in my drawer, took off my clothing, let it fall to the floor. Naked, I walked into the bathroom, turned on the tap, and got into the bath. I let the steam surround me. I felt weak, alone, incomplete.

When I came out wrapped in a towel, I didn't go to Lucas's room, where I'd slept for weeks, but to my own room, putting on a clean T-shirt and getting into bed.

The silence and the darkness settled over me, and I felt myself floating in the nothingness. A cold nothingness filling with chaotic emotions and spinning in a whirlpool of pain.

How quickly we get used to the good things! The pretty things, the nice things. Feeling complete. How soon we forget that it can all come to an end.

I hugged myself tight, feeling an agony in my chest I could hardly bear. Lucas had kicked me out. He wanted me to go. It was over before it started. So why did I feel like I was about to leave half my life behind?

I sank my face in the pillow and muffled a sob. How I regretted not doing things differently. I was a disaster... But the past can't be changed, can it? All you can do is accept it and take the pain, even if your whole life's been turned upside down. For a second time.

I gathered my strength and told myself I could do it. I'd gather my things and go. To where? I didn't know. And I didn't have the least idea what to do about everything else.

I was tired from all that thinking. I didn't even know what time it was when I heard steps on the stairs and a key in the lock. Lucas's door opening and closing. I closed my eyes tighter and curled up into a tiny ball, unable to stanch the tears that burned my cheeks.

I had nearly fallen asleep again when I heard the door to my room open. I held my breath and stared straight ahead as I felt his weight on the mattress, his body next to mine, the way it fit mine like a piece in a puzzle. He wrapped his arm around my waist and pulled me to him. His skin was hot, and he smelled of tobacco.

"You're right. He looks a lot like you in the photos," he whispered.

"I know."

I could feel his breath on my neck as he whispered, "It's not true what I said before. I don't want you to go. I want you to stay."

"And I want to stay." My voice cracked, and he pressed his nose into my hair.

"Maya, I'm pissed."

"I know."

"All this has fucked me up bad."

"I know."

"And I want you to know I don't agree with you. But I'm willing to respect you."

A profound sense of gratitude overtook me. I grabbed his hand

and laced my fingers through his, feeling a little more whole, more me, truer, the way I always did with Lucas.

"So no one else knows about this?" he asked.

"No, only Matías."

"Your family hasn't gotten in touch since you left?"

"No, but I haven't really pressed them either. I called my grand-mother a few times to talk to Granddad, but she didn't pick up." I sniffled. "It's OK, though, Lucas. It doesn't matter."

"It matters, Maya. Trust me, I know that better than anyone."

He turned me around, and I tried to see his face in the dark.

"When I was little, I thought she loved me," I said.

"Your grandmother or your mother?"

"I don't know, both I guess. I thought they loved me and they always would. Because that's how it's supposed to be, right? Your family loves you. But it wasn't that way, and there are times when I feel like I just wasn't good enough."

Lucas pressed his forehead to mine and rested a hand on my cheek as I stroked his face. "You don't have to be good for someone to love you. You don't have to do anything, so stop asking whether you deserve to be loved and let yourself be loved. Because there are people who love you, Maya."

Surprised, I asked, "Do you think that? That I refuse to let people love me?"

"I think you've convinced yourself that it's impossible that anyone would love you simply for who you are, and you somehow can't see that everyone around you already does."

They already do, I repeated to myself in my mind.

Lucas continued rubbing my cheek. We were so close, we were breathing the same air. One more millimeter, and I'd feel his lips. But that space between us, the space before a kiss, was so dense that I couldn't yet pierce it. I needed to dissipate in that silence that said so much more than words. In that longing that flew like a moth between his lips and mine.

One second. Two. Three…

How do you ignore what's throbbing inside you? Answer: You can't.

42

For the weeks that followed, we fell back into our comfortable routine as though nothing had happened. We didn't mention the photos or anything that had to do with them. But sometimes, I'd notice Lucas staring at Giulio with something like worry. Watching us when we were together, with emotions parading across his face that I struggled to identify.

I didn't want to bring it up, so I let it go, imagining that as time passed, he'd stop worrying about it so much.

Then I got up one morning and found him staring at me. I had started sleeping in his room—more and more, my room—again every night. He was smiling at me, and I smiled back. Our eyes roved each other's face, and I felt something new there, a vibration, an emotion that was emanating from our bodies and suffusing the air around us. Something soft, something pretty, something you could almost reach out and touch.

A warm expression appeared on his face. He bent over and kissed me, and I knew we were feeling as one. The world disappeared. But alas, time didn't stop, and I murmured, "I'm late, I'm late," as I stood and jumped up and down, trying to pull on my pants.

"'For a very important date! No time to say hello, goodbye, I'm late, I'm late, I'm late!'"

"What?" I asked.

"Come on, you know. The White Rabbit, *Alice in Wonderland*?"

"Oh, that," I said after a second. "Sorry, I never read the book and I only saw the movie when I was a teeny-tiny kid."

"Isn't there a ballet version?"

"Sure is," I said, bending over and kissing him. "Gotta go."

"Bye," he grunted.

I ran out of the bedroom and down the stairs, but before I left the building, I knocked on Giulio's door. I'd gotten an idea and I didn't want to let it slide. A few seconds later, Dante opened the door, still in his pajamas, hair a mess.

"Buongiorno," I said to him.

"Buongiorno," he responded.

"Is Giulio home?"

"Chi è?" Giulio said, walking up behind him. "Oh, Maya, hey. Everything OK?"

I nodded. "Remember how you said something about a performance at the Teatro Tasso for Christmas?"

"Yeah, of course," he responded.

"We should do *Alice in Wonderland*! There are lots of characters, so we can be sure every kid gets a part. We can draw on Wheeldon's choreography for the Royal Ballet, it was like clockwork and full of beautiful colors. What do you think?"

He took a minute to consider my proposal, but soon I could tell he was more overjoyed than I was. "I love it!" he exclaimed.

I could tell he was imagining the same things I was: the costumes, the stage, the steps…

I pedaled off to the florist with the sun on my skin and the sea breeze on my face, smiling like an idiot, feeling wonderful. Full of relief, full of gratitude for the life I was enjoying so much it was hard not to shout it out to the world.

I was learning not to ask myself questions there were no answers to. To stop doubting everything. To stop trying to fill every little hole in my life, to realize I needed those empty spaces to make room for the unexpected. I was learning to let myself go, to let things be.

Lucas came into the shop in midmorning with a coffee and a box of pastries. I hadn't expected it, and I was excited to see him there in his sunglasses and his wrinkly T-shirt. He almost always dressed carelessly, and I loved it.

"Are you alone?" he asked.

"Yeah, Monica just left with Tiziano. They've got a doctor's appointment."

"Is she OK?"

"Yeah, it's just an ultrasound to see how the babies are. She's getting close."

He smiled a little awkwardly and put the coffee and pastries on the counter. Then he took out some sugar packets and stirring sticks. I could see he was tense. It was something in his movements. I wondered if it had to do with Monica.

"You look nervous," I told him. "Is everything OK?"

"Sure."

"Are you sure? Because as soon as I mentioned the doctor, your expression changed."

It was odd. Lucas was normally so relaxed, and I hadn't seen him show any particular concern over Monica. But now I knew what had happened to the baby that he had thought was his for so long, so I thought there might be something else there.

Stirring his coffee, he said, "Here's the thing. I wasn't happy when I found out I was going to be a father. I wasn't ready for anything like that, and I didn't know how to face it. But everything changed when

Claudia did her third ultrasound. That's when I started thinking of him as my son, and in that moment, I began to love him. He became the most important thing to me."

"Do you still think of him?"

"Sometimes."

"I'm so sorry you had to go through something like that," I told him.

"Me too." He exhaled and then his face lit up as he pointed at the box of pastries. "Cream or chocolate?"

"Chocolate!"

He stuck around for a while, sometimes observing the customers as they trickled in, other times staring at my shorts or the neckline of my shirt. I tried to swat him away when he made it too obvious and smiled at Lola, one of our regulars, who was Spanish, too, and stopped in sometimes just to chat. She was inquiring about something, and I couldn't quite hear her, so I asked her to repeat it, and slightly impatiently, she said, "I was wondering if putting aspirin in water really helps your roses last longer."

"Honestly, I don't know…" Lucas slid his hand into my shorts just then. Lola couldn't see it, but that didn't make me any less nervous. "We've got a product though. If you use this, your roses will easily last for two weeks."

I passed her a little packet, and she asked, "Is this the same one I took for my carnations?"

"I think so."

"Well, they sure as hell didn't last two weeks."

"Got it," I said. "Maybe I should call Monica and ask her."

When Lucas's finger tugged at the seam of my underwear, I stomped on his foot, and he whimpered softly, pulling away. Lola asked him if he was all right, and he told her, "Yeah, I've got a bunion. It's killing me."

"Oh, you should get that operated on," she said. "I had them on both feet, and getting them taken off changed my life. Maya, just give me the preservative you were talking about. But I think I'm going to try the aspirin thing, too."

I rang her up and handed her a receipt, then ran out from behind the counter to hold the door for her. As she said, "Bye," I turned and scowled at Lucas. "You're acting like a child!"

He giggled, walked over, grabbed my wrists, and wrapped my arms around his waist. "Aren't you getting bored here?" he asked me. "The minutes are just creeping by."

"I'm not a busy bee like you. Anyway, nobody's forcing you so stick around," I replied.

"Ouch."

Looking at the clock, though, I saw it was time to close, and I pulled away from him and started cleaning up. He sat on a stool and stared at me as I did so. Then he asked, out of nowhere, "How come you never say goodbye?"

"What do you mean?"

"Just that: You never say goodbye. You never even wave. At most, there's a teeny-tiny movement of your lips when someone else says it."

"I never realized," I confessed.

"I don't buy that. You know, because you get tense right when you're supposed to do it. You've been here for months now, and I've never seen you say goodbye to anyone."

I hung the CLOSED sign on the door and lowered the blinds that covered the glass, asking myself when Lucas had gotten to know me so well. When he'd started picking up on those details no one else noticed.

"I just don't like that word," I said. "I don't like what it means, what it implies... I don't know. It's so...absolute. Definitive."

"Definitive?"

"Like it's forever. Or maybe it's not. Not always. But still."

"Does it make you feel like you'll never see the person again?" he asked.

"Sort of."

I could tell he was trying to understand, that he really wanted to, so I explained further. "I've never forgiven my mother for up and disappearing without telling me bye. She just ran away. Maybe that's it. I'm aware of how silly that is, that it doesn't make any sense. Even I can't really understand it, but it's just the way I am."

"Sure."

"Sorry for being so complicated."

He got up and pulled me into a hug. "I like you being complicated."

"Liar."

"I really do. Trying to unravel you is super-interesting, it's like trying to solve some complicated puzzle."

"What if you never do?"

"It's fine," he said. "There's nothing sexier than a woman of mystery."

I think that was the first time I realized I had fallen in love.

For that matter, it was the first time I had fallen in love.

For real.

Because the sensation was utterly new.

Lucas was what love meant for me.

43

People are nothing but layer after layer of secrets. Motives hidden in our hearts that we're too scared to share. And yet we expect everyone else to trust us fully, not to hold back, to take a leap of faith with their eyes closed.

44

We all find moments in life when control slips from our hands. Sometimes we see them coming and we manage to get a grip in time. Sometimes we're paralyzed and there's nothing we can do. I was in one of those, surrounded by chaos, knocked totally off balance. Unsure what to hold on to, flapping my arms and legs, but nothing could keep me from hitting the ground.

And so, in one of those moments, you hold on to the one thing that's left: fear. The most chaotic instinct we have.

I should have seen it coming. But I didn't pick up on the details. The insecure looks.

The doubts.

"The pas de deux between Alice and Jack has to be spectacular. The sautés perfect, the turns dramatic, and we need elevés!" Giulio said as he knotted his sweatpants a second time.

It was a Sunday morning and we were on the patio at the villa working on choreography for the ballet. Christmas was still three months away, but we wanted everything ready as quickly as possible so the kids could have time to rehearse.

"We should keep the elevés simple, Giulio. They still don't know what they're doing," I replied.

"You're too soft. Come on! Diagonal, three piqués, promenade, pirouette, pirouette, and porté…" He lifted me up.

I rose as high as possible, arched my back against the hand that was holding me, and began a slow descent until he caught me in his arms.

"Perfect." He sighed.

He hugged me and I hugged him back with closed eyes, then walked shyly to the table and took a sip of water. I saw Dante doing yoga under the tree. He looked like he was concentrating. Lucas had been napping in the deck chair in the sun, but had disappeared.

Giulio's phone rang. He picked up, talked to someone briefly, then told me, "We've got to leave it for today."

"No problem, I'll see you again soon."

I walked inside and hurried up the stairs. I pushed open the door, which we usually left cracked when we went outside, and noticed Lucas's keys on the table as I went to my room for clean clothes before taking a quick shower.

"Cosa fai?"

I turned around, scared to death, to find Dante standing at my bedroom door.

"Dante! What…?"

"I asked che diavolo stai facendo?"

His face and posture were aggressive, his tone suspicious, his stare almost frightening. I barely recognized him, and he kept mixing his Spanish and Italian and talking so fast I didn't understand him.

"Dante, slow down. I don't know what you're saying!"

"I asked you what the hell you're up to. I see how you've been talking to him since you arrived. How you watch him all the time. The way your occhi, your eyes, shine when you're with him. I see it all, tutto."

"Are you talking about Lucas?" I asked. I was so confused. Why would he care about that?

"Don't you make fun of me."

An alarm went off in my head and all of a sudden, everything was clear. "Are you talking about Giulio?"

"Sì, il mio marito. You're in love with him."

"What? Are you crazy?"

"You're calling me crazy? No, you're crazy, tu sei pazza. Stay away from him," he shouted with venom in his voice.

"Dante, listen…"

"What do you think's going to happen? You think you're going to turn a pirouette and fall in his arms and he's going to start loving you?"

"No!" I shouted, my throat stinging.

"You think he's going to stop being gay for you?"

"Dante, please," I begged him with tears in my eyes.

"This is patetico. Triste. And he has no idea…"

I shook my head, feeling powerless. I'd never really seen before what jealousy could do to a person. How irrational it could make you, how it could drive you insane. "None of what you're saying is true."

"I'm sick of this!" he shouted. "I'm sick of you."

He wasn't even listening. I could tell all he could think of was the next cruel word he would lash out with. He came into my bedroom, cursing at me, using words I didn't understand, apart from *Lascialo in pace*—leave him alone. I felt cornered, shut up in a building in the middle of an earthquake with every exit sealed. It was like a bad dream that wouldn't end.

"He's not going to do it. Capisce?" he growled.

And then I broke down. Shattered. Exploded. "It's not what you think. It's disgusting, what you're implying. I'm not in love with him, dammit. I think he's my father! My father, get it?"

Sometimes the truth comes out like that, carelessly, an avalanche no one can stop. And once it's out, there's no way to catch it and hide it away again.

"What?"

I looked into my doorway and saw Giulio standing in our living room. His eyes were wide, his face was pale. Dante stepped back, looking at him and then at me.

In Italian, he asked him, "Is she your daughter?"

Giulio responded, "What are you saying?"

"Now I understand. You don't want kids because you already have one!" Dante screamed.

"Dante, per favore…" Giulio looked so devastated that I pitied him.

"He doesn't know, Dante." I interrupted them. My hands were shaking as I opened my dresser and took out the photos before handing them to him and saying, "Here."

Giulio looked me in the eyes as he grabbed them, his entire face frozen apart from a slight twitching in his jaw.

"Remember her?" I asked in a near-whisper. He nodded almost imperceptibly. "Daria's my mother. She got pregnant the same summer you were in Madrid."

Dante asked, "Giulio, who's Daria?" But he ignored the question. His eyes opened wider, his pupils dilated, and a flood of contradictory emotions crossed his face.

"She told you I was your father?" Giulio murmured.

"No. She always said she didn't know."

He laughed bitterly. "Then why do you think it's me?"

"She'd kept these photos hidden, and the dates coincide, and…we look alike." I pointed to the mole on my brow. "See? It's identical."

I felt so stupid when I said that aloud. All of a sudden, nothing made sense. It was all so ridiculous, a castle in the air, with a foundation of dreams and walls made of my neediness and inadequacies. A fantasy I had built up day after day and had somehow allowed to turn into a certainty. Now it was crumbling. I could see the cracks getting bigger, the light filtering in.

"Impossible," Giulio whispered.

Dante, on the verge of breaking down, asked in Italian, "You want to tell me what's going on?"

"Do you think I know?" Giulio replied.

"She says she's your daughter. È possibile?"

"No!" he shouted. "No... I don't know."

"You don't know, do you? Did you sleep with her mother?"

Giulio raised his hands, as though asking for space, for time to think. I tried to tell what he was thinking, what he was feeling behind that look of panic. But I couldn't. Dante asked again, and Giulio told him to shut up, and finally he confessed. "I was eighteen years old! I thought it would fix me!"

"Babe," Dante said compassionately, "you were never broken."

"I didn't know that then." He turned to me. "Maya, I don't know what makes you think I could be your..." He couldn't bring himself to say it. "It's just not possible," he continued. "It isn't. I don't have children. I don't want children. It's not who I am."

"What about the photos, then?" I asked, feeling the cold claws of doubt digging into me.

"You're wrong." He looked cruel now, and I wasn't sure I how much longer I could take this. "A mole doesn't make you my daughter. Not even close."

He stared through me as if I were no one, as if I wasn't even there, and I was so overwhelmed that I didn't know what to do. He chastised me. "You showed up here with that crazy story in your head, didn't you? I was so stupid. There were too many coincidences; I should have known. For weeks, you've been faking with me and my family..."

"I didn't know how to tell you!" I protested. "One minute I would say to myself it was time, but then it all struck me as so…"

"Ridiculous?" He cut me off contemptuously. "Because that's what it is. And another thing: it's over. This issue doesn't leave this room, and I don't ever want to hear another word about it."

"Giulio, please…"

"Shut up. You're not mine." He barely pronounced those words, but the desperation in his tone cut through me like a hatchet blow.

He stared at me for a moment longer, then turned around and disappeared. Dante followed after him and I heard their voices echoing in the stairwell.

I couldn't take it all in. I felt as if I were in a movie. None of it was real. My mind seemed to be floating over my body, observing it from above.

I sat on the couch and cried and tried to get ahold of myself. But I was sinking. The sobs got worse and worse. I couldn't get one out before another came, and then I heard a voice, Lucas, asking me, "Maya, what's going on?"

I was too broken up to answer, and I saw the worry in his eyes as he ran over, crouched down, and cupped my face. "Why are you like this?" he continued.

More tears, a waterfall, bellowing, coughing. He hugged me, and I told him, "It was horrible. I admitted everything to Giulio. It went really, really bad."

Squeezing me tight, he asked, "Why now?"

"Dante showed up here out of his mind and being super nasty to me. Cruel, like he was trying to hurt me, and I had to make him stop. It's disgusting. He actually thinks I'm interested in Giulio. He thinks I like him. How could he imagine such a thing?" I sniffled and rubbed my face and went on, "And so I just blurted it out. I told him Giulio was my dad. And Giulio heard me."

"And he took it badly."

"Terribly," I replied. "He doesn't think it's possible that I'm his daughter. He doesn't believe there's even a remote possibility. And he doesn't want to hear more about it. And he doesn't want anything to do with me, either."

"Maya," Lucas said, "give him time. Put yourself in his shoes."

I shook my head, still feeling the memory of the moments before lodged inside me like shards of glass.

"You didn't hear him. He never wants to see me again."

Lucas sighed, leaned over, and kissed my forehead, leaving his lips there for a long time. They were trembling; his hands were trembling, too. When he pulled back, I saw his eyes were red and gleaming with tears. But when I asked him what was bothering him, he wouldn't tell me. I pressed him, and he tried to shrug it off. "It's not important. You're what's important."

But when I wouldn't let him kiss me, he sighed and opened up. "My sister called me. My dad's had a heart attack. He's in the ICU, they just operated on him. They don't think he's going to make it this time."

"Oh, Lucas, I'm so sorry. How are you taking it?"

"I don't know. My sister says I should go see him."

"What do you think?"

"It was so hard leaving them behind, and to go back now... I don't know. But..."

He rubbed his chin and I told him, "Maybe they hurt you, but they are your family."

"I know. But they were never a good one, and they don't deserve anything from me. That's a fact."

I reached up and pushed his hair away from his brow. "Whatever you do, Lucas, do it for you. Not for them or anyone else."

I'd never seen such vulnerability in those beautiful eyes. He asked me, "Do you think I should go?"

"I don't know. If he's dying…" I paused to try to get straight what I wanted to say. "If he dies and you're not there, will you regret it? Because you're a good guy, too good, and we human beings are stupid like that."

He sat on the floor, contemplative. "I have no idea how I'll feel. I don't even know how I feel now."

"Your parents were cruel to you, and you were right to leave, but that doesn't erase what they are. You and I both know that. So the question is: Do you want to say goodbye? Do you want to try?"

"A part of me thinks I should, but…" His face was distorted with despair. "Goddammit!"

"Lucas, you left without saying anything, and you haven't spoken since. Maybe this is an opportunity to fix things and relieve yourself of that burden."

He was fidgeting, twisting his fingers. The mere idea of going back to Madrid tortured him. I could tell even thinking of seeing his family again took him to the edge of panic. He looked like a lost little boy. Scared. In need of protection.

"I could go with you," I said. He looked up so relieved that I almost laughed. "If you want."

"Are you serious?"

I nodded. "And if at any point you stop and say, 'Never mind, I can't do that,' it's fine. We'll go somewhere else. We both could probably use it."

He grinned. "I can't ask you to do that, Maya."

"What else am I going to do… Stay here with Dante and Giulio and just hope everything magically gets better?"

"Maya." That was all he said, my name, his voice muffled, moved, as he pulled me into his lap and embraced me. We didn't do anything more, and yet it was the most intimate moment the two of us had ever shared.

45

The next morning, we packed our bags and called a taxi to take us to the bus station. I know I shouldn't have, I know it was selfish and cowardly, but I asked Lucas if we could go without saying goodbye to anyone. I didn't know if what had happened between Giulio and me was going to stay buried, as he'd said, or whether everyone might already know.

I'd made a mess, but I wasn't ready to face up to it.

Once we were in Naples, waiting for the train to Rome, Lucas called Catalina and told her why we had stolen away like that. What he didn't tell me was her response. And I didn't ask.

We got tickets for an evening flight taking off at nine.

We took off on time and landed in Madrid around midnight.

It was weird to be back in the city I'd always called home. Only a few months had passed since I left, but they felt like an eternity. I felt so distant from everything around me and from myself. The Maya who had come back there was nothing like the Maya who had left. There was something different inside me, and even the air felt different on my skin.

We caught a taxi. Lucas rested his hand on mine, and I squeezed his to reassure him. At that moment, he mattered more to me than anything else.

The taxi stopped, he paid, we got our things out of the trunk, and we walked toward the door of his building. He'd inherited the apartment when his grandfather died, and had lived there from the time he began his studies until the day he left with no turning back. No one had been there for two years.

We took the elevator to the top floor and he announced, "Here we are." He turned the key in the lock, and the door creaked as it opened, letting out stale air as Lucas entered, feeling around for the switch and turning on the lights that illuminated the hallway in front of us. "Home sweet home," he said.

I followed him to the master bedroom, where we dropped our bags. The place was an old two-bedroom with a living room, kitchen, and bathroom. The furnishings were simple and functional, and there was no decoration apart from a couple of framed pictures on the wall above the sofa. It amused me to think Lucas and I had lived so close to each other for several years. We might have even crossed each other on the street without knowing we would one day share so many tender moments.

Lucas opened the windows, and fresh night air filled the apartment. Used by now to the silence of the villa where we lived, I found the sounds of so many voices and cars unnerving.

"Should we order takeout? I'm hungry," he said.

"Isn't it a little late?"

"This isn't Sorrento. There will definitely be something open." He yawned.

I frowned. He was right. It wasn't Sorrento. And I already missed it.

The next morning, we got up early and went to the hospital.

"Are you sure you want to come?" he asked. We were waiting for the subway, and in the ten minutes it took for the train to arrive, he had asked me four times.

"If you weren't squeezing my hand so tight, maybe I'd say no," I responded, and when his grip loosened slightly, I added, "Don't be silly, Lucas. I'm not going to leave you alone."

He nodded and exhaled. He seemed to have been holding that breath in a long time. He was nervous. I was, too. After all he'd told me about his family, I knew it wasn't going to be an easy reunion for him, but I swore to myself I'd be there for him, no matter what happened.

When we got to the hospital, we headed to the cafeteria, where Lucas's sister had agreed to meet him. I asked him if he could see her, and he gazed around the room, which was full of people eating and drinking coffee. After a few seconds, he spotted her.

"Yeah, come on, she's in the back."

We zigzagged between tables and he stopped next to a brown-haired woman, her hair pulled up in a bun, absorbed in whatever she was typing into her phone.

"Hey, Lucía," he said.

She looked up, and I noticed her eyes were identical to his, light blue bordering on gray. She stood and rubbed her hands on her stomach. They were both tense, uncertain, as if neither knew how to act around the other, and only after a few apprehensive smiles did they lean in and give each other a kiss on each cheek.

"You look good," Lucas said.

She looked back and forth between us before answering, "You too."

He waited a few awkward seconds before introducing me. "Oh, and this is Maya. She's...a..." He hesitated and looked at me, seeming to wish I'd respond for him, before finishing the phrase, "She's a friend."

I don't know what I thought he was going to say, but that designation—*friend*—disappointed me. And it made me wonder if there were worse surprises in store.

Lucas and I had been going out for three months. We'd shared a home, a bed, and our deepest thoughts and feelings. But we'd never actually defined our relationship. It didn't have a name or label. We had never asked what *we* were, or if *we* were anything at all. So I didn't have a justification for getting mad. But who can control their feelings?

"Hi," I greeted her, and she smiled silently in response.

"How is he?" Lucas asked.

"He's still in the ICU. He's been there since they operated. His doctor says all we can do is wait to see how things develop."

"What about Mom?"

"She's in the waiting room. We spent the night there."

Sliding his hands into his pockets and gazing lost around the cafeteria, Lucas asked her, "Does she know I'm here?"

Lucía nodded and asked if he was going to see her.

"I don't have a reason to hide," he responded.

"If that's what you say," she told him, and the room seemed to darken a bit. Those five words concealed a profound resentment, I could tell, but Lucas didn't respond. He looked down, trying to restrain himself, on the edge of lashing out, and I almost wanted him to. He didn't deserve to be treated that way.

Lucía led us to the waiting room, which was on the same floor as the ICU. All through the hallways, I felt uncomfortable. I remembered my own week in the hospital, the pain I felt in my body and soul. The smell was the same. Maybe all hospitals smelled the same. Of disinfectant, fear, uncertainty.

There were around twenty chairs in the waiting room, a few tables, lots of people. But I saw her right away, and I knew who she was, though I'd never seen her. She had the same eyes as Lucas, the same nose, the same mouth. The same posture. And her perfectly calculated appearance and her coldness reminded me of my grandmother. She stood when she saw Lucas and glared at him as he approached.

"Hey, Mom," he said, and she inspected him as if he were a stranger before her eyes filled with tears.

"Two years, Lucas. Two years…" She groaned. "How could you do this to us? After we sacrificed so much for you."

"Mom, we agreed we wouldn't talk about the past," Lucía whispered.

"How am I supposed to not talk about the past?" Angrily, his mother stood close to him and looked up into his eyes. "Just running off that way, without saying a word, dropping all your commitments…"

"They weren't my commitments, Mom. They were commitments you made for me," he responded.

"You had obligations, Lucas! We could at least have talked it over."

"What was there to talk about, Mother? What did you expect of me?"

She admonished him, "The Lord commands us to forgive."

Impatiently, Lucas fired back, "He also commands us not to lie or bear false witness, but you would rather do that than let people know Dad's best friend's daughter had been sleeping around on me."

She pretended not to have heard him, squeezed the little cross hanging around her neck, whimpered again, and continued. "We could have worked it out, but you only thought about yourself. You vanished, and people started asking questions. Just imagine how ashamed I was when we had to call everyone and tell them the wedding was off. And Claudia…"

"Don't you dare, Mother." Lucas stopped her, his voice cracking like a whip. "I'm your son. I'm the one you were supposed to be protecting. How do you not understand that? And you wanted to force me to keep going in a relationship that was a lie."

"The poor girl, she made a mistake, and she regrets it. And she has to live with what she did."

I had to bite my tongue not to intervene. Lucas was tense, and he didn't look like himself. His shine was gone, a cloud was casting a shadow on him, and all his energy and verve seemed to have vanished. That was normal, in those circumstances, but it still struck me as unjust.

"She regrets exactly one thing, and that's the truth coming out, goddammit."

"How dare you speak like that in my presence," his mother murmured, and all at once, all the tears, all the pleading, were gone.

"People are watching us," Lucía remarked.

Their mother grimaced. Her expression was revolting.

"At the very least, you could have phoned and let us know you still cared for us," she told him.

Lucas replied, "That's a two-way street."

Finally she looked at me for the first time, knitting her brows. "And who are you?"

Lucas went to answer, but his sister cut him off. "Her name's Maya. She's a friend of Lucas's."

Seeming to apologize with his eyes, Lucas introduced his mother. "Maya, this is Águeda."

"It's nice to meet you," I said. "I'm so sorry for what's happened to your husband."

Ignoring me, her face emotionless, Águeda turned to Lucas again as I felt my pulse pounding in my temples, and said, "Son, I need to talk to you about your father. In private, if possible."

His cheeks reddening—I could tell he was angry at how his mother was treating me—he started to reply, "Whatever you have to say…" but I interrupted, telling him I would wait outside. He asked me not to, but I said it was better that way, and anyhow, I wanted to get a coffee from the machine. He walked a few steps away, apologizing over and over, telling me I should just ignore his mother.

"It doesn't matter," I said, trying to calm him down. "I'm fine. But I really do think you two ought to talk alone. Please, don't worry."

Ashamed, flushed, he whispered that he didn't want me to go.

"I'm not going anywhere, I promise."

I squeezed his hand and walked off, weak in the knees. I needed to get away from that woman as quickly as possible before I said something I'd regret.

I pushed open the door, closed my eyes, and counted to ten. Then I kept walking until I found the vending machines. Money in my hand, reading the options, I changed my mind and put my money away. That encounter with Lucas's family had made me almost sick to my stomach, and I had the feeling a coffee would only make it worse. I collapsed into a chair, and a thought crept into my mind and started settling in there.

Maybe I had been wrong, convincing Lucas to come back to Madrid.

Maybe I had pushed him to close a chapter of his life he wasn't ready to turn back to.

Maybe he didn't need to get over what had happened. Maybe all he needed was to forget about it and stay where he was, safe from that family that had hurt him so.

Maybe he had done it for me. Because he thought it was what I needed. An excuse to run away without looking like that was what I was doing. In fact, I was sure it was that when I looked deep into my heart, but that knowledge made me feel so miserable that I ignored it.

46

"Are you going to be OK?" he asked me for the third time.

Seeing the kindness, the vulnerability in his eyes, I nodded and stroked his cheek. "You're the one who's going to have to spend the night in the hospital."

He lifted my wrist and kissed it. "I don't know how long this is going to take, but we should talk about what we want to do afterward."

I knew what he meant. Going back to Sorrento. Where his things were. His home. His life. My life. The life I had built without realizing it and had lost before I'd really known what I had.

Going back wasn't an option for me anymore.

But neither was losing Lucas.

I felt so selfish, but in that moment, I couldn't help it, and I wasn't sure I wanted to go back. We had to find a way. Another path. Start over, the two of us, together, somewhere. Because whatever you want to say about the world, that's one thing it's got going for it: It's big, and you can always begin again.

"We'll talk," I whispered.

"Listen," Lucas told me, "don't lock yourself up in here. Go take a stroll."

"To where?"

"Go hang out with your friend Matías. Call him and tell him you're back."

"How do you know I haven't?"

"Because I know you, Maya."

The way he said that, I felt exposed, as though he had seen through the shell I hid behind to pretend that everything was all right. That shell without which I was just a bundle of emotions that spun around uncontrolled. And that meant Lucas was starting to understand the chaos inside me.

"I'm not sure that's a good thing," I told him.

"Why?"

I looked down at the Chinese writing on his shirt. "Maybe you'll stop liking me when you really get to know me. I've got a lot of defects, and I'm pretty sure the bad outweighs the good."

"And what about me?" he asked.

"You're perfect."

Forcing me to look up at him, he said, "You want to know the first thing I noticed about you?" I shook my head. "It wasn't those precious eyes. It wasn't those lips that drive me wild. It wasn't these." He grabbed my breasts, making me laugh, then brought his hands down to my waist. "It was the cracks in you, Maya. The wounds you tried to hide and I wanted to lick until they healed. The first day you opened your mouth to order that pizza, I could tell how fragile you were."

"Lick?" I asked sarcastically. "You mean like a cat?"

He leaned over and ran his tongue across my lips. "I love cats."

"I'm starting to like them, too," I said.

"We should get one and give it a funny name, like Aires or Odin or Thor."

"What if it's a girl?"

"Cookie," he responded without hesitation.

"What the hell kind of name is Cookie?"

He kissed me and I felt my bones turn to jelly. That was just the effect he had on me. I walked him to the door and stood there as he called the elevator. And I stayed there as he disappeared. I sighed and thought of Matías. I had been since I'd gotten to Madrid. I was dying to see him, but I wasn't ready to hear him say *I told you so*. With Lucas, I had to be strong, sensible, but with Matías...

With him, I could break down, and I was afraid I would.

I closed my eyes tight and told myself I was acting like a fool. If there was anything I needed just then, it was that slightly introverted, slightly rebellious guy who had been by my side since we were kids.

I wanted to surprise him, so I took a risk. I sat at the bus stop in front of his house and waited for him, hoping his routines and his schedule hadn't changed. He was predictable, always had been; improvisation was never his thing.

I saw him turn the corner in his athletic gear with a canvas bag on his shoulder. He passed right by me, distracted as ever, not even looking over. I walked behind him, trying not to burst out laughing, until he stopped in his doorway and started digging for his keys.

"You know, you and I would make the perfect couple," I said.

He froze. Inhaled. Turned slowly. Looked me in the eye. "No fucking way. What are you doing here?"

"Surprise!"

He hugged me so tight my ribs cracked, lifting me effortlessly off the ground. "I can't believe you're here!" he shouted.

I wrapped my hands around his neck and sniffled. I'd waited thirty seconds to start crying. A record. "You look amazing."

"You're the one who looks amazing. You hightailed it out of Madrid looking all depressed, skin and bones, and now..."

I slapped his shoulder. "What do you mean, skin and bones?"

"I'm just saying, you look gorgeous. That place is working wonders for you. But wait a minute... What are you doing here? Did something happen?"

"Lucas's dad is sick. They've operated on him, but they're not sure if he'll recover. I don't want him to have to go through this alone. He doesn't have what you'd call an amazing relationship with his family."

"Well, I'm not glad his father's doing badly, but I'm so happy you're here!"

"Me too. I was dying to see you, Matías. You want to go have a bite or something and catch up?"

"Sure. I just need five minutes to drop off my stuff and change."

I grabbed him by the elbow and pulled him away from the door. "You're handsome enough. Don't overdo it. I don't want all the boys interrupting us."

He obeyed cheerfully and followed along. With Matías, things were always simple like that. Comfortable. Familiar. It didn't matter that three months had passed since we'd last seen each other. Time was just a concept. It didn't have anything to do with the feelings that joined us.

We went to a tapas bar and settled down at a table, ordering a couple of dishes with nonalcoholic beers. The clink of silverware and glasses, the voices of the other diners, the TV in the back—all of it felt so much like home that I started turning nostalgic. Bittersweet. I was happy to be back, but it saddened me to realize this was no longer really my home.

"Tell me now," I said. "When do you go on tour? Do you already have your dates?"

He nodded and took a sip of his drink. "Beginning of November. We'll start in London, and yes, our dates are set. It's a packed schedule—more than I could have hoped for. So I won't be back in Madrid for a while."

"Why the frown, then? You should be happy?" I asked because he looked like he was getting ready for a funeral.

"I *am* happy, I can promise you that, but…" He stopped himself and started blushing like a child. And I'd never seen anything make Matías blush. "I met someone. And I can't believe I have to turn right around and leave."

I choked on a bite of asparagus and started coughing. "You met someone? Who?"

"His name's Rubén and we have absolutely nothing in common. But I like him. A lot."

"When did you meet?"

"Just three weeks ago."

I pretended to be indignant and threw a wrinkled napkin in his face. "Three weeks! And you didn't tell me anything?"

"I didn't want to jinx it, Maya!"

"So you really *do* like him," I said.

"He's perfect, and he's so sure of himself that I feel like an idiot when I'm with him. I swear, I've never had anything like this happen before."

It was hilarious, seeing him so excited like this. "Tell me more," I said.

"Well, he's twenty-nine years old, he's ungodly handsome. He works at a consultancy, but he loves music. He plays bass in a band with some friends."

"What kind of music?"

"Hard-core. Don't laugh! I actually had to go to one of his rehearsals a few nights ago, and oh my God! I wanted to die!"

I couldn't imagine anything more awkward for Matías. All he listened to was classical and easy listening, and then that playlist with nature sounds that he went to sleep to. He went on talking: about their first date, the first kiss three nights later, his body… It was so nice, seeing him all excited like that. I'd never known him to really like another guy. But at the same time, I couldn't help but feel scared for him. I didn't want anyone to hurt him. He was my little boy.

After eating, we wandered around for a while holding hands. I smiled, remembering other times we'd walked together. We'd always enjoyed that, and there was never any need to fill the silence with words. We understood each other the way few people did, and just a touch, a fleeting glance, or a cleared throat was enough to read each other like an open book.

But finally, he did ask me something, "Are you going to tell me what happened, or am I going to have to force it out of you?"

I conceded, "You were right. I should have told him as soon as I got there. It was wrong of me to keep my mouth shut, and now I've ruined everything."

Matías stopped and studied me for a few seconds before pulling me in for a hug. "Oh, girl, I'm so sorry."

"I screwed it up bad, Matías."

"Everything has a solution, babe."

"I'm not sure this does…"

There was a little playground behind us. We walked there and sat on a bench, close together, so he could wrap an arm around my shoulders. "Come on, now, get it all out," he said.

I did. I told him about Dante and his misguided jealousy. How Giulio had burst in and heard everything. How badly he'd taken what I'd revealed to him. The intensity of his rejection, his refusal even to admit that I might be right.

"Maya, you shouldn't have left," Matías responded.

"Why not? He didn't want me there."

"So? Fuck him!" he shouted. "He had sex with your mom and nine months later, you popped out. Maybe he's not your dad, but it damn sure seems like it. That's his responsibility, and he needs to face up to it."

"I can't force him, though. Not now."

"Force him, maybe not, but you've damn sure got a right to try, and if he isn't your father, great, you can both get on with your lives. If he is…"

"It's not that simple," I countered him.

"Maybe not, but you should have stayed there and tried, because—I know you're going to argue with me here—you didn't do anything wrong."

"Maybe not, but it's weighing on me. Anyway, I couldn't let Lucas face this alone. And, don't roll your eyes, it's not an excuse. If you knew what I know, you'd get it. You can't imagine what his family's like. And I know he'd do the same for me."

"OK, so what happens when Lucas solves his problems here and decides to go back?"

"Maybe he won't?" I mused.

I didn't bother concealing my apprehension. Not that there would have been a point. He always knew when I was hiding something from him. But maybe it was me I hoped to hide from? Because I had changed. I was hardly the same person I had been when I left. I had learned to let go, to let the mood carry me, to let my instincts hold the reins and my desires mark my rhythms, to let my impulses move me without thinking of tomorrow. Living for the minute. Flying high. Too high, maybe.

"I finally found my wings, you know," I told Matías.

"You never lost them, hon."

No, there was nothing he didn't know about me. He remembered every single crazy thing I'd told him through the years.

"But now I wonder if they're breaking," I said.

"It wouldn't matter. You'll always soar, Maya, even with broken wings. But just so you know, everything that's broken can be mended."

"Are you sure?"

"Of course I'm sure, dummy. And I can sew my ass off, so if those wings ever tear, just bring them my way and I'll have you airborne again in no time."

We laughed. It was that easy. Because I knew what he said was true. He would never let me crash into the ground. His arms would always be there to catch me at the right second.

47

I woke feeling his body sliding between the sheets. His hand reached under my skirt and rested on my stomach. He pulled me in to him, his chest resting against my back. His nose was in my hair inhaling softly as he said, "Hey."

"Hey."

"What time is it?"

"Almost nine."

I closed my eyes and relished the heat of his body as I asked, "How's he doing?"

"Same. A nurse let me in to see him during their shift change. I didn't think he'd look like that, you know? So...withered. He looks like he's aged ten years."

"How are you?"

"He was happy to see me though," Lucas said instead of answering. I turned and tried to glimpse him through the darkness, running a thumb under his eyes as if I could erase the bags under them.

"That's a good thing, right?" I asked.

"Yeah. I guess so."

He hugged me and kissed my forehead. It was warm, nice; his

heartbeat was slow beneath my hand. I closed my eyes again as I heard him confess, "I saw Claudia. She came by the hospital."

Those words were like a kick to the stomach, and I shivered, unsure how to respond in the silence that followed, unsure if I should say anything. Lucas added, "It was super uncomfortable. She started crying and asking me to forgive her in front of everybody. All I could do was drag her out in the hall so she'd stop bothering everyone. But even there, she kept putting on a show and I finally had to promise her we'd talk."

"Are you going to do it?"

"I said I needed time."

That was a yes. Lucas had only told me about his ex once, on a July afternoon, when we were sitting in a tub of cold water trying to keep cool. It was a short tale, brusque, but enough to know she had manipulated him as long as she'd known him. She'd played with his feelings, taken advantage of him, left him a shell of a person. And then he'd had to put himself back together all on his own.

And there she was, two years later, putting on an act, and that was all it took to bend him to her will. I was shaken by how easily she'd done it. "If that's what you want…"

"It's the last thing I want, Maya, but maybe my sister's right, maybe I really do owe it to her."

Another light went off in my head. "Your sister told you that?"

"She says Claudia and I never truly broke up because I refused to see her after I found out the kid wasn't mine, and then I left. She thinks we need to get closure on that. Maybe she's right. Maybe now's the time."

I was nearly hyperventilating. The possibility that I might lose Lucas was suddenly becoming real, and I was panicking because that brought home how much he mattered to me.

"I guess…" I said.

"What do you really think?"

"I mean, if she just wants to say she's sorry, maybe you can listen to her, maybe it will reassure you that you did make the right choice two years ago. Maybe it will make you feel better. She doesn't matter to you anymore, does she?"

"No, Maya, of course not. I never had any doubt about leaving her, and I have even less now that I've seen her again. I don't feel anything for her. Nothing at all."

"Nothing?"

He smiled and pulled me in to him, and I curled up into a little ball and let him run his fingers through my hair.

"Unless you count anger and resentment... But even those I don't feel the way I did before. And maybe forgiving her will help me shed those bad feelings too. And once that's done, the whole thing will be over forever."

I wanted to believe him, I really did. I wanted to believe it was as simple as it seemed to him. But a little voice in my head was whispering things I didn't want to hear.

"I'm so glad you came with me," he said a few seconds later, sounding like he was about to fall asleep.

"I couldn't abandon a friend like that," I said on purpose, throwing an obstacle in his path to see if he'd stumble or skip past it. Because I didn't know what I was to him, what I meant, and I was too much of a coward to just ask him. If I did, his answer might be the end of me, and I'd have to tell him how I really felt—and the mere idea of doing that paralyzed me.

"Friend," he said, and patted me on the head.

Disappointment ate into me like acid. I felt love. Pain. Anxiety. Insecurity. Loneliness that wouldn't end.

Lucas started breathing deeper, and his hands went limp on my body. Mine, though, were holding onto his like a lifeline. And that's how I fell asleep.

48

Fifteen minutes passed as I tried to decide whether or not to look at Monica's message. I was scared of what I might find there. The guilt and remorse didn't help. The realization that I'd screwed up. And that I might have screwed things up for Giulio and Dante, too. I'd run away from everything and everyone, and I hadn't even bothered looking back.

What did that say about me? *That you're human*, Lucas told me every time I brought it up.

But that was no consolation. Life had put me to the test, and I'd failed. And then I hadn't bothered to face the consequences, even though I knew people were hurting because of what I'd said and what I'd decided not to say. But was I going to keep sticking my head in the sand? Avoiding things had gotten me into this, so I decided to open the message.

It stirred me deep inside. All I found were words of care, a friend concerned about Lucas and me, someone who just wanted everything to be resolved as quickly as possible so we could come home soon.

Home.

That word was like an arrow in my flesh.

She sent me greetings and good wishes from Catalina, Marco, and everyone else. I had to dry my tears with my sweater sleeve. I took for granted that *everyone else* didn't include Giulio and Dante. It was childish of me to even hope it might. It made me think maybe they'd kept what had happened between us secret, and I didn't know if I liked that or not. A part of me wanted everything to explode, to come out, so I could get out from under the weight that was crushing me. Of course, I could make that happen, but I was incapable of taking the step on my own.

49

I had just emerged from the shower when the doorbell rang. I took the bathrobe down from the hook on the door and threw it on. Lucas was still asleep, and I didn't want anyone to wake him. Or so I thought until I turned the doorknob and heard a woman's voice.

"I just want to see you."

"Claudia, I told you I needed time."

"I know, Lucas, but it's been two years. Isn't that time enough?"

"You can't keep doing this, always imposing on me like this. I'm not going to allow it."

"I'm not imposing," Claudia said. "I just want us to talk. It can't be that hard, Lucas."

I cracked the door a little wider and heard Lucas respond, "Actually it is that hard. So look, I *will* have this conversation with you, but I *won't* do it right now. Understand?"

"No, I don't understand," she insisted. "Lucas, do it for me, please, for all that we've shared. Give me a chance… Let's go out to eat. Just listen to me. I'm not asking you for something impossible."

"Maybe, but you don't have a right to ask me for anything."

"I know I didn't treat you right. I know what I did was horrible, and I regret it every single day. But I learned my lesson. I swear. Losing you…losing you was the worst…"

"I can't do this again," he interrupted her. "I can't let you come back into my life and try to make my whole world revolve around you."

"It's not that," Claudia said. "I know that would be pointless."

"What is it, then?"

"I want you to forgive me. I want us to be friends the way we were before. At least to try. I've changed, Lucas, and I want to show you that."

"You don't have to show me anything, just respect what I say."

"I am. I will. I did for two years. I accepted that you were gone, and I admitted my mistakes. But you're here now, and…if only you knew how excited I was when your mother called and told me you were back! I've been waiting for this opportunity forever."

"Well, then, you can wait a little longer."

I heard the front door opening, and I held my breath, waiting for her to go. I was tired of her whiny, cloying voice and I wanted her as far from Lucas as possible. But no, I heard her again, "Why is it so hard for you to do this one little thing for me?" She was so irritating that I wanted to scream.

"Because I don't love you anymore," he responded calmly. And I knew I couldn't stay on the sidelines anymore. She wouldn't give up even if he screamed in her face and threw her out by force.

I walked out of the bathroom and down the hall with a sure step, and when I rounded the corner, I saw her: tall, with straight blond hair and bangs. Her eyes were honey-colored, and she had dimpled cheeks. She was wearing a snug red dress, short, and matching high heels. She was beautiful. I hadn't realized she'd be so pretty, and that made me conscious of what I must look like then, in a bathrobe three sizes too big with my hair still damp and unbrushed.

Claudia looked me over smugly, then turned back to Lucas as

though I didn't even deserve her attention, and she snapped, "Fine, I'll go, but call me, please. I still have the same number. I'm sure you remember it, even if you deleted it from your phone. I miss you. A lot." She rested a hand on his bare chest, and he stepped back. Then she walked out, her shoes sounding like firecrackers on the floor of the hall.

Lucas shut the door and looked at me red-faced with countless emotions in his eyes. He rubbed the back of his neck, then stretched back both arms.

"That was Claudia," he said. I nodded, wanting to vomit.

I told him I was going to dress, and I stood there confused, trying to contain myself. Then I walked back into the bathroom and tried to hold back the tears.

I wonder now if it was right of me not to say more. If things would have gone differently if I'd told him everything I thought then instead of remaining silent.

I think now of all the details I decided to ignore. How I let him walk alone, lost, when he must have needed me to be his compass. But how could I guide him when I didn't know where I was either?

I realize now that it had to be that way. We were naive. We thought we were walking side by side, and I guess we were, for a while. But we couldn't see the road forking up ahead, pushing us in opposite directions.

50

Despite all prognoses, Lucas's father started to get better. A few days after we arrived in Madrid, they transferred him out of the ICU and into the cardiology unit. They'd need to continue monitoring him constantly. He needed help for almost everything, and Lucas started spending more and more time at the office.

He didn't talk much about his family. Not with me, at least. But not with them, either, I'm pretty sure. It was as if they'd reached a tacit agreement to leave behind the past and start over. But it's dangerous to start over when the wounds are still raw and words still burn, when mistakes weigh heavy and *I trust you* is still just a three-syllable phrase.

The ugliness doesn't disappear just because you turn away from it. You can't rub out mistakes with an eraser. And when you push all that stuff off into a corner, eventually it overflows. Or maybe it doesn't, and that's even worse. Because then that inertia takes you over. You close your eyes, cover your ears, bite your tongue, forget what your senses were even for, and you disconnect from life, surrounded by fog.

Then one day, your life ceases to belong to you, and others dictate to you what you should do.

And that's when you disappear.

I could see that. I could see Lucas fading away at the edges. A little bit more every day.

And I was watching it happen. Motionless. And it was happening to me, too, and the person I was faded away like chalk streaks under rain.

51

I was trying and failing to screw on the top of the Moka pot when Lucas appeared in the kitchen. He stopped behind me, and I felt his lips on my shoulder.

"You want me to help you with that?"

I stepped aside to make room for him. "Yes, please."

I nearly choked on these words as I saw how he was dressed: in a dark gray suit with a blue shirt, hair combed and gelled, taming his dark curls. He looked like another person. That was the first thing I thought. But then, he seemed so comfortable in those clothes that it was almost as if he'd been born in them.

He screwed the cap on deftly and placed the coffee maker on the stove. He'd told me the night before that he'd be going to a lawyer with his father to fill out a power of attorney for the business. Supposedly it couldn't wait.

He'd be busy, but only for a few days. He had some meetings to attend, some documents to sign, and then he'd make sure everything at the business was running as it should. His father had asked him, and he couldn't say no when the man was in such a delicate state. Besides, he knew how the company ran. It was the only thing that made sense.

"Stop staring at me that way," Lucas said.

"I'm not!"

He turned and leaved against the counter. "Do I look that weird to you?"

"Your clothes are pressed. It's unnatural."

"My mother would die if she heard you."

"She nearly died when she saw me," I said.

He laughed and hugged me, and I didn't resist. I loved having him close. Kissing him… All those things we barely did now, because we barely saw each other. And when we did find some time together, nothing was the same as before in Sorrento. Lucas talked less, laughed less. He was colder, more introverted.

And I…

All I could think about was how much I missed what we used to be.

I couldn't say what would become of us.

I couldn't even say what we were then.

It hurt me, feeling that way. Having those thoughts. Doing nothing about it. Because I wouldn't tackle the issue and I had no idea what was stopping me.

Hours later, Lucas wrote me to let me know he'd be having lunch out with his father's partner before heading back to the hospital. A part of me got angry with him. I knew it wasn't fair, but emotions aren't something you can control. They arise, they grow, they extend like roots, enveloping you and sucking all your energy. You can pretend you don't feel them. You can convince yourself they don't exist, but that won't make them disappear. They are shadows with a life of their own. Run as far as you like, get as far away as you can, but they'll still be there, clinging to your feet. Even on the darkest days.

That anger stayed with me the rest of the day, and grew when I thought of Sorrento, Giulio, Catalina, and everyone else. Of evenings in the garden, days on the beach, nights curled up next to Lucas's body. I wanted that life back more than anything. And losing it was killing me. There was no getting around it.

Matías called me in midafternoon. It was Rodrigo's birthday and they were going to give him a surprise when the rehearsal was over. I said I couldn't go, and that made me feel even worse. Moreover, it was pointless. Matías was an expert at dismantling my excuses, and for ten minutes, he parried every attempt I offered to get out of it. He made me feel like an idiot for avoiding Antoine and Sofía, and like a bigger idiot for ducking the people who had been my friends for so long. For hiding from everything and everyone like I was a criminal.

"You win," I told him, "I'll be there."

"Eight o'clock at La Cantina, then. Don't be late."

At ten to eight, I was walking into Matadero, a former slaughterhouse that had been converted into a series of arts spaces and bars, and was walking toward our meeting place. I liked it there, down in the old boiler room, but even better was the patio with its plants everywhere and its furnishings made of cast-off shipping pallets.

Everyone was already there when I arrived, and soon I was being kissed, hugged, greeted on all sides. It was moving—how couldn't it be? And I felt stupid for almost missing out on it all. For being so weird and antisocial. For giving up so quickly what mattered to me, for not staking my claim to what was mine. Especially when nobody had forced me to go but myself.

"Maya!"

"Fyodora!" I exclaimed.

She kissed me all over my face.

"You bitch! How am I only just now finding out that you're back?"

Before I could answer, everyone fell silent, apart from soft murmurs and chuckling, and I looked around and crossed eyes with Sofía. Strangely, I didn't feel anything at all. Nothing good, nothing bad.

Just nothing. Whatever wounds I'd had before were healed over. There wasn't even a scar left. Barely a memory of why she might have ever mattered to me.

I laughed when I saw Matías guide Rodrigo in with a blindfold on his eyes. Antoine was with them. Antoine looked shocked when he saw me. Clearly, Matías hadn't bothered informing him or Rodrigo, who rushed over as soon as he could see again. I hugged him tight and said, "Happy birthday!" Then I frowned and apologized for not bringing a present with me.

"You're my present. I'm so happy to see you!"

I laughed and let myself be hugged again.

As the night went on, I was surprised to realize I was having fun. At some point, I got up to go to the bathroom and stopped at the bar for an iced tea. The place was crowded, and I didn't think anything of it at first when I felt someone behind me. But then I turned and saw it was Antoine with an awkward grin on his face. "Hey," he said.

"Hey."

He sighed and responded, "Well, that's a start. Honestly, I didn't think you'd talk to me."

"And yet, here we are."

"Yeah." He shifted his weight from one foot to the other. "I've called and texted you I don't know how many times these past few months."

"I know. But I didn't feel like talking," I admitted.

His green eyes looked down and he prepared himself for his grand declaration, "I'm sorry, Maya. I was stupid for not valuing what we had, and not a day passes when I don't regret what I did. And if you wanted, I... We—"

I raised a hand to stop him. "I'm with someone, Antoine."

He nodded several times, squeezing the bottle in his hand. When he opened his mouth, I thought he would say something vengeful, but instead, he struggled meekly to get out the words, "Is it serious?"

"I don't know, honestly. But I hope so."

"Where did you meet?"

"In Italy."

"Italy. Wait a minute. Is that where you've been all this time?"

"Yeah, you didn't know? Matías didn't say anything?"

I had just taken it for granted, with Matías living with him, that where I was would have come up between them at some point during those past few months. They were friends, after all.

"No! The son of a bitch has kept the whole thing to himself. I guess you did want to get away from me then."

"It wasn't about you, actually."

Again, he looked at me with surprise mixed with disappointment. It was hard for him, learning he wasn't the center of the universe. I'd always hated and loved that in him in equal measure.

"Why'd you go then?" he asked.

"Because..."

And without my thinking about them, the words flowed out of me, and he stood still, absorbing them as though he were afraid of ruining something if he spoke up. He gave me his full attention. I think it was the first time he truly ever listened to me. Tried to understand me. Took an interest in what I was saying. All things Lucas had done from the very beginning.

Lucas... The thought of him opened an enormous hole in me. I glanced at my phone and saw I had it on silent, so I'd missed several calls and messages. I wrote him quickly, and he responded immediately, letting me know he had left the hospital and was taking his mother home to get some documents he'd need the next day. He told me to enjoy my time with my friends, and that was the end of the conversation.

I stayed there another hour, then said goodbye to everyone and told Matías and Rodrigo we'd be in touch soon to hang out. Then I caught a taxi back to Lucas's place.

As soon as I arrived, I showered and got into bed. The sheets were cold when they touched my skin. Autumn had brought with it a drop in temperature, but it was the absence of Lucas's body that made me shiver.

He arrived maybe half an hour later. I heard him making a racket in the kitchen and then entering the bathroom, where the shower soon started hissing. Afterward, he opened the bedroom door. All he had on was a towel around his hips, and he dropped it on the floor before getting into bed. I didn't move, even though I was dying to wrap myself around him and feel his warmth. I was angry. Very angry. Whether or not it made sense.

"I'm sorry," Lucas said.

Hearing my pulse in my ears, I turned and saw him lying on his back looking over at me.

"Sorry for what?"

"Everything. Not being with you, leaving you alone, not having time for us… It'll just be a few days, I promise. Dad's getting better."

He leaned over me, touched my cheek, touched his hot, damp lips to mine. I didn't want to kiss back, but my will broke when I felt his tongue working its way into my mouth. I moaned: from love, from pain, from anger, from need. When I leaned back to look at him, he was gazing into me with such desire that I trembled. We were hungry for each other.

I shoved my fingers into his hair and trapped one of his lips between my teeth. I kissed him with rage. I needed to let lose everything that was burning inside me. All those feelings boiling up, setting me alight, feelings it was hard to distinguish, separate, name… feelings I myself didn't understand. I felt and felt, and I didn't know how to stop feeling, how to silence the voices in my head commanding me to say things I couldn't.

Suddenly I found myself naked. I pushed his chest and forced him onto his back. He watched me as I climbed on top of him and slowly took him inside me. My muscles were tense. His fingers dug into my hips, guiding me. He clenched his teeth and held his breath as I moved back and forth on top of him. I did it for me, not for him. I needed this, and Lucas seemed to know, because he didn't hesitate to let me take control. He opened up to me, gave himself to me with each and every gesture, molecule by molecule, until he was entirely mine, without the need for words.

I went faster, he thrust deeper, and amid the whirlwind, I found his lips. He groaned, a loud moan erupted from my throat; I shook, he shook too as I collapsed onto his chest.

We remained there, holding each other in silence as he drew shapes on my back with his fingers, making me shiver. I closed my eyes and dreamed that we were elsewhere, in another room, in another bed, where it smelled of lemon and salt.

52

Monica wrote me.

> *They're here! Let me introduce you to Ezio and Velia. I feel like*
> *I've been run over by a truck, but when I look at them, I know I'd*
> *be happy to do it all over. Now you have to come back soon. There*
> *are two little people here dying to meet you. I miss you both.*

I looked at the photo of the babies and had to blink over and over to clear the tears from my eyes. They were so precious, so little... I wished I'd been there. But I wasn't, and I wasn't sure I'd ever go back.

I sat on the sofa for hours.

And on the other side of the wall, the world kept turning. The days passed. Life passed me by.

53

Sometimes, life transforms into a big wave. All you see is water and foam, and you tell yourself not to be scared of them. That there's nothing there that can hurt you. You feel confident. You stand on the shore, watching it come close.

But what's actually approaching you is a solid, impenetrable wall, and you'll never survive the impact. And that's what life is like, right? Nothing lasts. Even the wave, big as it is, breaks on the shore and disappears. And it all happens in an instant.

54

I woke, and Lucas was already gone.

I stayed in bed, hugging the pillow and staring at the wall. It wasn't like I had anything better to do. We'd been in Madrid two weeks, and the time was starting to weigh on me like a stone. The days passed, I did nothing, I just waited and waited, and there was nothing else for me but to try to be patient.

Supposedly it was temporary. Lucas's father was much better. The doctors would send him home any day now. When that happened, Lucas and I would need to talk. About my options, his options, how compatible they were or weren't. In the meantime, all I could do was think. Too much. And wait.

At least I'd be seeing Matías that night for dinner. He wanted me to meet Rubén. And it was the perfect moment to introduce him to Lucas, who had promised he'd come along.

My phone rang, forcing me to drag myself out of bed. It was Fyodora. We decided to meet for lunch at a place close to the conservatory. When I got there, she was already at a table waiting for me. She got up to hug me, and I took the chair next to her, holding her hand on top of the tablecloth.

We ordered and brought each other up to date on our lives: what

Italy was like, what was happening with Lucas and Giulio. How badly things had ended, the reason I'd suddenly come back.

She told me this was her last year as teacher at the conservatory. She was also leaving behind her post as répétiteuse at the ballet. She didn't have the same energy as before. Her body wasn't as agile. She was looking forward to retirement. She needed to spend time with her family.

"I could propose you take over for me. You'd be good at it."

"As répétiteuse? But I'm not trained for that!"

"You have everything you need, and as long as you're careful, your injuries won't hold you back. If I can still do it, you could do it a thousand times better. We could try."

"Listen, it's an opportunity," I said. "I won't argue with you about that."

"It's a job, Maya. It means stability, independence, a future doing something you love."

"I don't know, though, Fyodora..."

"You've still got three months to think it over."

I looked down at the bread crumbs on the tablecloth and started crushing them with my fingertip.

"I don't even know if I'll stay in Madrid. I really have no idea what I'm going to do."

She shook her head and grinned as she studied my face. "Can I give you some advice?"

"Of course."

Squeezing my hand tight, she said, "Don't follow anyone. Especially not a man. If you're on the same path, fine, walk it together. But if you aren't, as much as it hurts, you need to find your own way."

Her words made me shiver. "Why do you say that?"

"Because you deserve a life that belongs to you! Time passes, Maya. It doesn't stop, and it doesn't turn back. It only goes in one direction: forward. And one day you're my age and all you can do is look back. Now when you do that, what would you like to see?"

I remembered something she said to me one day, how vehemently she had uttered it, and I repeated it back to her. "I want to be the hero of my own story, not a bit actor in the stories of others."

"Exactly. No matter how much Lucas means to you, you can't base your choices on the role he's going to play in your life. Only you can decide where you'll go and when, and who you want to be. And as for Giulio, don't forget that your right to know matters as much as his right to ignore the truth. And there's nothing wrong with being a little selfish in a situation like that."

I thought her words over, started seeing myself through her eyes, started realizing that we all have to make our place in the world, and saw that I had been waiting for other people to do that for me. I had thought that the past three months had changed me, that I was a new Maya, a different one, but it wasn't true. What I'd thought life was— something easy, something that was in my hands—was a mirage.

I felt edgy all afternoon, and when I got home, I kept walking back and forth unsure whether to stand, sit, or what. All I could think about was that feeling of tension that was growing inside me.

Then the doorbell rang.

I looked at the clock. It was almost seven. I assumed it was Lucas, that maybe he'd forgotten his keys. He was a little late, but that was fine. We still had plenty of time to get ready and go to Matías's place.

I unlocked the door and opened up, and my blood froze in my veins as I saw Claudia in the hallway. "Is Lucas here?" she asked.

Hello to you, too, I thought.

"No."

She glared at me and said, "It's OK, I'll wait." Then she tried to walk in, but I stood in her way, instinctively, as if doing so were a way of defending myself.

"Sorry, I've got to go out," I told her.

"And?"

"And I'm not sure Lucas would agree with you being here by yourself."

She smiled mockingly at me and pushed her hair out of her face. It was impossible not to notice her fresh, expensive manicure.

"I hope you're aware that you're just some girl he's met. And this used to be my home."

She'd said that to hurt me, and it worked. I felt as if a knife had been plunged into my stomach. "You said it," I replied. "It *used* to be your home. It's not anymore."

Her nostrils flared and her tongue poked from the corner of her mouth. She shook her head and said softly, "Don't get too comfortable here." Then she turned and walked to the elevator. I pushed the door closed and hurried over to the window, where I saw her crossing the street and stopping on the opposite sidewalk, where she remained, waiting for Lucas. It was obvious she wouldn't leave until she saw him.

I stood behind the curtains, the pressure in my chest making it hard to breathe. Lucas appeared a few seconds later, as though summoned. He looked up at the building, walking quickly, jacket slung over his shoulder, holding his computer bag in his other hand.

Then he saw Claudia and stopped and she ran over to him. I watched, hypnotized, as they talked. Lucas stepped back every time she tried to get close to him. Their conversation stretched on, and at times it seemed they were arguing, and Claudia started flapping her arms.

Then Lucas raised his hands in surrender and nodded. After a few more words, he took out his phone and typed something. Seconds later, my phone buzzed. They walked off together. I wanted to scream.

I closed my eyes, but the image still stung. I tried not to be scared.

I knew I could trust Lucas, but we had never really talked about our relationship, and we definitely hadn't placed a label on it. I had taken for granted that we were exclusive, that we respected each other too much for games.

But now I felt like I was losing him. All I knew of his past was what he had told me. I thought that was enough, but now I had the suspicion that the way he'd let his family bully him and bend him to their will was happening again. They were good at manipulating him. I'd seen that in the two weeks since I'd been there, and Lucas was going back to his old self. Always acting for them, not asking himself what he needed.

He was turning back into the very person he swore he'd never be again.

55

Lucas's message was short and didn't give any details.

> Something came up, you go ahead. Send me the address
> and I'll be there when I can.

That's what I did. I sent the address. Just the address. No kind words, no reproaches, even if I was dying to say so much to him, and most of it wasn't good. Maybe a part of me thought that he didn't really deserve that. Maybe I too was letting myself be carried along, keeping my mouth shut, not complaining. Putting up with each setback. Accepting whatever happened. Just dealing with it, just getting by.

I rang the doorbell. My best friend opened up with a huge smile on his face. But then he looked over my shoulder and saw there was no one else there.

"You're alone?"

"Something came up. Lucas is going to be late," I responded as if it didn't worry me a bit. Matías's eyebrows rose. I hated him knowing me so well. I added, "Look, he may not even come, OK? His ex showed up to get him, and..."

Matías hugged me, and those words died against his chest. "It's his loss. Fuck him. You're the only one I care about."

I gave him a smack, but I was grateful. As I peered into the living room, I saw Antoine sitting on the couch. "What is he doing here? You told me he wouldn't be here."

"He said he was going to hang out with friends, but they canceled. Anyway, he *does* live here. It's not like I can kick him out."

"Fine."

"Are you sure?" he asked.

"We talked at Rodrigo's birthday, and it was all right. Don't worry about it."

"Great! Then get inside, I'm dying to introduce you to Rubén."

Matías was right when he told me they had nothing in common. He and Rubén were polar opposites. And yet, if you looked at them closely, you could see they were really two halves that fit together effortlessly. Their differences complemented each other, and right away it was hard to imagine one without the other. They were perfect for each other, the way they shared everything: laughter, looks, caresses.

"They look good together, don't they?" Antoine asked, taking a lemon cake out of the refrigerator.

"Matías looks happy."

"I think he is. Will you pass me some plates?"

I opened the cabinet, grabbed a stack, laid them out on the table, and waited for Antoine to cut us each a portion. The doorbell rang, Matías scurried off, and a few seconds later, I heard Lucas's voice. That irresistible voice. Rodrigo hurried into the kitchen. "Your guy's here," he said. "Antoine, do we still have some beer in the fridge?"

"There's a six-pack in the bottom drawer," Antoine responded. He smirked at me as though to say, *Everything's OK*, and then asked me to help him carry out the cake. I nodded and we walked back out to find Matías and Rubén sitting at the table talking to Lucas. They had pulled over a folding chair from the balcony and made a space for him. Lucas caught my eye as I set out the plates, and he smiled and said, "Hey."

"Hey," I replied, and I admit it sounded cutting, but I was tense, angry, and incredulous. He must have noticed. After all, he always knew what I was feeling. He could see straight through me, but I also wondered if a guilty conscience had put him on high alert.

Antoine introduced himself and told Lucas it was nice to meet him and he'd heard so much about him. Lucas responded with a typical manly handshake.

I was uncomfortable, but the rest of the evening was relaxed. Lucas was spilling over with charm as always, and soon my friends were in love with him. He was like that: He never needed to try, he effortlessly drew people in. He was so self-assured, so seductive, and his presence filled the room. He was himself again, and that somehow disconcerted me even worse. I didn't get it. I didn't get what his family and Claudia did to him to split him into two different people who just happened to inhabit the same body.

"Should we catch a cab?" he asked when we walked out.

"It's not far. I'd rather walk."

We crossed the deserted street and headed to his apartment. Lucas's hands were in his jeans pockets. He had changed before coming to Matías's, but I chose not to say anything about it. I wasn't going to force the conversation, I'd decided not even to ask him what had happened that afternoon. If he wanted to bring it up, he would.

"I thought you didn't want to see him again," Lucas said.

"Who?"

"Antoine."

I didn't like that at all, and I think my expression showed it. And under the circumstances, I found his reaction out of place, to say the least…

"Things change. We have friends in common and I thought it was best to play nice."

"Since when?"

"Since the other day, when I ran into him," I replied.

"And now you've run into him again. Will there be more times? Have there been?"

I stopped and looked him in the eyes, saw the storm brewing behind them, but didn't care, because I had a storm of my own. "What are you insinuating?"

"Nothing."

"You want me to spend every day alone, shut up in your apartment, with you barely ever showing your face?"

My cheeks were hot, but I saw a regretful look on his face that made me ease back a bit.

"That's not what I said," he responded.

"Good, because I'm not doing anything you haven't done first. And at least I'm not seeing my ex without telling you."

"What does that mean?" he asked suspiciously.

"I saw you talking to Claudia and then walking off with her, and you didn't come out and tell me. Instead you just said something had come up."

He exhaled and shook his head. "I was going to tell you."

"When?"

"Now. At home. That was my plan."

"Why not here? On the sidewalk?"

Open, sincere, the way he always was with me, he admitted, "I found her waiting outside for me when I came back from work."

"I know. I already told you that I saw you. She showed up at the apartment. She wanted to wait inside, but I didn't feel comfortable letting her in."

Looking uncomfortable, he said, "She went inside?"

"I told you, I wouldn't let her in."

He looked up into a tree that was rising over us in someone's yard. I knew he had something he wanted to say, and I was thinking the same thing: In many things, he and I were exactly alike. Claudia, with her sweet little face and her big eyes, was bad news: malicious, and a pro at sowing misunderstandings when she felt like it.

"Maya, all we did is talk, I promise. She's been chasing me down ever since I got here, and I finally folded. I thought it was the best thing that I'd give her what she wanted and she'd leave me alone."

"So what *did* she want?"

"She wanted to justify everything that happened, ask me to forgive her…and I did. I told her I was over it. I told her whatever I thought she wanted to hear to put all this behind us for once. I'm tired, OK? I'm tired of feeling uncomfortable every time I see her. I want to go to my parents' house without worrying I might find her there, because whether I like it or not, she's part of my family. I'm doing the best that I can…"

"So you say," I told him.

He rubbed the back of his neck. "She fucked my life up, OK? And I used to hate her for it. But now…I just don't feel anything. Pity, I guess. Do you believe me?"

"I don't have any reason to doubt you, Lucas."

"I'm just trying to make things right for everyone. Do the right thing. Even if I don't always know what that is."

"It's fine." I bridged the distance between us and cupped his face.

"I don't want you to be mad at me, Maya."

"I'm not mad at you. It's just everything: the situation, being alone… I've basically had my arms crossed for two weeks and I don't know what I should do, I don't even know if Madrid is an option for me."

"Well, for me it isn't," he said. "I've been thinking about selling the apartment even. This is temporary. I'm not staying here."

Those words helped me pull myself together. They gave me hope. I didn't want to lose him. I wanted to stay with him. I wanted to find some corner of the world where we could just be, where we could let life happen. That was all I needed.

"Are you telling the truth?" I asked him.

"Yeah. But Dad said something, and he's right: It's not a good time to sell. I should probably wait a few months."

"So you are making progress, you and him."

"I'm trying," Lucas said. "I just need you to hold on a little bit. My father will go back home soon and he'll take up the reins again. My sister will help him. She's more qualified than I am, and now he seems ready to let her be part of the business."

"He wasn't before?"

Lucas shrugged. "He's always been a little sexist in that way. But I guess almost dying changed his perspective. What I mean with all this is…that I love being with you, and I don't want to fuck up what we have."

"What do we have then, Lucas?" I asked.

"This. You and me."

I didn't like that answer.

It wasn't enough.

But I didn't push it.

And by letting it slide, I allowed all my doubts to overtake me again. The insecurities that consumed me a little more every day. I should have opened up to him. That I didn't was my fault.

I let him hold me, but I didn't say a word.

56

The morning sunlight was glowing through the curtains when I woke. I opened my eyes, expecting to find Lucas next to me, but his side of the bed was empty and his clothes were gone from the chair where he'd laid them.

He was getting up earlier and earlier every morning.

I walked to the bathroom, where the tile was cold under my feet and gave me goose bumps. It was freezing in there, but there was still vapor on the walls and mirror. I turned on the heater next to the door and waited for it to heat up before stripping off my clothes and getting into the shower.

It was a cold October, and I didn't have anything warm to wear. After getting dressed and eating a quick breakfast, I walked to my family's neighborhood, where I had lived my whole life. It was strange, going into my old building and smelling that familiar scent in the vestibule.

I went down to the storage room, got the door open on the third pull, and felt the brief fear, as the light flickered on, that my things would no longer be there—that my grandmother had flown into a rage and decided to get rid of everything that had anything to do with me. But the fear vanished as soon as I saw all my boxes were exactly where I'd left them.

I pulled the ones with clothes in them onto the floor and cut the tape with the corner of one of my keys. I'd brought a suitcase with me, and I filled it with pants, long-sleeved shirts, and a couple of jackets. Then I put the boxes back where they had been.

I stared at the room for a moment.

It was still hard for me to accept the reality it represented.

That time passes, dies away, doesn't wait. And I was moving in circles.

Three months before, I'd been in that same room, looking at those same boxes.

Nothing had changed since then, and nothing was the same.

Least of all me.

57

The days passed, and finally they discharged Lucas's father. But nothing changed. Lucas kept working at his family's company, had his meetings in the evenings, had lunch with buyers and suppliers. And apart from all the work, there was his family always on his heels. His phone never stopped ringing. If it wasn't his mother, it was his sister or his father, and Lucas never said no to them, no matter the time, the place, or what they wanted.

Claudia was the same way.

And every day, Lucas was less connected to me, less connected to his emotions. He was so good at hiding his feelings that not even he was capable of finding them inside himself. An invisible wall rose between us, and I was the only person who seemed to notice or care.

One day I was watching him dress, missing him already, missing being beside him, talking laughing, doing nothing. Entrusting him with my thoughts, him entrusting me with his.

He was buttoning his jeans and he looked at me sweetly, and I wanted to let out everything that was inside me, but I couldn't. The words got caught in my throat.

He threw on a leather jacket and put his phone and wallet in his pockets.

"Shall we?" he asked.

"Sure."

He came close, touched my face, kissed me, looked at me as if trying to read what was going through my head. But at the same time, he looked scared of it. He was baffled and resorted to silence: a silence of a kind that was now starting to define the way we related to each other. A silence that said too much. Much more than any words could.

"It's late," I whispered.

He nodded and took my hand.

We walked out of the apartment and to a crossing where we waited for a cab to come. We were supposed to meet Matías and Rubén at a restaurant on the Plaza del Carmen. That night, Rubén's group was giving a concert nearby at the Wurlitzer Ballroom, and they'd invited us to come. I looked out the window on the ride over, feeling the tension in me give way. I was about to see my friends, chill out, have fun. Do something normal with Lucas for the first time in ages.

I saw Matías sitting at a table on the patio. He stood when he saw us and hugged me tight, rocking me back and forth and saying, "There's my girl."

Rubén then gave me a kiss on each cheek and I sat down next to him. He had his hair pulled back in a bun—sort of, because it was sticking out in all directions—and was wearing a gray hooded sweatshirt. His fingers were covered in rings and he had a piercing in his lower lip. I liked his style, but what I really liked was how much Matías liked him.

"What time's the concert?" I asked.

"Eleven thirty," Rubén answered.

"You look nervous," I said.

"I always feel hysterical when I have a show. Fortunately, it all goes away once I'm onstage."

A waiter came and took our order. "What's your band's name?" Lucas asked. "I can't remember if you told us last time."

"Bad Sirens," Rubén responded.

"Any albums we can check out?" Lucas inquired.

"I wish. For now, there's just a demo with five songs we recorded last summer. You can find that on Spotify, Apple Music, Deezer, and so on. It's doing OK, to tell the truth. So maybe we'll record an album soon. We're writing songs now."

Lucas's phone started ringing while Rubén was speaking, and he pulled it out and looked at it, then begged our pardon, stood, and walked away. I followed him with my eyes while remarking that it sounded cool. Then I squeezed Rubén's hand and thanked him for inviting us.

"No worries," he said. "I hope you like it, but if not, you can always do like Matías and wear earplugs."

"That's a lie!" Matías responded. "I love you guys' music. I've never put in earplugs in my life!"

"Liar," Rubén said. Then he bent over as if to tell me a secret, "Last time, he forgot to take them out, and I thought he'd gone deaf because of the speakers. I was actually scared!"

I laughed as Matías pretended to feel embarrassed, and just then, the waiter laid out our dishes and Lucas returned. I asked him if everything was all right.

"It was my mom," he responded. "She wasn't sure which medicine my dad takes before he goes to sleep."

Throughout the meal, Lucas's phone rang every ten minutes, making me more and more uncomfortable, for Matías and Rubén especially. I could see them shooting glances at each other across the table, and then they'd look quickly back at me. When there was half an hour left before the show, we asked for the check, then walked to the concert hall, which was just five minutes away. It was packed like a sardine can inside, and there were still dozens of people waiting in line at the door. Rubén walked us to the bar and said something to the bartender before vanishing into the multitude, heading for the stage where the rest of the band was tuning their instruments. The bartender wiped the bar with a rag and served us drinks.

A DJ was playing music as we waited for the show to start, and it was almost impossible to talk with the noise and all those people around. Lucas wrapped his arms around me and kissed me on the temple. I leaned back into him. I loved smelling him there, I loved tasting him when I kissed him, I loved feeling his pulse.

I felt him pull away and watched him reach into his pants pocket. He brought out his phone, and on the screen I saw the word *Mom*.

"I'll be right back," he said.

"Is everything OK?" Matías asked when Lucas walked off.

"It's his mom."

"Jesus! How many fucking times has his phone rung tonight?"

I shook my head. I'd lost count.

I could hear the singer roaring through the speakers and the public quieted down long enough to hear, "How are you guys tonight? We're Bad Sirens and we hope you have one hell of a good time with us!"

The first chords rang out, and Matías grabbed my hand and guided me toward the stage. All around us, people were drinking and dancing. A group of girls yelled the chorus, and Matías rolled his eyes when one of them shouted Rubén's name. I couldn't help but laugh.

After a few minutes, a pair of hands wrapped around my waist and I felt lips on my cheek. I leaned back into Lucas and we swayed to the rhythm of a slower song. Then I turned. He smiled at me and pressed his forehead into mine and we kept dancing. His mouth was close to mine.

One second. Two. Three…

He kissed me.

His tongue tickled mine and I quivered. He slid his fingers under my sweater and touched my skin. He was gripping me so tight, I thought our bodies would melt together. And in that instant everything ceased to matter apart from us and the feelings making us turn and turn…

But of course, his fucking phone had to start vibrating again. I could feel it under his clothes.

One time. Two. Three…

He grunted and took a look at the screen. *Claudia.* He put it away.

Four. Five. Six…

"Goddammit," he grumbled, taking it out again.

Why wouldn't he just turn the damned thing off? It was just one stupid button. All he had to do was flick it and be done with it.

Our eyes met: mine angry, his pleading, and I told him, "Turn it off."

"What if it's something about Dad, though? Listen, just give me a minute." He had to yell over the music. I followed him out. We pushed through the crowd and made it outside. He had rushed ahead of me and was standing some fifty feet away, leaning against the wall of a shop with his phone pressed to his ear.

"What do you want me to do about it?" he asked. "I mean, Claudia, if he's got a fever, call a fucking taxi and take him to the emergency room. Or call your parents! I'm sorry, but I can't… I didn't say it didn't matter… I don't hold what happened against the kid. How can you say that…? Stop apologizing for it. We'll deal with it…" Not knowing I was there, Lucas turned and started bumping his head against the wall. I got close enough behind him that I could hear Claudia's whiny voice, though I couldn't tell what she was saying. Lucas went on, "Don't cry, dammit… I know he has problems. I'm not insensitive, it's just… I know I said we'd try to be friends… Fine… Yes. OK, get him dressed, I'll be right there."

Pale, he hung up the phone, squeezing it so tight his knuckles turned white.

I was furious. I could feel anger radiating from my core and over-taking my entire body. My eyes stung, and I had to clear my throat before asking him, "You're going?"

"Her kid's got a fever, her parents are at their place in the country, and she's all alone. She's nervous and worried. I told her I can't, but…" He shrugged, as if there really were no other option.

"What about the kid's father? He *does* have one, right?" I asked. Did he really not see where all this was going? Was he honestly that naive?

"He does, but he's not in their life."

"So you're actually going to go?"

"I don't want to," he said, "but…"

"But what?" I exploded. I didn't care anymore about being sensitive.

"What if something happens to the kid?"

"Lucas, you can't make everything your responsibility. The entire world doesn't depend on you."

"So what do you want me to do, Maya? Just ignore her, ignore my family?"

Much as it hurt me, I glared at him. I knew I was getting mad at him for being a good person. But at the same time, it wasn't that simple. No—our entire situation was anything but simple.

It was dark on that street, and I felt alone with him and the tingling in my hands, the sound of blood rushing through my head, the heat spreading upward from my neck. I could have told him to stay. But I refused to lower myself in that way.

"Whatever," I said. "Just go."

"Maya… Maya, please. Maya, talk to me!"

But I had already turned to walk back into the bar. I ran through the door before he could catch up with me. Right away, my phone started ringing. Lucas. But unlike him, I knew how to turn it off.

58

I spent that night sitting up in bed. I couldn't sleep. I blamed myself for everything with Lucas a few hours before, but at the same time, I knew I had good reasons for being pissed.

I was disappointed. Hurt. Sad.

And I was tired of walking in circles. Feeling unsettled, uncomfortable in my own skin. Scared, confused, anxious. I couldn't untangle all those feelings I was lost inside of, as if I'd wandered into a no-man's-land.

Outside, I heard voices and got up. I cracked the door and listened to see who it was. I didn't want to bother anyone. Then I walked down the hall of that unfamiliar apartment and peeked into the kitchen, where Matías and Rubén were sitting at the table, Matías in a robe and Rubén in his pajamas. They were talking softly, leaning in toward each other and holding hands. I was starting to envy how happy they seemed.

"Hey," I whispered.

"Hey, honey. How are you doing?" Matías asked.

I shrugged and frowned.

"Come on, have a seat. It's nothing a little coffee can't fix," Rubén responded, standing and popping a capsule in his Nespresso. "With milk?"

"No, as is, please."

"Make me one, too?" Matías asked.

"That and anything else you want," Rubén said.

Matías blew him a kiss. His phone rang, and he disappeared down the hall. Soon he returned, talking with someone. After mouthing the words *Antoine*, he continued. "Yeah, she's right here, she's fine. We slept at Rubén's place… Tell him she's with me… Sure… See you at rehearsal."

"What's up?" I asked.

"Lucas is at my building. He showed up there. Apparently he's been calling you for hours."

I covered my face with my hands. "Yeah, I turned it off last night."

"Antoine says he was freaking out because he had no idea where you were." Matías sat back down as Rubén served our coffees, then excused himself, saying he needed a shower. "What's going on, Maya?"

"Things aren't good with Lucas and me. There's too much distance between us. I think it's over."

"Are you sure?"

"No, of course not! But I don't see a way out, either. You saw what happened last night."

"You mean the phone calls?" he asked. "Yeah. I get it. It was even getting on my nerves."

"And then he just abandoned me there and took off running when his ex called him crying about a kid that isn't even his."

"I'm sorry, babe," Matías said.

"I felt terrible when it happened, and I feel even worse because he did it for her child, and he's just a little baby, Matías. It's not his fault!"

"It's not your fault, either, Maya. And if I were in your shoes, I'd feel the same as you do. The whole thing is just crazy."

"How long have we been here now, a month and a half?"

"More or less," Matías replied.

"And in all that time, the only thing Lucas has done is scurry off whenever his family's opened their mouths. If they say stand, he stands. If they say sit, he sits. He spends his days in the office glued to the phone, running errands, solving problems... I get that it's his family and I have to respect them. And I would if he was doing all this because he wanted to, but he doesn't! I know he doesn't!"

"What do you mean?"

"I told you, Matías, his family's a mess."

"Every family is, though, Maya."

"Yeah, but these people are something out of a horror movie. And his ex... She's just a bad person. I don't know any other way to say it. And it's not that I'm jealous, it's that she's been playing Lucas their entire lives, and he's just gone back to letting her manipulate him like an idiot."

"What do you mean, gone back?" Matías asked.

"Why do you think he left Madrid two years ago? Everything went to shit and he took off running to get away from all of them."

I told Matías everything Lucas had admitted to me about his family. I knew it wasn't right to do so, but I needed to get out all those things that had been torturing me for weeks, and I trusted my best friend more than I trusted myself in that moment. I talked about Lucas's childhood, his father's illness, the heart attack that had almost killed him and how Lucas felt responsible for it. Matías was shocked at the whole story of Claudia, her pregnancy, and the paternity test. By the time I finished, he was cursing out loud.

"And you think history is repeating itself?" he asked.

"I don't think it. I know it."

"Then you need to talk to him."

"You think I haven't tried? He just keeps asking me for time, but I don't have time. I can't waste my life waiting for him to be brave enough to confront them. I'm living in his apartment, I don't have a job. Even if I wanted to, I couldn't just stay here indefinitely."

Matías stared into my eyes. "Do you love him?"

"A lot."

"But you're still willing to end it with him?"

I'd been trying to hold the tears back, but now there was no point. "End what, Matías? We may look like a couple from the outside, but in reality, we're nothing. Every day when he walks out, he makes a choice, and that choice is not to stay with me."

"You need to tell him this, Maya. Everything you've told me. He needs to know that you love him and that losing him is hurting you."

I shook my head, voice cracking, and said, "I can't."

"Why?"

"Because I've spent my whole life begging for others' affections, struggling to deserve them, and losing myself in the process. And for once, I need to feel that I matter. I want to be someone else's priority. And I want to know that I am, understand?"

Matías took my hand and guided me to my feet, hugging me and resting his chin on my shoulder. He asked me if I wanted him to tell me the truth, and I nodded, wiping my nose on my sleeve. He went on, "You're right, Lucas needs to resolve some things before he can move on. And he's got to do it on his own. But the same is true of you."

"What do you mean?"

"You've got problems of your own, and until you get out from under that weight on your shoulders, you can't be with Lucas or anyone else. He's not your life preserver, and you're not his, all right? You have to learn to swim on your own. If you don't, one day you'll end up drowning each other."

"What do I do then? How do I break free?" I cried, striking myself in the chest from frustration.

"Be brave, Maya. But be selfish, too. Stop bowing your head and waiting for instructions from someone else. Ask questions. Shout. Make demands. Get mad. Blow up. Let out everything you were holding onto."

I knew what he was doing. He was pushing me toward the edge of a cliff. To a place I'd been scared to approach on my own. In his arms, as we dried each other's tears, I knew that he was right, that this was the only way.

Go back.

To the beginning.

No matter how scared I was of hitting the wall.

No matter how much I wanted to stay.

Because I was drowning.

Because I was starting to hate Lucas as much as I loved him, and he didn't deserve that.

He didn't.

But I knew leaving meant going back when there were no more stars left to count.

59

I found Lucas sitting on the couch in one of his suits. He was wearing a tie this time, and his briefcase was at his feet. It was almost ten and he hadn't left. I guess he was waiting for me. He looked lost. Vulnerable. That was the worst thing. Knowing that, without wanting to, I had manipulated him with my attitude, my moods. That I was another obligation. One more thing that was demanding something from him.

It wasn't fair for either of us.

Our world was tipped off its axis and we couldn't manage to set it aright. Sorrento had been a dream, a wonderful dream, and we'd been determined to keep it alive in a Madrid full of ghosts and memories that wouldn't leave us in peace.

A mirage.

A fantasy starting to crumble.

I tried to pull myself together as I walked into the living room. Lucas didn't say anything. The silence was painful, deafening, for both of us. He grabbed his briefcase and stood.

"I need to go," he said, passing by me. "I just wanted to make sure you were OK."

"I'm fine. I'm sorry I worried you."

He stopped and turned and took a deep breath. He was angry. I could tell from the wrinkles in his forehead and the way he was clenching his jaw. He knew I was angry, too. We would only go on hurting each other, I was certain of it, unless we found a way to communicate.

He turned back and stared, and though it was hard to look, I did, and I felt his presence, powerful, painful, seeping into me. He closed his eyes and leaned his forehead into mine. "We need to talk, Maya," he said.

"Yeah, we should."

"I've got to work till three today, then I have to go with Dad to an appointment. I'll be back around six. Will you be here?"

"Yeah."

"All right," he said, sounding relieved.

His fingers gripped my waist.

His breath tickled my lips.

We almost kissed.

A million dreams lay in waste around us.

One second. Two. Three...

There are moments that should last for an eternity.

60

He didn't come back at six. Or at seven. Or at eight.

And all that time, his phone was off.

I tried him again. Got his voicemail again. Sank back into the sofa. How many more signs did I need? To know that no matter how much Lucas meant to me, this wasn't our time.

That maybe it never was.

That maybe it never would be.

I was scared, and I felt trapped between those four walls.

And alone. Oh so alone.

My phone rang.

"Where are you?" I blurted out.

"I'm sorry, I'm sorry, I'm sorry... My battery died and I didn't realize it."

"Where are you?" I repeated.

"At my parents' place. We got back from the appointment, and the whole family was here. My aunts and uncles, my cousins…they wanted to surprise him. And Dad asked me to stay the night. He looks so happy that I don't want to upset him. He's still not completely well, though."

"Sure," I whispered.

"I'm sorry. I really am. I'll be there first thing in the morning, I promise."

An invisible hand squeezed my throat so tightly I couldn't respond. I heard voices through the phone. Some deep, some old, some young. And hers, telling them to cover the pool so her son wouldn't fall in.

Everyone has a weakness. Lucas's was his family.

"Maya?"

"Right. Tomorrow. I heard you." I hung up. I wanted to hate him. I wanted to erase him from my memory, him and everything else, so I could stop feeling that way. I wanted to accept that what we'd had was temporary, fleeting. A handful of moments that stung just then, because they represented a different him, a different me. Because we hadn't loved each other the same.

Maybe I was making love, and he was just fucking.

Maybe I was thinking of tomorrow, and he only saw now.

There was Lucas, his family, and me. And one of us had to go.

I gathered my things. I couldn't do it anymore. I felt a sharp pain in my ribs. I was having a panic attack. I knew it. And in my head, I kept telling myself it would pass. It always did.

Acting more determined than I felt, I walked into the spare bedroom where there was a desktop computer and a printer. Telling myself I'd use my head this time, that I'd think before acting, that I'd plan as coldly as I could, I clicked through the links. I selected my origin and destination. I checked the schedule. I bought a ticket for the first train headed out the next morning. Then I called Matías.

"I'm going. Alone. But I promise you, I'm not running away this time."

"Where are you going?"

"You know where. You're the one who gave me the idea. I'm going to be brave. I'm going to swim on my own."

"That's my girl," he said.

I smiled to myself. "I don't know if it's going to work. Maybe it will blow up in my face. But what I know is I need to learn to love myself. And that's all I need right now."

"And I know you'll do it, babe. You'll fall in love with every part of yourself. Because you're marvelous."

"I love you."

"I love you, too, dummy," he said. "Be careful now. And call me every day."

"I'll call you *almost* every day," I said.

And hearing him starting to tell me off softly, I let him go with the words, "See you soon."

61

I woke up to the sound of rain drumming the windows. I didn't move for a minute. I just listened to that soft plunking sound and looked over at the empty side of the bed. I reached out and rested a hand on his pillow.

Slowly, the room was brightening.

I needed to go if I didn't want to miss the train.

I dragged my bags to the door and took one last look at the place to be sure I wasn't forgetting anything. Of course, there was one thing I was leaving behind, but I had to. I didn't know how to say goodbye. I couldn't call him. Because he'd ask me to stay, to wait for him, and I knew I'd end up giving in.

For the same reason, I couldn't send a message.

And so I did the cowardly thing. The thing that eased my conscience without forcing me to take a serious step.

I looked for a piece of paper and something to write with, and I tried to translate into ink the emotions that were overwhelming me, the hard edges that cut and jabbed me, opening wounds through which my dreams, my yearnings, and my hopes were trickling out.

I'm sorry, Lucas, but I can't stay. Not like this. It isn't fair to either of us. We're going in opposite directions, and dragging this out is hurting us. You matter too much to me, and I think this is the best thing for you. For me. For both of us.

Thank you for these months. They've made me more me than I've ever been.

Thanks for taking me in and letting this happen.

Take care of yourself.

I reread the note and left it on the bed, taking one look back to store away that apartment and the moments that had occurred inside it. Then I dropped my keys on the table, walked out, and closed the door.

The taxi was already waiting for me when I walked outside. I got in and turned off my phone.

It was still raining, and the streets were slick, looking blurred through the window, with little gleams of light. Inside me, everything was silence.

The taxi soon left me at Atocha Station. The morning trains were arriving, and people were all over, rushing toward the exits to head to work. I checked the time. I still had forty minutes till my departure.

I sat on a bench by the indoor garden and waited patiently, watching the travelers move to and fro. Some were alone, some accompanied. Some were reuniting, some were saying goodbyes. *See you later, so good to have you back.* Because that's what it all is: people and coming and going in our lives, us departing or arriving in theirs. And no matter what, life goes on. It doesn't stop, doesn't break off. It just follows a different rhythm, turns in a different direction.

On the screen, the track number for my train appeared, and as I got in line for security, I heard my name, "Maya…"

My heart ached and I turned to find Lucas just a few feet away, sopping wet. Water was dripping from his hair, and his chest was rising and falling from the effort of running. He opened his mouth, but struggled to get a word out. Then he held up the note I'd left him, wet, the ink running, and said, "Are you serious? This is it?"

Everyone was looking at him, but he didn't seem to care. "How did you know I was here?" I asked.

"You left the computer on with your travel receipt right there on the screen. Are you serious, Maya? A note? A note is all I deserve?"

"No. But this is the best thing."

"For who?" He looked at me with glassy eyes. "I thought we were going to talk?"

"Yeah, that's what you said. That we were going to talk. Yesterday."

He blinked and tugged at his hair in frustration. He stepped closer. I saw so many things in his face. Most prominent among them: fear.

"Is this because of yesterday? I told you I was sorry."

"It's for yesterday, and the day before, and the day before that, Lucas."

"I know I've been busy, but this is temporary. My father..."

His phone started ringing. I noticed how nervous he was as he tried to pretend to ignore it.

"Lucas, this isn't going to work," I said.

"Not if you give up."

"I'm not giving up. I'm accepting the truth."

His phone kept ringing. He pulled it out and rejected the call. "What truth, Maya?"

"That you're in the same place you were in two years ago, before you left here. You're still the same person that you told me about in Sorrento. The person you couldn't stand being."

He looked down as if he'd looked at himself in a mirror and hadn't liked what he'd seen.

"That's not true," he grumbled.

His phone rang again. It was driving me crazy. He rejected the call a second time.

"It is true, Lucas, and you know it. As soon as you set foot in Madrid, you went back to your old ways. And I can't do anything about it. I can't help you. You need to change, but it has to come from you."

"Fine. I'll do it. I promise. I'll fix things. Just give me a couple of days, until my sister can take over at the company."

"I can't."

"Why not? Where are you going?"

"I've got my own problems to solve," I said.

"Maya, dammit, we can fix this! Just stay a little longer. We'll… We can go somewhere and talk. Shit!" His phone rang a fourth time. He picked up, enraged, and brought it to his ear, saying, "What? No. It's a bad time. Because I said no… I'll call you when I can."

I was crushed. I could have broken down right there. But I kept the sorrow in and let the anger out. The rage. The indignation. I didn't hold back. I reminded him that this was the best thing for both of us. He needed to find himself. And I damn sure hoped he did.

I would miss him. I knew I would. Or rather, I'd miss the guy I met in Sorrento. The one who made me crazy thinking about a piece of chocolate cake. The one who danced to a love song with me and whispered the words into my ear. The one who kissed me under a stormy sky and showed me what sex could really be. The one I learned to make love with, the one who taught me to let go. To count the stars and to dream of two points in the universe.

I turned and handed my ticket to a railway worker who scanned the bar code and told me to put my suitcase on the scanner belt.

"Maya!"

I turned. The worker stood in front of Lucas when he tried to reach me, telling him, "I apologize, but you can't come any further without a ticket."

"I'm sorry, Maya. I just…" He stopped, realizing he was just going to try to justify himself one more time, and that this showed that everything I'd said to him was true.

"Don't go," he said.

"I have to."

"Please, please…don't break up with me."

"I'm not breaking up with you, Lucas," I said.

"No?" he asked, clearly confused.

"We've never truly been together. All we've done is go with the flow. There never was an us. I never knew you wanted there to be."

"I do, though, Maya. Of course I do."

They announced my train's departure.

I took my bag off the belt when it emerged from the machine and looked at Lucas, whose expression was lost, powerless. Nothing has ever made me as sad as that image of his face. But I forced myself to take a breath.

"Stay," he said again. And I tried to smile, though inside I was breaking into tiny pieces. It hurt: every word, every glance, everything that came between us. Everything that wouldn't be. My top lip separated from my bottom one, and I could feel it forming in my throat, rising, sliding off of my tongue. A single word.

A word that meant a world.

A word he couldn't mistake the meaning of.

"Goodbye."

And then I left him behind.

62

We spend our lives wanting things. Some pointless. Others grand. Some that are simply impossible.

And there are many other things we try to forget.

But the only thing we ever truly forget is the fact that we only have one life. One life that we let pass by, doing nothing but wanting, desiring, as if our thoughts were a magic wand that could just make all our wishes magically come true while we stand there with our arms crossed.

And we take this life that's been given to us and turn it into an endless wait where nothing happens, because the things that really matter are things you have to create on your own. Yearning doesn't make them happen, whining doesn't make them happen, and self-pity, cowardice, and passivity sure as hell don't. Life owes us nothing. Absolutely nothing.

I was like that all those years, waiting, despairing. Always standing in front of a door waiting for someone to invite me in. Tiptoeing around, trying not to make any noise. Not understanding that there are doors that you just have to knock down, that sometimes you have to trespass. That you can't expect doors to open for you just because you've shown up.

It's not enough to want to change things. You have to move them, turn them around, transform them into what you need them to be. Realizing that no matter what you do, the world keeps turning. It's not a carousel you can get on and off of whenever you feel like it. But you can choose which horse to ride.

And you know what? When you change, everything else seems to change, too. That's the truth. But once you set out on your path, you shouldn't stop until you figure out who you are. Until you've accepted your contradictions, your fears, your desires. Until you've admitted that not everything makes sense. But when it doesn't, you can always dance. I'm serious. Dance. Giving up is the easy thing, but dancing... dancing requires you to stand up.

I don't remember when I started to change. When I took the first step. And it wasn't so much steps as it was little glimmers of clarity that opened my eyes like a camera flash and slowly awakened me. I started to belong more to myself and less to others. I became my own superhero and understood no one could save me. I had to do that myself.

Defending myself is my responsibility.

63

I leaned my head on the cold window and watched the drops fall on the glass, spreading out into a thin film as the train left Madrid behind. It ached terribly to think of Lucas, and remorse consumed me inside. We deserved better than the goodbye we'd shared, but it was too late to change it.

What's done is done.

And if I thought of it objectively, Lucas had been the first one to leave, weeks ago, even if he was physically present.

As for my decision, I had no doubt whatsoever. I had been right to take my own road. It wasn't our moment. It probably never would be. Staying with each other would have destroyed us. Yet there was a truth that remained through that realization—in fact, it grew stronger. I loved Lucas. I loved him a lot, and I knew I'd always have him inside me. And hopefully, after a while, when I thought of him, I'd do so with a smile and not with the tears that I could barely hold back just then.

I closed my eyes and let the movement of the train rock me.

I woke when the other passengers stood. Through the window, I could see we were in Alicante. I walked my bags out to checked luggage and left them there before continuing with my plan.

I wasn't scared, but I was nervous. I had decided to be brave, to confront everything that had held me back, to turn the page on all that had made me suffer and were still doing so. From now on, I would do things right, even if that meant I'd have to go it alone. Anyway, wasn't that what I'd always done? The answer was yes, and knowing this gave me the strength to continue.

I exited the station and walked to the taxi stand.

Fifteen minutes later, I was in front of my uncle's house in a development outside of town near the beach. I rang and waited. Soon, the iron gate opened and my cousin peeked out.

"Yes?"

"Hey, Iván," I said.

"Whoa! Maya!" He slung the door open and stood there slack-jawed, unable to believe I was really there. "I hardly recognized you!"

"I know," I responded, "it's been ages since we last saw each other."

"Years, for sure. You're all grown up."

"You, too. I'm here to see Grandpa. Can I come in?"

"Yeah, of course. Just be careful and don't trip on anything. He's sitting out on the back porch. He likes to listen to the radio out there."

He stepped aside and I walked over the paved path through the front yard and into the two-story home, kicking the hose that lay in my way.

Iván added, "You look good."

"Thanks. Nothing compared to you, though."

He shrugged as he guided me inside and toward the kitchen. "I can't complain. I'm getting married. I don't know if you heard."

"Honestly, I don't talk much with anyone in the family."

"Sure, I get it. Anyway, my fiancée's name is Elena. We met at an internship in the hospital. I work in a laboratory, I guess you didn't know that. We still don't have a date set, but the wedding will be sometime in the spring."

I didn't know about his job; I barely knew anything about any of my cousins. But Iván had always struck me as one of the nicer ones, and he was confirming that impression now. I congratulated him.

"Thanks. You should come!"

"Is this an official invitation?"

"You're my cousin," he replied. "Of course it is."

Looking around, I noticed the house was silent and felt empty, and I asked, "Aren't your parents or Grandma here?"

"Nah, they're all at the market in Teulada."

As we walked out onto the back porch, I could smell freshly cut grass and the sea. It was calming. I saw my grandfather there, sitting in a wicker chair next to a table, and could hardly contain my joy. Iván announced my presence. "Grandpa, you've got a visitor."

"Visitor?"

"Hey, Grandpa," I said.

He straightened up immediately and turned toward us. "Maya, is that you?"

I ran over and kneeled next to him. "Hey," I asked, barely able to speak. "How are you?"

His eyes began to water and he reached up to feel my face. I grabbed his hands and placed them on my cheeks. "My little girl," he said. "It's been so long. I can't believe you're really here."

"I'm sorry I didn't come before. And I'm sorry I didn't call," I told him. "Grandma wouldn't pick up, and after a while I quit trying."

"I know, honey, it's fine," he said. "How are you, though?"

"Good."

"Well, have a seat beside me and tell me all you've been doing these past few months."

With a smile on his face, my cousin headed back toward the kitchen and said, "I'm going to go grab a bite. Do you want something?"

I nodded. I was dying of hunger. Then I dragged a chair next to my grandfather and sat down, holding his hand. Iván returned a few seconds later with coffee, orange juice, and toast. He sat with us a while, but soon got back to his yard work.

That was when my grandfather started in with the questions, and I tried to answer as honestly as possible. Of course, I left a lot out. I didn't want to worry him. It didn't make sense, not at his age. I asked him if he'd heard from my mother.

"Not really. The only person she really talks to is your uncle Yoan. She calls once or twice a month on Sundays, when she knows she'll catch him at home, and then we exchange a few words. But that's it." He joined his hands over the blanket covering his legs. "She'll never forgive me, and I understand."

"Don't say that, Grandpa."

"I understand you, too," he said, reaching over to turn down the radio. "I didn't protect her. That's the honest truth. I knew what was happening in my home wasn't right, but I didn't do anything. I took it for granted that caring for the kids was a mother's job. That's how it was back then, and since I was a man, I didn't think anything else about it. Maybe it was just comfortable that way. I don't know. I worked all day, and the children were Olga's responsibility. All I wanted when I came home was to have dinner in peace, watch the TV with my wife, and tell myself the kids were happy and didn't lack for anything. And Andrey and Yoan were happy.

"Daria wasn't, though. I could see that every time I looked at her. We'd sit at the table and she wouldn't even eat the same thing as anyone else. I saw that, and I let it happen. The same way I let her go off to dance every weekend morning when she was just ten, while her brothers slept in and lived normal boys' lives. Daria never got to be free and she slowly stopped glowing, like a candle burning out. The same as you did."

I didn't know what to say. That was the first time my grandfather had ever spoken so openly, with so much pain and regret in his voice. It was also the first time I'd seen him as a real person. I'd always adored him. He'd been the man who hugged me, who gave me advice, who was always there for me. But he was also a man who had closed his eyes and ignored too many things, bad things that had frustrated and wounded me. Things that came back to me now clearer than ever.

I'd always blamed the woman who hurt me and forgotten that bystanders share the guilt. Especially if their passivity allows the situation to continue and becomes a habit, something that helps normalize cruelty.

But there was no point in blaming him now. And I was tired of carrying that weight around. The time had come to let it go, not add to it. I needed to forgive. For my sake. I reached out and touched his hand. "Have you told Mom all this?"

"No. She wouldn't listen to me."

"Do it. For both of you, but especially for her."

He nodded and smiled bitterly, and I heard the door open. My aunt and uncle and their other kids came in with my grandmother behind them. Everyone froze when they saw me. We were tense as we greeted each other, but the mood calmed when I announced that I was only visiting and wouldn't be there long.

That was depressing, but I didn't let it get to me. I couldn't let that kind of thing matter anymore.

Being family isn't a guarantee of unconditional love. Blood is just a fluid that runs through your veins. Plasma and hemoglobin. Something that keeps you alive. Thinking it binds you to someone is an illusion. It had been hard for me to admit that, but seeing Lucas's relationship with his family had helped me see the chains that kept me bound to mine.

And it wasn't worth it, giving so much in exchange for nothing. Suffering with the thought that I deserved something in return. Making sacrifices for the sake of the impossible. Giving in to blackmail. Begging for something that a person either feels or they don't—and when they do feel it, you don't have to ask for it, it's just there. And they offer it to you because it's a part of them, and it just comes out naturally.

They told me I could stay for lunch—you could tell they felt they had to—and I accepted, just to be able to spend a little more time with my grandfather and Iván. He was a good guy. We exchanged numbers and he told me I should call whenever I wanted, to check up on Grandpa or even just to talk.

My grandmother hardly opened her mouth the whole time and pretended, as much as she could, that she didn't realize I was there. I didn't mind. It wasn't my problem—I knew that now. I thought of Catalina, of Angela, of Marco and the kids. Of Monica, Jules, and Roy. Of Giulio. Bad as things had ended, I felt like part of a family when I was with them. They had nothing to do with the people who surrounded me now.

And I didn't have anything to do with them either.

When lunch was over, Iván offered to take me to the station.

I said goodbye to my grandfather and the rest of the family, who were sitting on the porch drinking coffee. My cousin went upstairs to change clothes, and I walked to the door to wait.

Then I smelled it. Intense. Heavy. My grandmother's perfume. She sprayed on so much of it, it surrounded her like a cloud and never dissipated. The air around me froze. The whole house seemed to. And I shrank like a deflating balloon. I couldn't help it, but I tried to remain firm and tell myself she no longer had any power over me.

"Why did you come here?" she asked. "Because it clearly wasn't to ask my forgiveness."

I turned to face her. I don't know why, but she seemed smaller. More fragile. Older. As if the four months since we'd last seen each other had passed more quickly for her than for me.

"I came to see my grandfather. I wanted to know how he was, and I wanted to talk to him a bit. And this was the only way to do it."

"It's inappropriate, barging into someone else's house like this."

"Why would I call? So you could find an excuse to keep me from coming? No thank you."

"Don't you speak to me in that tone, Maya."

"Did you honestly believe for one second that *I* would come here to ask forgiveness from *you*? I have nothing to apologize for. I never did anything wrong."

"Oh, you did nothing wrong? You've always been an embarrassment, and you've never appreciated everything I…"

"Listen to you: I, I, I, me, me, me. Just stop it! It's not about you and it never was. It was always me: my life, my career, my efforts."

"How dare you say that!"

"It's the truth, though. You treated me like a thing, as if you owned me, and you toyed with me and you broke me and didn't even care. Who does that to another person? Only someone who's cruel. Wicked."

"I'm sorry, what did you call me?"

"Grandpa always forgave you. He used to tell me that if I'd seen the environment you grew up in, you with your family, I'd have understood. I believed that, and I ignored all the times you shouted at me, humiliated me, punished me. But that's over. I tried to force myself to be better for you. No more. You want to know why? Because I suffered, too, every minute I was growing up with you, but I'm still a good person and I could never deliberately hurt anyone. And that means you don't have an excuse."

My cousin came downstairs just then, and I looked away from my grandmother and up at him. I could tell he'd heard most of what I'd said, but surprisingly, he seemed pleased by it as he said with a grin, "Come on. Otherwise you'll miss your train."

I nodded and we walked out. I turned back once before the door closed to see my grandmother standing immobile in the doorway, as though she were truly seeing who I was for the first time.

For me, though, this was the last.

64

When you're living through things, they always seem enormous, but as time passes, they shrink and go blurry at the edges, and eventually you even forget them.

My grandmother had always been like a wall holding me back, one I was incapable of jumping over. And now she was just the dust that floats in the air after that wall has collapsed, and I knew a breeze would soon come through and carry it away.

I realized I was breathing lighter now, that I no longer felt corseted. I had left something behind in that house, a burden, a sense of things undone, and being free of all that was wonderful. The pain I'd carried around my entire life was gone.

My cousin turned to me. "She's…complicated, isn't she?"

I had been watching the city pass outside the window. I turned to him now and said, "I wish she was just complicated. But it's so much more than that. You can't even imagine."

"My parents talk about you two. My mother never liked how she treated you. It actually worried her, but Dad always told her it was none of her business and she should stay out of it."

It was nice to think my aunt had cared enough to say something, even if just a little. "She couldn't have done much for me," I responded.

"We'll never know. They don't get along well—my mother and your grandmother, I mean. As soon as Grandma showed up here, she decided she was the boss and everything had to be done her way. She cuts Mom down all the time. It's gotten a little easier, but at first she caused all kinds of fights between my parents."

"I'm sorry," I told him.

"Why are you sorry? It's not like you did anything."

"Yeah, I know," I said. "I guess it's just a habit, apologizing for everything. And it's a hard one to break. Things didn't seem too tense in your house, though."

"We've worked it out. I mean, Mom's not alone, she has me and her other children, and we supported her as soon as we realized what was happening. I would never let someone run my own mother down in her home. By the way, I heard everything you said."

He took a hand off the wheel to switch gears.

"I know."

"I had no idea she treated you so badly," he admitted.

"Honestly, for a long time, I didn't, either. I always thought it was my fault. Now I know otherwise."

"So what are you doing? Heading back to Madrid?"

"No," I said. "I've still got to see someone."

It had been four months now since I'd set out on my journey. It had its bad days, its sad days, its complicated ones. But there were also happy days, marvelous days when I learned how to live, to dream, to discover how small things can turn to big ones.

It was a journey that hadn't yet ended, and who knew if it ever would.

Because getting to know yourself can take a lifetime.

Because some journeys take you deeper and deeper into yourself, and inside your heart is an entire universe.

65

I walked through the train cars till I found the least crowded one, then flopped down, and soon I was asleep, faintly aware of the conversations of the other passengers around me.

Trains had a sedative effect on me, I'd realized. My mind would think of nothing, and soon I'd fall asleep. And I was scared to think just then. Scared of hesitating. Scared of reaching the end and regretting it. My longings had already made me suffer enough.

I arrived at the station in Murcia, and the PA announced the regional train headed to Águilas. I ran with my bags to the ticket counter as I heard the message: *Local train for Lorca-Águilas, departing from Zone C, Track 2.*

"Shit!"

I snatched away my ticket, stuffed it between my teeth, and ran off, making it in just before the doors slammed closed.

Breathless, with a pain in my ribs, I sat on the floor between two cars, where I remained a moment, thinking about how this was my last stop on this trip. I felt the most terrible anxiety, like a rope tightening around me as I asked myself whether I was really ready for what I was about to do. Probably not, but probably there would never be a perfect time.

After a few minutes, my legs stopped twitching, and I looked for a free window seat.

I'd turned off my phone that morning. Now I took it out and turned it back on. Several notifications came through, none of them from Lucas. I didn't know what to think or feel about that—or everything I thought and felt was contradictory.

Had I really expected him to contact me after the way I had run off? And why would he? So I could hurt him by not giving him the answer he needed, telling him no, there was no way I'd go back and wait for him?

Maybe I did want him to do that, just so I'd know that I mattered to him, that he hadn't given up on me like so many others.

But he had.

I put away my phone, leaned my head on the window, and stared at the countryside passing by.

As we passed from station to station, thoughts and emotions flooded me, and I didn't know what to do with all that chaos. What if this was the worst idea I'd ever had? So what, I reminded myself. It wasn't like I had anything to lose.

The grain fields and hothouses thinned out and gave way to the first buildings of the town, and soon the train was making its last stop in Águilas. I grabbed my bags and got out. There was a clock in the station that told me it was a quarter to nine. In the sky, I could already see stars, and they seemed to whisper to me that what I was doing was insane. To start with, I didn't even know where to go. All I had was the photo of a town and a couple of photos I'd found on Instagram. I'd probably end up spending the night on the beach. Except this time, there would be no blue-eyed boy with a precious smile who would swoop down and come to my aid.

"Calabardina, please," I told my taxi driver.

"Street?"

"Uh, just a sec." I slid my finger across my phone screen and found what I was looking for, turning my phone sideways so he could see. "This place."

The taxi driver, a man around thirty, squinted at the photo with his dark eyes, lifted his brows in confusion, and scratched his chin. "You know, Calabardina's not small, I don't know every street or house. If you had an address, maybe…"

"Sure." I bit my lip, nervous. "Wait, I've got more. Let's see if any of these ring a bell." I showed him the rest of the photos to see if anything looked familiar to him.

He smiled and nodded. "I think I know where the place you're looking for is."

"Amazing!" I shouted. "Is it really far from here?"

"Eight miles, maybe."

He got in gear and I sat back and took a deep breath, unable to free myself from the tension that had overtaken me. We left the city behind on a long, lonely highway, then soon exiting into a small town full of empty streets.

"I think this is it," the taxi driver said.

Through the windshield, I saw a two-story house with a stairway outside and a white stone balustrade. On the corner by the beach, surrounded by a short wall, it was identical to the photos.

I paid and got out, and the taxi driver took my bags out of the trunk. I started hyperventilating as I threw my purse over my shoulder and dragged along the two suitcases.

"You want me to wait?" the man asked, sounding a little worried. I shook my head, and he took out his card and offered it to me. "This is my cell number, just in case."

"Thanks."

"No worries." He got in his car and drove off.

I looked at the house again, saw the light in the windows, noticed shadows moving behind the curtains. I took a deep breath and pushed open the gate. My heart was pounding as I knocked on the door. Three times. Then waited. I could hear voices and music inside. A few steps. Then the door opened.

Her gray eyes stared straight into mine. She'd opened up with a joyful look on her face; now it turned surprised, tense, scared. She stood there holding the door, unable to move, as if I were a ghost, and she couldn't grasp what I was doing there.

"Hey, Mom."

"Who is it?" her husband asked from behind her.

When he saw me, he was just as shocked as she was. He looked me up and down, then his eyes settled on my suitcases. He rested a hand on my mother's shoulders as though trying to give her courage.

"Hi, Alexis."

"Maya…hey."

I looked down at my feet. I certainly didn't feel welcome. I don't know what I was expecting, honestly. I didn't care, though. I had gone there for one reason and one reason only, and I wasn't going to turn back now. Not yet.

"I don't have anywhere to go, Mom," I told her. "And I need to stay a few days."

Myriad emotions streamed through her eyes. Hesitation. Uncertainty. Fear.

I thought for a second she would shut the door in my face and leave me outside. And that suspicion made me clench my jaws and my fists. What the hell had I done to make her reject me this way for so long?

But then she surprised me, stepping aside and saying, "Come in."

66

I followed them into the living room. My legs were heavy, and my shoulders ached from dragging around my bags.

"Where can I leave this stuff?"

"Let me take it upstairs to the guest room," Alexis said.

My hands were shaking so much that I dropped my bag. Alexis grinned and picked it up. Then he vanished down the hall with all my things.

Mom and I stayed in the living room. You could have cut the tension between us with a knife. It felt hard to even breathe. Then a door opened and Guille ran in, wearing his pajamas with their dinosaur print. His mouth was covered in toothpaste. He stopped and stared up at me and I smiled at him. He had his father's curly hair and dark skin, but the same eyes as my mother, maybe even more piercing than hers. They shone like two streetlamps.

"I know you," he said.

"Do you now?" I asked.

"Yeah, your name's Maya."

"How do you know me if the last time I saw you, you were a baby?"

He smiled, revealing his tiny teeth. He was so handsome!

"I saw pictures." He pointed to the bookshelves where I saw

something that made me weak in the knees: a dozen photographs, all of them of me at different ages.

Then Guille asked me, "Do you know me?"

It was hard for me to answer him: I didn't know what to think when I saw those pictures or what they meant. Were they a cruel joke, or a missed opportunity, or the seed of a chance to make things better? I had no idea.

My mother was looking at Guille as he scratched his head and I told him, "Of course I know you."

"You want to see all my dinosaurs?" he asked. "I've got lots of them. My favorite is the diplodocus."

"Guille, it's late and you've got school tomorrow. You should be in bed," my mother admonished him. He grunted and crossed his arms angrily.

"Pay attention to Mama," I said, being especially careful with that phrase, because I wasn't sure whether he knew if we were related, and I didn't want to confuse him. Feeling my mother's eyes on me, I added, "You can show me your dinosaurs tomorrow, OK?"

He shrugged, and Mom said, "I'll be right back. I'm just going to put him to bed."

When I was alone, I looked again attentively at the photos, and a million questions popped into my head.

Alexis said from behind me, "She's got an album with many more in the closet."

"Why?" I asked, sounding bitter, almost disrespectful.

"It's her way of keeping you close." I laughed almost contemptuously at that response, but Alexis ignored it, asking if I'd had dinner and offering me a sandwich and some juice.

I *was* hungry, and I *was* tired, so much so I was starting to sway and my vision was unclear. I nodded, thanked him, and sat on the couch to take a look around. There were toys all over, folded clothing in a chair, and on a table, a sewing kit and a half-finished scarecrow costume.

It was all so normal, so authentic.

A home. It even smelled like home.

Alexis soon returned with my dinner. I thanked him and wolfed it down. I could hear giggles coming from one of the bedrooms flanking the hallway. Alexis smiled and said, "It's hard to get him to sleep some nights."

I swallowed my last bite and washed it down with a sip of juice. I could hear my mother reading him a story, and Guille replying to some of the dialogue. He must have known the book by heart. In a way, it hurt, hearing her be the mother for him that she'd never been for me. It was an ugly feeling, but I couldn't help it. She *had* been mine first, hadn't she?

I was jealous of Guille. There was no point in lying to myself about it. And realizing it brought up feelings I'd kept suppressed for a long time, feelings I'd rejected when I told myself she didn't matter to me anymore, that she was no one to me. That was just another lie I'd swallowed to try to deal with the anguish, my inability to understand why she'd rejected me, why she hadn't loved me as I'd wanted to love her.

I'd gone there to get closure on our relationship and lift that weight off myself, and I'd told myself it would be easy because I thought I was over it. But I was wrong. It was as if I'd traveled back in time, and was a teenager again. That was when it had been hardest for me. There hadn't been space for anything but anger and hatred, which ate at me at all hours, making me ask questions and look all over for somewhere to cast the blame before concluding I could only blame myself. I was the problem she'd run away from. That was what I always believed.

"I'm pretty tired," I said. "If you don't mind, maybe I'll go to bed."

"Sure, it's the last door on the left, and the bathroom is right next to it."

"Thanks."

I walked down the hallway in the darkness. Through the sliver of soft light coming from the right, I could see my mother and Guille curled up in bed, almost hidden behind a gigantic book with dinosaurs on the cover.

I walked into the guest room, where my things were sitting by the door. I left again to brush my teeth, then slipped into bed. The sheets were cool and slightly damp from the humidity. I balled up and closed my eyes, feeling terribly empty inside, and asking myself how it was possible that an emptiness could hurt me so—how a void could take up so much space.

67

The next morning, I had to nearly drag myself out of bed. I had struggled to get to sleep, and when I did, I kept having the same strange dream: I was on a stage beneath a blinding spotlight, and I could barely see the audience. And yet, I knew who was out there: everyone. My grandparents, my aunts and uncles, my cousins. Catalina, Giulio, and Dante, and everyone else I'd met in Sorrento. My mother, Alexis, Guille…and Lucas.

They were all watching me try to do a pirouette. But every time I tried, my knee crunched louder and louder, until it finally broke and I fell on the floor and cried out in pain. Nobody moved to help me. They just watched me like mannequins.

When I woke, I needed what felt like ages to gather the courage to get up and face what lay past the door. I had told myself I wouldn't be weak, that I wouldn't allow it, but I felt small and vulnerable and, worst of all, adrift.

I walked out to find the house silent, but with the strong scent of coffee in the air, and found my mother sitting at the kitchen table staring out the window. She turned, swallowed, and stood.

"Are you alone?" I asked, uncomfortable.

"Yeah, Alexis took Guille to school. Do you, um… Do you usually have coffee in the morning?"

"Yeah."

"How about toast? Or cookies?"

"Just a coffee's good, thanks," I said as I sat down.

She nodded and poured me a cup, setting it down before me. Then she did the same for herself. Her expression was cautious and almost disoriented as she sat across from me. For a moment, we just looked at each other. She was waiting for me to take the first step, but I wasn't there yet. I wasn't even sure what I was doing there.

I looked at her hair, her eyes, the wrinkles around them; her nose, her thin lips, the fine contours of her cheeks. I could see she was doing the same. It was as if we were looking at each other for the first time.

"How do you forgive someone?" Those words came out of my mouth with a life of their own.

She started wringing her fingers. "I don't know. I never made it that far. Fyodora used to tell me that you have to start by accepting that someone hurt you and just living with the pain until you don't have any other choice."

"You know Olga threw me out?"

"Yeah."

"Did you ever ask yourself these past four months what might have happened to me?"

"Yeah."

"Didn't you care?" I was trying to shake her out of her passivity.

"I did."

"Well, you sure didn't—"

"I called and wrote you, several times." She interrupted me, defensive.

A cold, disdainful smile pulled my lips upward. Then I realized she wasn't lying. But how could she be telling the truth? In that moment, I remembered I'd blocked her.

I took a sip of coffee, not knowing how to continue. Thousands of words were swirling around in my brain. I wanted to say them all, but none of them would take shape.

I thought of what she'd said about forgiveness. Fyodora was smart, she gave good advice. At least, she'd always known how to help me out. But this was asking a lot. It's hard to admit someone's hurt you, even if the ache is there every single day. It's hard to open yourself up to your own pain: Your conscience always tries to protect you, throwing layer upon layer of white lies around you, scraping together the pieces, telling you you're still whole. And all the while, you keep shattering, and the pieces get smaller and smaller, and a day comes when they're too tiny to even pick up.

And that was where I was: a handful of dust, waiting for the wind to come along and blow me away. But I refused to disappear, and I was ready to face my fears if it would give me the opportunity to move forward, alone if I had to.

"Do you remember the last message I sent you?" I asked.

"Yeah."

"You didn't respond."

"There was nothing to say—"

"I found your music box and the photos hidden inside it." I interrupted her, seeing she didn't know what to do but keep lying. "As soon as I saw his face, I knew. I look too much like him for it to be a coincidence."

She closed her eyes, and a few tears escaped her. And I kept talking, because I couldn't stop myself. "I know his name's Giulio. Giulio Dassori. He lives in a precious villa in Sorrento with his family and his husband. In the mornings, he gives diving classes, and in the afternoons, he runs a little ballet school. He's forty, but he looks way younger, and he has a mole over his eyebrow just like mine. When he smiles, the left side of his mouth lifts up more than the right. He cuts his toast into four pieces before eating it, and he puts the jelly on first, and then the butter. He has the sweetest laugh I've ever heard. He hates liars. You want to know how I know all this? Because I was as close to him as I am to you right now."

Scared but resigned, Mom asked, "Have you been with him all this time?"

"Almost."

"Does he know who you are?"

I nodded. If I'd ever had any lingering doubts, they were gone. "You always swore to me you didn't know who my father was. Why?"

"When I got pregnant, the whole thing was so complicated, and then...you tell a lie so long, and it kind of becomes truth, you know?" Her voice was wavering, and she took several breaths to try to control herself. "How is he?"

"He's good," I said. "He has a nice life and he's happy. Or was until I showed up and fucked everything up for him. I guess I'm more like you than I realized."

"I never hurt your father."

"You did now. Thanks to me," I responded, intending to cut her deep.

Starting to cry again, she said, "I had my reasons for not telling him."

"Well, it doesn't matter now because he knows, and it's all blown up in my face. He doesn't even want to hear from me."

"Why not?"

"Why would he?" I shouted. And I wanted to keep shouting. Wanted to shout that it was her fault, that she'd caused all this by being a liar and playing with people's lives. I wanted to show her how much I blamed her and how resentful I was against her for having been the worst mother in the world. She had never shown any interest in anyone but herself and had pushed me aside so she could continue on her way, as if I were a dog abandoned on the side of the road.

What kind of mother does that?

Mine. Mine did it.

And yet, instead of letting out all the rage that consumed me, the disappointment and reproach I'd swallowed down, I told her the story of my life as it had gone since she'd taken those photos of me.

The words came out, and I watched her shrink and grow weaker before my eyes, especially when I got to the part about the life I'd discovered in Sorrento and how happy all the people there were and how, for once, I'd been able to fantasize about a family where I finally fit in.

I told her about Dante and the misunderstanding that caused everything to collapse. About Giulio's reaction and what he said before he disappeared through the door.

"I couldn't stick around after that," I whispered.

Then I bent over and pressed my hands into my eyes till I saw stars. I wouldn't do it. I wouldn't cry again.

"I'm sorry things turned out that way," she said.

"It was me, though. I'm a disaster. I fucked everything up from the beginning. No matter how I try, I always pick the wrong road."

"That makes two of us," my mother responded.

"It's shit," I hissed, feeling disappointed as my mother sat back and sighed.

"What do you want from me, Maya?" she asked.

I blinked and stared at her, shocked by the question. Then I asked myself the same thing. I had gone there to free myself from a weight that was keeping me from moving forward. But the problem was, I didn't know how. What did I actually need to bring that story to an end?

Was I looking for reconciliation? Had I gone there to renounce her forever? Would either of those make up somehow for an entire life of abandonment? I didn't know. All I could say was I was tired: tired of an entire life of revolving around that infinite circle that was my mother, looking desperately for a way out, an escape hatch from those emotions that had always dug into me with their claws.

I studied her, asking myself: What do I really want?

Then the answer appeared like a lightning bolt. *Nothing.* I knew nothing about the person who had carried me in her belly for nine months and then had decided to shove off and live her own life.

I read somewhere once that the truth will set you free.

Maybe. And maybe that was all I wanted.

"I want you to tell me the truth. The whole truth."

68

My mother said we should take a walk on the beach. I agreed. The walls in her house were starting to close in on me, and it was getting hard to breathe.

The sun shone and the air was cold and damp coming off the sea. I was chilly, so I flipped up the collar of my jacket as I crossed the street. Mom walked beside me, hands in her pants pockets, eyes lost on the horizon.

I saw her from the corner of my eye: sad, but cagey.

Neither of us said anything for a while.

The sea was calm, with faint traces of foam on the waves that lazily lapped the shore. I tried to swallow, to get rid of my nerves, and waited for her to say something as I watched the tiny bubbles pop on the sand.

She exhaled, then started to speak. "When I saw Giulio for the first time, I thought he was the handsomest guy in the world. Right away, I was hooked. I couldn't even look at him without holding my breath. We got to know each other from one class to the next. He was funny, he was nice, a sweetheart—he had everything. When the first summer semester was over, we organized a farewell dinner. Giulio and I sat together, we got to talking, and the hours just flew by. I don't know how, but we ended up in the bedroom at his dorm, and… Well, you know the rest."

"You went to bed with him," I said, just to make sure, but from the way she'd smiled subtly as she remembered him, there wasn't really any doubt.

"Yeah, we went to bed together. And after that night, we went out a few more times, and I guess you could say I got hung up on him. He stayed longer to do another class. I wound up falling in love with him. I even told him so. And then he started getting weird. He avoided me and spent all his time with another one of the students, a guy. I didn't get it, and I ended up confronting him. We argued, and he confessed that he was pretty sure he liked men. I got angry, of course. Furious. But then, how could I blame him for being human? After the auditions, he left, and we never saw each other again."

"You didn't try to stay in touch with him?"

"He did, but I never responded. I was still stupidly in love with him, and I thought I needed to try and forget."

"And after?" I asked.

"I learned I was pregnant when I was eleven weeks along. I'd always had very irregular periods, so the fact that I'd missed a couple hadn't really worried me. My mother lost her mind when she found out. She moved heaven and earth to try to make me get an abortion, and she nearly threw me out of the house when I told her I wanted to keep you."

I felt a sharp jab in my chest. "She wanted you to get an abortion…"

"Yes."

"Why didn't you?"

"Because…" she said, closing her eyes. She was hesitating. Doubtful. Trying to think of something. I wasn't sure what I felt just then, but I knew I was ready to take whatever came out of her mouth.

"Tell me the truth, please," I asked her.

"Because I wanted to stop dancing. I couldn't take it anymore. The pressure she put on me, her demands, her expectations... It was impossible to live up to them. You were my way out."

That hurt. Bad.

I cleared my throat to try to relieve the tension. "I remember you always dancing. Rehearsing with her at the school."

"She forced me to as soon as I'd recovered from giving birth. It was that or move out with you, and... I was just eighteen years old, I didn't know how I'd take care of us." She wiped away the tears that were dripping down her face.

"It never passed through your head to get in touch with Giulio and ask him for help?" I asked.

"No."

"Why not?"

"Because I was a scared little girl and I had lied about him from the beginning. I made the wrong decisions, and there was no undoing them, and it was all just too much for me. So I put my head down once more and did everything my mother asked of me. That meant going back to the ballet, back to auditions, just trying to get through each day as best I could."

"But..."

"You should understand that better than anyone. Why did you come back from London? You had made it. You'd escaped," she said with a tormented expression.

My breathing kept speeding up as we locked eyes. She was scared, terribly scared—and I was, too. Scared of everything that brought us together, everything we were feeling. That fear was a bond stronger than blood and would tie us together forever.

Because we were two versions of the same story.

Trained animals scared of their master's hand, even if they were stronger than that master would ever be. Obedient, waiting to be petted. Afraid of punishment. Thankful every time they were tossed a rotten morsel of love, because the pain of hunger was so much worse than the pain of eating those poisoned crumbs.

My rancor, my rage evaporated in waves, and all that was left was my vulnerability, and I saw that she was as fragile as I was. I looked out at the sea. Then I asked something. I don't know where it came from.

"Did you like dancing?"

"Yeah, at first, when it was fun and it made me feel special. But then she turned it into hell for me, and I wound up hating it."

"Why is Olga like that?" This was the thing I truly needed to know.

"Maya, my mother isn't a good person. That's the truth. I know it's hard to accept. It took me years to. Olga has never loved anybody except herself, and because of that, she's never known remorse or restraint. Having a child, giving birth, those are just biological processes, they don't mean love is necessarily there. The instinct to protect and care for your child when the doctor first lets you hold it... That's something not every mother has."

A moan escaped me. I knew she was right. But that made me ask another question. "You ran away, though. You left me with her. So that instinct, that love—do you not have it, either?"

She nodded, her face the very picture of grief, and I thought for a moment that maybe the blame wasn't all hers, that we aren't much more than the circumstances we find on our path.

"It's true. I had you because I saw you as a way out of that hell. But when you were born, I did everything I could to take care of you. I tried, but I didn't know how to be a mother, and Olga wouldn't let me. And I just had to go. I didn't have another option."

"And now?"

"I still don't know how to be a mother to you."

Those words burned into me like acid, through my skin and muscles and into my bones. Straight through to my heart. Something broke in me, I swear I could hear the cracking sound, and she burst into tears as I confessed, "I always thought you stopped coming to see me because I'd done something wrong."

"No, Maya. You never did anything wrong."

"What was it, then?"

"I never stopped feeling guilty for abandoning you, and when I'd spend a few days with you, it just hurt too bad. I saw you growing up, but at the same time withering under my mother's cruelty, and I knew I was the one responsible for it. And so seeing you was no relief. It actually made me hate myself more because I wasn't strong enough to take you away from there."

I lashed out. "So you just stopped seeing me and didn't even give me a reason that might help me understand why?"

"I was a coward. Again. I'm still ashamed of it."

I felt sorry for her, even though I knew I had every right to hate her. At the same time, I just wanted to erase all that from my memory, go to sleep, and wake up with it gone. Life would be so much easier that way. But my childish side, my malicious side, the one that wanted to hurt her, reappeared, "I never opened any of the presents you sent me all those years."

"I know. Your grandfather told me."

"And I only came here to tell you I hate you for abandoning me. I blame you for everything Olga made me suffer, and I won't waste another second of my life thinking of you."

"I understand. And you're perfectly right to feel that way."

I was right. I was right in everything I said. I was right to want to turn around and leave without looking back. I knew everything I'd come there to learn. I had answers to my questions, and what I'd thought was just a possibility—that Giulio was my father—was now a certainty. I could turn the last page, put down the book, and start another story, as if none of that mattered anymore. Start over, from zero, with a new story.

Except that I couldn't…

A new question, one I hadn't seen coming, rose up inside me, not from my head, but lower down, behind my ribs, in the center of my chest. In that emptiness that at the same time was always spilling over with longing, desperation, and fear. A question that didn't make sense because it contradicted everything I was feeling. I managed to get out the word *Then*, but the tears burst through and stopped me, and the sobs started strangling me, and I cursed.

"What, Maya?" my mother asked. She, too, was suffering.

"Then why…why do I want you to hug me?"

Trembling, wiping her face, she looked at me like a startled cat ready to take off running. But then her expression changed subtly. If I hadn't been looking close, I could have missed it. I saw a spark of something: determination, inspiration, courage. And she rushed over to me as if an invisible hand had pushed her. She wrapped her arms around me and squeezed me tight. My arms hung at my sides, my face was buried in her hair, her scent filled my nose, and I cried. I remembered when I was a little girl. The feeling was agonizing, but I must have needed it. And she held me, her embrace never slackening.

"I'm sorry, honey. I'm so sorry. I hope one day you can forgive me."

For once, I was really, truly her daughter. Knowing that was crushing, but at the same time consoling. Like a scalpel that cuts you open, but at the same time cauterizes the wound. We held each other a long time in silence. Then she took my hand and we walked together.

We talked. Strolled. Talked more.

I realized something that day: that we only see one side of things, but we live as if that small something we know and perceive is absolutely everything. We think *our* truth is *the* truth. That the reasons that make sense to us are the only reasons. But it's not that simple. We forget that every person has their own perspective on things, that they too confuse what they see and believe—their truth, their reasons—with everything.

My mother had her reality. One that was hard for me to understand, but that didn't make it less true. It was just different. I had suffered because of her; she had suffered because of others. She'd made mistakes, the same as me. Those errors had caused terrible pain to other people, but also to ourselves.

How do you forgive a person? It depends. There is no magic formula. Some people never do it. Some people need a lifetime. Some people can do it instantly. But the important thing is to truly forgive, with no conditions, no expectations, without looking to get anything out of it. To forgive for your own sake because you need that to keep going. Forgiveness isn't something you concede to another; it's a privilege you allow yourself. A freedom that doesn't cancel suffering, because your suffering will always be there inside you. The past can't be erased. But the wounds can close and scar over, and life can go on.

I started to forgive my mother on that beach, at the same time as I realized something important. She didn't know how to be my mother. But I didn't know how to be her daughter, either. I had never been a daughter. But still, we could be something. Something different. Something new. Something that was real and truly mattered.

69

My mother asked me to stay with her. At least until I could figure out what I wanted to do with my life. I accepted. I didn't have anywhere else to go. But what mattered more than that was my desire to get to know her, to learn who she really was. To find out if we were similar or completely different. If we liked the same things.

I wasn't scared anymore to make things up as I went along. I wasn't so afraid to go with the flow. I didn't need to control every last detail. I didn't need to know where I'd be in a week or a month or a year to feel secure.

I could move on if I chose to. I knew that now.

I wasn't scared to be alone anymore if that solitude would make me the owner of my own life. If it would help me love myself and be the person I really was. We have this absurd belief that it's other people who make us complete, but there's no one who's been put on this earth for the sake of our happiness or fulfillment. That responsibility is too big for any other person to take on.

I had held on to Lucas as though my whole world would crumble if I didn't have him. I had been waiting for him to walk in step with me. And while I was waiting, I'd almost disappeared.

Love doesn't justify everything, and it isn't always enough. It isn't a sufficient reason for two people to be together. Loving sometimes means letting the other person go before you hurt them more. Love can mean distancing yourself and choosing yourself above others.

Even if it hurts.

Even if it seems like you won't be able to take the absence.

I could hardly think of Lucas without breaking down. A week after I'd left him at the station, I could feel the emptiness where he used to be like alcohol in a wound. It got worse every day, and I kept asking myself when it would finally stop hurting. When I would stop loving him.

And the answer was always the same.

When there were no more stars left to count.

70

Guille lifted another shell he'd found and I smiled at him. We had been on the beach for a while, playing in the sand and splashing on the shore. I liked watching him, and it was a big help to his parents, since Alexis and my mother both worked from home.

A few years before, Daria had started making necklaces and bracelets with beads and charms as a hobby, and now she had a little online store that made her enough money to pay the bills. That surprised me. I could never have imagined her doing something like that. Alexis was a freelance translator for book publishers. They were doing well, and they seemed satisfied with the calm, simple life they had created.

I looked at the sea and held my phone close to my ear, listening to Matías's detailed account of the pros and cons of moving in with Rubén.

"I think you're starting to lose it," I said with a laugh.

"I just want to really think it over. It's a big step, and I don't want to rush it."

"You can make twenty lists and go through a thousand scenarios, but the only way to know if it will work is to try."

He sighed. "You're right."

"I know I'm right," I said, looking over at Guille. "You just have to be honest with yourself, OK? Do you want to live with Rubén? If it's a yes, then dive in headfirst. If it's a no, don't. Rubén's a good guy, he'll understand."

"What if he thinks me not wanting to is me having doubts about him?"

"You adore him. Everybody knows that."

I walked over to the water's edge and let the waves tickle my feet. Matías changed the subject and asked me how I was.

"Good," I responded. The breeze blew my hair in my face, and I pushed it aside. "I felt out of place the first few days, but now it's like I've lived here my whole life."

"So everything's better with your mom?"

"More or less. Let's say we've started from zero. We're trying to be friends."

"Is that enough for you?"

"It is."

"How long will you stay there?" he asked.

"I'm not sure. Maybe till the end of the year. Then I might listen to what Fyodora said and try to take that empty spot at the dance company."

"That would be amazing!" Matías exclaimed.

"It would, right?" As I asked that, I noticed a silence on the other line that I knew all too well. A silence that said Matías had something to tell me that he was struggling to get out. I nudged him along, asking, "What?"

He tried to tell me it was nothing, and when I pressed him, he admitted, "I saw Lucas yesterday."

My heart skipped a beat. "Is he still in Madrid?"

"Yeah."

I didn't know if that relieved me or made me sad. But it did hurt. It hurt to think that he was still in the very same place where I'd left him, with his family surrounding him and pulling the strings and telling him where to go and what to do and when.

"Madrid's a big city, but it's still one of those places where you randomly bump into people, huh?" I said, just to make conversation.

"I didn't run into him by accident, Maya. He came to see me."

"Why?"

"Why do you think? He wanted to know if you were OK."

"He could have asked me."

"That's what I told him, and he said leaving you in peace was the best thing he could do for you. And I think he was right. He's a good guy, Maya, but he isn't good for you. He isn't capable of giving you everything you need."

"I mean, he made a choice, right?" I said, my voice cracking.

"And he hasn't changed his mind, babe. He's still here."

"I convinced him to come, though. He left Sorrento because of me."

"You gave him the best advice you could give him. His father was dying, Maya. Everything that's happened since he got to Madrid, though, all of that's on him. He's made these decisions, he's acted, and he could have guessed what the consequences would be."

"I know, Matías, but it's his family. They've got him wrapped around their fingers, and…"

"Lucas is twenty-seven years old. He's an adult. He should be capable of dealing with this situation. He needs to defend his independence, live his own life, not ask other people's permission for everything he does. And he hasn't even tried. He never fought for…"

Matías stopped himself. I could see he didn't want to hurt me. "You can just say it," I told him.

"He never fought for you."

He had hit me where it hurt, but he was right. Lucas hadn't fought, he'd given in, and that was what I couldn't accept. Not after everything we had shared.

"You're right," I whispered.

"And don't you dare blame yourself. You tried, and it didn't work out. These things happen."

"I know they do, but it hurts, and I miss him, and I'm angry because of the two of us, he was supposed to be the strong one."

"Those are the side effects of love," Matías said. "Didn't you read the manual?"

I was laughing and crying at the same time. That was the best I could hope for just then, I guess. My phone beeped. I was running out of battery.

"I've got to go, Matías. My phone's almost dead."

"Call me soon, OK?"

"Will do, bye."

I hung up and caught my breath, as I looked again over at Guille, who was running toward the boardwalk, where I could see my mother's outline. There were two other people with her. I squinted, trying to see who they were.

Then I shuddered, and I felt a tingle all over. Impossible, I thought. I must be imagining things. But the closer he came, the more real it all was. I was stunned, and all I could do was watch and tremble. He stopped and looked me over. I felt smaller than I ever had and wrapped my arms around my body instinctively, as if that could protect me.

His hair was longer and hung loose over his forehead. He was wearing a white sweatshirt, and that made his tanned face look darker. His jeans were baggy and hung off his hips.

He smiled at me.

"I should tell you something," he said. "Your grandfather had a mole just like ours. In the very same place." He reached up and touched his brow. "It's funny, but I was looking at old pictures, and you look much more like him than me."

"What are you doing here?" I asked.

"Daria got in touch with me a few days ago at the school. We've talked a couple of times since then."

Now I was starting to understand. But this was crazy! My mother had actually gotten him to come here?

"She shouldn't have called you," I said. "You were under no obligation to come."

"And no one made me, Maya. I'm here because it's where I need to be. Coming here was the right thing to do…"

I stopped him. "You never wanted children, and I'm old enough to deal with my issues on my own. I didn't need you to do this, OK? You don't have to make something up for me. Go back to your family and forget all this."

He stepped forward and tried to look me in the eye.

"You didn't let me finish, Maya. May I?" I nodded, and he went on. "I'm here because it's the right thing to do *and* because I want to be here."

"You were so mad when I left."

"I was caught by surprise. I didn't know how to handle it. I was scared." He looked up into the sky, as though to draw strength from it.

"No, it was my fault," I told him. "Right from the beginning, I screwed everything up. I'm really sorry."

"Maya, it's not your fault. You're not responsible for anything. I can't even imagine how hard it must have been for you."

"I mean, I can't really act like you were responsible either…"

"Maybe not, but here we are, right?"

I nodded, gulped, tried to slow my racing heart. "I hope everything's OK with Dante."

"Dante and I are doing great. He asked to come along."

He pointed behind him and I looked over at the boardwalk, where my mother was talking to someone. Was it him? I wasn't even sure I wanted to know. Our last encounter had scared me. Nor did I really know what Giulio was doing there. I looked at my father for a moment in silence, and then he began speaking. "What I said about not wanting to have kids… I didn't get the chance to explain."

I held myself tighter and tried to hold in my tears. "You don't have to explain anything to me. We are who we are."

"It's got nothing to do with who I am. It's more complicated than that," he said softly.

He walked toward a boat that was stranded on the beach, and I followed him. He leaned against the hull and motioned for me to come over, and I stood next to him, so close that our arms touched. I observed him in profile. It still didn't seem real that he was here, that he'd just shown up after I'd convinced myself I'd never see him again.

We looked out at the sea for a few moments, and then he turned to me and confessed, "My father's name was Vicenzo, and he was the greatest guy in the world. Never in my life did I meet another person like him, and I adored him. I know there are millions of kids who say that about their dad, but mine was special. You can't even imagine. We were close, and I was a wreck when he died. I never got over it. The pain is still with me today. And that's why I promised myself I'd never have kids. Not because I didn't want to, but because I refused to bring a person in the world whom I might make suffer the way I suffered over my father. It didn't seem fair, causing someone else that kind of pain, no matter how much people say life is just like that."

I blinked, confused. Was that really it? He didn't want to make another person suffer? Hearing that was like meeting him again for the first time. I'd never experienced the death of someone I was close to. I didn't know what it felt like, but the despair in Giulio's eyes in that moment gave me a sense of how it must feel.

"You must think that's absurd, right?" he added, smiling.

"Of course not. Losing your father when you were a boy was a traumatic experience. It's normal that it left a mark on you. I can't judge you for that."

"And I can't judge you for wanting to find me."

"I shouldn't have done it."

"You should have, Maya. Of course you should have! I'd have done the same thing in your place!"

"How do you know?" I asked.

"Because I haven't stopped thinking of you even for one day since you left. Thinking about all you told me about your family and the way you grew up. How alone you must have felt to leave everything behind and take off running because you glimpsed a possibility, just a possibility, in a photograph."

I dried the tears stinging my cheeks with my sleeve. "I needed to find out if there was a place for me out there. Somewhere I could fit in."

"There is, Maya," he said, so energetically he almost sounded angry. "It's called Sorrento. And I want you to come back there with me."

"Are you serious?" I asked, partly timid, partly excited.

"We all want you there. Dante, your grandmother, your aunt, the kids... You're part of our family." He reached up and touched my brow, and I shivered. "You're a Dassori."

"But...I'm sorry to come back to this... You said you never..."

"That doesn't matter anymore. You exist. You're my daughter. And it's not like I even need any proof. I mean, look at us! And I missed out on so much: being with you, watching you grow up... I don't know what you were like as a little girl, I don't know what kind of father I would have been, but there's one thing I do know: I don't want to miss out on all the other things I can still experience with you."

I struggled to stop the torrent of tears, and they kept flowing, but I was smiling, too. So was Giulio. He wrapped his arms around me and pulled me in. Waves of emotion washed over me, and all I could do was say yes. Yes to life, yes to everything that was happening to me.

Because I didn't want to miss out on all the things he and I could share, either.

71

It was hard to say goodbye to my mother and Guille. It wasn't sad, though. It wasn't a *goodbye*, it was an *until we meet again*. We were a family now, and I wasn't going to lose them again. I would stay in contact. I would be sure I was always a presence in their lives.

Madrid was far, and we decided a train ride would be much more comfortable than a bus. Giulio fell asleep almost instantly, his head leaning on Dante's shoulder. I wasn't so scared of Dante now. We'd had the chance to talk things over the night before. It was uncomfortable at first, but we were united by a person we both loved a lot, and we promised each other we'd do what it took to make our relationship work.

We had to change trains in Murcia, and we had enough time to grab a bite to eat in the bar there. We talked about the rest of our trip over sandwiches and soft drinks. Our idea was to spend one night in Madrid before flying to Rome.

I could hardly contain my excitement about going back and seeing Catalina. My grandmother. I never imagined I'd be able to say those words and feel my chest swell with joy instead of fear.

"What are you smiling about?" Giulio asked groggily, woken up by the jarring of the train. I had been looking outside through the window. Now I turned to him.

"I was thinking of Catalina. I've really missed her."

"She missed you, too. You and Lucas… Sorry, I shouldn't have mentioned him. It came out before I could stop myself. Your mother told me you were having problems."

"It's fine," I said.

"Are you no longer together then?"

"No, we split up. It was better for both of us."

Giulio bent over the table that was between our seats. "You don't think there's a chance you could work it out? You seemed perfect for each other."

"We were, but…" I shrugged and noticed Dante had stopped reading his book and was peeking up at me. "There are other things in life that matter more to him right now."

"Like what?" Giulio asked as if he were struggling to believe that.

Dante said something in Italian that started with *Amore* and ended with *disagio*. I was pretty sure he was telling Giulio I might be uncomfortable, so I let him know I was fine, then told Giulio, "It's complicated…"

As the train came closer to Madrid, I told them about the weeks I'd spent with Lucas there. It was hard at first to order my thoughts and transform them into words. It was hard just to remember it all. Three weeks had passed, and my feelings were still just as raw as the day I'd left, if not worse.

Dante and Giulio didn't respond, but their expressions said more than their words ever could. My voice cracked as I reached the point in my story where Lucas came to find me at the station. Dante reached out and held my hand, squeezing it tight and giving me all the comfort I needed just then.

"I haven't heard from him since," I concluded.

"Oh, Maya…" Giulio said.

"I'm fine!"

"You're not," he responded. "And none of this is fine, either. And you can't just leave it this way."

"What do you mean?"

"Sometimes we need someone to give us a little push so we can make the necessary change. Lucas doesn't need a push, though. He needs someone to shake him until he opens his eyes. Did you do that? Because if not, maybe you should have."

I didn't like that. I didn't like the suggestion, or the turn the conversation had taken, or the doubts I was starting to feel. Had I not done everything possible to change the situation? Was it possible that I'd just been waiting for Lucas to react on his own?

"What are you getting at?" I asked.

"Maya, Dante and I are here with you right now because your mother found me and forced me to talk to her. She gave me things to think about. She made me face reality. When I hesitated, Dante pushed me. I would never have done it on my own. Lucas is trapped again. Maybe he doesn't have the strength to run away a second time. Not without someone there to motivate him."

I grunted. This was so frustrating! I'd gotten out of one mess and back into another.

Dante squeezed my hand, and I looked him in the eyes and asked if he felt the same.

"I think Giulio's right," he said. "I know Lucas. I've been his boss and his friend for two years. He's not as smart as you think."

We both laughed.

The train stopped at Atocha. We got our bags and left from the main exit. When we were stopped in Murcia, Dad—could I call him that now?—had made a reservation at a nearby hotel. We checked in, dropped off our bags, and went for a walk. Dante wanted to get to know Madrid.

I called Matías and asked him to come meet us. I wanted him

to meet my father, and I needed to see him anyway to say goodbye before I left again.

He showed up right away, with Rubén.

I tried to be good company, take part in the conversation, enjoy the time we had together. But I couldn't. I couldn't even concentrate for more than a few seconds. Lucas was casting a shadow over me. He had been since we got off the train, and my doubts and dark thoughts clouded my mood.

Late in the afternoon, we said our goodbyes and walked back to the hotel, taking our time, stopping to look in the shop windows, snapping photos in all the places that awakened memories for Giulio.

I heard my name, "Maya! Maya!"

"Yes?" I answered distractedly. I had gotten lost in my thoughts again. Dante and Giulio asked if I was all right, and I smiled and told them I was, but it felt like a dagger was twisting inside me. So I stopped and corrected myself, "No, sorry. I'm not all right at all."

Giulio seemed frightened, and hurried to put an arm around me. "What is it?"

"What if you're right?" I asked. "What if I was just sitting there waiting for him to take a step when I needed to be the one to help him to do so?"

"Parlate di Lucas?" Dante asked.

I nodded. Of course we were talking about Lucas. My father told me, "You've still got time to fix it."

I stared him in the eye. And what I saw there quelled my fears and calmed my nerves. I could feel his touch supporting me, telling me I could trust him. Determination and self-assurance flowed from him.

It was true. I needed to resolve this. Or at least I needed to try.

"You're right. I can't just leave things this way. I can't go back to Italy without opening up to him completely."

Giulio held me close, smiling... Was it proudly? I didn't know.

I'd never seen that expression on anyone in my family before. But I loved it, and I loved feeling him so close. We had a lot of lost hugs to make up for.

"Are you going to give him that push?" Giulio whispered.

"I'm going to shake him till he gets whiplash," I said.

He cracked up laughing. "Do that. And tell him we miss him."

72

I took a deep breath, tucked a strand of hair behind my ear, and rang the doorbell again.

Nothing. Not a single noise.

Across the hall, the door opened, and a guy came out with a trash bag in his hand. I knew him. We'd run into each other many times coming in and out. "Hey," I said.

"Hey."

As he passed by me on his way to the elevator, I rang the doorbell again, and he told me, "Lucas is away. He won't be back until tomorrow."

"How do you know?" I asked.

"He asked me to keep an eye out for some packages for him."

"Got it…" I bit my lip. "Did he say where he was going?"

"His parents' place. They've got some celebration or other."

He must have been able to see the disappointment on my face as I stepped away and said, "Thanks."

"No worries. You going down?"

"Yeah."

We said goodbye to each other outside and I started walking back to the hotel. I felt as if my life consisted of junk that I was constantly trying to put in order only to always have someone step in and knock it all over again.

And I was tired of the disorder. Tired of going round and round. Tired of getting stuck in dead ends and wasting my time on winding roads that took me away from the things I had to face.

My fears. The fear of a broken heart.

That fear that makes us wound ourselves, because sometimes running away from what we really want is easier. Resigning ourselves to loss. Pretending what happens to us is just fate.

What idiots we can be!

Well, I was tired of being an idiot. I was tired of being stupid, being scared.

So I caught the first taxi that came past.

Lucas's family house was in a development in Alcobendas. I'd never been there, but I remembered the address because he'd mentioned it to me. I clutched my bag as I looked through the window at the empty streets.

"Would you mind waiting for me here?" I asked the driver.

"No problem," he said.

I got out with my heart pounding and stopped in front of a tall iron gate with a wall on either side of it. I couldn't see what lay past it, apart from the tops of trees swaying in the cold November wind. I pushed a button on the call box and a woman responded on the other line, "Hello?"

"Yes, hi… Good evening, I…I'm looking for Lucas. Is he in?"

"Lucas? Yes, that's my grandson."

This was his grandmother? The thought made me grin, and I replied, "It's a pleasure to meet you."

"Did you bring cake?"

"Excuse me?"

"You're not from the pastry shop?"

"No, sorry, I'm a friend of Lucas's, and I need to talk to him. Could you tell him Maya's here?"

"Tell who?"

"Lucas."

"Lucas is my grandson. He's a good boy."

I sighed. I had a bad feeling that this conversation wasn't going anywhere. "He is a good boy. But I was wondering…"

"Just a moment."

The light on the screen went out.

I stuck my hands in my pockets and waited, feeling the cold soak through my clothes, and every time I exhaled, a cloud of vapor escaped my lips. I jumped nervously, walked back and forth. Time passed, no one opened up.

A minute went by. Then another. Then another.

He wasn't coming.

Sad, disappointed, I turned and walked toward the taxi. At least I'd tried. I'd failed. And I was frustrated, and I could have broken down then and there. I wished I'd done something earlier. But I'd tried.

Then the gate opened.

"Maya?"

I turned, almost terrified. Lucas was there on the sidewalk looking at me. He was wearing a knit sweater, a button-down shirt, and chinos. He looked too formal. I could see he'd started growing a beard, and his eyes looked tired. I must have been the last person he was expecting, but I didn't see any sign of happiness in his face.

"Hey," I whispered.

"Hey."

"How are you?"

"Getting by," he said. "What about you?"

"I'm good." I motioned toward his house. "Big party tonight?"

"It's my birthday," he said hesitantly.

I was so nervous, I didn't know what to say, but I managed to get out, "Happy birthday."

"Thanks."

"It's funny, we've talked about so many things, but never about when our birthdays are. Mine's in April."

He sucked in a breath, and his eyes lit up with fear, suspicion, doubts, confusion. "What are you here for, Maya?"

I had been chilly on my way there, but now I was burning hot: in my cheeks, my hands, all over. "I wanted you to know I'm going back to Sorrento. Giulio and Dante came to see me. We've worked things out, and they want me to go back there. To stay."

"They're in Madrid?"

Still feeling insecure, I responded, "Yeah. They want me to tell you everyone at the villa misses you."

"They could have called me," he said almost scornfully.

"Yeah. And you could have called them. You've basically fallen off the face of the earth."

He looked down. Was that shame I saw? He nearly said something, but then he thought better of it and closed his lips. That irreverent attitude he'd been trying to put on vanished.

I was getting impatient. I hadn't gone there to argue. I stepped toward him. He looked cautious, vulnerable, fragile—just as fragile as I felt.

"Lucas, I'm here because someone told me once I needed to live according to my instincts. That person told me intuition is an impulse born inside us. A desire. A thing we really want, more than anything else. And my instinct brought me here to tell you something: that I don't regret leaving, but I do regret not telling you some things before I did."

His eyes looked distrustful, but he asked me, "What things?"

I took a deep breath and gathered as much strength as I could.

"There's lots of them. I honestly don't know where to start. All this, everything here, you don't want it, it isn't you, and you know that. Obviously your family matters to you and I know you're worried about what might happen with your father, and that's a good thing. But that's not what's keeping you here. It's guilt. And that's not fair, because you never did anything wrong and you don't have anything to make up for! It's not fair for you to make these sacrifices.

"This is your life we're talking about, and you've given it away to people it doesn't belong to. For weeks, I've been watching you become a different person. You're not yourself anymore. You're someone you promised yourself you'd never be again. Slowly you've been disappearing, to the point that I hardly recognize you now, and what I regret the most is that I stood on the sidelines watching it happen when I could have helped you. I'm sorry I left like you didn't matter to me. I'm sorry I told you there was never an us. That was a lie. Of course there was. And there could still be one."

My eyes were burning. In a hoarse tone, Lucas asked, "Still?"

The taxi driver called out, "Hey, just so you know, my shift's about to end."

"I'll be right there," I said.

Lucas's shoulders were tense, and he was looking past me rather than at me, while my emotions were like a choppy sea inside. I added one last thing. "I love you, Lucas. That was the other thing I needed to tell you."

His eyes opened wide, showing me all the mixed emotions he felt. He blinked and shook his head as if he didn't believe me.

"You say you love me, but you're leaving again? Is this some kind of cruel joke?"

"It's not a joke. I love you so much, but I'm going because my place, my family, my home is in Sorrento. It's where I belong, and it's where you belong, too, Lucas. In that villa full of people who truly love you, who only want you to be happy. A place where the mornings smell of sea and coffee and the nights of barbecue and limoncello. Where we can take naps in the cool bathtub and whisper songs into each other's ears. Where…where you don't need wings to fly."

My voice was cracking, and we looked at each other with glassy eyes. Then someone appeared behind him.

"What are you doing out here? You need to come unwrap your presents." It was Claudia. She froze briefly when she saw me, but soon she regained her composure.

"Oh, hey," she said. "Sorry… What was your name again?"

I looked away and pretended she wasn't there. With my eyes, I begged Lucas to make a choice, knowing the taxi driver was getting impatient. I was terrified: I kept telling myself that this was our only opportunity. "Don't stay," I told him. "No matter how much you think it's your duty. Don't stay."

Claudia grunted and said, "Lucas…"

I smiled at him as if it were just the two of us and that farewell could only be temporary. "Goodbye," I said, turning to the taxi.

"Goodbye? I thought you didn't like that word. I thought it was too *definitive*."

I felt a spark of something just then. Was it joy? Because his voice told me he wasn't just sad, he was amused.

"And I thought you liked complicated things. That you had a talent for unraveling them."

He smiled—a real smile—and with that, I felt he was giving me my life back. I held on to that image like a treasure in my mind as I got into the taxi and closed the door. Leaving him behind. Traveling away.

I'd be lying if I said it didn't hurt to go. That my heart didn't ache. That I didn't want to tell the driver to screech to a halt so I could jump out and run back to him. That it didn't cut me to the core to think that this might be the end for us.

But it was a risk I had to take.

They say with time, everything ends up where it should be.

And I hoped we'd wind up at each other's side.

73

We landed in Rome early in the afternoon.

I walked toward the double glass doors with Dante behind me pushing a cart with our luggage while my father talked on the phone. I was anxious. I had dreamed of coming back so many times, but for a while it hadn't seemed real, and it almost didn't seem true that I was back in Italy.

It was as if the time hadn't passed.

As if nothing had happened at all.

I walked through the doors and made my way through everyone waiting there. Then I met eyes with someone I knew. "Chabela?"

She turned. A few wrinkles appeared in her forehead. Then her face was transformed by an explosion of joy.

"Maya! Is it really you? It's so amazing to see you again!"

I ran over and we wrapped our arms around each other.

"I'm happy to see you, too," I told her. "How are you?"

"Great, dear, just great. As always."

"Are you here for your daughter?"

"I was, but I'm leaving now. My plane departs in a few hours."

Giulio and Dante appeared next to us and they and Chabela looked each other over.

"Guys," I said, "this is Chabela. We met the first time I flew over here, and she was so nice to me. These guys are… They're…".

"Her parents," Dante said, reaching out his hand. "Buonasera, I'm Dante."

My cheeks were trembling with happiness. All my life, I'd wanted a father, and now I had two, and they were better than I could ever have hoped. Giulio reached out his hand and introduced himself, before warning me, "Maya, we should get a move on or we'll miss our train."

"I'll be right there," I said.

Chabela watched them walk off through the bystanders and asked with surprise, "You've got two fathers?"

"Yeah, Giulio's my biological father and Dante is his husband, so I guess you'd call him my stepdad?"

"They look so young. I was wondering if one of them was your boyfriend. Good thing I didn't open my mouth!"

We laughed, and I told her she was right, that it was hard to believe he was that much older than me.

"So he's what brought you to Italy," she said. "Well, it seems to have turned out well. I'm glad."

"How do you know?" I asked her. "I never mentioned that!"

"It was obvious you were looking for something. I just didn't know what it was."

I hugged her. "I've got to go, Chabela. I hope we see each other again."

"Me too, Gorgeous. You take care."

"You too."

I ran off toward the tracks as I saw on the monitors that the train for Naples was leaving in just a few minutes.

Seeing her again brought back to me the first time I set foot in that airport: who I was then and the different person I was now. An eternity seemed to have passed since then. For all I'd lived through. All that had happened. All those important moments.

But it had just been a few months, followed by weeks when I'd fallen and gotten back up and become a much freer version of myself. A version that was much more me.

It had been worth it.

Once the train arrived in Naples, we went to the parking lot, where my *parents'* ATV was parked. *Parents.* I loved saying that. The very word tasted sweet.

Dante got behind the wheel, Giulio sat next to him, and I got in the back.

I tried to take part in the conversation for a few minutes, but the closer we got to Sorrento, the harder it was for me to speak. To say I was worried was an understatement. I was terrified to see all those people I had lied to and deceived. I hadn't thought about that, but Giulio and Dante weren't alone. Every single person there had thought I was someone I wasn't, and they might not care how good my reasons were for doing so.

We got into town and turned down the narrow side streets, where everything now looked like autumn. I was coming home. I realized that now, and the thought made me shed a few tears.

My father turned back to see if I was all right, "Are you nervous?"

"Yeah."

"You shouldn't be."

"I lied to them, too," I said.

"That doesn't matter anymore."

I smiled and looked back at the wondrous panorama of the cliff-sides. How I had missed those views.

Giulio wrapped an arm around me and pulled me into his side as we crossed the yard and reached the villa.

Nothing had changed.

It smelled the same: of lemon and sea.

I pushed the door to the vestibule open, and the memories rained down on me, full of laughter, magic, talk.

Full of life.

Giulio stopped me before I started to head upstairs, taking my hand and guiding me out to the patio, where I saw the table where we'd enjoyed so many dinners, the trees with their garlands of bulbs, the wicker chairs under the branches.

Unconsciously, I brought my hand to my chest as I crossed the threshold and felt the world start to spin around me. All of them were there: Angela, Marco, the kids, Monica and her babies, Tiziano, Roy, Julia, Iria, Blas… They looked almost like they were posing for a photo.

I held on to my father to keep from stumbling.

Catalina broke away from them and came to meet me, and everything I'd done to keep my emotions in check failed. She opened her arms and I ran to let her hold me. We remained that way a long time, her gripping me tight, me swaying against her body.

I felt so little. Like a baby girl. And also so loved.

When we separated, she dried my tears with her fingers as I told her I was sorry.

She smiled and shook her head. "You don't have to say sorry for anything. Your mother told me all there was to tell, and all I care about is whether or not you're OK."

"I am."

She took my face in her hands and kissed me on the forehead. "I'm so happy to have you back."

"Thank you, Catalina."

"No more calling me Catalina. Nonna, you can call me Nonna. It means Grandma, but I guess you know that by now."

I laughed, and she hugged me again, and finally I felt home.

74

That first night back in the villa, I couldn't sleep. I spent hours awake, walking around the apartment, then, finally, I got into Lucas's bed. I curled up and hugged the pillow, thinking of all the time we'd spent between those sheets.

His things were still there, his clothes still in the closet, his scent still lingering all over. Every corner of that apartment belonged to him, and his presence hovered there like a ghost I couldn't see but could feel. I couldn't even conceive of that space without him, and the mere idea that he might not come back was a torment to me.

I wanted to smell his skin at dawn.

I wanted to feel his hug before I slept.

See his eyes in the silence.

Talk with him till the morning, fending off sleep.

Sense his body on mine.

His mischievous gaze.

His desire to know me.

I wanted him to come back.

I wanted him to stay.

I needed him in my life so bad…

75

Time passed slowly, and I returned to that routine I had missed so much. I got my job at the florist back and started giving ballet classes again. On the weekends, I helped my grandmother in the garden and she told me stories about our family and my father's childhood. She had boxes full of photos, and I never got tired of looking at them.

On Sundays, I'd call my cousin Iván and chat for a while with my grandfather.

I also made a habit of keeping in touch with my mother, and our relationship started to flow effortlessly.

I stopped asking myself questions. Stopped looking for that *something* to fill the void I had always sensed inside myself. I stopped feeling lost and alone. Stopped living halfway. Stopped sleeping curled up in a ball.

The only thing I couldn't break free of was the feeling of expectation that was crushing me. The waiting. The fear, the uncertainty of not hearing anything from Lucas.

Every day, I wanted to call him, but I knew that wouldn't be fair for either of us. Freedom is a right, and you can't take it from someone. The person who wants to go back always can. The person who wants to stay can stay. If you want to, you can look for me, I thought. You can find me and never let me go.

My door was open. It was now up to him to decide if he wanted to come in.

In the meanwhile, I missed him.

Maybe I'd have to miss him forever.

76

What gives meaning to life are moments.

That truth became more and more mine as the days passed.

Little moments.

Simple moments.

Moments that fill the emptiness, overflow, make it disappear.

I learned to enjoy those moments. The details. What I had in front of me.

I learned to be that girl I wasn't allowed to be back when I needed it.

77

Christmas lights, Christmas trees, nativity scenes had decorated the streets of Sorrento for weeks. It was cold, but there were still tourists everywhere. They always invaded the town for the Feast of the Immaculate Conception. People milled about in the markets, took photos under the giant Christmas tree in the Piazza Tasso, lined in front of the pastry shops for their Christmas treats. My favorite were the struffoli, little sweet balls of dough covered in honey and sprinkles.

I popped one into my mouth and chewed as we crammed together next to the tree. There were too many of us to fit in one photo, and no matter how far out Dante stretched his arm with his phone, he couldn't catch more than the tops of the children's heads, and Roy and Julia looked decapitated, and all you could see of Blas was one shoulder.

Finally, a woman selling chestnuts offered to take a photo for us.

"Sorridete!" she said, meaning *Smile!*

I didn't need her to tell me to. I hadn't felt that happy in forever. I squeezed my father's hand and pulled my grandmother in close.

"Un'altra," our photographer said.

It was my first family photo. Because for me, every single person there was my family. We were parts of a whole. Family isn't blood; it's a feeling, a warm emotion that wraps around you and keeps you feeling safe. It was perfect, but there was something missing. A hollow I couldn't ignore. Keeping on without him was getting harder and harder every day.

"Are you all right?"

The question dragged me out of my thoughts. I looked up and saw my father with a worried expression on his face. I had lingered behind while everyone else walked away. I forced a smile. "Yeah, I'm fine."

He and I walked together, side by side.

"Maya, you know you can talk to me about anything, right?"

I nodded. "He's not coming back, is he?" I asked. "I feel it, that he's not coming back."

"I don't know."

"It's been weeks."

His expression darkened. "Sometimes, the people who matter to us don't show up in our lives to stay. They just pass through and teach us to grow up."

"Growing up is horrible," I hissed.

"I know," he replied.

"So what do I do now?"

He winked and grabbed my hand. "When you don't know what to do…" He pulled me into a pirouette and we both shouted, "Dance!"

We laughed. It was one of those small, ineffable things that are somehow bigger than anything you can touch. He sighed and hugged me again and guided me through the packed market.

"If it helps, I'll stick around here forever," Giulio said.

Trying hard to hold in all the emotions I felt, I responded, "Yeah, Dad. It helps."

78

They say love is something living, and like every living thing, a time comes when it has to die. I took consolation in that. One day, I told myself, that feeling that was devouring me inside would be diluted into a mere memory, a scar, one that would lighten until one day it would hardly be visible. And then it would just be history.

I climbed the stairs slowly, lost in thought, the way I often was. The way we often need to. Because our feelings are only true if we allow ourselves to feel them, if we learn that they can hurt us but never kill us, even if we're scared they might.

I slid the key into the lock and pushed the door open. Then I stopped. The lights were on. Everything around me seemed to melt as I asked myself what that meant: the strands of lights, the decorations, the garlands, the tinsel. Who had put all of it up?

I had an idea, but I shoved it aside. I couldn't allow myself to feel that excitement. Because if I was disappointed, it might well destroy me.

I threw my purse down and walked around with fear. It smelled like plastic and something delicious coming from the kitchen. But there was another thing, too: soft, subtle, but an aroma I would recognize anywhere. An aroma that was entirely his and, at the same time, entirely mine.

I walked into the kitchen. On the counter were bags of food, in the oven some kind of puff pastry. I didn't know what to think or what to feel. The possibilities were overwhelming.

I felt him behind me, tried to breathe, couldn't.

And slowly, I turned. Very slowly. Almost clumsily. Uncertain. Scared. And so much more.

He was so close that I found myself staring at what was right in front of me: his T-shirt, his neck. I looked up and saw the stormy blue of his eyes. His face was strewn with freckles like tiny stars, his lips were fleshy…

"What is all this?" I asked.

"Around here, we normally put up our Christmas decorations on the Day of the Immaculate Conception. I've still got to do the tree, but I was waiting for you. I thought we could do it together."

Hearing his voice again was like hearing music for the first time. I didn't want to cry, but I couldn't stop myself.

"Hey!" he whispered, drying my cheeks with his hands. "This isn't the time for that."

"I thought you'd never return."

"I had a lot of things to take care of."

"You took forever," I moaned.

"I know, and I'm sorry."

He cupped my neck with one hand and wrapped the other around my waist. I touched his stomach. I needed to make sure he was real. He was. The heat of his flesh radiated into my fingertips. My body reacted, absorbing him, recognizing him, submerging myself in him. Following his movements.

We looked at each other for an eternity, so close together that we were sharing the same air.

"Are you going to stay?" I asked.

He leaned his forehead in to mine. "With you…? Forever." His gravelly voice was like a caress filling all that emptiness I had carried around inside me. "If you want that," he added.

"I do," I said softly. "Please stay."

He pulled me in and I felt complete at last.

"I will."

"Stay," I repeated.

"Forever."

His lips brushed mine.

One. Two. Three…

I loved that tiny space that remained there.

Four. Five. Six…

Just before we kissed.

Seven. Eight. Nine…

And now it was gone, and we were close, and I closed my eyes and trembled. I was airborne. Flying high.

Sometimes, letting things happen is all you need.

79

There are people who think we are the circumstances life confronts us with. Others think we're the decisions we make every day. I don't know what I am—a handful of circumstances or a bunch of decisions. Maybe both, maybe neither.

I don't know who I am. I don't know what I'm doing or what I want to do. I don't know anything. That's the truth. And I'm not worried about finding out. But if anybody asked me about myself, I know what I'd answer.

Giulio says the past is made of memories, the present of moments, and the future of dreams. And that's what I am: memories, moments, and dreams.

Epilogue

Lucas

The sky surrounds us like a black velvet blanket and the sweet air of summer is dense as we walk hand in hand on the beach. It's been almost three years since I came back here. Since I chose to stay. Three years, and I still don't have a profession or any of that adult stuff that tells me who I am. But I don't care.

I'm still living for the day, and I'm not worried about it, because life is perfect as it is. I don't need to look for meaning in it, and there's nothing I'm waiting for.

This is perfect. And what will happen afterward is perfect, too. And the same for whatever comes after that. Because *she* is the moment. The girl who saw love and jumped. The girl who used to live in my dreams and then became reality.

I decide to hug her. Feel her. Show her every day what matters.

I pull her along, holding her hand. She looks me in the eyes and smiles. She has a special shine to her, and it makes my pulse race. She's just a few inches away and I can feel her breath on my skin, and it tickles me, and that feeling shoots through my body, lights me up, drags me along, lifts me into the sky.

I bend down and look at her lips, and my fingers caress her thigh and climb under her skirt. She trembles and pants—I can't hear it, but I feel it.

One second. Two. Three…

If I had to choose a moment, this is the one I would choose to hold onto forever. I have all that I need: sea, stars, and her. More than anything, her. My compass. My anchor.

I kiss her. I look her in the eyes and kiss her again. Hungrily, lustfully, with everything that words can't express.

It was so easy to love her that there are times when I think I must have been born with this love already in my heart. For her. For us. Because I love her in every way possible. Inside. Outside. Every single part of her.

It's so easy. So nice. So true that it scares me sometimes, and I wonder if this feeling will last forever. Or if one day we'll have to go in different directions. When might we stop loving each other?

The fear kills me.

But then I look up and there it is.

A tiny spark in the sky.

Then another.

Then another.

Then thousands.

Millions of lights shining in the universe.

And I calm down, because I find the answer:

When there are no more stars left to count.

Acknowledgments

My thanks go to my publisher, Planeta, which has become a home for me and my stories, and for Sourcebooks publishing my books in English.

To Irene, my editor, for her unconditional support, her care, her trust.

To Míriam, for taking such good care of me, and for the incomparable job she does.

To my family, for always being there for me.

To Dani Ojeda, Iñigo Aguas, and Andrea Longarela. I couldn't hope for better colleagues. Let alone better friends.

To Alice, always, for trusting me more than I trust myself.

To my H girls. I love you a lot.

To my little stars, for shining so bright.

To you, my readers, because without you this book wouldn't exist. Thank you for giving me wings.

About the Author

María Martínez is the successful Spanish author of *You and Other Natural Disasters*, *The Fragility of a Heart in the Rain*, and *When There Are No More Stars Left to Count*, among other works. She writes sensitive stories that address the complexity of emotions and issues like family and identity. When she is not busy writing, she spends her free time reading, listening to music, or watching series and movies. Her favorite hobbies are getting lost in any bookstore and having fun with her daughters.

Facebook: María Martínez
Instagram: @mariamartinez.itsme

You and Other Natural Disasters

Until she can figure out what she wants for herself, love will always be a disaster.

Twenty-year-old Harper Weston always wanted to be a book editor. But when she inherits her grandmother's beloved bookstore, she must decide between carrying the legacy forward and the carefully planned life she had envisioned for herself. After all, her love for reading came from her grandmother, who always supported her dreams. But grief, sadness, and resentment resurface every time she steps foot in the store.

Amid her uncertainty, Harper struggles to welcome all her family who are in town for not only the funeral service but also her older sister Hayley's wedding. But she was not ready for the event to bring back Trey Holt, a close friend of her siblings who broke Harper's heart. Faced with many conflicting thoughts and decisions to make, Harper takes a trip to get away from it all, to think. Little did she know it would change her life and send her right into the arms of Trey, the person she needs answers from the most.

For more information about Sourcebooks books and authors, visit: sourcebooks.com